PRAISE FOR MIKE CHEN

A Quantum Love Story

"*A Quantum Love Story* is a delight of a novel. Mariana and Carter join his pantheon of richly drawn characters in a story that offers freshness and surprises throughout a time loop."

—Kat Howard, Alex Award–winning author of *An Unkindness of Magicians*

"This emotional new novel from Mike Chen combines what is best about science fiction, mystery, and romance. . . . The result is a world rendered in Technicolor, every corner lit, every scene set so that the reader can walk right in. Chen's charming characterizations are at their best."

—*Scientific American*

Vampire Weekend

"A love letter to the power of music, this thoughtful, humorous exploration of what constitutes living versus mere survival sees Chen at the top of his game."

—*Publishers Weekly* (starred review)

"Mike Chen is at his best here, with a sharp-as-fangs reinvention of the vampire mythos centered on the power of family, born and chosen, and, of course, punk rock. This book will sink its teeth right into your heart."

—Gwenda Bond, *New York Times* bestselling author

A Beginning at the End

"If you're tired of grim, grueling apocalypses with high body counts and bleak horizons, *A Beginning at the End* offers an intimate, surprisingly gentle vision of post-disaster humanity, less concerned with how we might survive than with why—and for whom."

—Alix E. Harrow, *New York Times* bestselling author

"Chen manages to imbue his apocalypse with heart, hope, and humanity. Sci-fi fans will delight in this lovingly rendered tale."

—*Publishers Weekly* (starred review)

"[T]he best kind of dystopian novel: one rooted deeply in the hearts of his characters and emphasizing hope and connection over fear. Chen has a true gift for making the biggest of worlds center around the most complex workings of hearts, and his newest is compelling, realistic, and impossible to put down."

—*Booklist* (starred review)

Light Years from Home

"All the stars for Chen's warmhearted space-travel story."

—*Kirkus* (starred review)

"So good, sweet and funny and dark and weird, *Light Years from Home* is a tense family melodrama wrapped inside a wild alien abduction story. I could not put this book down."

—Annalee Newitz, bestselling author of *Autonomous* and *Four Lost Cities*

"A heartfelt novel of family dysfunction wrapped in an intergalactic cloak . . . Chen's strength in writing poignant character arcs, especially within family dynamics, shines here, as does his ability to craft intriguing blends of literary and speculative fiction with compelling, character-driven plots."

—Library Journal

We Could Be Heroes

"A delight from start to finish even if, like me, you don't know the difference between Batman and Robin."

—Riley Sager, New York Times bestselling
author of Home Before Dark

"The story of deep friendship and the sheer power that comes from feeling less alone in the world. . . . An overall enjoyable, exciting, and action-packed read."

—Associated Press

Here and Now and Then

"This gripping, fast-paced time-travel thriller is also a warm, moving story of a man pulled between two lives and families. With plenty of humor and suspense, Chen has crafted an original and captivating story."

—Shelf Awareness (starred review)

"Chen does what the very best sci-fi writers do—he takes a fascinating concept and elevates it with brilliant execution and deeply heartfelt plot twists that make this story less about the (fun) conventions of the genre and more about the profound experience of being human. *Here and Now and Then* is a page-turner, an examination of love and loss, and, most of all, a dazzling debut from a wonderfully unique new voice."

—Michael Moreci, author of Black Star Renegades
and canonical stories for Star Wars

BY MIKE CHEN

THE

PHOTONIC

EFFECT

MIKE CHEN

SAGA PRESS

LONDON **NEW YORK** TORONTO
AMSTERDAM/ANTWERP NEW DELHI SYDNEY/MELBOURNE

SAGA PRESS

AN IMPRINT OF SIMON & SCHUSTER, LLC

1230 AVENUE OF THE AMERICAS, NEW YORK, NEW YORK 10020

 Let's stay in touch! Scan here to get book recommendations,
exclusive offers, and more delivered to your inbox.

For the doers.
You build us new solutions to old problems,
and we need you now more than ever.

EXCERPTS FROM OFFICIAL RETIREMENT FILE

Demora Kim

Final Rank: Captain, Galactic Cluster Fleet—Starship Horizon

Advanced materials from retirement file—DO NOT DISTRIBUTE

Final Starship Command Specifications

Name: GCF Horizon
Registry: GCF HP2X19
Class: Pathfinder 2
Length: 243 meters
Width: 75 meters
Deck 1: Bridge, Captain's Quarters, Crew Quarters
Deck 2: Stellar Cartography, Mess Hall, Crew Quarters
Deck 3: Runway/Docking Bay, Storage Hangar, Science Lab, Observation Lounge
Deck 4: Engineering, Crew Quarters, Senior Officer Quarters
Deck 5: Brig, Medical Bay

Key Dates During Command (Earth Standard)

January 16, 2291: Launched for deep space exploration to establish and map a new trade route for Cluster systems on trajectory 8793, bearing 9701 (crew count: 72)

February 10, 2291: Pulled into photonic gravity well, approximately 20,398 light-years from Sol System

April 20, 2293: First deaths of original crew members (3)

March 20, 2298: First recorded activity of volatile energy within gravity well

May 18, 2298: First contact with Lumersian photonic species

August 25, 2298: First implosion of neighboring craft within gravity well

November 29, 2299: Death of First Officer Grant Singh

January 30, 2300: Initial development of photonic engine begins in conjunction with Lumersians

May 21, 2301: Return to Cluster space (total passengers: 93—over capacity; 33 original crew members, 12 field-recruited crew members, 48 refugees requesting asylum)

April 4, 2301: Assigned for specialized research (crew count: 18; 13 original including captain, 5 field-recruited)

October 28, 2301: Incident at Base Theta Seven

Selected Excerpts, Exit Interview (December 15, 2301)

On the gravity well

Kim: Lost. Stranded. Stuck. Whatever you want to call it. Neera would say we got caught in a photonic convergence point as the Lumersians were running an experiment. Like flooding an interaction of photonic and physical space. Great science for them, bad gravity for anyone else. We got trapped. Other ships got trapped. Some from parallel universes. In the gravity well, the only way to survive was to lean on one another. And it worked, until the well itself began collapsing on us.

On returning to Cluster space

Kim: Well, GCF ships greeted us with guns. That was our introduction to the war. You ask why it was so disturbing, I mean, war was ancient history to us. The Expansion Frontier War was a school lesson! Then we see even science and research officers on front lines against the Withdrawal Movement? Sometimes I still can't believe it happened.

On Photonic Being #910047

GCF Command: What is the significance of Photonic Being Number 910047?

Kim: We wouldn't be here if it wasn't for Chuck. When the gravity well collapsed, he sacrificed himself.

GCFC: I'm sorry, did you call him "Chuck"?

Kim: That was my nickname for him.

GCFC: A nickname. So you were friendly with this photonic being? Why aren't there more details about him?

Kim: (Long pause) With all due respect, that's private.

On the incident at Base Theta Seven

GFCF: Can you explain why you chose to disobey orders at Base Theta Seven?

Kim: You want my polite answer or my honest answer?

GFCF: It's for the official record.

Kim: All right. It's gonna make some of you look bad. Don't say I didn't warn you.

TWO
MONTHS
EARLIER . . .

CHAPTER 1

DEMI

Captain Demora Kim never expected to be a mechanic on board her own ship. She didn't have the qualifications—she wasn't an engineer or a technician. She studied cartography at the Galactic Cluster Fleet Academy, which didn't really apply to repairing hardware.

But things always broke on the GCF Starship Horizon, often leaving the closest person available to fix the problem.

In this case, she'd told the crew that she'd meet them down at the mess hall for ramen night soon. Classified war intel was coming through, and she just needed a minute. But a minute didn't suffice, because the message wasn't processing at her private station. So she'd walked down the hall from her quarters to the bridge, though at the path's end, the elevator tempted her to just leave and go get ramen. However, she did the responsible thing—the captainly thing—and stepped forward.

Two doors slid open, revealing the large—and empty—bridge of the Horizon. Through the wide front window, a blanket of space and stars lay ahead. In front of that, a floating hologram of the ship's statuses projected from the large square data table. Normally, she'd head right to the captain's chair near the back of the rectangular space. But instead she turned immediately to the corner comms station. She knelt down to the access panel, a sheet of alloy covered in magnetic decals of rock bands spanning nearly three hundred years—a giveaway that Lieutenant Lynn Kohli was both the ship's communications officer *and* resident music buff. Demi unlatched the panel and slid it off to expose wiring and hardware, then got onto her back for a look.

There it was.

Just as she'd suspected, the chip that drove routing of incoming classified messages had simply fallen loose. It happened every few months, like many other things on the Horizon, because parts wore down, got damaged, needed haphazard fixes. Ten years stuck in a mysterious gravity well would do that to hardware. Demi traced her finger along the edge of the chip until she got to the exact right angle to lock it in, then pushed.

It clicked into place. She sealed up the panel and stood up, then tapped the console to process the message right here on the bridge.

Stuck, then unstuck. Kind of like the Horizon itself.

And just like the Horizon, the chip saw *war* when it got unstuck—here, in the form of communications regarding the ongoing civil war with the Withdrawal Movement. Demi went to her seat and glanced at the clock, a reminder that her skeleton crew were down in the mess hall.

A captain and her crew of seventeen didn't exactly fill a starship built for seventy-two. But when things actually worked, Demi found the empty ship a peaceful, almost stable environment for the greatest of scientific endeavors: to restore the photonic engine that brought them home. Such a project proved a blessing: scientific progress *and* a reason to stay far away from the front. None of them needed the turmoil of the war; they'd seen and lived worse.

Because those seventeen people down at ramen night were more than just crew members.

Getting trapped with no outside communication or support caused all sorts of things to claim the lives of their colleagues. And when other spacecraft got pulled into the well, distrust and sabotage took more of them until Demi forged truces between the often at-odds groups.

Then the well grew unstable, eventually imploding neighboring ships, and panic took over: skirmishes over supplies, emergency repairs that wouldn't quite hold, and long, empty nights debating whether it was worth it to go on.

No, they weren't just crew. Or friends. Or family.

They were *survivors* together.

Demi lingered on that when the wide holographic display shifted from ship status to an incoming classified message about a war she wanted no part of.

Or at least, it started to. CLASSIFIED—FOR YOUR EYES ONLY appeared before dissolving to the sight of Galactic Cluster Minister of Defense Cabell. Cabell opened his mouth before the image froze and a system warning appeared, along with a schematic of comm array hardware.

Primary classified decoder failing—rerouting to secondary array

This issue had nothing to do with a loose chip. It flashed several times before *Rerouting successful* appeared and the message played out.

"*To all fleet captains. I apologize about the mass outreach, but it was the most efficient way to reach all of you given the rapidly unfolding situation. An incident occurred on the central mining station of the gas moon Ark Getru in the Nedotia System.*" The image changed from Cabell to the station itself, a diamond-shaped conflux of alloys designed for mining gas and supporting a massive civilian community. "*This is a select edit of security footage. I am warning you that this is not easy to see.*"

It started out innocently enough, a view of a factory floor where staff stood lined at machines, holding pumps and nozzles. Then the image shook, the feed becoming blocks of colored and distorted pixels for a moment. Then *everything* moved—workers, equipment, hardware, safety helmets, all of it flew in a strange way, a sudden jolt that tossed everything toward the left side of the image.

It took Demi a second to realize what happened. The people didn't fly horizontally; no, the station *tilted*. And the people dropped due to gravity.

Suddenly, ramen night seemed so very far away.

The footage changed to a courtyard view of a park near the station's upper floor. Residents milled about, some walking along the gardens, some seated around a fountain with a picnic blanket, and others playing with pets or children.

Then the same thing happened—first, a massive shake, then everything lifted and flew to the left side of the image. Except this time, the yellow clouds of Ark Getru rotated nearly ninety degrees, as if someone turned the background sideways. And against those clouds, tiny dots began to trickle from background buildings and structures, a line of specks floating helplessly out of the station, like insects crawling out of a flooded rock face.

The image switched again, this time to a flying security vehicle hurtling toward the station. A nonhuman voice spoke, her words tinted by both concern and curiosity as a single explosion fired off near the station's lower levels. Soon another bomb went off, and another and another, until the station's multiple rings of stabilizers and magnetic repulsors—originally designed to work with Ark Getru's significant magnetic fields—all exploded, a one-by-one line that created systematic rings of destruction around the station's middle and bottom.

The repulsor tech that defined the very existence of the Ark Getru central mining operation simply vaporized. And with it, the gas planet's natural gravity pulled at the superstructure, first causing it to tilt on its axis before a rapid descent into the whirling gaseous core of the planet below, leaving the security vehicle's camera to stare at an empty location of puffy clouds and several blinking beacons.

Seconds ago, the pilot's voice cried out. But now her vehicle hovered, the only noise the panicked radio chatter over her comms.

"Internal view. Surface view. External view," Cabell said as he faded back in, his broken gaze betraying his otherwise stoic voice. *"There is more recorded, of course, but it's not necessary for our purposes."*

One explosion wouldn't do it. A dozen well-placed bombs wouldn't do it. This required a massive coordinated operation, and Demi guessed possibly seventy or eighty bombs were needed to take out the station, her mind racing through the logistics necessary to attack one of the Cluster's most historically lauded resource stations.

And how the hell did someone get past security?

"Here are the facts of the event." As Cabell spoke, text appeared across the hologram: Ark Getru population statistics, demographics, mining output. One line in particular was highlighted—*Exports impact 15% of Cluster non-FTL propulsion.*

Demi figured that in a war over resources, anything impacting Cluster-standard faster-than-light systems was probably pretty important. Though not as important as the bold words at the bottom of the hologram, a line of characters with the most harrowing, stark text any captain could ever see:

Estimated destruction rate: 100%
Estimated casualty rate: 100%

Just like what happened to ships in the gravity well. The damage was the same, the only difference being that in the well, implosion crushed people instead of tossing them into the atmosphere.

Demi thought she'd left that level of destruction behind. But in a way, it felt like it followed her home.

"Prime Minister Kentworthy put out a statement on behalf of the Withdrawal Movement neither confirming nor denying involvement. However, our intelligence believes this attack was in response to our last attempt at negotiation—specifically, the claim that the WM lacked the organization to produce coordinated efforts and should release territory as such. It is likely that similar large-scale, quick-strike attacks are in the

works." Cabell bit down on his lip, hesitating for several seconds, and during that span, a gnawing realization hit that, unlike what Demi witnessed in the gravity well, this was self-inflicted, a byproduct of hubris and stubbornness playing with risk.

The Cluster bluffed its position, thinking it might strong-arm the WM into concessions. The WM responded in the worst possible manner. And now an entire station was destroyed.

"*We have instituted a Cluster-wide media blackout. Now*"—the old man's gaze narrowed, a tension coming to both his eyes and the bushy white brows above them—"*the official story is that a severe and unexpected series of ecological events ignited a storage room of collected gas, setting off a chain reaction. Select footage will support this. And you, as fleet captains, hold a responsibility in maintaining that narrative.*"

Demi realized her fingers were tightly pressed against her knees. She relaxed them, then a breath as well. Everything she'd known about the Cluster fractured. Impenetrable security of high-value resources. Truth, justice, honesty, and all the other supposed virtues of being in the fleet. Of course politics existed, but a cover-up of this scale? *Mistakes* of this scale?

"*Word of this incident has spread much faster than anticipated. While it is known that WM attacks have always disregarded civilian safety, this escalation exposes the Cluster's weakening security, cumulative loss of resources, and weakened bargaining posture. If those facts get out to the public, it will, at best, drain support for the war.*

"*At worst, it will give the WM a strategic advantage on all fronts— tactically, culturally, politically. We cannot allow the public, even rank-and-file crew, to know—*"

Data stream halted displayed across the frozen image. Demi tapped the console on her chair again, this time to reroute enhancers for signal stability. The transmission stalled on Cabell's mouth in mid-sentence. Which was kind of good, because as she waited for the system to recover, Demi really needed a moment to process the way that her government and its opposition both treated civilians as war fodder.

In the well, every single one of her decisions clawed back a little more stability, a little more *life* out of the impossible. Here, everything seemed to spiral in the opposite way.

Despite the violence, despite the death, Demi froze at a sudden thought: horrifying as it was, destructive as it was, maybe it all existed outside of the Horizon. Since they'd returned to Cluster space—raw, traumatized, lost—she'd pushed Command to keep the Horizon *out* of the war. The ship, the crew, they were all anomalies that just popped up in the middle of an ongoing conflict, one that threatened to swallow each of them whole.

With everything Cabell just revealed, that might have been the right decision all along. Her decade-old ship carrying a patchwork crew and their shattered emotions couldn't shift the war in any way, not when the Cluster goaded the WM into more deadly attacks. All Demi could do was keep everything at bay long enough to . . .

Long enough for something *better* to happen. What that was, she wasn't sure. But she owed it to her crew to find out.

It was the only thing she could control. She had to stick to it.

Demi took a breath, then told herself the next time she listened to classified war material, make sure her dog was around to help steady her racing pulse.

"—*stage of the war,*" Cabell continued, though the visuals remained paused. "*As fleet captains, there is no doubt these discussions will reach at least some of your crew. Your orders are to—*"

Suddenly, the entire holo disappeared, leaving only the front window and the vastness of space. On Demi's console, the comm array schematic lit up with all types of unhappy flashing—plus a new message: *Secondary support maximized. Attempt internal repair?*

Demi hit an icon to start the Horizon's self-repair processes and watched as an estimated completion time fluctuated between ten minutes and three hours. That was a good prompt for Demi to stand up from the captain's chair. "Computer, reroute comm array status to the mess hall, primary display."

Her crew expected her. If she didn't show up, they'd suspect something. It was ramen night, after all.

Demi gave herself a few breaths to absorb the lies, the death, the chaos sent in a single message. Then she tamped it down. She had to. For one hour, because reality would come soon enough. Word of Ark Getru would surely trickle in from outside colleagues, from news broadcasts, from family and friends. And then Command's orders to lie would kick in.

For that hour, she wanted to give everyone on board freedom from everything that was soon to come.

Including herself.

CHAPTER 2

DEMI

Not every GCF officer was allowed to have a dog on a starship. But when Demi stumbled upon an illegal greyhound racetrack operating near the Mars orbital repair dock, she watched as rescue teams took in scared animals unsure of their surroundings and apprehensive of a new life.

Demi understood that. And as a relief worker struggled to corral six dogs at once, one broke free and sprinted directly at her.

Demi opened her arms and held the trembling greyhound until the dog calmed down. Then she immediately requested an animal companion exception for her starship.

Now Indy walked patiently by Demi's side as they entered the Horizon's mess hall on the second deck. Prior to escaping the collapsing gravity well, crew dinners had filled the space. A mix of original Horizon crew had welcomed refugees from imploded community ships along with walking mech suits housing the strange planes of pink light that made up Lumersian bodies—if you could even call those bodies. Bodies usually meant something tangible, something you could feel or hug.

Light wasn't exactly a body. Even with Chuck, his brilliant mind resided in the sentient square of photonic energy, but Demi sure missed holding that mech suit's robotic hand.

Those days were loud, raucous, and busy, and the mess hall's air was often thick from so many beings from so many universes, everyone trying to make it to the next day, the next minute. One night would have a culturally themed meal, the next would host a movie night from a parallel universe, and other times the mess hall and the hangar bay on deck three would be turned into a massive round of hide-and-seek. If the bridge was the Horizon's brain, then the mess hall was its heart, the place where culture, species, tastes, and emotions flowed together, giving the Horizon's crew and its multiversal visitors a place to exist outside the empty glowing void around them.

All of that came courtesy of one man, a former rock star who arrived via another universe's cruise ship. Tanav Lexin's knack for understanding people may have also explained why he now sat surrounded by the crew's wide grins and bright eyes.

Even with a smaller crew, the place still came alive—a little quieter and certainly less messy than before, but in some ways even more vibrant. Standing at the back of the mess hall, Demi caught the black, compound eyes of Neera, rows upon rows of visual receptors lined together on each eyeball to give him a unique sense of vision—highly effective for working on intricate ship systems. Though maybe more importantly, the tall Dywan engineer with an inhuman skull was Indy's second-favorite person on the ship. Neera mixed back into the crowd, either to avoid the dog or focus on the test data in his hand, or both. Demi let him be, instead turning to the unfolding action.

Tanav didn't notice her come in, instead focusing on the bowl in front of him. Lieutenant Aurora Sterling, one of the Horizon's system engineers, offered him . . . something.

Demi squinted to be sure, but it looked like the green-haired lieutenant carried several glowing peppers by their thin stems.

"All right," Aurora said, "the challenge is *three* of these. So hot they can disrupt the ship's power lines." The proclamation sparked a mix of whoops and applause. "Don't ask me how I know."

Oddly, Tanav looked at Lynn during all of this. Not at Aurora, who described how her family farm grew the spiciest peppers in the Milia sector; not at the glowing white peppers themselves; nor at the ship's captain, who'd just entered the room.

And it wasn't just a glance. Lynn stood directly in front of Tanav with a finger on her chin and giant smirk, leading to a locking of eyes—the lingering type that sent messages. In this case, the message might have been, *What have I gotten myself into?*

"All right, all right," Tanav said, putting one hand up. He took a deep breath and raised a single finger. "First one."

Aurora plucked a pepper off the stem and handed it to him. He held it between his fingers, staring at it with an intensity that even pulled Demi's thoughts away from Ark Getru and into the immediate drama. How did Tanav get roped into *this*?

In one motion, he popped the pepper into his mouth and chewed. A flush came to his cheeks, darkening his already brown skin into a richer hue, and he squinted, deep lines forming in all sorts of angles across his eyes. He chewed in large, quick gestures, and though his eyes stayed shut, he held up two fingers and nodded his head.

"Second one!" Aurora yelled, prompting more cheers, and even Indy got in several deep barks. Tanav took this one down, speeding up his chews. Lynn waved a glass of water at him, though with his eyes closed, he missed it.

The status display on the wall showed that the internal diagnostic and power rerouting were still processing. Demi reminded herself that allowing one hour for this was as much for her as it was everyone else. And she couldn't review Cabell's message while the hardware rerouted.

So, hot peppers it was. It had to be. She needed it to be that and nothing else right now.

"Now," Aurora said, "my family stops at two peppers. Does our

Cultural Counselor dare for more? He always talks about finding opportunities. I guess that means he's done that here. Last pepper—but, maybe we give him a choice with it. Fair?" By now, tears streamed out of Tanav's eyes and sweat matted his thick black hair. "He's been such a good sport, how about for this last pepper, he can choose to eat it whole or break it apart and put it in his ramen." Murmurs swept through the room, and Tanav ran a cloth napkin over his face, the top of his head, the back of his neck before giving a thumbs-up. Aurora gave him the final pepper. "You do the honors."

Tanav held it steady over this bowl and inhaled—sniffled, really—before cracking the pepper and dumping its seeds into his noodles. He dropped the remainder in and swirled his chopsticks to stir the dish. Just as he took a bite, he said in a low voice, "Gravity-easy."

Demi doubted the scientific accuracy of "gravity-easy," given that gravity wasn't exactly easy; the well proved that every day. But who was she to question the idioms of someone's home? One time, she'd told Chuck she had a bone to pick with a neighboring ship, and when Chuck asked for its literal meaning, she had no answer.

Tanav came with his own set of references, just like he came with his own quantum vibrational frequency. For the latter, his comm integrated a signal booster so the ship's sensors could better identify him. But no piece of tech constantly translated his cultural sayings.

They all just had to *learn*.

"Four bites, to be fair," Aurora said, and Tanav obliged, taking in the noodles while sweat rolled down his cheeks. The crowd counted each one, Tanav taking one very deep, messy breath before the final bite caused the crew to cheer.

Not bad for eighteen people and a rescue dog.

Lynn waved the glass of water again in front of Tanav, who drank the whole thing in several gulps. She took the empty glass and dashed off while Tanav slumped away from the crowd to the sink behind the main counter. As he splashed water on his face, Demi decided to make her presence known.

"We make it out of the gravity well and you decide to immolate yourself with Aurora's family peppers? There are easier ways to do the whole 'bringing the crew together' thing." Despite possibly melting his mouth, throat, and intestinal lining, Tanav mustered a laugh. It came with coughs, and he ran the damp napkin over his face again.

"Ah," he said, the top part of his face still covered with the napkin, "well, I wanted to help Aurora out." It dropped down to reveal a clarity in his eyes despite the redness and tears. "You didn't hear this from me, but she's thinking of leaving the ship."

Demi paused at the statement but quickly stifled any further reaction to it. She knew not to take these types of things personally, even though they always stung at first. When they arrived in Galactic Cluster space as a starship packed with refugees, many people asked for immediate transfers. Some wanted to get the hell away from their floating space prison. Some felt the need to support the Cluster in its surprise civil war with the Withdrawal Movement.

Some quit the fleet altogether, having been through enough.

For those who stayed, though, Demi's mission was to give them stability in an uncertain galaxy—difficult already with the war relentlessly encroaching upon *everything*. The war had been ongoing for two years when they'd landed, and she quickly discovered it to be as meaningless as it was vicious, and the last hour cemented that belief even more. That take was probably the one thing she'd agree on with her parents—if she ever talked to them again.

Stability would probably be even more difficult after Ark Getru.

Demi rubbed her chin at the thought.

"You all right?"

Tanav was the only current crew member to dare ask her that question. Grant Singh, her former first officer, would ask during private conversations. But since his death, only Tanav went there, and while he always seemed to denigrate his lack of military *everything*, Demi saw it as a kind of license to go where others would avoid. Cultural Counselor, after all, was a made-up title.

She rarely replied with full honesty. But she appreciated that he tried. And that he seemed to *know*. "She wants a transfer?" Demi asked, a conscious deflection back to Aurora. "I can contact—"

"No." Tanav shook his head, though a quick grimace showed that maybe his stomach was feeling all the peppers. "The Milia sector joined the Withdrawal Movement. The Cluster has cut off trade with her farm. She wants to go home to help her parents."

"I can get her over there . . ." Demi started. And even though Tanav often talked about how war in his universe was more about corporate takeovers than guns and bombs, he understood enough to send a knowing eyebrow at her. Demi couldn't cross official lines like that.

"It's weighing on her." Tanav stirred his noodles around, though he hesitated to take another bite. "These walls"—he gestured around them—"can't always keep the war out, no matter what you say. People have family and friends out there. So tonight, she arrived with her family's peppers, and I wanted to distract her for a few hours. Clear her mind." Tanav laughed, then rubbed the sweat out of his eyes. "It was—" A rapid blink interrupted him as his hands patted around, searching for the napkin. "My eyes. I shouldn't have touched my eyes."

Demi grabbed napkins from the counter, and right when he took them, Lynn showed up with a tray of chocolate chip cookies and milk.

"Sorry," she said, "had to search for milk. Oh, hi, Demi. Did you catch the show?"

"More like the aftermath." Tanav groaned as he wiped his face.

"Milk helps with the heat," Lynn said. "And cookies to go with them, of course. He baked these." Demi couldn't stop the surprised look on her face. "I know, right? Though a little undercooked. He forgot to test them, he's gotta slow down"—she thumbed at Tanav—"and don't rush the bake. Sometimes it's better if you don't jump to the next step. It needs five more minutes."

There it was again: that *look*. These two weren't just flirting. They were a *couple*.

Demi didn't want to show her epiphany. Or the grin on her face. That part needed her hand as a cover, and she considered what she knew about them, how Tanav struggled being marooned in this universe apart from Thaddea, his ex-fiancée and his ex-bandmate. And Lynn, despite her friendly exterior, always carried a tension in her. Maybe they both had to be here, in Cluster space, before they could relax and let someone else in.

"Right. Like the Supermercado song 'Five More Minutes.'" His voice carried a playful tone, like he said that just to annoy her. And she responded in kind.

"I swear those songs aren't real. I give you three hundred years of music, and you're just making up shit to mess with me." Lynn turned to Demi, her long dark curls falling over her GC Fleet uniform. "As ship's captain, did you ever wonder if maybe he's not really a rock star? Like, he's just a waiter who found a situation? 'Cause we've known each other for how many years, and I've still never heard you sing?"

"You sing first, then I'll sing." Their debate highlighted the contrast between them: the musician versus the music fan; Lynn's decade of fleet dedication versus Tanav's fell-into-this-role duty; Lynn's polished, sharp diction versus Tanav's sometimes unexplainable pronunciation from another universe. "Different life. Different universe. Maybe my calling is baking here."

But that wasn't true. Demi knew what Tanav's calling was, just by the very fact that everyone in the room watched him eat three of Aurora's super-peppers. "Whichever life, don't melt your intestine before you make it back home."

Normally such a quip would get a laugh in return from both of them. This time, they just turned to each other, an awkward pause saved by the ship's status chime ringing through the mess hall.

A flashing red *X* over the comm schematic said it all. No internal rerouting would get this thing fixed. Demi fought off a sigh, mind already thinking about the next makeshift fix for this crew, and as if the ship's computer wanted to make sure she didn't miss the point, a new message arrived:

Internal repairs unsuccessful. Hardware replacement necessary. Purging cached transmission.

She raised a hand to excuse herself without taking a single bite, then she heard a familiar voice:

GC Minister of Defense Cabell.

She turned to see the same classified message from before broadcasting out over the mess hall. Somehow, the combination of hardware damage, software limitations, and dumb luck broadcast a very classified, very not-good war message to the crew.

As footage of Ark Getru came to life, conversations fell away, voices exchanged for gasps and whispered chatter. The video paused and stuttered, right when Cabell said, "We cannot allow the public, even rank-and-file crew, to know—"

Then the transmission hung, just like before. And even though Cabell's words eventually continued, the minister couldn't be heard over the shouting of crew members—shouting at her, shouting at the screen, shouting at each other.

Demi wanted a peaceful hour for everyone before the impact of Ark Getru wormed its way into the ship. According to the clock, she only got twelve minutes. And from the sudden fierce anger around the room, no matter how bad she originally anticipated, things were going to get much, much worse.

CHAPTER 3

✳

TANAV

Tanav had never seen anything like Ark Getru before. His universe was far from perfect, with its economic caste systems and corporate control over large regions of space. Accidents certainly happened, as did tragedies. But the thing about corporate control was that military forces usually focused on local skirmishes and border enforcement; everything else negotiated through boardrooms as populations and communities stayed in their respective roles.

So intentional destruction on that level was beyond understanding, those images rooted deep in his mind. And the GCF official who talked so *clinically* about the whole thing . . .

As with the war itself, the whole thing felt like a whirlpool sucking in innocent bystanders. He couldn't do anything about it; he didn't even know why Ark Getru itself was so important. He just knew that something horrible happened and the reason behind it was top secret. Others in the crew had stronger opinions—he overheard Casey Tarell in particular say something about calling her grandfather to "tell the old admiral that this is bullshit."

Demi shouted to bring order to the mess hall. "Everyone settle down! I don't like this any more than you do. But this is a classified message, and it only slipped through because of a damaged comm array. If you need someone to yell at later, you know where to find me. But for now, we need to fix our home. We can't ignore that. I need everyone's help."

That got people going, even if they grumbled about it. Discussions about who would do what and where started with an underlying tension. Words came out clipped, responses came with hesitation, and extra glances were traded in all directions. No one was happy, yet everyone needed to get involved, which happened more often than not on the Horizon. Tanav thought of a phrase from his universe that his parents particularly liked: "Pulling the debtors *and* creditors into the ledger."

In this case, that meant people got tasked with things they weren't necessarily suited for. "Outer hull array repair" meant a space walk with *two* crew members, each carrying and installing equipment—plus the necessary crew to monitor systems.

Commander Neera, the Horizon's chief engineer, was the logical choice for the space walk. The would-be first officer—would-be, as in he would be if he'd stop turning down the promotion—agreed to the request and immediately left the mess hall to prepare.

For the second spacewalker, Lynn volunteered. Which surprised Tanav, given the zero gravity environment and her sensitive stomach. "I worked with the transmission array the most. I've studied the hardware—like fifteen years ago, but it's burned in my memory. I just need Neera to guide me on the repair part." Though she didn't look at Tanav, the next line felt like a direct response to the expression on his face. "I'm the best person for the job, despite being prone to motion sickness," she said, which cascaded into quiet laughs around the room.

"Macek will be in engineering to power cycle the circuit at the array," Demi said. "Aurora, check the stability of the decryptor. It's got outdated transmission protocols, so we need to integrate that cleanly." She rattled off other orders, Tanav missing the technical details, though his ears perked up when she called his name. "Tanav, how would you like a temporary promotion to GCF communications officer?"

Lynn flashed a grin his way, and for that brief instance, it was like they hadn't seen the horrors of Ark Getru.

"Whatever you need," he said, and with that, Demi sent everyone on their way. He followed her to the bridge, a place he hardly visited due to his lack of training. Reading subtext, thinking ahead, remembering what people liked or wanted, he excelled at the things that weren't part of ship operations. And while no one else ever mentioned it, his inability to grasp those things always stuck out in his own mind.

Forty-five minutes later, he sat at Lynn's station, a clear view of the live holographic feed projected out from the front data table: the blanket of space, then the shape of a human silently coming in from the right side. To his left, Demi sat in the captain's chair, a tablet in each hand. They watched Lynn stumble forward, magnetic boots clamping onto the outer hull by the main transmission array. She moved steadily, step-by-step, as her legs swung slowly in the very strange environment of outer space.

"I am so nauseous," Lynn said over the comm system. "Why did I volunteer for this? Don't worry, everyone, I know we've got limited laundry resources right now. Trying my best not to throw up." Her heavy, regular breath broadcast, soon followed by barely audible words in melody. "'The execution of all things,'" she sang quietly. "'The execution of all things.'"

Whisper-singing her favorite songs, rambling, and cracking jokes—all of Lynn's coping mechanisms activated at once, pushed by nausea, the space walk, possibly even Ark Getru. He'd caught her reaction to the broadcast, a wide-eyed look that crossed horror and anger and disbelief, yet she'd managed to stuff it all down and break into duty.

Tanav *could* have made a crack to keep the mood light, about how he still really never got to hear Lynn sing, and space walk whispering didn't count. Except saying something probably would have only distracted her, and the outer hull wasn't a place for that. Instead, he focused on the various panels monitoring the status of intra and external ship communications.

"Thirty steps farther is all we will need to traverse." Neera's voice came first, then his familiar silhouette. He moved with more confidence than Lynn, thanks to his previous experience on the outer hull repair. They'd adapted the puffy white space suit to Neera's needs: taller, slight diamond-shaped skull with a ridged forehead coming to a peak, and two opposable thumbs on each side of his large hands. Kind of like the way Neera adapted his speech to the basic English used by the mostly human crew of the Horizon—though the syntax of Neera's native species still carried through, giving his sentences an odd format.

Tanav once told Neera that Dywen phrasing reminded him of a term he learned in his upper-school years: idling format. Demi said that in this universe, they called it "passive voice," and her dad—an Earth-bound high school teacher—would mark it on her childhood writing.

Which, Tanav supposed, made "communicating while walking in space and carrying a lot of equipment" the ultimate exam, given that brevity would have worked better for all involved.

"This is the point where we will split up," Neera said. "Upon reaching the secondary range booster, the security decryptor must be set and plugged into the base module. The same step will be done at the primary range booster by me."

"That's when you'll need me to activate the decoder?" Tanav asked as he watched the flashing red text that loudly proclaimed *ERROR* over the monitor for encrypted priority communications.

Another notification flashed on the screen, and while this one provided more details, it still didn't make sense to Tanav. So many statuses, messages, displays, *things* to keep track of, the whole thing started to push his thoughts into a growing panic. Every light, color, and character flooded his senses, an overwhelm that drilled down to the fact that he didn't really know what he was doing there. He forced a calm wave to Demi, who read it aloud: "'Data within embedded layer stuck in cache.'"

She huffed softly, giving away more of her frustration than she'd usually let on. "No idea what that means. I'll borrow Lynn from you for a minute later to see if she knows."

Borrow Lynn.

Demi normally wouldn't reference a personal relationship among the crew. What could cause her to slip like that?

Maybe they all felt overwhelmed. And if so, did *he* contribute to that in Demi?

Everyone else shifted into duty mode with ease, even with the shadow of the Ark Getru disaster. But he'd just put on his best front, and though Neera said his task would be easy, the relentless displays at the station made Tanav feel like a child among adults. He sat taller in his chair, like good posture would fool the rest of the crew.

Lynn didn't seem to notice Demi's slip—or she didn't care, given the potential space sickness at play.

"Affirmative," Neera said. On the holographic screen, the two silhouettes ambled toward respective transmitter modules on the hull, each carrying a booster pole of three feet in height. The engineering station on the other side chimed, and Tanav craned his neck to see a bunch of blue lights flashing.

Blue was usually good. Red was usually bad.

That didn't change across universes.

"Clickity-click," Lynn said. "My pole's plugged in. Demi, Neera is just about there. I'll give you the play-by-play. I'd sing more but I don't want anyone to hear me off-key. About ten feet now." Onscreen, Neera moved out of camera range. "Five feet. You know, I've never watched people spacewalk before, but this definitely makes them look kind of ridiculous. Like a gingerbread man bouncing off a starship hull." Her rambling meant that she really must have been terrified now. "Oh, my stomach is going again."

"My module is now active," Neera said. "Tanav, you should be activating the reset process for the encryption decoder and priority transmitter now. Gratitude is owed to Lynn for volunteering to assist with this step."

"Gratitude doesn't settle the nausea."

Despite the tension of the past hour, Lynn's joke received low chuckles across the bridge. At the helm, Hikaru's head bobbed with a snicker, and at the front data table, Lindsay and Karl both wore grins under the projected hologram feed. Somehow, Demi had turned around a worst-case scenario in the mess hall into this—a frayed and messy family that edged on broken but found its way back.

Yet one glance at Demi showed that she still carried it all with her: furrowed brow, arms crossed, and jaw clenched with an intensity that went beyond a standard repair situation, even one involving the outer hull. With that, Tanav once again pictured the images from Ark Getru.

Maybe Demi did too. Maybe she pictured *worse*. They all knew Demi shielded them from the war, allowing the Horizon crew to work on getting the photonic engine back online. Now Tanav had to reconsider everything he'd seen from her in the past six months. Other things must have bubbled beneath the surface, and how much of that pressurized her from within?

And what would happen to them if that pressure finally broke?

"Focus, people," Demi said. "Tanav, start the reset."

Tanav obliged, and despite his misgivings, Neera was right: his task was actually very simple. He tapped two different buttons on the comm display. "Resetting the system." His fingers held against the screen until the status indicators appeared. Was that all it took? It sure looked that way. "It's working," he said, as much to reassure himself as letting the others know. A quick glance caught a shift in Demi: her shoulders *finally* relaxed, and she settled back into her chair, probably a response to something actually going right today. The bar on his screen filled up, and a new message appeared:

TELEMETRY CONNECTED. DATA TRANSMISSION IN PROGRESS.

"We've got messages coming in," he said. "I'm just seeing them with an ID and no actual message. Are you sure it's fixed?"

"It's 'cause this is the priority array for classified information," Lynn said, her voice in an exaggerated know-it-all tone. "Guess I'm getting my job back. Sorry, that was mean, wasn't it? I wasn't trying to—"

"We're good," Tanav said, and he could practically see her smile form in response. Demi's personal tablet pinged, likely receiving detailed versions of the messages he just saw.

Demi's sharp inhale seemed to confirm that. And that worried Tanav on multiple levels.

Earlier, in the mess hall, he'd asked Demi if she was all right. She clearly was not, except this wasn't the time or place to bring it up. Tanav forced himself to focus on Lynn's station, though he knew better than to touch any of her settings. The comm display chimed, a new message loaded with technical language, and he projected a tone like he understood it. "That other error is back. Looks like a new process is starting. It says 'archiving data within embedded layer.'"

"Wait, what?" Lynn asked.

"'Archiving data within embedded layer.'" More text displayed, a dense wall that he couldn't decipher. "It says something about 'backup cache,' but I can't make out the blue from the green." With Lynn's linguistics background, he'd expected something snide whenever phrases from his old life snuck through. Yet Lynn's voice came over muffled, more like a collection of rapid curse words than anything else.

"Cabell's message hung up on data caching," Demi said. "Something's still stuck in there."

"Repaired equipment appears to be functioning at nominal levels," Neera said. "The vacuum of space is something I am ready to leave, as it is affecting my digestive system."

At least Neera told a joke. Or at least tried to. Lynn had mentioned that she'd really tried helping him to understand the timing of humor. Though given the backdrop of everything right now, maybe Neera still didn't grasp it.

A sudden sound pierced the comms, and after a second, the noise registered: a human scream. But there was only one human out on the hull . . .

Lynn.

Tanav stood up, his chair still swiveling as he turned to the holographic projection.

With the secondary transmission module still out of view, only spiraling debris pushed silently across the screen, little trickles of energy charges wrapping around the larger pieces.

And just behind all of that, a limp floating figure came into view: first the head, then the shoulders, then the bent legs, all static as it drifted. They didn't need the computer to run an identity scan. It was already clear:

Lynn floated into the empty expanse of space.

CHAPTER 4

NEERA

In some ways, Dywen physiology was similar to human physiology. Bipedal, two arms, two legs, basic bilateral symmetry. As Dywens and their pack-based, hierarchical society began exploring the galaxy in Neera's universe, their scientists theorized that this commonality across encountered species came from the fact that it was a nearly ideal model for living on solid land.

The details, though, differed.

For Dywens, their compound eyes offered a wider field of view yet worse low-light vision. Despite that, his species remained extremely sensitive to sudden flashes of light and high-contrast environments. Which meant that tracking Lynn's location was a challenge. The outer hull's spotlights illuminated the locations that required intervention and installation. But their bright lamps against the vast blackness of space created a contrast stark enough that Neera squinted to find Lynn.

Then the blast—a flash of energy rather than an eruption of burning gas. Neera's vision blurred in response for several seconds. It took a conscious effort to grasp that pieces of equipment had fractured into hundreds of tiny bits, all twirling away into space. Followed by Lynn's limp body, the magnetic boots somehow losing their grip and causing her to drift upward. Neera quelled his growing panic and remembered they had emergency space walk protocols in place.

He could rely on those. He moved immediately, one magnetic step at a time.

"What's going on?" Demi called out. "Lynn? Lynn, are you all right?"

"An accident has occurred," Neera said, and though his sentences got longer, the clip of his voice sped up and his fingers started to fidget. "Unconscious appears to be Lynn's current state due to an explosion of some sort." His eyes focused, the details gradually coming in. "A tether was applied to her belt right before this happened." Her body drifted until it hit some twenty feet over the hull, the slack of the tether tightening, then holding her still. "Lieutenant?" Neera called out over the comm.

"We need support crew over there. Get the rescue grapple," Demi ordered the monitoring crew members. "Neera, can you keep her safe until we get out there?"

Could he? Previous space walks were solo—he never worried about anyone else. Here, all the risks stood out: oxygen in the suit, internal injury, damage to the suit, damage to the tether . . .

Neera forced himself to stop and attach a scope from his equipment belt to his helmet's face shield. The projected image zoomed in, and Lynn came into focus. He scanned the tether's clamp on either end, one locked onto her belt and the other anchored at the transmitter's base module.

Both clamps looked steady.

But halfway up the tether lay a different problem—a clear fraying of the cable, likely impact damage from exploding debris. Neera tapped the side of the scope, and numbers and lines highlighted across his view, all to analyze the integrity of the cable.

Sixty-four-percent cut. With exposed electrical flow eating away at it, combined with the pressure created by Lynn's upward float, that number was gradually ticking toward one hundred.

And numbers never lied.

"An unexpected issue has presented itself in Lynn's tether."

"Can you fix it?"

"Further damage may occur with attempted manipulation." Neera sped up his march toward her.

"Lynn?" Demi called out over the open channel. "Lynn? Wake up! Rescue team, give me an ETA." Indistinct muted chatter came over the comm, though Demi's response gave away their status. "Not good enough. Get there faster."

Neera analyzed the problem the same way he would approach fixing a broken power conduit: initial condition, goals and objectives, and possible bridges between all of that. The zero gravity environment could be solved by a pull. But a delicate one, to avoid even more decaying of the cable, along with some guidance on Lynn's side of the tether.

Which required her to be conscious.

The scanner showed the fibers of the cable gradually deconstructing. A decision was needed—the rescue team wouldn't arrive in time.

Neera took one more look at Lynn's limp body and considered how the strength of their friendship might assist this task. As an original Horizon crew member, Lynn had been Neera's first alien contact when his Regent Empire freighter was pulled from his universe into the gravity well. He'd expected conflict in that new space, but Lynn had initiated communications and used the Horizon's translation matrix to establish commonalities between their languages. Eventually, she'd been the first to welcome him aboard the Horizon. Lynn always claimed she was just doing her job, but in that action, she made him feel a little less alone in a very strange place.

Their friendship started there and only grew stronger. This depth allowed another way of connecting, even if it meant putting himself in danger.

Neera closed his eyes, a wave of his emotions reaching out, like a radar sending a ping signal. Her presence came through to him—faint, but there. Usually, Dywen empathic connections happened between two conscious receivers, the comfort of each other's existence allowing for a deeper bond to form, like neurons tying into each other. With Lynn unconscious, Neera hoped that their bond was strong enough for her to accept him, like how his species considered others in their pack.

If not, his own sense of self would shatter. Temporary, only for several minutes, but problematic given that they were both on the outside of a starship.

Lynn seemed to recognize this strange semiconscious presence, and fibers of connection formed—not the same as the natural connection to other Dywens, but enough to achieve a temporary shared empathic experience. Loyalty to Demi, friendship to Neera and crew members like Aurora, grief for Grant Singh . . .

And for Tanav, Neera read a deeper bond, feelings very foreign to what Dywen families knew.

Through this came a strange hiccup of discomfort; as its wave struck Neera, he sensed that whatever caused it had little to do with the space walk and in fact seeded far deeper, perhaps being with Lynn for months.

That would be a conversation for another time—if Lynn even wanted to discuss it. Perhaps she found the return to Cluster space disquieting as well. A place so *different* from the stories Lynn had told him.

Their emotions wove into each other, Neera sending an intentional calm to establish himself, an empathic way of holding someone's hand. Then he projected out something sudden and new, a transmission wave of *urgency* directly to Lynn's very core.

His eyes flew open.

And he knew—he *knew*—hers did as well.

"Neera?" Lynn suddenly said. "What am I— I feel weird."

"Indeed you do. I have connected to your senses using a process known to Dywens as empathic imprinting." Lynn groaned at this, and Neera wasn't sure if that meant she remembered the details he'd explained about his native society years ago. "It is a connection often created by Dywen families and their pack. The aftereffects of it can be difficult for non-Dywens."

"Empathic . . . what?"

That meant she did not remember.

"Explanations will come in due time. For now, your alertness is the most important part of this plan." Neera moved into position at the base of the tether clamp. "Damage has put your tether at risk. I will pull you toward the ship, but you must orient yourself in order to take my hand. The integrity of the tether is almost gone. We must do this now."

"Now?" She huffed out a short laugh. "Told you, you'd make a good captain."

Captain. Before becoming a captain, GCF officers needed to be a first officer. Demi had offered Neera the position months ago. He'd declined.

He fixed things. He didn't give orders. He didn't know *how* to.

This, however, was a fix. "Now," Neera said, and he pulled. Not too hard—snapping the final threads of the cable might create a whiplash effect that sent Lynn spiraling away. And not too light, as he needed her to have enough pull to float toward him despite the dampening effect of the Horizon's shield bubble. Lynn inched closer, her arm outstretched toward the safety of Neera's hand. They connected, and Neera gripped her hand tightly, though Lynn only offered a weak return. He pulled her in, twisting her body until he could reset her magnetic boots. They came to life with blinking green lights, and Neera dragged her legs toward the hull until they locked on.

Now they waited.

Except Lynn slumped in an odd way. Neera twisted to see her eyes had fallen half-shut, beyond empathic calm. Neera pulled out his scanner and soon understood why:

A cut in the space suit.

"Almost there," Demi said over the comm. "They're preparing the grapple drone."

A small cut, no bigger than a few centimeters, but enough to start draining air faster than it pumped in. Lynn needed to stay awake. Neera closed his eyes, transmitting his own internal urgency at the situation like a bolt of energy to her. Her eyes snapped open again, though they quickly fell.

"The most important thing is for you to remain conscious right now," Neera said. "Help has almost arrived, but oxygen is leaking from a puncture in your space suit. Talking must be your priority to stay awake."

"Talking?" Lynn said slowly. "About what?"

Neera didn't have a good—or quick—answer to that question. So many choices floated through his mind, but with time running out, he forced an arbitrary choice. "Tell me about the song you were singing."

"Oh," she said with a small laugh. Her eyes half closed, and even though she seemed to force them open, they gradually sank again. "Rilo Kiley. A band from Earth's peak rock music era." She took in a slow, even breath. "Jenny Lewis was their singer. A poet for generations."

"Drone's firing up," Demi said. "Hang in there."

"Neera. Your turn. You tell me something. Tell me . . ." Lynn said, a smile forming even as she slowed down. Some distance away, a hatch slid open, the light from inside cut through by the silhouette of a circular drone. ". . . about the photonic engine. Something I don't know. You love talking about that." Her question came with a curiosity somehow echoing the deep anxiety from earlier. But whatever kept her mind awake would work.

He thought back to the last conversation he had with his friend Colin Sadler, a GCF engineer who studied the photonic engine as Neera did, despite his war-support tasks. That would work here.

"A system reset exists for the pressure release cycle," Neera started. With one hand still holding on to Lynn, he raised his other arm to hail the drone. "The cycle is necessary from the collected heats of the engine's different modules. Because they were not designed to work together, a partial reset is not possible. A cycle initiation causes a reset delay of approximately thirty-two . . ." The drone arrived, a circular machine with small propulsion jets at different angles and several robotic arms. In this case, each carried rescue cables tied to an anchor within the ship. "Thirty-two to forty hours. Accidental cycle initiation is to be avoided," he said as he undid Lynn's damaged tether and attached the rescue line, "to prevent significant delays in engine experiments." As he took the secondary line to his own belt, the drone's arm grabbed Lynn and fired off a boost, expediting her back to safety.

While her body tugged away, her voice came through the comms—weak, slow, but still undeniably herself. "That all sounds really boring," she said through huffs. "Thanks for helping me. Can you show it to me?"

Lynn drifted away, tugged forward by the drone toward the open hatch, where an emergency crew awaited. "You are welcome to a complete demonstration once you are safe and recovered."

CHAPTER 5

DEMI

Twenty-four hours after Lynn's semi-disastrous space walk, Demi called an emergency meeting in the Horizon's observation lounge. The full orders from Minister Cabell had been curt and simple: captains were to show a compilation of selected footage from the incident, cite it as an environmental accident, and say that any crew members that lost family in the "accident" would be granted emergency bereavement leave upon request.

Well, that wouldn't work. The damage was done, so she presented the crew with a choice:

"None of us can unsee that message. It's horrific. I'm sure it recalls bad memories of being in the gravity well. However, Command wants everyone to believe it's an accident. I'm sure there is tactical thinking behind that decision, so I'm asking you to respect that." Classified intel was classified for a reason, except classified munitions deficiencies were a bit different from covering up the truth behind a terrorist attack. This marked the first time Command asked for an active, clear lie. Ten years ago, she'd see this as an order.

After everything, it wasn't that simple.

A long pause stretched through the group, and while they looked at one another, none of them looked at Demi.

"What the fuck?" Casey asked. "Are you listening to yourself?" Her crossed arms, matched by a scowl across her face. "What is this statesman bullshit? People are dying!"

Demi knew *exactly* what Casey was talking about. Her words had been her own, but they acted as a filter for Command's message. And everyone saw through that. "This is a little more complicated than that."

"No it's not. This is a cover-up, plain and simple." Nods circled among the crew, and Demi could feel immediately that she was losing them. "We know you. You don't talk like this. You *didn't* talk like this when we were in the well. This is Command putting words in your mouth. This is Command telling you to lie. A 'tactical' lie is still a lie."

Grumbles turned into agreement turned into shouting. A barrage of words flew at Demi, and as she glanced at these faces she knew so well, a deep shame welled within her gut.

Aurora yelled to be heard, and that gradually brought a quiet, but not a calm. "If this hadn't leaked, would you even talk with us about it? Or would you just tell their lie?"

On the surface, Demi remained controlled. Not even an extra exhale or scowl. But inside, anger gathered momentum. It started small, a simple irritation at the way dumb luck and chain of command collided to create this mess. But it rolled into a pointed, desperate fury aimed at Command for putting her in this position. *They* wanted her to act like any other captain of any other crew, like none of what her crew did mattered, and everyone on the Horizon could just jump at orders. For six months, she'd stood in front of her crew, taking the jabs and shrapnel from within GCF, even playing the role of the dutiful captain to keep things as status quo as possible.

"I don't know," Demi said after several seconds. More shouting rained down on her, though Aurora yelled to let Demi be heard. "You wanted honesty, I am being honest. I don't know. I didn't have time to think things through before it happened."

A clamor of voices rose quickly, words meshing into a wall of sound without any distinct purpose. Casey stepped forward with a hand held high, and that tamped down the arguing enough for her to speak. "I remember when the well started collapsing, and I told you about how every generation in my GCF family lived by their code. This idea that nothing from above was ever wrong. My grandparents, my parents, my aunts and uncles. All those admirals and vice admirals, so wrong. So often, they just went with it." She faced Demi with sharp eyes. "You remember that?"

Demi did. She nodded and gave Casey the space to finish her thought.

"It was just me and Demi," Casey said as she looked around. "Standing in the captain's quarters. Staring at the lashes of red energy. Terrifying. I remember realizing that was why I didn't look out any of the windows. But that night, I forced myself to look. Because that was our reality. And I asked you to never be like them. Never be just another officer. Not to us. And you promised. And you weren't; we saw your honesty every day. You never lied." She came back to Demi, her expression somewhere between challenging and pleading. "I like to think you haven't changed since we've been back. We trust Demi, but can we trust GCF Captain Kim?"

"'A military's a military, even in peacetime.' That's what I always heard. 'You can't trust them.' I thought I knew better. It's why I joined the fleet. And now we're at war," said Lindsay Ballard, the Horizon's chief of environmental operations. "Can we trust *anyone* in the Cluster? I defended you to my parents last week. Now this? The WM was goaded into Ark Getru. What is Command even doing? What other deaths are they responsible for?"

Demi saw it now, like her vision suddenly focused with startling clarity. Casey was right: in the well, she could protect them because it was only the Horizon, the colony ships, and the Lumersians. In Cluster space, eventually *something* would break through. The attacks came from too many sides, in too many ways. Military commands, war resources, the drip of information to and from friends and family, the needs of people who stayed aboard . . .

Follow command or serve her crew. It had to be one or the other, because satisfying both in a time of war was impossible. The soldiers dying on the front lines, the civilians caught in collateral damage, the politics squeezing the life out of both sides, she couldn't dent those losses. The Horizon couldn't dent those losses.

But as she looked at the people who survived with her, the choice was easy. And the choice was right. She owed them, for every single loss under her command.

"You can trust me," Demi said slowly. This lowered the volume—and tension—enough to be heard. "Command asked me to lie to you. I won't. The way I see it, you, me, this ship, we're not changing the course of the war, so I'm choosing to prioritize *us*. Life is different within the Horizon's walls. I say that all the time and I mean it." The murmurs finally settled, and Demi saw her opening. "It's not always going to be clean. But if we want to protect ourselves, sometimes things go sideways. Here's what I'm asking of you—I talk about the difference between the Horizon and life out there; I'm asking you to treat this the same."

Now everyone's eyes turned to her: Neera in the back, Tanav and Lynn off to her right, Casey still in front, and the rest of the group. Demi took a moment to look at them, to really take in their faces and understand them. Because this was survival too, but messier and more complicated. She couldn't control that, but she could at least give them stability. "With each other, whatever you need to say or feel about Ark Getru is fine. Your opinions are your own. But to keep Command out *there*, you must use the cover story in any communications to family or other crews."

"It's being complicit. You're asking us to lie," Aurora immediately said, and others agreed.

Demi looked at Aurora, noting the tension in her shoulders, the harsh flattening of her lips. "If we want to keep this ship, this *crew* together and safe, then sometimes it calls for going with orders. It's a compromise to prioritize *us*." She gauged the reaction again, logic tipping things her way. Not necessarily enthusiastic approval, but at least something between understanding and acceptance.

They'd skirted guidelines before, taking shortcuts or fudging reports. None of those moments came with this contention, and Demi didn't know if that stemmed from the scope of Ark Getru's destruction or from the fact that those choices often came as a group. For now, she needed to lower the tension and give everyone some breathing room. "This isn't over. I suggest we all sit with it for another day or two. Can you give me that? Have I earned that?" Several affirmatives rippled through the crowd. "We'll know when the time is right. Until then, I'm available for private discussions. Or gripes. Or yelling, if you need it. Or if you need to pet Indy." A greyhound mention grabbed enough laughs to settle things down, enough that Demi dismissed the crew and very quietly exhaled. They shuffled out, and as she observed, Demi caught herself alone and wondering about ramen night.

Were they trying to capture something that didn't exist anymore?

Grant would know. And while she missed Grant's friendship the most, his sensible grasp of the crew really, really helped in moments like this—and with the upcoming Command status meeting. Because the topic of Ark Getru was sure to dominate.

Except she *wasn't* the only one in the observation lounge. Tanav had disappeared with the rest for a moment, but then came back. Of course he'd be the one to break protocol. He'd probably ask if she was all right. She told herself that, given everything, it was okay to let some reality through in her response. She kind of owed him that, given their big crew talk about honesty.

"You've had easier days," he said, empathy laced into his tilted brow and soft smile.

"That obvious?" Demi asked, rubbing her face in her hands.

"I get the feeling that it's been a rough twenty-four hours for you. And I don't exactly have any crew duties right now, so . . ."

Tanav always downplayed his role, despite the fact that it took on more importance the smaller the crew got. He just couldn't see that. "I just wonder if I've lost all their trust," she said.

"I had this moment yesterday"—Tanav started as he leaned against one of the lounge's tall, thin tables—"when I realized how tightly you've been holding it together."

He noticed that? "I should deny that."

"I think that's the problem." Tanav gave a small laugh, which caused a matching chuckle to sneak out from Demi. "Everyone's used to you being impervious to stress. Sometimes they don't re-member that you're actually a person underneath that." Her sigh filled the empty lounge, and as much as she tried, snapping back into captain mode suddenly didn't feel as easy as it normally did. "They're shaken," Tanav continued. "I am too. That footage. I've never seen anything like that."

"Things like that aren't supposed to happen." Demi paused, sur-prised at the low tone in her voice. "I'd be worried if that *didn't* shake them."

"Hey," he said. She'd heard that word said in that way before—Grant used to do that before imparting wisdom. Did Tanav pick it up from Grant, or was this just the standard operating procedure for talking down a stressed captain? "You didn't cause that. You know?"

Which was such an odd thing to say. Of course she didn't cause that. Maybe that meant something different in Tanav's universe, a whole separate meaning to phrases. Tanav's words almost worked opposite than intended, and Demi assumed the strong shoulders and straight back of her rank and role. "It doesn't matter who caused it. It affects all of us. My job is to keep those ripples at bay."

"You're asking for a very reasonable thing. People are in shock. They need to let it wear off first." He offered just a hint of a smile at that. "That's my official, non-military-yet-military perspective."

"Noted." With that single word, Demi's inner switch flipped, mind revving up to meet with Command. "Tanav, you're a good officer," she said, emphasizing the last word as she gestured toward the exit.

He averted his eyes, and his pace dropped slightly behind her. "I'm not really an officer." Which he said from time to time. And sometimes she tried to engage him about how value on the ship didn't need to come from technical know-how or things like that, but here she chose to stay quiet and instead offered a warm look.

The observation lounge's doors slid open, and they stepped out. Several steps ahead, Lindsay stood with eyes trained on a tablet. They turned to Demi and Tanav but diverted their look right after meeting Demi's. Instead, as they passed, Lindsay said hello only to Tanav before turning back to the screen.

Demi didn't exactly ignore things during the weekly war status meetings, but her ship didn't carry troops, equipment, or frontline support, which usually put it far lower on Command's priority list. Near each meeting's end, Demi usually provided the latest information on the photonic engine tests, usually on things like synth generation efficacy or examination of current jump-cycle stages.

This time would be different. Something had changed. Because a flurry of messages arrived right upon leaving the observation lounge, all involving the photonic engine. At her desk, she called Indy over and sat with each message. The greyhound leaned against her hip, and Demi found that the deeper this went, the tighter she hugged her dog.

Command asked how much of the Horizon's resources were taken by photonic tests. Research & Development asked why the synthetic photons developed by Cluster scientists kept failing. Stellar cartography asked what a successful jump range might eventually look like compared to standard FTL. Even Advanced Security Measures got in on it, with a curt demand for all the reasons why the engine wouldn't jump.

And just to rub it in, Tactical Resources asked how much time was lost on this "science experiment."

THE PHOTONIC EFFECT   41

"Indy," she said, kissing the dog on the nose, "a walk in the California redwoods sounds good about now, doesn't it? A *long* walk. My childhood dog loved it."

A long walk was better than the alternative, which would have been screaming so loud the bridge crew on the other side of the deck would have heard her.

The Horizon had just gone from being the fleet's footnote to the thing that every department suddenly wanted. Which would further complicate the growing unease among the crew, especially since Demi had no answers. Neera spent entire days testing different stages of the photonic engine, yet acquired no firm explanations. Or solutions.

It really was too bad the engine didn't work. Because if it did, they could at least take it somewhere far away from this cycle of escalation between the Cluster and the WM. At the end of it, asking her crew to repeat a cover story suddenly seemed like it might be the least terrible thing to come out of this.

All for a "science experiment." But much more than a mere science experiment.

Demi looked at the corner table underneath the room's large glass dome, eyes focusing in the dim light. On it sat a metallic unit of sorts, a cuboid with a frontal square, two feet each way and a depth of one foot—not too different from the units in engineering.

This particular photonic containment unit captured a single purple spark, a dot of energy that used to be a square plane but now was barely strong enough to glow. Even still, it existed, and that meant part of Chuck, or Photonic Being #910047, still existed, despite being used up, dead, or however Lumersians addressed the state of being deceased.

She missed him. So much that staring at the barely visible purple glow pulled her mind away, long enough for Indy to decide to lie down on her bed.

Long enough to remain lost until a chime yanked her back into reality.

It rang again from her desk, and Demi squeezed her eyes tightly shut and held in a breath that lasted for two more chimes.

Her eyes flew open and she stuffed all of that emotion right down. Duty called.

The room lit up with the desk's display, but rather than Minister Cabell, vice admirals, or admirals, Demi stared at charts. Ark Getru's death toll, Ark Getru's resource impact, Ark Getru's social awareness, Ark Getru's supply chain impact; *everything* tied into the disaster and its fallout. For forty-five minutes, voices narrated over numbers and graphs, with the occasional map of troop movements and related intel swapping into view.

Turned out, Demi's hunch was correct: this only created more chaos, with GCF resources being shuffled to and fro but without any true *purpose*. If the WM meant to bring the Cluster back to negotiations with such an act, it failed. If anything, this might extend the war. That realization sunk in, and right when Demi let out a sigh, she heard her name.

"We're running long," said a voice she didn't recognize, and with the display still full of charts, it remained unidentified. "But we need to hear from Captain Demora Kim of the Horizon. Captain Kim, does the photonic engine work?"

This was bait with no good answer. A quick, obvious reply downplayed Neera's work. A long-winded response would paint the Horizon as an ongoing waste of time. "Our progress has been more theoretical than practical since my last report. We continue to test in stages per safety and security protocols," she said in careful cadence. "But we've had comm array repairs this week. That's been where a lot of our efforts have been."

"Isn't the Horizon's entire purpose to get the photonic engine online? And you're saying you can't even support that? Then what will finish this science experiment?"

There it was again—"science experiment."

Hearing the phrase said out loud touched a nerve deeper than reading it in a message. The photonic engine started as a grand effort that blended tech from different cultures, and its repair followed suit with Cluster standards. Science experiments through and through, but for Demi, the only science experiment that mattered was her relationship with a photonic being.

She'd even jokingly called their relationship just that, to which Chuck replied, "Experiments are defined by their hypothesis, controls, and metrics. Have we applied that to our time together?"

To hear their term twisted into condescension ignited a raw wound upon so much more. Her home was unrecognizable and growing more alien by the minute. Now Ark Getru, then the mess *about* Ark Getru, then the near miss with Lynn, and Chuck was *still* gone. Demi's internal defenses broke. Her face flushed, frustration and disappointment clouding her ability to put together a single coherent thought.

A rare moment of pure sarcastic impulse broke through. "More engineers. We're not even a skeleton crew."

A deep breath later, a wave of regret.

She shouldn't have done that. And she knew it right away.

"Understood, Captain Kim. We'll take that request under consideration. Apologies for running long, let's hope the galaxy has a better week when we speak next."

Under consideration.

What had Demi unleashed?

Three days later, Demi got the answer when a new message arrived:

PRIORITY: Imminent Crew Transfer to Horizon

Captain Kim, per your request, Command has expedited
authorization for the transfer of eight support engineers and
analysts to support the photonic engine project. In addition, under
the supervision of Commander Jonathan Matthews, an additional
complement of thirty-three crew will be assigned to bring the

Horizon closer to its preferred capacity for standard operations, including a new first officer.

"Expedited authorization." Could they even do that?

Demi laughed to herself at that question. They asked the entire fleet to cover up a terrorist attack. So transferring support staff to an under-resourced ship with highly prized experimental tech, she supposed, was nothing in the scheme of things.

Demi sank into her chair, a pit in her gut pulling her down harder than the ship's artificial gravity systems. She had pledged to keep everything outside the ship, and in her moment of weakness, *she* was the one who invited it in. Tension already ensnared the group. This wouldn't help. If anything, it showed how much was out of Demi's hands—out of all their hands.

And Commander Jonathan Matthews?

Was that the new first officer? Or was he just overseeing this transition?

Either way, life on the Horizon was about to change—and whoever took the first officer chair wouldn't fill the shoes of Grant Singh. Not even close. Demi read the orders one more time and wondered if she could convince Neera to accept a promotion before all this went down.

CHAPTER 6

DEMI

Demi gave herself an evening's sleep before informing the crew of the impending changes. "Sorry for ruining breakfast," she started, with everyone gathered in the mess hall.

That joke didn't save the discussion from accomplishing just that. The reactions went somewhat as expected: Neera and Macek asked about the kind of engineering support they would be getting. Tanav asked if she needed help onboarding new crew. Lynn tried to talk up a positive spin to things. Karl, the ship's eldest officer, even said it might feel good to support the fleet, given the recent attacks. Which drew all sorts of looks.

Others, like Casey, stood stone-faced at the news, staring at their oatmeal or pancakes like Demi didn't exist. Lindsay simply left the room.

But at least they didn't outright argue with one another. Despite the growing fractures between Demi and the crew, if they still trusted one another, then that would be a win for now. The rest would figure itself out over the coming days. That was how Demi and Grant handled it in the early days of the gravity well, when they made the decision to share resources with the other colony ships. That worked out in the end, so maybe this would too.

Of course, that was still under the context of survival. This was the fleet and the Cluster worming their way onto the Horizon. This dichotomy played out as transfers gradually arrived over the following days: engineers, technicians, new faces that arrived with the most unexpected realization:

To them, Demi was something of a celebrity.

Crew members unloaded, bringing awkward smiles, stumbled introductions, lingering glances; the story of returning the Horizon from hell must have captured their awe. Too bad reality didn't come close to the myth. Demi began adapting stock replies, counting down until this moment when the final shuttle docked.

A headache brewed as Demi waved to the craft's final passenger, a young, starstruck ensign named Diaz who'd given an enthusiastic if rehearsed speech: "Captain Kim. I just wanted to say, I've read all the details about your time in the gravity well and your encounters with the Lumersian species. They sound fascinating." Demi tried her best for a calm, neutral pose—a bit of practice for her newfound commitment to protocol. "At the academy, I specialized in both piloting and xenobiology. So I'm a bit of a fan. If that's okay to say so."

"Two specialties in the academy. An overachiever. You'll like our resident xenobiologist," Demi said, and Diaz laughed much louder than a person normally would.

"If the Horizon has to evade a WM attack, you'll be in safe hands with me."

Diaz couldn't have been more than a year or two out of the academy, especially if he was in the rotation program for new graduates.

An entire generation so used to war that they casually discussed it. What a waste.

Diaz saluted and left, and Demi was about to follow him when her eyes hung on the corner of the docked craft. The bottom-left corner of the outer hull carried the cracks and scorch marks of an attack, the burnt discoloration overtaking the last two painted digits of the shuttle's registry number.

Plenty of transport ships brought supplies and equipment over recent months, each craft arriving in pristine condition, with war scars patched up prior to their next assignment. Now it appeared no one was hiding from the reality of the war. Not even new recruits.

More mechanical noises came, a mix of grinding gears and released hydraulics, followed by the sound of boots on metal. The footsteps echoed before a silhouette appeared on the shuttle's loading ramp. Shadows covered their identity until he got all the way down and turned, pausing only to survey the Horizon's docking bay, though the deep blue trim of GCF Command stood out on the uniform. He took several steps closer, the docking bay's light casting over close-cropped hair, tanned and scarred cheeks, and creases that seemed permanently etched around his eyes.

Commander Jonathan Matthews.

Demi had spent the last few days perusing his records, at least what she could access. Born in the extra-system colony of Barnard, a childhood survivor of the HBT attacks, a member of the local military that liberated Reflex Point—and from there, he moved to the Cluster, eventually joining the Advanced Security Measures division.

Also, people considered him "matter-of-fact."

From his scowl to his lumbering walk, he seemed more of a military stereotype come to life. Which made his interest in a science ship even more confusing.

"Commander," Demi said, hand to brow in a customary salute. Mathews's hand came up in return, though it stopped halfway, turning more into a casual wave rather than an official gesture. "Welcome to the Horizon."

He spoke as he walked, making fleeting eye contact with Demi. "We barely made it. Nearly ran out of fuel." His words came with a slight drawl that confirmed the extra-system upbringing in his record. "Either our onboard computer forgot how to count, or the depot manager did." His gruff chuckle filled with annoyance, though

Demi couldn't tell who its target was. "Maybe both. Transports don't have time to get prim and proper these days." His gaze dropped to the metal panels of the docking bay floor. He knelt to swipe a finger against the floor, then stood up again. "Not like this place. Not a speck of dust here."

"A lot of equipment comes through. We try to keep it clean, ensure that particulate matter and other debris won't cause interference." Demi caught herself being defensive, a position usually saved for meetings with upper tiers of GCF Command and their requests.

"I'm sorry," he said, as if he sensed her annoyance. "I'm being petty, aren't I? I'll try that again."

"Tensions are high right now," Demi said, much quicker than she'd intended.

"Yeah," he said, looking around. "Ark Getru will do that to people." He nodded toward the docking bay's exit and set out, Demi tracking his pace. "Your crew buying the cover story? I hear it's not going over in a lot of places. Footage is leaking, people are finding out."

Was this a test of some sort from Command? Or was this why his profile noted his reputation for being "matter-of-fact"? Demi gambled on the latter and decided to offer honesty in return. "We're a ten-year-old science vessel equipped with hardware from multiple universes. Sometimes things don't work." *Some* honesty, at least. She wasn't going to explain that she refused to lie to her crew. "A technical issue led to some of the crew being exposed to Cabell's message. They know to keep it quiet to newcomers. I've put in a request to upgrade outdated comm hardware but—"

"Don't do that," he said, his voice sharp with clipped words. "For now, this ship needs to stay exactly as it is."

His statement was so unexpected that Demi waited to respond. He pulled a tablet off his belt and began thumbing through schematics.

Schematics of the Horizon's comm system.

Why would he have that already loaded?

"Your opinion is noted," she finally said.

Matthews offered a half smile in return. "Look, you can probably tell that I'm really not good at small talk, so I'm gonna be direct. It'll save us time. Fair?"

On the one hand, this was probably the most honest conversation Demi had ever had with external officers since they'd returned from the gravity well. On the other hand, she was certain Matthews had bad news in store.

"Fair."

"Your job is to either get your engine working or not." Matthews at least paused his schematic reading to look her in the eye. "The clock is ticking. Don't ask why. I can't tell you."

Demi was used to some measure of disrespect from GCF Command since coming home. The Horizon's arrival seemed to be more nuisance than anything else. When she pushed back against transitioning to war assets, they begrudgingly agreed—mostly because the Horizon's sudden return made for great publicity, a victory against impossible odds. But every message from Command since came with the implication that *they* had done *her* a favor. Still, that tone came from admirals and other senior officials. Who was this random commander to come in and give obscure orders to her, on *her* ship no less?

"Commander Matthews, I have received no such timetable from GCF Command. If you're expressing an *opinion*, consider it noted."

He raised his hands, head bowed in contrition that seemed sincere. "I promise you, I'm not being insubordinate. Now look, I go ship to ship, sector to sector, captain to captain. I evaluate what we need to save lives and protect people. Command was already reviewing your ship's specifications when your engineering request came in. They asked my opinion. I looked over this ship, this crew. It's a hell of a history, I have to say. I'm trying to respect what you've been through. But you've had your time. There has to be a cap, especially when there aren't any results. They're giving you days for a live test of the engine. Full cycle. Not stages or simulations."

"Days?" Demi scanned his face for clues, while her best instincts muted the logical follow-up: What could possibly make them want something so soon?

It didn't matter, though. Matthews practically read her mind. "Yes, days. Your ship is needed. One test. It jumps or it doesn't."

Demi tamped down her shock, tapping into years of training under Captain Hayes, her former superior and mentor. She figured this was coming. She'd gotten enough side-eyes and pithy comments from Command not to suspect it was in the works. But she'd made a promise.

The war wasn't supposed to exist. This wasn't their fight. She tried to keep them away from the chaos, yet her own mistake let it in.

"With respect, Commander—" Demi started, but he put up a hand.

"You don't have to respect me. You outrank me," he said, pointing to the blue stripes on her uniform's arm. "I'm just the messenger."

"The Horizon is not a battleship. It never has been. It has standard defense and minimal attack capabilities." Demi opted not to rattle off the ship's specifics. "Its charter was exploration, mapping, and data collection. It's not going to turn the tide of *their* war."

As soon as she said the word "their," she knew it was a mistake. *Another* mistake. She'd talked about it as a separate issue for so long, a slip came out naturally. But she couldn't give Matthews any advantages, not with tension already tightening his jaw and brow. He stared blankly at her, as if he needed a moment to reset.

"This morning, I saw an entire ship go down because the WM bombed a munitions transport. A week ago, we all saw a space station crash into a planet without a single chance to rescue thousands of lives," he said slowly. "They make quick, destructive strikes. They're not waiting for orders like we are. Intelligence thinks they have new FTL tech far faster than Cluster standard. And it is costing

us. So it's *everyone's* war, until it isn't. Science ships support the front
line. Repairs, medical staging, resource conversion. Meeting places."
Matthews bit down on his bottom lip, like he tried to contain something about to burst out.

Everyone's war.

Was it really? Demi grounded herself, sensing the stability of the
floor beneath her to stem the oncoming ire in her gut. She felt control
slipping away, putting her in the role of innocent bystander against
the inevitability of the war, like a virus replicating out of control.

Though she wouldn't let Matthews see it, Demi kicked herself for
ever being so naïve.

"Like I said, you put in a request. Then I put in a request. You
outrank me, so if you don't agree, take it up with Command and put
in another request. I respect the chain of command." He turned away
from her, finishing his sentence as he started down the hall. "Let's
leave it at that. I can't tell you anymore."

"Can't or won't?" Demi probably could have phrased it a little
better, but at this point, they were already butting heads, so why not.

It did make him pause, though. "A little bit of both," he said, his
tone humbler than she expected. "We should set course for Base
Gamma Twenty-One. It's the closest one to your mapped convergence point. You'll prep at Gamma Twenty-One, then FTL to the
convergence point and fire it up. If you'll excuse me, I need to check
out the hardware in stellar cartography."

Matthews's departure should have been a welcome sight, except
now he moved deeper into *her* ship. And an hour after Matthews
left the docking bay, a message from Vice Admiral Swapna Krishna
made the orders official:

The War Council decided the Horizon is a top priority to the war
effort. All imminent test proceedings will be monitored with elevated
visibility. Diagnostics are synced with the computers in our lab at
central command.

You are to contact us immediately following completion of the test—succeed or fail.

With the new goal announced, tasks were assigned and executed like an undammed current. Even the unhappy crew members did their job, and by all metrics, they did them well. Something about having a mission and a deadline lit a spark through the Horizon.

At the center of it was Neera and his mix of new and old engineers. Command suggested forty-eight hours before initiating the test; Demi negotiated it to seventy-two hours, with the excuse that most of the crew arrived on the ship days ago and they deserved the luxury of breathing room. In the middle of that, Demi checked in with Tanav to see if he'd heard rumblings among the crew, given the rapid changes. "I can't say who. And I can't say for sure. But I think you might hear of some transfer requests in the coming day."

None came through during that span. If crew dealt with misgivings or bitterness, they didn't present it to her yet. Strangely, everyone worked well as a team together, with Neera overseeing a plant for a full jump sequence built from individual test stage data. The truth was, however, that they'd learned little about what actually worked.

Rather, those tests eliminated *some* of what didn't work.

With the seventy-two hours nearly burned up, Demi arrived in engineering for a final check, or at least a pep talk. The double doors swept open, and she entered the tall bay where the standard GCF engine room held the pulsing white of standard plasma-based propulsion surrounded by an upper-level walkway. In the middle sat a system built up with the technology of far-ranging cultures, a variety of complexities that looked like a single large tube jutting out of a large glass case. But inside that tube sat all sorts of circuits and wires, conduits and power cells stitched together for a not-quite-perfected jump process.

The photonic engine.

And connected to it was a smaller module: the generator crafted over months to convert physical matter to synthetic photons. With the clock counting down, Neera and his team all hunched over it, tapping at interfaces or reading scanners.

"How is everything?" Demi called out, arms propped on the railing across the top perimeter. She waved Neera to join her at the vantage point, and the tall figure set down his tools to turn her way. She nodded once more and waved again, and only after that did Neera leave the team working their stations.

Part of the reason why Demi wanted Neera as her first officer was that he was the most capable: intelligent, thoughtful, analytical, and loyal. His intuition always rose to the moment, just like on the outer hull. His problem was that he remained blind to it, and even here, he still needed that extra push before breaking from his station. That type of *permission* came with the rank.

If only he would have accepted it—and accepted that in himself.

It was too late now, with newly assigned Commander Doug Connors taking the spot. They still worked on finding a rhythm, but at the very least, Connors's first days showed him to be amiable and sharp, and even now, he gladly went to the science lab to support the photonic test.

Connors's only issue was that he was an officer. A fine one, yet not a survivor. He'd simply never fully understand some things about her. Not like Neera.

"All stations monitoring," Neera said as he approached. "Pre-jump power cycling has completed. Final checks are being processed. Synth quantity has been generated to the proper amount."

"I figured that," Demi said, nudging him with her elbow. Which, given their height difference, connected with him more across the forearm. "When I asked 'how is everything,' that includes you. This is the culmination of everything."

"My thoughts on the process do not affect the outcome," he said after a long moment. "Command will be observing no matter what."

She hadn't explicitly told him that. Once again, his intuition proved correct. "You're psychic, then." A second passed before a small grin formed on his lips. He *almost* got it. "You're telling me you don't like how we got here." Demi took a deep sigh, one hand through her short hair. "No argument there. I don't know, sometimes things don't go right until they're forced to."

Neera stared straight ahead, though his weight tilted forward. Demi knew what this meant. If Neera was preoccupied with the test, he'd have worked the tablet in his hand or watched the large display on the far corner or possibly excused himself to go to the synth generator. "Something's on your mind?" she asked.

"The numbers are not lining up as we would like." His gaze remained, locked on somewhere past her.

"'We'?"

"Sadler." Demi recognized the name of Neera's engineer friend. It wasn't an official collaboration by any means, but at this point, she'd take any help she could get. "The previous stage four tests were reviewed by him. Decay issues still appear in—" Demi's sideways look stopped him before he got too deep in explanation. "Issues still appear. Worries have gripped me."

"You think the engine might be dangerous?"

"No. Shutoff gates and emergency venting mechanisms are built in." Neera's head fell, a sharp gesture that caught the eye of Macek on the lower level. He enunciated slowly, a clear effort in his cadence. "I worry about what happens to our pack if we fail. It does not sound like we will get another opportunity."

There it was—the rare vulnerability that she often urged Neera to embrace. She understood his struggle, though, since she shared it as well. Maybe that was why she admired him so. "I'm the captain. Those are my worries. Not yours."

"Yes." Sometimes Neera would say that and immediately switch back into being deferential. This time the word came with a weight of compassion, a subtle acknowledgment that he grasped what she faced. "The solution to the engine is something I wish for constantly."

"Chuck would know." Demi's hand gripped the rail tight enough that her knuckles went pale. From below, tools chirped and mechanical pieces groaned as they shifted into place. "Chuck would know," she repeated.

"A smoother jump cycle would benefit from Chuck's knowledge." Now Neera turned to her with a direct look and his large hand landed on top of hers. "Chuck made things better for the both of us."

They remained that way for a beat, sinking into the type of compassion built only through circumstance and mutual experience. Then she let it go, a single quick nod that sent her silently back to the bridge, while giving Neera permission to return to his work.

"Captain on the bridge."

Demi stepped forward, her posture and demeanor reflecting her official presentation. The doors slid shut behind her, and she locked eyes with the person making the announcement: a yeoman named Chambers.

Having a yeoman would take some getting used to.

So would this full bridge crew: busy stations, constant chatter, endless blips from consoles. But it was more than just the full crew. The full *protocol* of it all would take getting used to as well.

She strode toward the captain's chair, each step moving with the poise and authority expected of her rank. "At ease, everyone," she said, settling into her seat. The bridge crew responded in kind by returning to their stations. As Chambers walked over to the front data table, Demi caught the young helmsman from the other day hiding a beaming grin—Diaz, the enthusiastic xenobiologist and pilot.

On the surface, it was everything a GCF captain could want.

Yet it all felt half-steeped in a dream, like her imagination snapped up different pieces of childhood starship expectations and blended them with her memories for something that was as clean as it was uncanny.

"Ahem." The voice came from behind her, and Demi turned to see Commander Matthews standing in the doorway to the bridge. "Permission to sit in?"

He'd spent the seventy-two hours examining the different sections of the Horizon—reading schematics, examining the ship's comm arrays, and apparently chatting with a lot of the crew. They'd passed in the hallways but avoided conversation—intentionally or unintentionally, given that Matthews always seemed too engrossed by the information on his tablet to notice her. And now, he sat in on the moment that might decide the fate of everyone on the ship.

Demi gestured toward the first officer's chair that Connors now owned, though he continued his support work in the science lab. "I'm sure Connors won't mind if you keep his seat warm for a few minutes."

"It's good to see how a crew functions during pivotal moments," he said, shifting his gaze to Lynn's comm station as he sat.

"I have complete confidence in them," Demi said. The crew, yes. Even the new transfers.

The engine?

Neera's fears echoed in her mind. As did his comment about Chuck.

Everything would have been better if Chuck were here. In so many ways.

She pushed the thought away before it could color her emotions. "All right, everyone," she said. "Let's show our guest what makes the Horizon special. I hear we've got quite the to-do list today."

Chuckles rippled through the bridge, though Matthews stayed quiet. Even Lynn—Lieutenant Kohli, as per proper protocol—let out a small laugh before she hailed the station, fully recovered from her space walk incident.

They were ready. And that was such an *odd* feeling. This wasn't the crew or ship she was used to. This was more capable, more functional, more official. Part of this felt so very right, so strangely comforting.

Except deep down, she recognized a burn, like a subtle acid in her veins that rejected this situation, whatever it was. Because accepting it felt like it just might overwrite every single thing about the past ten years.

"This is GC Horizon to Base Gamma Twenty-One. We are ready for departure. Please release docking clamps."

"Acknowledged, Horizon," came a male voice, an unearthly growl to its deeper tone. The data table projected a new hologram of the live transmission, front and center with a thin comm officer, a layer of fur poking out from beneath a headband of goggles. "Docking clamps released. You are cleared for departure. Safe travels." The voice placed a strange affect on the last syllable in "travels."

The transmission closed, leaving a view of the yawning chasm of space, pinpricks of light cast in front of the ship. Everything ahead tilted as the Horizon pulled from Gamma Twenty-One.

"Captain," Yeoman Chambers said, stepping over from her station at the bridge's rear. She presented a tablet of glowing text, then stood at attention, her neck and shoulders in perfect alignment. "Command requests immediate communications following the test."

"Understood," Demi said before addressing everyone on the bridge. "An executed photonic jump requires us to be at a convergence of photonic energy. We've managed to properly identify a few of these points. We'll head to the nearest one to commence the full test of the engine. Commander Neera has a newly generated batch of synthetic photons." Nods circled from station to station. "Any questions?"

"Yes. Are the bridge stations all original hardware?" Matthews asked, still looking at his tablet.

Diaz interrupted them before she could make an appropriate response. "Captain, we're ready for FTL to the convergence point."

Matthews constantly inquired about the ship's hardware—probably gauging how battle-ready it might be. Demi tapped her finger against the chair's console, a tell of her frustration that she caught after it ran too long. "Those stations could tell stories if they could talk." She refused to let the Horizon's old bones give him any reason to doubt the integrity of the ship or her crew. Instead, she took Diaz's enthusiasm and rewarded it. "Ensign Diaz. They're still finishing in the science lab, so go ahead and pick a speed threshold you're comfortable with. I trust your training."

Diaz nodded, now a full grin visible in the rise of his cheeks. "Yes, Captain. Engines primed and ready, at your call."

"All right, Ensign," she said, adjusting the tone and pitch of her voice to exude full confidence. "Take us there."

CHAPTER 7

NEERA

Tests were usually one of Neera's favorite things. Trial, error, improvement, solutions—such a practical, constructive process. This time, it ate at his nerves. Something was wrong. Not in early diagnostics, or anything that would even affect engine operations.

This was different. It went beyond equipment or processes—something bigger. But for his immediate purposes, it was ultimately only a test.

Neera repeated that to himself, his height towering over the human-size station. Maybe this would have been just a test several months ago, when the Horizon was a playground for theories and prototypes. A life of science, *finally* achieved. That time seemed lost now, what little space he made for himself in this strange universe being eaten away by war.

War.

He knew war. At home, the Regent Empire crushed all oppositions and uprisings. Here, the Cluster and the Withdrawal Movement traded losses in ways that took up too many resources and spared too few civilians. Even in the gloating headlines—*GCF Forces Score Decisive Blow Against Withdrawal Movement Guerillas in Border Battle; Report: No Truth to Rumors of WM's New FTL Engine;*

Welcome Parade Set as Tirolian System Joins Galactic Cluster—Neera knew enough to see the undertones of wartime communication. Like when Demi acknowledged that Command watched the test closely, that meant more. The others around him might not have caught it.

But Neera knew. War made test results a demand rather than a scientific inquiry.

Support had arrived, which meant someone somewhere wanted the engine. Or the Horizon. Or both. Demands for results always came from that sort of ownership claim.

Matthews made it very clear that he had one concern, and it had little to do with photonic beings or mapping uncharted space. "I need to see the maintenance logs for the entire comm array and transmission system. Every record going back to launch, including any data on hardware used for repairs," he'd told Neera, completely ignoring the containment unit of glowing pink synth. Per his nature, Neera obeyed. That request still seemed odd, and he assumed that Matthews was evaluating ship functions on a section-by-section basis.

Neera blinked and focused on the test, both sets of his eyelids sliding over the glossy black of his eyeballs as he took in the displays in front of him. How did humans do this, with their narrowly set vision? They could focus on, what, two, maybe three displays at once? But engineering, of all places, had a dozen charts, diagnostics, and monitors flashing across a panel of six horizontally locking displays.

It was a wonder that more human ships didn't get stranded all the time.

As if his thoughts projected across distant space, text popped up in the corner dialogue window.

Good luck, pal. Try not to blow anything up without me. —S

S, as in *Sadler*. As in Colin Sadler, GCF scientist. More than a scientist. Neera would, in fact, say Sadler was a fellow science *enthu-*

siast. And while Neera's arrival in Cluster space came with uneasy glances by a lot of the humans who came and went, Sadler offered wide-eyed enthusiasm.

"You built this?" he had asked, the first thing out of his mouth upon seeing the photonic engine. No introductions, no greetings, no formalities, only excitement over the engine's modular nature, how it interconnected and utilized pieces of tech—a plasma conductor from one universe, a compression capacitor adapted from another universe, all built and integrated over a GCF thermal control system.

Neera liked him right away.

Maybe Sadler snuck in on some official GCF chatter to learn about this test cycle. Or maybe his friend just had really good timing—Sadler did have a natural affinity for calculations. Travel times, prep times, calibration times, and *bureaucracy* times, all that remained simple arithmetic for Sadler to precisely send a good-luck message.

Neera typed out a short reply, then hit send:

Thank you. This is only a test. —N

As it transmitted, Neera wondered where on the front lines Sadler currently served. He'd moved every few days, tweaking propulsion efficiency formulas or adding chemicals to increase explosive power. Did Sadler know the truth about Ark Getru? If he did, could they discuss it?

Wherever he was, Sadler managed to monitor this. And, Neera noted, did not mention his concerns about problematic decay rates from the last simulation.

Perhaps Sadler believed in this test.

The first full test, in fact, of the photonic engine using synth. They'd tested individual stages, of course, and ran a full-cycle simulation. And stability cycles for the energy produced by the synthetic generator. Yet for months, something always failed—a benchmark couldn't be met, or dry runs didn't complete. Nothing ever war-ranted them going to a convergence point and actually trying to jump. They never got that far.

And now, everyone watched.

"The engine is ready for initializing," he said to the panel's comm systems. To his left stood Aurora, who ran various instru-ments to monitor internal power fluctuations. Across the bay was a newer arrival, a human thermal engineer named Ayenew. Though Ensign Ayenew came a week ago, Neera had hardly seen him, his responsibilities clashing with Ayenew's onboarding training and protocols.

Macek came up to him, each hand carrying two scanners. "It's exciting, isn't it?" His wide grin marked the difference between the two; they'd worked together for years, and while Macek could exist forever in the *process* of it all, Neera's brain wired the opposite way, always focused on the goal.

Still, he didn't want his own anxieties to tamp down his friend's excitement. "This moment is what we have strived for."

"It'll work," Macek said as his grin broke wider. "It'll work. Be-cause *we* worked on it." He reached up to pat Neera on the shoulder, then did the same to the others in the room.

"Commander Neera and team, standby." Demi's voice shook him out of his thoughts, and through the small window on his display, the bridge cam centered her in the captain's chair, a familiar adjust-ment in posture—one shoulder forward and her chin tipped up, framed by her jet-black hair. That was her "on the bridge" look, a combination of steady and curious that he'd come to trust, even as outside pressures threatened it.

To shut it all down and march forward—maybe that was the true mark of a leader.

"The countdown can begin at your request."

"Diagnostic scans active and tracking," Lynn said from the bridge, just out of camera shot. "Data stream is flowing to GCF Command."

Demi said something to Commander Matthews, who sat next to her, then faced forward. "Understood. Neera, take us there."

Neera hit the button.

All of this buildup just for a button. The hard work—generating the synth, capturing it into a containment module, loading it into the engine, and calibrating the engine's intake for synthetic rather than organic photons, all of that happened in the hours prior. Neera pushed a slender finger against the display's glowing icon.

Now they waited. And watched.

First the engine room's deck plates rumbled. Then the conversion chamber glowed, the neon pink of the photonic energy intensifying to a blinding glare before darkening into a deep red hue.

Through the monitor, crew voices chattered, repeating the numbers and statuses flashing across Neera's display.

"Mix ratio is stable," Ayenew said.

Diaz's voice came from the bridge helm station. "Convergence point lined up with navigation."

"Photonic activation hitting threshold minimums," Aurora said.

"Gravitational pull detected," Neera read from the display, which prompted Macek to cheer from across the room.

The deck plate rattle grew louder, just as it did right before the engine powered them out of the collapsing Lumersian gravity well.

"Engine efficiency is at ninety-five percent of optimal," he said, though overlapping voices and updates came from both engineering and over comms. Neera tuned out, focusing on the dynamic bar graphs on his display, fluctuating blue digits next to them. Though the specific details didn't matter, not on a second-by-second level. The rumbling intensified, even shaking the scanning device next to him. As he held a hand out to steady it, he checked for consistently high bars on the display, their back-and-forth wavering never dipping too far off course.

Until they did.

With it came warning lights. And voices:

"Synth viability dropping. Eighty percent. Seventy percent."

"Photonic engine stalling."

"Reaction rate stuck in stage three."

So many voices, in fact, that any sense of pack got completely overwhelmed by emotions and inputs, enough that Neera almost craved the efficiency of the Regent Empire.

"Neera," Demi called over the monitor. "Give me your best take."

"Their assessments can be confirmed," Neera said, comparing displayed values to the hums and rattles in front of him. "Levels for key internal tracking are starting to drop." The engine's noise gradually settled, and Neera spoke into the shoulder comm link embedded in his uniform. "Transmission: Neera to Connors. A status check is needed for the power bay."

"Connors here," a voice said as he appeared via video display. Despite the awkward angle, the clear figure of the Horizon's tall, slim, new first officer sat at the science lab's secondary power station. "Power levels are nominal. Nothing weird here, so that's good. All fluctuations seem to be contained to the photonic systems."

Nothing impacted the other ship systems—a good thing. Yet the photonic engine didn't want to clear the final obstacle. Photonic space tugged at the ship, but the Horizon stubbornly refused to let go of physical space.

Which meant that the ship just might tear itself apart.

Sadler's concerns were right.

Warning lights still flashed across the display, though they gradually sunk to stable, most of the bar charts sliding downward into a more agreeable range.

One of them, however, increased.

"Connors, acknowledged," Neera said. "Captain, the absorption process is not executing quickly enough within the photonic engine. The energy remains stuck rather than fully activating with the convergence point."

"Staying in the chamber?" Demi's voice kept its neutral tone, but

Neera knew her well enough to identify the rapid questioning as a sign of tension. "Overheating?"

"Heat tolerance is now eclipsing nominal and at one-hundred-ten percent," Ayenew called out.

Which was out of turn, but Neera reminded himself that this new crew would take time to fall into rhythm. "The fast decay is re-appearing with unknown causes," he said. "The engine remains static when the energy decays too quickly."

"Helm, did we move?" Demi asked.

On the monitor, Diaz spoke. "No, Captain, jump state was not achieved. We're still within FTL range of Gamma Twenty-One."

"One-hundred-twenty percent," Ayenew said.

Neera's finger hovered over a single icon on the control panel, a button with the word *VENT* in all large, capital, Earth-standard let-ters. He glanced over his shoulder at the room's environmental mon-itors, the numbers agreeing with his own senses. Despite Dywen physiology being less sensitive to heat compared to humans and their thin epidermis, the sudden temperature spike caused a tingle to the top of his hand.

"Captain," Neera said, "dangerous heat levels are about to be hit by the engine. Venting is required once the process is aborted."

"Hold it as long as you can. I want to be certain this is what we're dealing with. We've only got one shot at this."

One shot.

Neera ignored that part and stayed focused. Suddenly, everything worked. The heat tolerance dropped, its value shifting nominally, and then a different type of vibration rattled the room, complete with a high-pitched frequency that Neera recognized.

The engine was processing photonic energy, a force powerful enough to break through the space-time barrier and pull them into another dimension. From the conversion chamber, the glowing in-tensified until its brilliance caused him to turn away.

Just like when months ago it brought them here.

As suddenly as it worked, everything stopped. The noise, the brightness, all of it. The display grew active, thermal charts spiking beyond their limits. Instead of opening a pathway between convergence points, energy stewed in the engine's chamber.

And it was *hot*. So much that a wave of heat caused Neera to wince, and he didn't even bother telling Demi that the engine sat at 145 percent of heat tolerance.

Almost there. But "almost" might tear the ship apart.

Neera's finger slammed the vent button.

Switches and mechanisms clicked, along with the pressurized whir of the engine's safety system. The temperature gauge on the wall rapidly dropped, and following it, the color in the photonic engine drained, the once-bright glow turning into a dull pink that gradually faded away along with the heat.

Neera's wide field of vision caught Macek looking his way.

Only a test. A failed one.

Within seconds, everything stopped. Beneath his boots, the deck plates steadied. And the temperature, the room's precise environmental control system, reset to the optimal standard for human work.

Quiet.

Neera had grown so accustomed to the status beeps coming from different displays that they didn't register anymore. He may as well have stood in a vacuum staring at a photonic engine that just tantrumed instead of jumping twelve hundred light-years away.

"Neera, the monitors show everything's down." Even through the comms, Neera heard the shift in Demi's tone, a slight acceleration to the way she spoke. "What happened?"

"The system needed to be vented."

"I . . ." *Now* Neera looked at the small image of his friend in the captain's chair, small lines forming between her brows. He understood the chain of command—it was a way of *life* from where he came from. In his native universe, he wouldn't have dared to make a decision like that on his own. And here, knowing he made that split-second decision formed a queasy pit in his stomachs. "Overheat was imminent," he said, words speeding up with justifications. "Heat tolerance at a hundred-forty percent due to a failure to mix with the convergence energy—"

"I see." Demi's eyes darted at the various crew members around her—most of which had not experienced life in the gravity well. To them, this was insubordination. And that made his friend look bad. Neera probably should have followed protocol.

"I am offering apologies, Captain," he said, both for their friendship and for anyone listening in. "A decision was required to save the ship."

"Understood." Tightness wrapped her voice as Macek ran over with a tablet of data. "Note it in your report, and I'll pass findings along to—"

"Incoming message from GCF Command," Lynn said off-screen. "Marked as top priority. Where should I patch it through?"

A little while ago, Demi had said that Command's opinion was *her* worry, not his. Now they intertwined.

"The report can be my top priority. I will put my attention on it for now," Neera said, tapping buttons to upload the test data to the GCF's science hub—most likely, Sadler just got a notification and was already digging through it. Maybe together they could take *one* thing off Demi's list. "Commander Neera out." The bridge camera disappeared, leaving only diagnostic displays and their associated status beeps.

CHAPTER 8

DEMI

In the quiet of her quarters, Demi took a second to stare at herself. Official demands awaited, but she squinted, studying her image on the screen, along with a GCF identification number and her full name in bold capital letters. And next to it, her official profile photo.

The side of her lip curled. Ten years ago, when the Horizon set out to map potential trade routes, she looked at this very same viewscreen, this very same image and nameplate, with pride. Even her uniform was the same: sharp lines of the dark gray overshirt and blue trim lining the vertical fold that sealed the double-breast flap.

That woman could have never imagined the Cluster being a war-complacent machine. Nor could she have imagined being trapped across the galaxy, leading twenty-two stranded ships to build a community of survivors. That woman could have never imagined Chuck.

Ten years later. Ten difficult, frustrating, and occasionally magical years. All that panic and frustration, all the scratching and clawing, all the arguments and disasters.

And joy, however fleeting it was.

To come back to *this*? Protocols and ranks and government-sanctioned cover-ups—government-sanctioned war escalation? Even some crew who survived a decade in a gravity well with her, barely even said hello to her now—all because of Command?

So much time passed, and yet the same photo remained: shoulder-length hair then, compared to her current short crop; a few less lines on her face; a polite smile instead of the smirk she felt in her cheeks. The eyes, though, they held the starkest change—a brightness lurked underneath, an excitement at the *possibilities* among the stars.

Demi had considered resignation once, shortly after they had escaped the well. The thought entered her mind—never documented in words, never spoken aloud. But one day among the crew was all it took to push that aside. Because if even a single member of her crew struggled, then she couldn't walk away.

That might have been the biggest lesson to pass on to the woman in the photo.

The monitor beeped impatiently again, and Demi sucked in a quick breath before tapping the screen. Vice Admiral Swapna Krishna immediately appeared, a war map displayed behind her, various icons and colors scattered across it—and a large jagged red line across the top indicating the front. For better or worse, Krishna was one of the few higher-ups Demi regularly spoke to, enough that she could try to read between the lines of Krishna's flat stare.

"I'm sorry for the delay," Demi said, aiming for a confident, assured tone. "The bridge was noisy and our conference room is undergoing renovation, so it made sense to take the call in my quarters, where I'll actually be able to hear you." Her hand went up to activate holographic charts and tables in front of her.

"How bad is the failure?" Krishna waved away Demi's apology, her focus shifting as the synchronized charts appeared on her end, tinting her brown skin and thick black hair with glowing blue.

"I haven't had a chance to break it down with my chief engineer yet." Demi grabbed one holographic table labeled *Photonic Decay*

Rate, then highlighted it for the vice admiral to see. "We've encountered this problem in simulations during stage four of the jump cycle. The additional personnel didn't put us over the hump. Perhaps," she said with strategic purpose, "they need more time to work together."

Krishna paused briefly at Demi's statement, then settled into her seat. "I see. Captain, did you not fully understand GCF Command's perspective?"

"I did." Demi bit down on her lip, considering the paths in front of her. None were ideal, but she had nothing left to lose. This failed test likely meant being called to the front and the end of the Horizon as they knew it. "Admiral, permission to speak freely?"

"Of course."

Demi thought of the crew transfers like Diaz and their rehearsed speeches—now she fired up something similarly prepared, though with far heavier consequences.

"Vice Admiral, I think using the Horizon for the war effort is shortsighted. It's the most unique scientific ship in the fleet— perhaps even in the galaxy. New engineers and science teams barely onboarded. Another test or multiple tests, with time for this new team to come together, that would put them in a position to succeed. Why waste them as just another support craft?"

It wasn't *technically* a waste. Demi understood why they wanted the Horizon—presumably both the ship *and* its crew. Tallied against their failed scientific endeavors, Command's perspective made sense. But they couldn't be the only science vessel away from the front—and it grated on Demi's nerves that they assumed the Horizon and its crew were just *numbers*, bodies to serve the war.

Which they weren't. Demi thought back to those final weeks in the gravity well, photonic volatility causing energy to thrash out in bursts and implode ships in their community. The storms proved unpredictable, and Lumersian scientists saw this as evidence of imminent collapse. Demi had stood on the bridge with Chuck, repeatedly calculating possibilities and risks over sending rescue teams.

Demi had made the call to go. She'd sent three crew members: Cam Flinders, a Dywen named Siedt, and Aurora Sterling.

Only Aurora survived.

Demi sent Cam and Siedt to their deaths. Did it matter that it was in service to community and life? She still wasn't sure. But several weeks *after* the Horizon landed in Cluster space, Demi organized wakes for each of them. For the survivors, their faces said it all: they'd traded one war zone for another, and that epiphany pushed aside any lingering thoughts of retirement. The crew needed more time.

Just like now.

"Captain, your test failed. Even your simulations failed. You've had chances," Krishna said, tapping her desk to accent her point. "I've read Commander Matthews's analysis. We need to bring the Horizon into the fold."

Right when Matthews arrived on the ship, he told Demi *not* to upgrade any equipment. And even in his analysis, he often asked about original systems and hardware age. The ship was a decade-old craft that barely ran—how did that warrant a take like "We need to bring the Horizon into the fold"?

None of this made sense. Really, nothing about the Cluster itself made sense these days, but especially since Ark Getru. Demi chose her next words carefully, swiping away the holographic data to make eye contact with Krishna. "The engine's very nature is a blessing and a curse. It's powerful and, at times, unknowable. Lumersian scientists helped us understand the intricacies of photonic energy, but they're not around. We can't snap our fingers and make it work. Not without reopening the collapsed well." Her gaze briefly drifted over to the purple spark in the corner of her quarters. "Reopen it and bring things back the way they used to be. But this crew—*my* crew—they have experience no one else can replicate. We are learning and we've made progress. Once we unlock its basic principles, it could be the foundation for new discoveries. They just need more time to come together. Whenever this war ends, the galaxy will move on. My job, the Horizon's job, is to support that life. Let us start now."

Krishna didn't respond, remaining still enough that Demi checked to see the transmission didn't freeze.

"Our focus is the ship and the crew. Not the engine," she finally said.

Demi considered launching into some impassioned, very Grant-like speech about discoveries and the possibilities of the photonic engine if they *just invested in it*. That wouldn't work here. She'd been back long enough to recognize that. Instead, she retorted with the question that had plagued her since that first conversation with Matthews: "Why is the Horizon so important?"

"Every ship is—"

"It's an old ship." Ten years ago, Demi would have never dared to speak to top brass that way. Such words invited immediate reprimands. Still, she felt like she'd earned the right to circumvent protocol. "This doesn't make sense," she said, repeating her epiphany from a moment ago before daring to add more. "I think I deserve to know why."

Krishna squinted, and Demi figured she might get relieved of duty then and there, or even discharged from the fleet entirely. Her mind wondered what that might mean, and the idea of a cabin with Indy among her native California redwoods didn't seem that bad, despite spending her entire childhood trying to reach the stars. But she had responsibilities to seventeen people. And if she held her ground long enough, maybe they could outrun the war altogether.

"I can't discuss that."

"What?" Demi's reply came out in a single dry word. "The war's going so badly that you need a ten-year-old ship with a broken experimental engine? I mean, if that's the case, at least be honest. I've seen your headlines: Ark Getru's an Accident. Systems Are Joining the Cluster. The WM's Rumored FTL Tech Is All False—"

"*Captain.*" The word was sharp, forceful, and Demi gave herself points for rattling a vice admiral. "I. Can. Not. Discuss. That." Krishna let out a heavy sigh. "Matthews warned me you might not be happy. But regardless of your feelings, the Horizon is needed, and its directive will be reclassified."

Frustration ripped through Demi. "If things are that bad, has the negotiating team tried the radical tactic of, you know, *offering* something instead of insulting?"

"Captain Kim." Calm neutrality slipped over Krishna's face, like she'd slammed an internal reset button. "Even though you were not here for the onset of the conflict, you are still involved. You are a captain in the Galactic Cluster's fleet. You cannot run away from that, nor can you be in denial. The Horizon has two days to perform final analysis of the failed test, then you're to report to Base Theta Seven to prep the Horizon for frontline support. And at Theta Seven, you'll be relieved of command and receive your new assignment."

Krishna's words seemed to float in space. Demi didn't react right away. Instead, she thought of the time she'd joked to Grant about all the ways she might lose her command. She'd gotten her ship and crew lost in space, after all. Yet she'd never believed it would happen. The Horizon was as outcast as any crew in the history of FTL travel, space exploration, ocean exploration, land pioneers. No one could actually want them or their damage. At least, that's what she'd told herself.

And now she was going to lose everything.

Not because she talked back to Command. Not because she didn't play nice with Matthews.

Because of this war.

Their war.

Disbelief. Grief. Bargaining. Demi had learned enough about human psychology to know that those *should* have been the emotions stirring inside her. Maybe they stewed in there, little bits waiting to emerge, but right now everything was completely and absolutely eclipsed by a very sudden, very incandescent rage.

It presented, though, in a short, calculated reply.

"Admiral, the Horizon crew needs me. No one in the fleet can understand what they've been through."

"Those aren't discussions for me. They've had their psych evals. Additional ones are available as warranted."

Krishna's words came out fast and clean, like she'd just commissioned a new fuel depot rather than shattered everything around Demi. Demi forced a response out even as her mind raced elsewhere. "What's my new assignment?"

"That's not under my purview. You'll learn more when you get to Theta Seven." The admiral glanced off camera, nodding at something. "For now, prepare a transition plan for the Horizon's new captain. You can brief Matthews on it in the meantime." A chime came from Krishna's side, stealing the conversation from the sudden questions prompted by that statement.

"Matthews?"

"Yes. He'll be acting captain until we assign a permanent one. Or unless he stays." Demi wasn't surprised by any behind-the-scenes activity these days. But for Matthews to actually take over her command?

She glanced over at Indy, who sensed the movement enough to open sleepy eyes and look back.

Well, at least *someone* in the Cluster liked her.

"We'll see if he earns a promotion," Krishna continued. "War moves things in unexpected ways. Learn to deal with it. That's an order, Kim."

The screen went dark, leaving only dim overhead lighting and the glowing font of her monitor's default display.

And, of course, Chuck.

Demi walked barefoot across the carpeted space, having ditched the standard-issue boots as soon as she got into her quarters. "Transmission: Kim to Connors," she said into her comm as she touched Chuck's containment unit, the uneven metal ridges of its frame digging into the meat of her palm.

"Connors here."

Demi operated for almost two years without a first officer after Grant was killed in a dispute between angered colony factions. They didn't have the means, so she simply got used to it—less structure for the rest of the crew, and more leniency to herself.

None of that was Connors's fault. If the situation were reversed, maybe she'd still be the by-the-book person who kept standard-issue boots on at all times. "I've signed off with Vice Admiral Krishna. Unless there's an emergency, I'll be back up on the bridge in an hour."

"No emergencies here. Take your time. Connors out."

The comm system beeped, and Demi crumbled to the floor. Next to her, Indy's deep-sleep breathing quickened, and she looked down to see big brown eyes emerge among the graying muzzle of the dog's long face. As if Indy knew the weight of her thoughts, the dog adjusted without getting up, just enough to rest her head across Demi's lap. Indy seemed to love naps on a soft bed more than any other creature in the galaxy, a life far removed from her time in a grimy, dank kennel connected to a racecourse.

Quite a life, being able to relax *anywhere*. Indy fell asleep again, the cadence of her breathing steady and deep, a meditation of sorts for Demi as she watched Chuck's remains, eyes trained on the lone purple spark. She leaned over to a small refrigerator adjacent to her and grabbed a bottle of *some* kind of chilled wine. The details were lost to time, Demi having been the third or fourth owner of it. A refugee from a collapsing nearby ship in the well gave it to her in gratitude, stating to only have some for special occasions.

Now seemed like a good time to sample it. She took a small glass off the top compartment and poured enough for something between a sip and a shot. "You remember the last time we had this?" she said to Chuck. "Low on optimism."

Two years ago, specifically, in this very same spot, back when Chuck had a glowing photonic body, mechanical limbs, and a digitized voice.

Most importantly, though, he had his mind.

Like now, she had sat cross-legged and barefoot, while Chuck stood, his alloy-composite legs hinged to mimic thin bipedal feet and knees. Above that, the operating mechanics and computer processing of the robot body sat encased below his true self:

A swirling plane of bright pink glow, compressed down into a two-dimensional square about two feet on each side; back then, his light was bright enough to cast a tint across the entire room. How the containment unit managed to interface with Lumersian physiology—was that even a thing?—Demi didn't know; she left that to cybernetics experts. But it translated his voice into a soothing tone, one that evolved from an initial monotone.

Servos whirred as Chuck's left arm raised a glass of this chilled wine. "A toast," he suggested, "as long as I'm understanding the meaning of the ritual correctly."

"A toast is celebratory. I thought we were just sampling because things are bad," Demi said with a laugh. "Sampling" was relative; while Chuck absorbed many details to bring him closer to humanity—including his name—eating and drinking remained impossible. But she appreciated his commitment to the gesture. Plus, more for her. "This seems like an odd time to celebrate."

"Why do you say that?" Chuck asked, glass still up.

Demi refrained from taking a sip, just in case Chuck had a point with this. "Well, let me see. The Carbarran group raided our supplies. That wasn't great. They're also our neighbors, so that's not great either. Less supplies on the Horizon means more crankiness. You like math, you can calculate the inverse relationship of those two." Though Chuck didn't have a head, his entire torso dipped in a move as close to a nod as possible, the green status light on the bottom left slicing through the dark. "Let's extrapolate that. Carbarrans raided our supplies because they're desperate. They're desperate because the well is collapsing and we have no way out of it. We'll implode in a year or two like that one ship did last week. See, we're a little low on optimism."

"Optimism," he said after a pause, and his vocabulator projected a laugh. Though the tech did wonders in terms of functional translation and even capturing the nuances of emotion, laughter still came out like a replicated simulation.

"Oh, and one last thing. You're here," she said, red wine sloshing as she pointed at him, glass still in hand, "to help us figure that escape out. But also, your own kind are confused by you grabbing an identity and discovering things like feelings instead of just disintegrating back into your big cloud of collective photons." Now she held up her glass, steady, matching his pose. "See? Low on optimism."

"Let me perform an analysis on this."

"This is why I love you; everything's a puzzle to be solved. I'm going to have a sip, though." She raised the glass to her lips, but just before the wine hit them, Chuck held up his free hand.

"Carbarrans are desperate because the well is unstable. Fixing that instability requires some way to harness photonic energy in physical space. That uses a combination of Lumersian science and your realm's science. Us Lumersians use these mech suits to allow for direct collaboration. Which led to *our* direct collaboration. Which led to me choosing to stay integrated in my mech suit. Because, while Lumersians exist for a finite span to fulfill a purpose, I have discovered mine was different than originally planned. My purpose is to be here with you." Chuck's glass raised an inch higher, and Demi swore the pink glow of his cube intensified. "As long as you will have me. Everything else that happened before or comes after is incidental. So, I am not low on optimism."

"You should have been a speechwriter," Demi said in a quiet voice. "If Grant were still here, he'd be impressed."

"There is no need. This is all straightforward mathematics."

"Right." Demi nodded. "One plus one equals two."

"Everything in the known universe ultimately comes down to that."

In that moment, somehow all her senses dialed up—the feel of the carpet beneath her toes, the blow of ventilation through her hair, the low hum of Chuck's inner instruments, the ever-present rumble of the Horizon's thrusters as they strained to hold the ship steady against the pull of the well's superhot core.

And Chuck. The glow of his true self, the slightest variations across the spectrum of neon pinks, boldly coloring everything in her life.

"So," Chuck finally said, "a toast."

They clinked glasses, and Demi took her sip, while Chuck did the ceremonial action of pouring his back into the bottle.

That plane of bright energy—so vibrant, so *alive*—now a dim purple dot.

Demi's head tilted back, closing her eyes to lean into the silence. "I could use some of your optimism now. What would your math tell you?"

Demi felt Indy jolt, a whole-body tremble followed by an eyes-closed whimper. Her dog was dreaming. Maybe she had the right idea. Demi could feel the weight of the world settling on her shoulders.

"Shhh, it's okay, girl," Demi said, petting Indy's soft ears before turning back to the spark. "Okay, I mean, I have a dog now, so it's not *all* bad. But still. You know what—"

She stopped, then blinked several times to make sure her eyes were *not* playing tricks on her. She squinted, forcing her vision to adjust and confirm that yes, a green light suddenly glowed on the bottom left of the containment unit's frame.

Was the unit *active*?

It couldn't be. And yet, there was a clear difference between now and before. The light hadn't been on; she would have noticed that green dot sometime within the last six months.

She was *certain*.

Demi inspected the unit's interface module and small maintenance panel, the green dot indicating that something in the cubic mess of technology *worked*.

As she leaned closer, a high-pitched squeal came, a series of tones at different pitches and intervals—all sharp enough to unsettle Indy. The dog craned her neck upward, one floppy ear perched up quizzically at the noise.

Then a synthesized voice spoke, a tone that Demi had last heard six months ago when Chuck entered the photonic engine to power the final steps of the Horizon's journey back to Cluster space:

"Home."

CHAPTER 9

TANAV

Shortly after arriving in Cluster space, Demi told Tanav that she understood his goal: find a way to return to his universe. "A way has to exist. We just have to discover it." She'd joked that "if I ever send you an urgent transmission out of nowhere, I found your way home." Every time Neera completed a test, Demi let him know whether it succeeded or failed. She left out the technical stuff, but he'd always gotten a sense about whether the engine was closer to working—or not.

Since the failed jump at Gamma Twenty-One, Demi didn't say anything.

Much bigger things were at stake than his own quest to go home. So Demi staying quiet about that wasn't an issue. The fact that she seemed to cut herself off from *everyone* . . .

That was concerning.

When she wasn't on the bridge, she locked herself away in her quarters. Tanav had reached out to Demi twice in the last day. He didn't want to pry into issues of Command—he wasn't qualified to understand them. However, he did fully understand when things failed and authority figures weren't happy. His whole life had been kind of built around that.

Except Demi didn't answer and Tanav knew her well enough to wait. In one short day, rumors rippled through the ship, whispers of heading to the front or the science lab being turned into weapons research or even the crew being dispersed and the Horizon being commandeered. Ensign Diaz even mentioned a rumored black ops group possibly using the photonic engine for military purposes.

GCF culture was still new to Tanav, but even Lynn laughed at that one. "All the new grads fall for that," she'd said. "Then they start their rotations and realize how ridiculous that is."

Those rumors all circled around the ship or the crew—not Demi. And that, along with her self-sequestering, really worried Tanav. So when she reached out with an urgent, out-of-nowhere transmission to come to her quarters?

She didn't say why. And the only thing he was certain of was that it had nothing to do with finding a way home. But given how everything right now was military or science, why would she need someone like him?

That thought pushed him as he walked quickly through the crew quarter hallways of the Horizon's fourth deck, politely sliding between the middle of shift changes until he reached the elevator. He wasn't alone, though; Aurora stared at an engineering tablet while she waited. The display glowed with all sorts of green graphs and charts, which reflected off the green already in her hair. But then the device shut off, and Tanav caught that the green in her hair had actually faded a little bit, dulling it toward her natural brunette.

For years in the well, Aurora used hair dyes from vegetables and other natural sources. Getting back to Cluster space meant deliveries of modern supplies, including her special request of a hair color infuser. Yet here, either the infuser broke or . . .

Or she hadn't made a choice about her future.

Or perhaps she did.

Tanav's upbringing recognized the next step in a conversation as a piece of strategy instead of mere discussion. Even when he wanted to, he couldn't turn that off, which meant his playful tone was equally genuine and calculated.

He kind of hated that about himself.

"You're not hiding any peppers are you?" he asked with a wave. A targeted question that gave the option of letting her open up or keep things hidden.

"Sorry." She patted her uniform pockets. "All out. Have to commit treason to get some more. Oh wait, are we allowed to talk about that? Or not? It's so hard to keep track these days." Venom laced her voice, though Tanav didn't know at whom. In her position, her anger could be targeted at anyone.

"Demi will help you—"

"I haven't talked to her," she said. "No one has, if you haven't noticed. The engine. Commander Matthews. Environmental *accidents*. New crew. Guess we're all busy." As if on cue, several new crew members lined up behind them for the elevator. She gestured to take a step back, and while the elevator saw an exchange of incoming and outgoing unfamiliar people, they waited for everyone to clear before resuming.

Despite her posture and tone, Tanav recognized that Aurora's anger was a front more than anything else. Her next words came low and quick, with a surprising softness. "I know it's not really Demi's fault. I shouldn't blame her. I don't even really want to go. I just have to. You know, crossing over there"—her words came with cryptic meaning and a knowing nod—"means I can't come back until this is over. And when will that be? These new transfers have all the gossip. They say none of the negotiating is real, and the war's just at a standstill, Ark Getru is just a symptom. Why are we even doing this? No one has a good answer."

Tanav shook his head—he didn't have an answer either. He didn't want to think about it more because that just pulled flashes of Ark Getru, and the way the bodies had floated so unnaturally into nothing . . .

"I should try giving all the leaders some of my family peppers," she said. Her eyes brightened in response, a quip against the backdrop of horror. Maybe that horror felt more real to him because it was so otherworldly. For Aurora, her jokes might have come from the way the war wove deep into every one of her decisions.

Inside the gravity well, there were moments when the crew talked about how they'd give anything to see friends again, to smell natural flowers and plants again, to swim in an ocean again. Yet now, things almost seemed better over there. It was at least clear—no worry about politics or new transfers or messages from family to muddy up where to go, what to do, how to feel.

The elevator doors opened again, except this time it arrived empty. Demi waited with something she'd deemed urgent, but Tanav chose to make sure Aurora didn't need an extra second of camaraderie first. She stepped in, and he followed suit.

"Deck three," she said, putting her at engineering.

"Deck one," he said, and she shot him a knowing look. "Do you want me to—"

"It's my responsibility. I'll talk to her. I owe her that," she said. The doors opened at the engineering deck, and she took a step out. "But thanks for asking. Complimentary peppers if I ever get them back to Cluster space."

Demi wasn't even there when Tanav arrived, apparently pulled into an off-shift resources meeting with Matthews. Instead, the doors to the captain's quarters opened to reveal Neera, diagnostic tools and connection cables in his oversize hands. He hunched over, midway through scanning a metal frame.

A metal *containment unit* that held Chuck's spark and, at one time, sat in the heart of Chuck's mech suit. Now it might as well have been his urn, with his lone remaining purple spark floating in the middle of it.

So why was Neera scanning it?

Then noises arrived—a high-pitched frequency, clearly generated through the containment unit's speaker module.

And a single word:

"*Home.*"

While Neera looked to Chuck as a living wealth of scientific information and Demi had her own unique attachment to him, hearing that single word conjured up a rapid-fire set of memories: *What is culture?* and *Why is this culture so different from yours?* and *What makes music so pleasing to the senses?* So many off-duty hours spent crammed into Lynn's small quarters next to Chuck's standing mech suit as she played song after song from her catalog of historical rock songs.

"We are tasked," Neera said as Tanav stepped in, "to find out, as Demi put it, if her boyfriend is back from the dead. However, scans are continuing to present readings that are . . . confusing."

Tanav realized that they just jumped into this without even saying hello. Lynn kept telling Tanav that Neera was very nice and very caring in his own way, but Neera's technical nature and Tanav's very-much-the-opposite life experience meant that they'd never gotten past polite interactions. Even being here felt strange, like a quiz he was destined to fail. The unit in Neera's hand chimed, prompting him to put it down and change it for another from his equipment bag.

"How so?"

"The energy levels from Chuck's spark remain the same as they have emitted since the last scan. No noticeable change has been detected within the actual photonic state." Tanav nodded like he understood, which prompted Neera to continue while bringing up holographic numbers from his scanner. "The difference appears to be hardware based. Active detection is what the readings show."

Tanav wanted to ask Neera if Demi was all right, if she'd dealt with the crew's next steps yet. He'd even considered using the moment to ask how Neera felt about Ark Getru and the ensuing fallout.

In front of him, Neera moved with a singular purpose, scanning and analyzing and repeating that over again.

Tanav chose to leave it and not detour Neera's work.

"I'm, um," he started, before he found the best way to convey this given how Neera missed subtleties in communication. His next step needed to be direct, for both of their sakes. "I'm not sure why Demi called me. I'm not exactly good with scanners."

Before Neera could respond, the high-pitched noise returned. Tanav closed his eyes and focused on the noise: an electronic screeching that varied in pitch and intensity, speeding up and slowing down, even pausing for skips before the vocabulator plainly stated the word *home* again. Several more short bursts arrived before everything abruptly ended, leaving only the chimes of equipment.

"I have become accustomed to this noise with each passing playback," Neera said. "The starts and stops appear to drive a power current spike that cannot be replicated. A timer has been set to check for regular transmission intervals. But for now"—he tapped his tablet, and the noise played back from the device, not Chuck—"the raw audio has been captured by my scanner. You have asked about your purpose here. Demi recalled your discussions with Chuck about the nature of audio variations in frequency and rhythm."

It took Tanav a second to realize that Neera gave a definition of *music*—nearly the same way Chuck had described it. The first time Chuck heard a passing crew member whistling in the docking bay, he'd stopped and asked for an explanation—and after hearing several songs, Chuck had proclaimed, "It is a confluence of mathematics, dynamics, emotion, and language, in infinite combinations."

Was that what made up this screeching sound?

"Demi wants you to consider if this recording matches any possible songs that Chuck may have heard. Though I have thought of another reason." Neera let out a Dywen version of a laugh, an alien-like chortling that sounded more like asthmatic grunts. It even made

Chuck's synthesized laughter sound human. "Can you learn how Demi's dog has managed to remain asleep during all of this?"

Lynn mentioned that Neera had been attempting humor more, to which Tanav responded that not even humans always got it. Here, Tanav reminded himself to laugh, which in itself changed Neera's demeanor in subtle ways, despite the strange and almost grim circumstances.

Dywens telling jokes, dead Lumersians humming songs, and so many new crew members—things were changing aboard the Horizon.

Several years ago, Demi pulled Tanav onto the bridge to get his opinion on a strange message. He'd only arrived shortly before but had his role quickly defined, the constant influx of new faces needing someone to listen to their various needs and demands. With twenty-two ships stuck in the gravity well, he'd told Demi a saying from his universe: "Broken links can't form a chain." Dywens spoke with deference to authority and hierarchy. Maltrotish stated their requests first, then offered reasoning behind it. Humans, regardless of universe, seemed to operate more on emotion than anything else.

Despite those different backgrounds, Tanav was able to recognize how those traits wove into communications. Demi attributed this to his background as a musician, like the arts magically made him more attuned to emotional conditions.

But actually, it was his parents. Sure, they were his parents, but Nova and Rolf were head of Lexin Industries first and foremost. And they'd modeled for him early on that every culture and every individual, no matter species or age or gender, had a tell. They used that to exploit industries and companies.

Tanav used it for endless lyrical fodder.

And on the Horizon, he used it to connect strangers across stranded ships.

Demi had asked if such intuition could figure out some meaning in those flashing lights amid the endless glow of the gravity well. They repeated, one flash and then another flash, then two rapid flashes.

"Is it biological, like a heartbeat?" Demi mused, standing in front of the captain's chair with hands clasped behind her back. "Or perhaps a vibrational frequency?"

"There may be a species attempting to manipulate photonic energy," Neera said. He held up a tablet that projected out a hologram of data. "This species may be using a device giving off those flashes as a natural operating frequency. The flashes may be a byproduct rather than directly signaling intent."

They watched again as the flashes came, and for this next round, Tanav tapped his finger against his hip, and despite being very mediocre at drums, the move stemmed from a lifelong instinct to connect with beats. *Tap. Tap. Tap-tap.*

The timing of it was precise, like the click track to a song demo. *Tap. Tap. Tap-tap.* He repeated this, his fingers moving at the same cadence even though they sped ahead of the flashing phenomena, and it repeated even while Neera and Demi discussed what kinds of devices might possibly cause photonic energy to flash.

Then it hit him. Tanav blurted out the next few words without even really thinking it through. "Beats. Like a beat calculator."

Everyone on the bridge turned and faced him—Lynn at her comm station, Lindsay filling in at helm, Siedt, a Dywen, at the data table, Demi and Neera in front of him.

"Sorry," he continued, "it's called a metronome here. Click, click, click, to keep the beat. These beats," he said, holding up a finger, "are precise. A quarter note, a quarter note, two eighths. They're exact. I bet if you look at a recording of these, the timestamps would be exact."

"The flashes are confirmed to be that precise," Neera said as he stared at the tablet.

"Try this." Tanav pointed at the bridge's window. "Flash a signal back. Two, then two, then four."

Demi looked out at the glowing expanse, then back at Tanav, then over to Lindsay. "Concentrate low-energy weapons bursts to do that, as even in pauses as possible."

"Mathematics," Neera said.

"I see it." Demi stepped between the front consoles, moving as close to the window as possible. "One plus one equals two. Two plus two equals four. The most basic logic in the universe—in any universe. Tanav." She spun on her heel and looked directly at him. "When we get you home, you can tell your parents that all of that music paid off after all."

And now that intuition paid off again. Almost.

When Demi returned to her quarters an hour later, she lacked the awe and curiosity of their moment back in the gravity well. Instead, her posture collapsed as soon as she entered her quarters, like all the adherence to order and rules had knotted in an invisible string. Indy stretched and yawned, except instead of going to her, the dog waddled her way over to Neera. She shoved her long snout in Neera's face, which prompted a pained but polite expression, followed by two very mechanical pats on the head.

Tanav knew he had an opportunity to ask Demi if she was all right. But given the late hour and her long day, he went with more urgent matters. "It's not Chuck," he blurted out, causing her shoulders to drop further. "I'm sorry, I know that's not what you wanted to hear. I thought I should put it up front."

Neera tapped the scanner in his hand and out shot a holographic projection showing a schematic of the containment unit, various circuit paths lit up, and a star chart. "The unit's capabilities have been usurped." Demi crossed her arms at this, and her grave silence played so differently than the woman who quipped her way through life in a gravity well. "We know the Lumersians can identify convergence points. Being at one puts us in signal range with them. The evidence leads us to believe that the containment unit is doubling as a transmitter."

Tanav met Demi's eyes, the same way she did on the bridge years ago. Unlike before, all he caught was fatigue. "That's why it sounded like him," he said. "It's a message played through his body."

"The vocabulator was calibrated for accumulated knowledge. *Home* was the only word that became cleanly translated upon receipt," Neera said. "The rest of the translation is being worked on by Tanav."

"This timing," she said slowly, "is difficult." Indy finally broke from Neera, and Demi knelt down to meet her. Tanav watched as her gaze drifted out the large domed window, even as she rubbed the dog's ears.

Everyone hesitated. Tanav took that as an opportunity. "Demi," he started, "are you all right? Given everything?"

The question got Neera to freeze. Demi's shoulders rose and fell with several long breaths. "I can't think about that." Under her words, Tanav heard the faintest crackle, though it disappeared swiftly as she continued. "How much have you translated?"

She wasn't budging, and maybe that was the only way to keep things together against the failed test, the new crew, Command, and whatever this was. "Some of the important parts. I think." He handed a tablet over. "These are my notes. I've assigned a tone and length as a value and checked it against our archive of Lumersian communication, and Neera's been tweaking the vocabulator to adapt to it."

Neera nodded in agreement, and Tanav stood quiet, waiting for Demi's reaction.

She held the tablet close, her eyes tracking from left to right, the glow from the tablet casting a blue tint against her cheeks. "'Photonic energy . . . will face eventual collapse . . . return home,'" she read aloud. "This is a distress call."

Tanav glanced at Neera, but the Dywen didn't react. Which might have meant that he agreed. Most of Demi's face stayed absolutely still, but the glint in her eyes changed in ways that he'd rarely noticed.

"I have to make a choice," she finally said. "And fast." She handed the tablet back to Tanav and walked to the corner of the space, eyes turned up through the glass dome. "I'm being transferred off the Horizon," she said flatly.

Tanav glanced at Neera again, whose mouth dropped open and dark eyes grew deeper.

That meant that Neera believed her. Which was bad for all of them.

"I need to talk to Krishna," she said quietly. "They have to hear me out."

Demi's next step was clear—she needed space to think and to steal a moment with high-ranking officials. Tanav couldn't talk politics with Command or do a single thing about Ark Getru, but he could help her right now. "I'll keep working on this. Lynn's shift is almost done. She can help."

"This is a good point by Tanav," Neera said, picking up on this. "I will transfer appropriate data to stations in the science lab and Tanav's quarters." He tapped away at several displays, which then chirped with successful actions. Neera stepped to leave, then turned around to give Indy one last pet before exiting the room.

Tanav was on his way out when Demi interrupted him. "You asked if I'm all right. I don't have an answer for you," she said. "But thanks for asking."

CHAPTER 10

NEERA

Under the Regent Empire, roles came clearly defined and orders were followed. Dissent was quickly squashed, confusion rarely occurred, and things never, ever changed.

Neera realized the odd comfort in that. Despite the constant sense of threat, he always knew what would happen the next day. Compared to right now, as he contemplated a Horizon without Demora Kim.

Someone else would be in charge. Someone who perhaps didn't understand where everyone came from, how the Horizon got there. They might even ship the Horizon's crew off to different ships.

They might even have to fight a war.

The irony was that while so many on the Horizon fretted about so many things upon arriving in Cluster space, Neera found himself probably with the most centered sense of peace in his life. He just wanted to build and test things. These last few months on the Horizon may have been the only time in his life when he got to do just that.

And now, governments were trying to take that away.

Galactic Cluster. Withdrawal Movement. Regent Empire. Was there actually much of a difference for someone like him?

Neera sat in engineering despite being off duty, every possible display with a different facet of test data. It was technically the late shift, and while three new transfers were supposed to be there, they were assigned to training sessions elsewhere at this time. And really, the time in the gravity well showed that engineering usually moved along smoothly even when no one was in it.

If he were human, he probably would have been in bed. But the Dywen circadian rhythm only needed four hours of rest a day when well hydrated, even when adapted to the Horizon's human-centric, twenty-four-hour cycle. Which meant he had another few hours to ponder the mysteries of the photonic engine.

The test data tempted him, but he'd given up reviewing it again. He turned to the end table next to the main workstation, where four palm-size repair projects sat in an open drawer: a pneumatic hammer with a broken recoil, a drone remote with an inactive holographic display, a replacement hinge for a chair axle in the med bay, and an automatic filter cleaner for Indy's water dish. Sometimes he worked on one of these in between calibrations and tests. Other times he sat during off-hours, fixing one little piece of the ship at a time. Yet now he couldn't even focus on one. He tried, picking up the filter cleaner and examining it up close. Something wasn't swiping the debris away, which probably meant a busted actuator inside. His mind froze there, though, pulling in quick thoughts of the worst possibilities until his mind went the opposite way, a panic-induced list of ways that might get them out of this situation. Sending a message back. Building a miniature version of the engine. Ignoring Command and testing the engine again—and again and again until it worked.

If Demi just said the word, Neera would do it. He told himself he could even do prep work for it now, and to prove it, he grabbed a tablet and accessed Sadler's most recent research analysis.

It loaded, and he blinked when he saw an unexpected message from an hour ago. Neera just forgot to check, given everything falling apart:

I looked at the test jump data. Too bad I'm stuck halfway across the galaxy because I actually have an idea. It would need real-time tweaking of the generator as it processes the energy conversion. I think our problem is that we're treating calibration as a sinusoidal oscillation, when it in fact it has varying shifts depending on environmental state. Got a way of plugging me in?

Neera was senior enough to grant remote access—but that bypassed several layers of encryption security. No way to get that approved with photonic engine research getting shut down, unless Demi authorized it. Chains of command existed for a reason.

However, his chain of command was getting broken apart. Or at least it would unless something intervened.

He could at least *listen* to Sadler's thinking.

"This better be good, I just fell asleep," Sadler said in a muted voice as he answered the transmission.

"Apologies should be made for the hour of this communication. Your message was just read. Your ability to learn so much so quickly about the photonic engine is very impressive."

"I pity anyone who *doesn't* want to think about the photonic engine all the time." Sadler laughed, and as he did, he activated his video feed to put them face-to-face. On the screen, the transmission froze, pieces of Sadler's image coming in from top to bottom: first his thick brown hair, then the tired lines that framed blue eyes and combat-tanned cheeks, then the stubble of dark hair over his long chin. "So, you got a way to make it happen? You're right there. Plug me in."

"Your goals are in direct violation of Cluster protocol."

"You didn't call me right now just to shame me for wanting to bend the rules?" Sadler said, with a very telling glance at his pillow.

"Perhaps your ideas should be communicated for me to consider." Sadler wiped his tired face, though when he finished, he revealed a smirk. "A way may exist to make it work."

"It's simple: let's tell Command how important this project is so they let us do it. Or they fly me out there. I mean, they're cutting off research; you'd think they'd try one more time with the right people."

Sadler apparently wanted to complain more than solve problems. Neera was about to reply when a new realization dawned on him:

"How did you know Command wanted to shut down the project?"

Sadler's chuckle came clear across the monitor. "My friend, you mean you don't know?" He wiped the sleep out of his eyes, then stretched back for a long, possibly exaggerated yawn. "Anyone who's studied the engine has heard about this. Both directly and indirectly. That's why I sent a message tonight. Let's prove to them that this works before we lose everything."

Neera thought of the conversations he'd overheard around the ship—beyond unauthorized discussions of Ark Getru, other rumors floated about the war, combat metrics, and political motivations. "The speed of word traveling among humans remains surprising to me."

"'Word traveling,'" Sadler said. "Yeah, that's one way to put it. Hey, you're the first to see but the last to know. That's what happens when you're off doing science projects while I'm calibrating bomb chemistry." He made a *poof* sound and gestured his hands into a mock explosion. "We should ask. Except bureaucracy would take two months just to respond. Good thing we don't need it for anything pressing, right? By the way, the displays behind you look already loaded with test data."

Anything pressing.

Neera's mind hung on that thought, and Sadler's head angled at his sudden silence. "Either you're thinking of something important or you're thinking about your table projects. If it's the latter, I'm going back to bed."

Unless something changed, the engine was likely gone. *Demi* was likely gone. Neera's entire life of just fixing and testing things was likely gone, replaced by being the only Dywen in a war involving governments he barely understood. The Horizon and its crew, he understood *that*—disjointed, sometimes messy, and certainly lacking protocol, but stable, supportive, and *known*. Even with the new transfers that arrived, he could adapt to that as long as his foundations remained.

A new captain. A new ship. A new *war*?

That foundation would crumble.

The orderly part of Neera touted the need of the Lumersians—their situation sounded catastrophic, and they deserved support. But deep down, Neera understood that taking action right here meant giving this life on the Horizon a final chance. "There is something new regarding our situation," Neera blurted out. Such a strange feeling, making such a big leap on his own.

"Now you've got my attention."

But really, this wasn't on his own. Demi once told Neera that part of leadership was knowing when to bend or break the rules. She'd been referring to her romantic entanglement with Chuck, but such a notion applied broadly. This marked one of those moments. Much like the decision to vent the engine, options were very limited at this point.

"A situation has arisen that requires the photonic engine." Different explanations weighed in his mind, but he opted for the most direct. "This news was sent directly from the Lumersians."

"From the . . . how?" Sadler's eyes sharpened, the fatigue vanishing suddenly.

Over the next few minutes, Neera explained the day's theorizing and reverse engineering, all leading to the partially decoded message about energy collapsing—and the goal of returning *something* to them. "Historically, the well appears to be volatile enough to risk photonic space, yet stable enough to exist in physical space. I do not know what they need returned."

"Right. Because the well acts as a conduit between both?" Sadler squinted, a hand running through his hair. "Your escape used energy mined from the well. Yet it didn't destabilize things worse."

"Yes, but remember that the Lumersians both exist in photonic space while also composing the very fabric of photonic space. It . . ." Neera's voice trailed off; Lumersian physiology or lack thereof was something he didn't come close to understanding. "It remains confusing. The Lumersians knew how to parse out their individual beings among their tapestry of existence. Chuck compared it to an exothermic reaction producing steam in the physical world."

"And?" Sadler asked. "There's something else too."

Neera occasionally let his emotions express. Sometimes to Demi. Sometimes to Lynn, who was forward in her probing when she knew he was upset. Strangely, even though he'd detected her own anxieties recently, he found it difficult to ask her in return.

It was just easier to discuss science. Like with Sadler, that was their primary topic of conversation. But right now, science and emotions intertwined. One depended on the other.

"Yes. I do not want to lose the life I have built on the Horizon."

"Well then, we have something to prove to Command, don't we? New plan," Sadler said slowly. "As a friend, as a fellow scientist—forget the bureaucracy. Give me remote access. We can simulate with live equipment. If my theory works, we have every reason to ask for another chance." Sadler must have seen the hesitation on Neera's face, because he leaned in closer to the camera. "Look, we solve this, you present it to Captain Kim, she presents it to Command, the Horizon doesn't go to war, and instead you zoom off on a rescue mission. Right? That was Command's whole ultimatum." Despite only talking over video, Sadler's presence carried a palpable weight, a gravity that drew Neera into the logic of his argument. "Come on, Neera. We can do this."

Neera's hesitations about protocol and chain of command evaporated with the strength of Sadler's argument. He stood and stared at the displays of numbers filling up his field of vision, and despite the draining day, not a single hint of fatigue affected him.

He tapped the nearest station to pull up the shift schedule. Leeds, Porter, Hayase—the new transfers were due back soon. "I will not be alone in this room."

"Yeah, but Neera, you're the chief engineer." Sadler's laugh was loud enough to fill the space. "Sometimes I think you forget that. Just tell them you're running a simulation. Hell, they can help if you show them how."

Neera looked at the data across displays now, the six stages of the photonic engine's cycle defined in clear charts. And stage four, where the decay issue kept showing up.

A simulation was not breaking the rules. It was bending them, at worst. He could do that. His life on the Horizon, with Demi, deserved that effort.

"I am swayed by your words." Neera nodded at the monitor, finally matching the intensity of his friend's gaze. "How shall we begin?"

CHAPTER 11

TANAV

Tanav had stared at the distress call's waveform for another hour by the time Lynn got off her shift. Then *they* spent several hours staring at the waveform together. It didn't produce much, though, the translation matrix seemingly stuck even as they fed in more and more archives—logs kept by Chuck, analyses by other Lumersian scientists, transmission records with the collective species.

The process did help in one regard, though: it kept Tanav from thinking about Demi's imminent departure. She'd entrusted him with this role of Cultural Counselor for a reason. One night in the gravity well, Tanav joked that he acted as the community spy, to which Demi gave him a very serious look and said, "I need to keep things steady for everyone. And not everyone's going to be honest with me. But they like you, they trust you, and you have a gift for understanding people. That is more valuable than any academy training could ever provide. Especially here. You are their voice. And I need that."

How would that even work if she left? Tanav wasn't loyal to the Cluster or GCF Command. His loyalties were with Demi *and* this crew. Which meant that a life without those, in this universe?

It took away all his options. And without the photonic engine, it also shut down any possibility of him finding a way home, even with the Lumersians reaching out.

Home was both closer and more impossible than ever before.

"We need a break," Lynn said. "Human brains from any universe need a pressure release."

Tanav knew she was right. But he also knew that switching out of this mode might bring new questions. Especially because he only talked about the distress call and avoided the part about Demi's departure. That wasn't his to reveal.

"We've gotta keep going." He rubbed his eyes as he said this, signaling that his body didn't exactly agree with him.

"That's super academic of you." She laughed, which shook him enough to laugh too. "I know this is big. I know the Lumersians helped us, and we should help them. But my brain can't anymore. They'd understand if we took a break." She stood, tossing her long black curls as she yawned. "I'm going to the med bay. Meet me there if you want."

Which was a really weird request. Ten minutes later, he showed up to find her holding an acoustic guitar of all things—a timeless, rich wood body with clean metal strings and deep tones. As he arrived, she struggled for a smooth transition between an A chord and an E chord, all while explaining that the med bay's shape had the Horizon's best acoustics, and the guitar itself belonged to Commander Connors, who apparently brought it when he arrived.

"There," she said, one strum in A and then another in E. "Look at that. You need three chords to write a song, right? What goes with A and E? Here," she said, abruptly stopping to hold the guitar out by the neck, "you show me."

Tanav hesitated, which only led to Lynn repeating the gesture. "You can learn chords from the computer archives." His words carried plenty of resistance, but he gave into the instinct that carried him through nearly every stage of his life—from his first guitar as a toddler all the way to, well . . .

The only time he lived without the instrument—without *music*—was his time on the Horizon. That was his old life. He'd moved on from that. He was different now.

"Yeah, but I'm a better learner when *you* show me," she said. "And we're not getting a new doctor until next week. And your brain needs something new. Unless you want to talk about what's really going on."

He didn't. Partly because he didn't know what to say. Which meant Lynn won this point.

Tanav rolled a stool next to her and took the guitar.

"Come on," Lynn said, a playful bounce to her voice, "try the first thing that comes to mind."

The first thing that comes to mind.

A riff appeared from the depths of memory. In the past few hours, he'd hummed it, dissecting the notes and beats in his head because those four seconds mirrored part of the Lumersian transmission. The riff was stuck in his head, a constant loop that led to a memory of the last time he'd played it . . .

Which was, actually, the last time he held a guitar—about four years ago.

The last time he existed in his home universe, in fact. That riff, backed by drums and bass and wrapped in lyrics he'd written about relationships that broke and mended and broke again.

It was intended to be about his parents. But at that point, it was about Thaddea too.

He was surrounded by backup musicians contracted by the Crystal Dreams cruise, house band members loaned out to hit notes and keep time rather than feel the music. It didn't matter, though, the people there just wanted one song, four minutes and fifteen seconds of the best and worst thing to happen during his career.

"Coming Home."

He'd agreed to do this, a forty-five-minute, eight-song set for a simple trade-off: stability. He thought Thaddea, of all people, would understand the value of that. Would Lynn have understood? He wasn't sure. They had similar stubborn natures, immovable when they considered themselves right.

That final night, Tanav chewed on what to say to Thaddea as he sang the final lines of "Coming Home," his hands sliding up and down the fretboard to churn out the tune's signature melody. The drummer hit one quick tom roll, then a pause, then two snare hits leading into the final cymbal, and Tanav strummed a final chord. Applause wrapped the stage, a wave of drunken noise from people too dressed up to be his usual audience. Tanav appreciated the level of blindness created by the shining spotlights; it let him do his usual thank-yous without having to see their apathy.

Tanav started his contracted mid-set banter about the cruise's entertainment lineup for the rest of the night when the stage shook—a harsh, violent shake, so brutal that his whole sense of balance tipped, and the guitar draped over his body went horizontal.

To his right, the drum kit's hi-hat flew past him. To his left, the bassist knelt down, hands on the ground for stability. A loud chime rang out in the theater's PA system. "Attention, passengers," a voice said, "an interstellar anomaly has affected our gravity generators. Please shelter until they come back—"

The words cut off with a burst of static, then another jolt twisted the axis of the ship further. Tanav's eyes went wide as concertgoers started lifting off the floor, the combination of faulty gravity generators and whatever tipped the ship. Arms and legs clambered, and Tanav locked onto the strange sight of a single wineglass floating across the space, somehow staying exactly level. A side door opened, letting in a beam of light that perfectly struck the glass, and even though it remained a distance away, Tanav saw every single bubble shifting in near pause within the liquid.

Then a voice yelled, "Watch out!"

He'd turned to see the drum snare flying right at his face, and though he blacked out, he swore he still remembered how the collision gave off a much deeper snare hit than usual. And one day, he'd figure out if that was due to the shifting gravity situation or the fact that it smacked his head.

When he came to, gravity was restored, but the world changed. Because the Crystal Dreams floated inside the Lumersian energy well.

In hindsight, playing "Coming Home" that night proved particularly fitting. He couldn't go home, no matter how much he wanted to. Demi, the Horizon, the engine, the Lumersian distress call, they might coalesce into a way home if they could just get *something* out of it.

Though Tanav did see the irony in having Lynn of all people help with this.

"What is that song?" Lynn asked, interrupting his memories. "It sounds familiar."

"Well," he said, instinctive movements playing the rest of the song's chords, "there's only so many combinations of notes and rhythm out there. Sometimes they overlap." He paused, then pulled over an idle data tablet in the med bay and accessed Demi's research materials. "It's from one of my songs." Lynn arched an eyebrow up at that. "Yes, *that* song. But also this is where you've heard it before." He played the short snippet of the transmission, several seconds of digital noise that just happened to replicate nine notes played as a riff from the outro of "Coming Home." "Like I said, there's only so many combinations."

"Yours sounds different, though." Lynn took the tablet and squinted at the transmission's waveform. "Play yours again." His thumb plucked at the strings over and over, the final time in sync with the Lumersian audio. "I think . . . yours starts soft and gets louder. This alternates between loud and soft." The stool squeaked as Lynn stood. "Humans use volume to express the context of the words. But some cultures use volume as part of direct meaning. Like saying something loud means *up*, but saying the same thing quietly means *down*." She turned the tablet so Tanav could also see the screen, the waveform now on full display. "Same notes, different meanings. Like when you talk about blues and greens."

Same notes, different meanings.

Tanav hadn't accounted for that when examining the Lumersian message. He'd processed it without considering dynamics at all—and how could he, of all people, miss one of the fundamentals of music?

"I just thought of something," he said, putting the guitar down.

Lynn was right. They just needed a break. Now back in Tanav's quarters, they repeated the recording over and over as he added new layers of dimension and reference to the interpretation algorithm. The text started off as three sentences, enough for Demi to deem the message a distress signal: *Photonic energy . . . will face eventual collapse . . . return home.*

Gaps filled the space between and around those sentences, passages where the original audio played noises of varying pitches and cadences. Bit by bit, details arrived, until a paragraph of holographic text floated in front of them. And it was worse than they thought.

This was more than a distress call. And even though Tanav didn't fully understand how photonic energy worked, he grasped the scale of the catastrophe at hand:

The photonic energy well has returned to physical space. It is growing in volatility, and photonic space will face eventual collapse. Our scientists believe it is because the remaining energy of Photonic Being #910047 still exists in physical space instead of being in our collective dimension. This has created a fissure to leak photonic energy into physical space. 910047 must return home to seal this fissure.

Tanav reread the message, this time Lynn gripping his hand. She probably thought about the destruction of all physical space. It was, after all, a pretty big deal. But something new slipped into his thoughts, a possibility hidden within the disaster.

If the gravity well had returned, it might also be a way home.

Upon arriving in Cluster space, Tanav told Demi that somehow, some way, he wanted to show his parents and Thaddea who he'd become. If they managed to help the Lumersians, what else was possible?

A full spectrum of paths pushed and pulled at Tanav, and he remained still, fully aware that Lynn quietly held his hand. Though he didn't say anything, he knew she'd put it together. Of course she would; she was the ship's communications officer.

CHAPTER 12

·······✳·······

DEMI

Demi had spent hours debating how to present this distress call to GCF Command, and if it might change *anything* about their situation.

Then *everything* about their situation changed. Tanav and Lynn arrived to share that they'd deciphered the message. A breakthrough, for sure, but also a problem—or a series of problems, because each piece of the message got progressively worse.

The gravity well returned.

It was unstable and growing.

It could eventually destroy the Lumersians' dimension.

To stop it all? Their only solution was taking Chuck's spark back to the well.

And that meant Demi had to make peace with returning to a graveyard—one that might still very well be capable of imploding the Horizon. Just like her commitment to her band of survivors, she recognized the right thing to do and the one thing she could control.

Even if it meant losing Chuck.

He'd want her to do this. And on every level—scientific, ethical, leadership—it made sense in so many ways. But just imagining him gone forever back into the blanket of photonic energy . . .

She wasn't quite ready for that. Except she needed to be. And as she pondered that, a chime interrupted Demi, followed by the unusual sound of *knocking* on the door—something she only heard during periods in the well when power rationing required minimal internal sensors. "Demi, an urgent revelation has been uncovered. These findings must be seen."

Only one person on the ship spoke like that.

The doors slid open and Neera burst through, three tablets in hand. "It is possible to execute the photonic jump," he said, words sprinting out despite the verbose Dywen syntax. "The issue is the use of steady state presented by the synth environmental controls." He held up a tablet, then tapped a button to sync it with her holo emitter; from her desk display, a hologram of data materialized. Neera's words came out at a faster clip than Demi thought was possible for him. "This configuration was confirmed through simulations by Sadler and and—"

"Slow down, Neera. That's an order," Demi said with a laugh. Neera stood with a rare downward head tilt—she'd come to learn that Dywens naturally reverted to a passive and hierarchical baseline, but this move seemed a rare bit of embarrassment from her normally methodical friend. "Now, tell me from the beginning." Demi stood and carefully stepped over Indy on the way to join him. "Without waking up my dog. If you're careful, she'll stay asleep and won't bug you for once."

Neera proceeded to give a very detailed, very technical description of what he'd conjured up with his brilliant engineering friend. But Demi didn't need most of it. All that mattered was knowing they found a way to make the photonic jump possible—and they had the simulation numbers to prove it. They only needed to give it a shot.

Pending approval, of course. And that was the problem.

Once again, she steadied herself for a conversation with Vice Admiral Krishna, who agreed to meet on short notice. As she awaited Krishna's arrival, Demi couldn't decide if the universe was ironic or cruel. They'd sacrificed so much to escape, and now she had scheduled a meeting to beg to go back?

Perhaps returning to the well was inevitable, like the fate of Demora Kim was tethered to this anomaly across universes, always ready to snap her back, possibly even hold her there. In a way, it felt like her story was always meant to end there, which made this whole thing seem fitting, even poetic.

That unnerved her more than anything else.

Krishna's image arrived. And Demi took a breath, reminding herself of her three advantages here:

Krishna had been the most sympathetic to her situation since arriving in Cluster space.

Demi had simulation data that showed why the ship wouldn't jump before and why it should now.

And she was going to only ask for one week to get Sadler aboard, prep the necessary test, and jump.

What was a week in the scope of the Galactic Cluster and this war with no end?

Demi was about to greet Krishna when two more people arrived: Penn and Baker, two civilian Cluster government officials.

Then Minister of Defense Cabell. All humans, all stationed at the solar system's GC Fleet headquarters on Earth's colonized moon. Another vice admiral faded in via hologram, a crystalline species closest to Earth's sector that shared resources—yet Demi could not remember the species name. Two more people arrived, one human captain and one with amphibious qualities, its head captured in a semi-clear helmet, both of whom were new to Demi.

Each successive arrival chipped away at Demi's confidence and heightened her nerves. But, she told herself, she had science and data on her side. She saw zero evidence that bringing the Horizon's old bones to the front would make any difference *anywhere* right now.

"Thank you for all assembling on such short notice," Demi started. She sat in her chair, the wide view of her display accompanied by floating holographic notes. "This is a bigger audience than expected, and I'll keep—"

A beep interrupted her, announcing the arrival of another person via hologram.

The new silhouette fizzled in, first as a burst of several vertical lines before settling in on the image of Matthews—who must have been joining them from his quarters below.

Demi reminded herself to stifle any reaction. She would present the facts and the possibilities as clearly as possible. A quick glance showed that Indy chewed away at a ship-synthesized bone, Chuck's spark looming over the dog, and despite the encroachment of privacy, she appreciated that the conference room's ongoing repair put calls directly here.

Those two sure made things a lot easier to handle.

"I'll keep this short," Demi said. "Two new developments have occurred regarding the photonic engine. First, we have received a message from the Lumersians. It appears the energy well that trapped the Horizon has returned. It is threatening the Lumersian dimension, and they are requesting aid." Why was she so *nervous*? She'd done plenty of debriefings, across so many situations, and yet here a bunch of neutral faces ignited her nerves and shortened her breath.

She forced herself steady and forward. "Second, my chief engineer has identified a new variable in the processing of synthetic photons within the engine. He has run simulations with this technique and believes it resolves the synth decay issue." Chirps came as Demi tapped icons around the holographic data. "I'm uploading the simulation records now." Almost in unison, brows furrowed, and Demi moved quickly before any questions could slow her. "Given these recent developments, I'm formally requesting a delay of one Earth-standard week for the Horizon's arrival at Base Theta Seven, along with the pending reassignment for both the ship and myself. In that time, I would like to lead new tests of the photonic engine." One breath, then two, then a third came and went, Demi steeling herself for the next ask. "And pending its successful first jump, an additional five weeks to continue with thirteen further jumps necessary for reaching the Lumersian energy well and to provide assistance."

On the display, two of the admirals whispered to each other. Krishna sat with her eyes down, presumably scanning the uploaded data. Even Matthews offered a thoughtful look at his tablet.

They could have said no right away. So this was a win. At least for now.

"Six weeks total," Krishna finally said.

"One week to prepare and execute a test jump under this new engineering development," Demi repeated. "Then if successful, five weeks for the aid mission."

"Let's assume your team gets the engine working," Krishna finally said. "Why should we commit the Horizon's resources to going there? The disaster at Ark Getru has severely limited our resources, leaving WM opportunities to exploit our current situation."

Demi had prepped for these types of questions and maneuvered into them like an academy quiz. Had the Cluster been operating with more altruistic guidance, she would have pointed out charter 16.3 for mutual aid. However, this was the same group whose negotiation decisions emboldened the WM to massacre Ark Getru. She needed to get more practical.

"I will point out again that I am only asking for one week. We spend more time doing debriefings and analysis." Glances were exchanged across the display, and though Demi caught creases forming on the brows of nearly all the attendees, they angled to show consideration, not resistance. "Remember, the Lumersians helped design the engine. Helping them might prove beneficial to Cluster ships. It may bring photonic tech to the whole fleet." That caught their attention. She decided to go for it. "This could change the war. This could win the war."

This wasn't an easy group, but Demi saw the shifts in demeanor— the focus of looks, the pursing of lips, the raising of brows.

All except one.

"Why now?" Matthews broke the silence. "They've given us no timetable. Your debrief even states that linear time is a new concept to them. Their panic could mean that we still have twenty years before they face catastrophic conditions."

"Or two weeks," Demi said, and though Matthews sat some unknown distance away, she looked directly at him as if he were on the other side of her personal quarters. "If we can get the engine running, we'd get answers soon enough. And the ensuing scientific collaboration could prevent any more Ark Getru incidents. What could the fleet do with photonic tech? How many disasters could we stop? How much faster could we execute?"

"Can you guarantee that?" Matthews finally asked. "You ask for one week, six weeks, all this time on a theory. Thing is, the Horizon by itself might be all we—"

"Commander Matthews," Cabell cut in. "I should remind all of us that there are different levels of classified clearance here."

Demi's gut churned at the possibility in front of her. She could ask, with all of upper GCF Command present, *why* Matthews was inspecting the Horizon's old hardware so closely? If it wasn't the engine, then what drove this? The ramen bar? Indy's fur in the first officer's chair? Clearly, Command knew something. Why else would Cabell cut him off that way?

But instead, Demi chose civility to win people over. And during the long pause, muffled chatter and thoughtful looks showed it was the right one.

"This technology is intriguing," said the crystalline vice admiral before Matthews broke in again.

"In theory, that's all well and good. But Ark Getru has shown how fast the WM can strike. We need to change our capabilities *now*." Demi hid her confusion at that statement—the Horizon's outdated systems wouldn't exactly achieve that. Matthews took in a breath with pursed lips, and for a flash, Demi swore she caught something, a flare of a grimace on his face. "And Captain Kim's ability to deliver on her promise is severely biased—I would say, even compromised, by her history with the Lumersians." The side of his mouth ticked down, and despite being a holo-transmission, he scowled at the others in the discussion. "You had a romantic relationship with one."

That was unexpected. And inappropriate.

And way out of character. Matthews had a reputation for being *matter-of-fact* and mission oriented. His behavior on the ship, his hours poring over the guts of old hardware and reading ship schematics, that lined up.

This did not.

This was a trap. For what purpose, Demi wasn't sure. "The nature of my relationship with Photonic Being Number 910047 is not relevant."

"But you do admit that you had a close relationship?" he asked. Why was he pressing this? "What was your pet name for him? Chuck?"

The audio feed picked up murmurs, though Demi couldn't pinpoint who said what. "Again, that is not relevant to the matter at hand."

"We're talking about bias influencing judgment—"

"Again, your points are irrelevant." Demi's words came out faster than she would have liked—and probably too fast to help her cause, based on the surprised looks. Matthews settled back with a nod, and now Demi had to justify her outburst. "Ultimately, we're closer to getting the photonic engine to work than ever before, and propagating it further might be fully realized by aiding the Lumersians. That is worth investing extra time in. One week."

"We are at war. That changes everything. That prioritizes all our assets, all our resources. The Horizon is vital to a winning strategy, but only if it puts the engine aside." For that moment, Matthews's composure returned to the person she'd met: gruff, steady, impassioned. But then he took a thorough breath before his demeanor shifted again. "Your hesitation at joining the effort is *very* well known. I hear the chatter among this crew. They think they're separate from the war. There's active dissent. Every judgment about the engine is compromised by her history with the Lumersian species and this so-called Chuck. She cannot be trusted with any decisions about this ship—"

"Commander Matthews. Captain Kim." Krishna's voice came out stern. "That's enough. Take a moment."

"I don't—" Demi shot out, like Matthews spoke with precision targeting to trigger her impulses. Except the words couldn't form, an uncharacteristic stammer coming at the worst time possible.

She tried again.

"You are asking me to abandon my ship, to abandon my crew, and no one will tell me why—the truth, not the official line. The photonic engine—"

"Captain Kim, you said this was going to be short," Krishna cut in, shaking her head with clear frustration. "I'm going to make it short. Your request is noted. We"—she gestured around her—"will deliberate and give you a response as soon as possible. Krishna out."

One by one, the images disconnected. As Matthews faded from view, she thought he'd carry an air of victory, or at least confidence. But right before he disappeared, she caught him with a thin mouth, weary lines forming across his face.

The display darkened, leaving only floating holograms of data and the sound of Indy snoring. Demi choked down her frustration. She'd been close. She could see the engine tempting them.

But then Matthews presented an argument that, taken line by line, held valid weight.

The declared state of war allowed for superseding other causes on a case-by-case basis. The Withdrawal Movement both hoarded resources and operated without bureaucracy, allowing for quick and deadly strikes. The WM didn't care. But, as she understood it, neither did GCF forces. She just didn't bring that up.

Demi didn't have any certainties. She just knew that doing *something* instead of being part of this escalating churn seemed like it made better use of this single ship. To everyone else, the Lumersians may have felt theoretical, intangible.

But to her, and possibly the seventeen people who'd survived the well, the photonic species deserved better. And now, she'd given her last, best chance at making sure that happened.

Twenty minutes passed, all with Demi sitting still in her chair, the hologram of data still floating by as she stared at the blank display. All that time in the Lumersian well taught her to make extreme contingency plans for the unexpected, but that only worked when she had the autonomy to move things forward. Without a ship, without command, without a voice, no possibilities existed. She was a cog in the GCF machine, and unless Krishna and the others approved her request, she'd be plucked from this particular machine and tossed elsewhere. Probably to hide her away in a corner of space where she would toil without any influence.

Things were so much simpler when all she wanted was to chart the stars.

A green square appeared on her display, black text buried within it:

Incoming Message—Classified.

"Computer, display message," she said, her pulse quickening. The screen flashed, a fraction of a second that stretched until words loaded:

Upon further deliberation, GCF Command has decided your original orders stand. The Horizon will transition to support service for specialized communications. You are expected at Base Theta Seven within four days. On a personal note, I will add the room was divided between the potential scientific benefits of and the need to support the front line, but ultimately, the war continues to supersede decisions and charters during standard operations.

That was that. Minutes ago, she'd wondered if the well was inevitable. Clearly, such a thought was delusional, a smidgen of romanticism activated by Chuck's voice breaking through for a few moments. The truth was much more dry and simple: no hand of fate led to the gravity well.

And somewhere, under the swirl of emotions and thoughts, Demi sensed the ultimate contradiction:

Relief. Relief knowing she wouldn't return to where so many friends and colleagues had died, where a single lash of unstable photons could destroy the Horizon. A surprising relief, one that immediately turned to the emptiness of guilt. And from that, she sat completely still, those feelings pulling at her until nothing remained.

CHAPTER 13

※

NEERA

It'd been so long since Neera felt truly hopeless that he'd almost forgotten what it was like.

During his time in the Regent Empire, life ran at a constant balance between numb and dread. He'd learned to focus on himself rather than the systemic brutalities out of his control—fixing one thing at a time, one step at a time. Fear or discomfort or fury were all stuffed down under compliance.

Until his freighter found itself damaged and floating into the gravitational pull of the photonic convergence point. First they lost altitude control of the ship. Then reverse thrusters failed to limit the gradual slide into nothing. At that point, a calm washed over him, the inevitable lack of control so much nicer than what he had come to know.

A bright pink flash of energy swallowed them, and suddenly they were on the other side of . . . something. Whatever it was, it brought a different sense, the disquieting strangeness of freedom. Technically, they were still a Regent ship, but they flew on a twenty-person transport craft of maintenance techs and a cargo of repair drones. Not exactly a representation of the best, the brightest, or the most powerful, and because of that, the chain of command struggled.

Then Demi emerged on their viewscreen with information. They were stranded. There were eleven other starships in a makeshift colony. And as the Horizon was the biggest ship with the most scientific resources, it formed the pseudo-capital, with its docking bay hosting regular trading bazaars for the small shuttles and fighters capable of traversing through the gravitational sludge.

Neera had never seen anything like it. Even when the well began its gradual collapse, he viewed it with a wistful sensibility, gratitude that he'd gotten to spend some portion of his life in a place free from Regent control.

Everything after that was a bonus.

Now the Cluster wanted to send the Horizon to war. Without Demi in the captain's chair. To feel hopeless, that produced another strange shift in emotion.

Anger. Anger at how Command turned down Demi, even with proof—*proof*—that they had solved the decay problem. In the Regent Empire, proof was ignored all the time. But here? This universe was supposed to be *better*.

How could it not be?

His body tensed. His mind raced. His jaw clenched. This seemed consistent across species, the way everything turned inward and bound harsher in reaction to the outside world spiraling out of control. Neera found himself standing in the middle of his quarters, not looking at diagrams or fixing the small projects he'd brought back from engineering, but just *existing* in this anger.

It boiled over, propelling him to do something wholly unexpected:

He chose to call Sadler.

He didn't know why. His message captured as much: "There is a significant setback. Something must be done. I do not know what that is."

Those few words depressurized everything, soon causing an unusual fatigue to wash over him. His breath grew heavy, and a stiffness took over his muscles. He sat down on his bed, staring at the wall, an inner voice chastising himself for falling apart in such an *unconstructive* way. This wasn't his call, these weren't his responsibilities, and he had to fall in line, like he did before, like he did for Demi, like he would do for Matthews or whoever his next captain would be. He just had to remain in his own scope.

He had to. Because that was how he always got through. Stay in his scope and fix things. Reaching out to Sadler was selfish, emotional, *impulsive*. If he could take it back, he would. Neera stared at the wall, lingering on this thought until his gaze stuck on a light on the wall.

A broken light.

A dead series of micro-bulbs in the panel next to the faucet in his quarters. They worked during the first four years of his stay until one of the first jolts of unstable energy shook the ship and jarred something loose. It flickered or dimmed over months before the micro-bulbs went out one by one, left to right, leaving Neera's quarters with one panel that refused to adjust its line of illumination.

Neera always meant to fix it. He'd just never had time. And when the Horizon docked for repairs following its arrival, a facility engineer told him the replacement parts were obsolete. So it sat.

Until now.

Neera got up and grabbed tools, ready to tackle this fix that he should have done long ago. A chime interrupted, though Neera chose to ignore it. He'd made a mistake in reaching out to Sadler, and he shouldn't give it any more time. The chime rang again. And again.

Sadler would not give up. And though Neera tried to ignore it, he finally gave in and looked at the desk display around the ninth or tenth time.

"Are you okay?" Sadler asked as soon as his image appeared. "You look . . . off. Even for a Dywen."

Perhaps Sadler had an innate sense of pack too. "The micro-bulbs in my quarters required an attempted fix for many years," Neera said.

"Micro-bulbs?" From the display, Sadler angled, though Neera wasn't sure if he'd actually be able to see the open panel on the other side of the room. "All this was for micro-bulbs?"

"Three years have passed since the micro-bulbs in that panel have worked properly."

"This is how you're coping, huh?" Several seconds passed before Neera understood exactly what Sadler was saying—and why he said it. Probably reading the confusion on his face, Sadler gave a quick confirmation. "Yes, I know."

"This information is limited to the crew, who heard it from Demi this morning." Neera leaned forward, examining Sadler's face in the display. "What was the source of your information?"

"I told you, word travels fast," he said with a shrug before pointing at Neera. "Okay, you wanted to do something about it. Good news, I've been thinking about it since I learned about Captain Kim."

This could only cause more problems. If they did anything now, Neera's next captain might discover his actions. He could not break the chain of command. Especially during wartime. "A mistake was made. I should not have bothered you."

"My friend, you are the only Dywen I've met. And probably the only one I'll ever meet. I mean, other than a few other refugees, who knows if you even exist in this universe? So I don't have a lot of experience reading your emotions." Sadler's voice softened, his mouth in a sympathetic diagonal. "Despite that, I want you to hear me:

"This isn't over."

Sadler's optimism was admirable but misplaced. "The age of conscription in the Regent Empire is similar to a seven-year-old human joining the military," Neera said, his words paced slowly. "Citizenship is earned through a process of service, then specialty, then field commission." In all the times he'd talked with Sadler, he'd never revealed any of this. In fact, only Demi may have ever heard it.

And Chuck too. He definitely told Chuck, probably during late nights working on the prototype photonic engine.

Neera realized he still held tools in his hands, and he set them aside. "The difference in war between here and my universe is something I have considered. Someone was always the target of the Regent Empire. A conflict always existed to squash out." Even saying that caused a tremor in Neera's voice, images of flattened villages flickering through his mind, and he considered his next words carefully, a mental strain to put them in as much human syntax as possible: "War is unavoidable. All I can do is contain its impact. There is no way around it."

"Neera, listen to me." Sadler's voice came with the undertow of urgency. "Very carefully. Understand? You're wrong. We've got a choice." Sadler emphasized his claim with a nod, and he continued nodding as he spoke. "We're gonna do this. A small window exists."

"The window to do something has closed. Your belief is appreciated but false."

Sadler's head tilted, three lines forming across his brow. "You're going to let that stop you?"

Such a strange question. Sadler asked about something so impossible that Neera considered if perhaps a word got lost in the transmission.

"The list of people Demi met with was lengthy, including the minister of defense. The answer they gave was clear." Neera glanced at the time in the corner of the display. "Scans should complete in about two hours before our final departure to Base Theta Seven."

"Okay, that's good to know. My estimates were right."

"Your statement is confusing to me."

"Hold on one second. I'm sending you something." A notification of *Synchronize Data Patch* appeared, along with buttons for Accept and Decline. "Hit Accept on my mark. Three . . . two . . . one . . . now." Neera did as requested, and Sadler's face distorted, pixels forming colored blocks of digital noise, followed by audio bursts of static and hisses. "Okay, now we're secure. Encrypted tunnel for just you and me. I'd estimated your arrival at Theta Seven. I'll meet you there. I'm already in transit."

"This continues to be confusing. Did you request transfer to the Horizon? I require an explanation."

"Okay. I'm on my way to Theta Seven." Sadler's words quickened with as much excitement in his voice as any scientific discussions they'd previously had. "No one knows. I've borrowed a light freighter, stocked it all up. Let's test the engine. I'm positive it'll work."

Demi's transfer. Matthews's takeover. A list of orders. All of those acted as barricades to keep the crew of the Horizon in line, and besides, when did military commanders ever listen to scientists and engineers? *That* part was not unique to the Regent Empire. "I have come across a human saying in your culture's archive that feels appropriate: 'The best-laid plans—'"

"It's not a saying, it's from a book," Sadler said with a laugh. "I've never read it, though. Too busy coming up with a plan to get the photonic engine online and jump us all the way to the Lumersian well so Captain Kim can answer their distress call. Now, come on." Sadler's face changed, a direct and serious look. "You *came* from conflict. Can you really go back?"

Neera did not know how to answer such a question. He knew how he *felt*, but expressing it proved out of reach. "Galactic bureaucracy and GCF security provide many reasons to argue with your intentions."

"I've thought about that," Sadler said matter-of-factly. "And it's really simple. Forget legalities. Forget orders. I know that's hard for you but just listen." He pointed to himself, then Neera. "*We* have the moral justification right now. That outweighs any chain of command. And that means we must do this. I'm going to meet you at Theta Seven." He leaned forward, as if he could pop through the display, blue eyes wide and brilliant, his presence more tangible. "Then we're going to steal the Horizon."

CHAPTER 14

※

TANAV

Tanav wasn't sure what stirred him out of sleep first, the door chime or Lynn's groan. But the latter definitely forced him into some measure of responsiveness. "There's someone at the door," she said in a half muffle, before putting the pillow over her head.

Bright digits cut through the dim room, though it took several seconds for his eyes to focus on the clock—2:28 a.m. on the ship's hours. "I thought we stopped extra shifts with all the new people," he said as he pulled the covers half-down, though he couldn't quite commit to the next step of getting up.

Another chime came, followed by another groan from Lynn. "My shift starts at six. Make it stop."

Sleep wasn't a privilege anymore, apparently. Recent nights ignited his thoughts: What might help the Lumersians? What was happening within the well? How could he possibly stay on the ship without Demi?

What did it all mean regarding the sarcastic drowsy woman next to him?

Tonight, he finally fell soundly asleep, so of course *this* happened. Tanav rolled out of bed, slipping a robe over his bare shoulders. The door chimed again, and Tanav waved his arm to trigger the proximity sensor.

Awaiting him stood Demi, in full uniform, with dog at her side. Kind of odd for this time of off-duty night.

"Agh, the bright," Lynn said from behind him, and her voice alone caused Demi to smirk.

"Couldn't sleep?" Tanav asked, a hand running through his thick dark curls as he stepped out into the hallway.

"I see you have company," Demi said with a nod beyond the door. "I'm happy for you. For both of you." Demi's expression softened, a two-in-the-morning look, and Tanav finally noticed the fatigue lines forming around her eyes and mouth. "You deserve each other."

"Yeah . . ." Tanav let his voice trail off; he was pretty sure Demi didn't mean for her compliment to spur heavy thoughts, especially at this time of night. But such things lingered right now. "I've been thinking about that part. Everything lately . . ." He glanced over his shoulder, as if he could see through the composite door at her slumbering in a slightly too-small bed. "It's gotten complicated."

That was the easiest way to sum up recent days. Tanav faced the entire spectrum of possibilities over that span. The Horizon, Demi, the engine, the Lumersians, the returned well . . .

A path back home. And a blockade in the form of bureaucracy and war demands.

His thoughts about Lynn shifted with each new revelation, a winding path leading to an epiphany as life-changing as deciding to take that gig on the Crystal Dreams.

Somehow, the more his future grew uncertain, the more he felt sure about Lynn.

"'Complicated,'" Demi said, and the late hour probably made it really, really hard for Demi to fight the grin sneaking out. "That's why I'm here. Have you spoken to Neera today?"

Neera? That could mean many things—all of which would *further* complicate things. Apparently, Tanav wasn't getting back to bed tonight.

"He seemed busy today."

Demi looked around the hall, and even though no one was within earshot, her voice dropped. "He and his friend Sadler. They think they found a way. You understand?"

A way. "I think I do," Tanav replied to Demi's cryptic words.

"The only way to go there means *not* going elsewhere." That took a moment for him to put together, but the context and her sudden intensity pointed him the right way. He nodded. "It means making very specific choices that many won't approve of, but I'm going to do this. I have to. I'm only taking people who want to be part of it. Everyone gets a chance to opt out."

Demi trusted Tanav to read others. But he could read her too. Particularly now, when fatigue or desperation or something else let her emotions slip through more than she'd ever like. She spoke with equal parts cryptic direction and diplomatic strategy, but her *tone* gave things away as much as the glow in her eyes.

She believed.

Maybe not in the certainty of whatever Neera and Sadler had conjured up. But with GCF Command trying to take away her home, her crew, her *purpose*, built on the chaos of an escalating war, she believed in the righteousness of this plan, whatever it was. Like executing all these things swiftly and decisively could strip away the stain of it all—not just for her, but for the entire ship.

In fact, the only time he could recall ever seeing her like this was around Chuck.

She had so much belief that she even started nodding as she talked. "Still figuring the plan out, but I wanted to talk to you. Two things. First, you know this crew. You know how they think. I'd like your opinion on possible reactions. Second, think about it for yourself. Tell me in the morning—"

The door slid open to reveal Lynn, her oversize T-shirt and shorts contrasting with Demi's fleet uniform. "Hi, Demi. Captain, ma'am," she said with a quick salute, a sudden sharpness to her previously drowsy words. "I'm in. I can help Neera with the engine too." She looked up, then pointed above them. "No space walks, though."

"That's my way home." How long until they were due at Theta Seven? It was far too early to crunch that, and besides, he was never a numbers guy. He just knew that everything important in his life hurtled that way, and the flutter in his chest meant that he'd already embraced this journey, even if he wasn't certain he was ready. Maybe, like Demi, he believed. Lynn hooked her arm around his, leaning against his shoulder.

He looked at her, so many things that needed to be said. And soon.

"Sorry, I mean—"

"You're stating a fact," she said. "That's your way home. I'm happy to help you get there. You deserve a choice."

Did Lynn mean a choice about going home and everything that entailed? Or a choice about them? Tanav tried *not* to overthink it all, yet knew he had to sort it out. Just not at two in the morning.

"I guess I'm in." Behind him, Lynn cleared her throat much louder than it needed, and Tanav corrected himself. "Her too. We're already at the gates," he said before shaking his head. "Sorry, home-universe saying. It's late. You know what I mean."

Demi nodded with a new seriousness—determination mixed with excitement mixed with the unknown. "I should let you two get some sleep," she said before clicking her tongue to get Indy's attention. "There's a lot to prepare."

With that, Demi walked away, Indy trotting alongside her. Lynn put her arm around Tanav's waist for a quick squeeze before heading back inside. "I'm gonna start the coffee," she said, breaking into a hum.

As he stood in the open doorway, Tanav recognized the melody as the outro to one of Lynn's favorite songs, a repeated refrain that led the tune to its final beats, and under his breath, he joined along.

"'The execution of all things,'" he murmured, "'The execution of all things.'"

TRANSCRIPT OF ARCHIVED PERSONAL LOG

Grant Singh

Commander, Galactic Cluster Fleet—Starship Horizon (Deceased)

I'm not sure how we're going to resolve this latest problem, but that's the nature of the well, I guess.

Oh, the strangest thing happened.

Demi stopped by tonight with a question that was . . . what's the phrase? Shocking, but not surprising? Shocking is a bit harsh. We all kind of knew about Demi and Chuck—I mean, her tone completely changes around him. There's this singsong quality to her jokes that never exists around us. The first time, I thought maybe she hiccuped. After that, I knew.

She had a very serious look on her face, more serious than normal, and asked me how I would feel about her having a relationship with an official member of the crew.

To which I answered, "Is Chuck part of the crew now? I thought he was just a visiting scientist."

Now, I've known Demi for, what, sixteen years now? And I have never—and I mean, never seen her blush. I didn't think it was in her DNA. The closest she'd come before was saying some quippy remark and looking away.

I gave her a minute to process my jab by making coffee. One for each of us. And when I returned, she goes, "Are we that obvious?"

I didn't even answer the question. But they are. Painfully.

I said, "Captain Demora Kim. You have kept us alive through hell and back. So, as your longtime friend, but more importantly, as your first officer and immediate subordinate, I have something very critical to tell you: "It's okay for you to be happy."

She replied with: "It's unexpected. I don't even know where it's going to lead. It's just that when we talk, everything feels right. Even when everything else is wrong."

"That's how I felt with Rand," I told her. "And if I ever get back home, I'm going to let him know that every goddamn day until he's sick of hearing it."

As Demi left, I made a joke about how I planned to give the toast at their wedding. She smiled at that. I can tell when those are authentic. They're less smirky.

She didn't even take her coffee. More for me, I suppose.

CHAPTER 15

DEMI

Demi spent a good minute or so pondering if she had gotten into the wrong line of work since she really, really hated giving speeches. Middle-of-the-night discussions with Indy at her side, sure, but standing in front of an attentive group? No thanks.

Eventually, every starship captain had to give a heartfelt speech, either in gratitude or for inspiration or whatever emotion the moment needed. Words designed to move, just like propulsion through space, except with dopamine in the brain.

For many years, she delegated speeches to Grant. Except for eulogies. Demi always took those on herself. When she spoke, a whole-body change occurred: how she stood, how she breathed, all ways that would have impressed her academy speech and rhetoric teacher. It worked, but it sure took *effort*.

She supposed in a different life, she might have been an actor, turning it on and off. Possibly on a community theater level. Or at least a tour guide.

On the other hand, Grant could have been a mayor with the way he just *said* the right thing. He'd had a natural way of connecting on a personal level. At the Horizon's initial launch out of dry dock, as the ship's propulsion came to life, he'd spied her checking system data and metrics on her tablet.

"Hey," he'd said, reaching over from the first officer's chair.

She thought he might have noticed an anomaly in the thermal systems or stability enhancers. Instead, he'd looked at her and then nodded to the wide view from the Horizon's bridge.

"The first flight of your first command. You might want to slow down and be present for it."

If only Grant could speak for her now. Or at least provide some words of wisdom. Because this was more than speaking to the crew. This was launching a massive plan with many unknowns, all on a collision course with the place that they never should return to. Demi blinked, and when everything went dark, her mind's eye filled with the bright, inescapable hell of the gravity well.

The hydraulics from the docking tube blew pressurized air, an outward curl of fog that eventually dissipated about five feet up. Above the hexagonal door, a light shifted from red to yellow, indicating that the tube bridging the Horizon and Base Theta Seven continued locking together. Several seconds later, a loud buzz rang out from the side of the port door, indicating that the passage had securely connected.

"I wanted to take a moment to thank you," Demi said as she looked at the fifty or so crew members assembled in the observation lounge. Fifty or so plus one, technically, as Matthews stood in the front row, though off center. "Some of you have been with me and this ship for ten years. Some of you have only been here for a few weeks, or even a few days. It's never easy to go through this kind of change; every crew and every leader has a certain rhythm to how they work. But I am confident that whatever the Cluster requires of this ship and this crew, you will make us all proud—as proud as I am to have been your captain, whether that was for a decade or days. This ship is special, and the rest of the fleet will soon understand that." Tanav gave the slightest of nods, a subtle acknowledgment that the words hit all the right marks. Though the side of his mouth tilted in a hint of a smirk, enough to show he saw through her front.

Connors led the crew in applause, which rattled through, the noise bouncing off the ship's walls, while Demi tried to do the Grant-esque thing of appreciating the moment, she also kept one eye on the far monitor to her left.

Because for anyone that looked closely, they might have caught flashes of notices identifying an incoming vessel swinging around Theta Sseven. In fact, both Tanav and Neera snuck their own glances as well.

The clapping subsided as Demi held up a hand. "Computer, open the port door to the secured docking tube. Authorization voice print check, Demora Kim, Captain." The ship's computer responded with several chimes before the clicks and thunks of locking mechanisms started. "I wish you all safe travels and good luck. And for those who have been on the Horizon since the beginning, I'd like you to stay a few minutes more. There are some things that I would like to share with you about our experiences together." Heads turned at this re-quest, and Tanav and Neera began to gather the small group of long-time crew members.

Most of the others departed, with Connors guiding them to the docking tube for a few welcome days of respite at a large station be-fore the ship would set out. The first officer gave one final wave, then followed the crew off the ship. However, Commander Matthews didn't budge. Instead, he watched as Lynn, Aurora, and the others re-formed into a smaller group. His eyes narrowed in concentration and his feet remained firmly planted, like he wouldn't move even if the airlock pressurization failed.

Neera angled his wide neck enough to catch Demi's eye, a telltale sign that his instincts picked up on her sudden discomfort. She shot him a quick nod and then stepped over to Matthews.

His stubbornness would *not* get in the way of their plan.

"Commander, I would like a moment with my crew," Demi said with as much harshness as politeness would allow.

"Go right ahead," he said without moving.

"In private." The words came out in a clipped bite, enough tension wrapped in a few short syllables for Matthews to reply with an indignant scowl.

"Captain, something's not right here." He finally broke from his pose, turning to look her in the eye. "During whole-crew changeovers, security teams sweep the ship for bugs," he said, drawing in a short breath. "Wartime protocols after Ark Getru. We need everyone off."

Demi thought back to the conference with GCF Command, where Matthews spoke almost with glee about her relationship with Chuck. All of this felt personal, like Matthews targeted her and the Horizon for reasons unknown. It hadn't come up again at all, and though they'd barely spoken since then, any passing moments were polite discussions of ship logistics.

Matthews had weaponized that knowledge. But why? She still didn't know; either way, it wouldn't matter given their other plans for the ship.

Demi's eyes bounced to the monitor in the far corner, fast enough that Matthews ignored it. Sadler was on course, and she needed Matthews off this ship, fast.

"This is an open forum with people who have been to hell and back together. There may be things . . ." Demi hesitated, her choice of words aiming for the perfect balance between professionalism and "get the hell out." "Things that they want to keep between those who have been on that journey. We may not be together again. I think they deserve ten minutes for that."

From across the space, Tanav fired an anxious look, then offered a not-so-subtle point at the corner monitor.

"I see. That is fair, I . . ." Matthews paused.

Demi traced his eyes to the back-corner monitor monitor where she'd snuck her looks.

If this had been the Cluster Demi recognized, the fact that Sadler piloted wide around Theta Seven probably would have been nothing more than a traffic curiosity. In this context, though, it caught Matthews's attention.

Matthews held up the tablet in his hands and accessed the ship's scanners. "Let's see. Daedalus-class light freighter, crew of up to ten plus cargo. But only one life sign aboard. And this craft's itinerary shows that there's *no* itinerary. Cleared to dock on the other side of Theta Seven. So why are they heading *this* way?"

He couldn't have known what they were up to, but whether it came from paranoia or prudent awareness, Matthews recognized something was afoot. Possibilities whirled through Demi's head, and she picked the easiest one to execute—though whether this offered the highest chance of success, she wasn't sure.

That was something that Chuck could have helped calculate.

"May I see that?" Demi asked, an intentional urgency in her voice as she viewed Matthews's tablet. With only seconds to decide, she made a choice. "We can access stronger scanners on the bridge. Come with me." Matthews raised an eyebrow but nodded at this, and she turned to the seventeen people awaiting her. "Commander Neera?"

He walked over, and though he wore concern across his face, his unfamiliar alien nature probably meant Matthews couldn't read it. "Captain?"

"Commander Matthews has identified an unsanctioned and unscheduled incoming craft. We're going to the bridge to see what the scanners pick up. Can you boost scanner depth from engineering?" As she spoke, subtle changes came across Neera's face, the angled ridges across the upper half gradually pulling in. She paused, giving him enough space to ad-lib.

Which wasn't a Dywen specialty, but hopefully his pack sensibilities could pick up on where she was leading.

"The situation is becoming clearer to me. Commander, you may not realize this, but my culture of origin was a place where deception and sabotage were commonplace." Neera pointed over their shoulders toward the direction of the engineering deck. "This is a science vessel. It has more powerful scanners than a space station. I will adjust and calibrate scanning parameters to check for threatening chemical compounds and any other signs of WM activity."

Constructive deception. Neera *was* learning.

"Forward thinking. I like it," Matthews said.

"You'll find Commander Neera is one of the best problem solvers in the crew, even beyond engineering systems. Good idea. Please tell Counselor Lexin to lead the discussion with the remaining crew." Demi turned to Matthews, chin high with determination. She caught herself, a sudden awareness of how it must have come across: stubborn, annoyed, a little pissed off.

All of that rang true. And really, he acted the same way to her. But she could at least dress it up a little for his sake. She stifled an oncoming grin, a flash of memory as she heard Chuck say, "I do not understand this human drive to be very stubborn."

Demi watched as Neera moved to Tanav, who then broke away and addressed the remaining crew in hushed tones. Whatever he said, Demi wasn't sure; perhaps it didn't even matter. Tanav knew what she planned and why. The outcome, though, remained unpredictable. Would Casey jump at the chance to defy Command— and in a way, her family? Would Macek just be happy to have more science-ing to do? Would Lindsay talk to her again?

Would anyone be terrified of going back *there*?

If Demi had spoken, all emotions probably would have heightened for better or worse. She didn't want Tanav to carry this burden, but Matthews forced her hand. And she needed to let the crew have that discussion as soon as possible. She didn't even wait for Matthews to approve or acknowledge her change in direction, instead taking the quick and wide steps toward the elevator.

"This freighter is flying wide. Halfway around Theta Seven," Matthews said, keeping several steps behind her.

"We'll transmit our findings as soon as we get detailed scans. Could just be a joyrider," Demi said as the elevator doors slid open. She stepped in with arms clasped behind her waist and back straight. "Bridge." As the elevator moved, she pondered the different ways to solve this Matthews problem. Getting him off the ship now seemed impossible.

The elevator chimed, and Demi motioned for Matthews to step out toward the bridge's double doors. Everything ran against the same clock: Tanav's crew discussion, Sadler's impending dock, and whatever happened to Matthews.

The doors slid open. The commander didn't budge. "Captain, we have reason to believe there's a WM spy on the Horizon."

That was unexpected.

Did Matthews refer to their ship-stealing plan? No, it couldn't be that. Their goals existed outside of the war. Which led to another question . . .

Did he suspect *her*?

She felt the weight of his stare, and his wrinkled brow probably meant that he was trying to decipher how trustworthy she was. "An encoded transmission was sent this morning from the Horizon to a known WM mole at Base Delta Nine. Not using the ship's comm arrays. Do you know anything about that?"

"No," Demi said quickly. Urgency chipped away at her, but speaking fast and acting quick would only ramp up his suspicions for something she was genuinely separated from. "This morning? Do you suspect one of the new transfers?"

"Unsure. *Everyone* is a suspect," he said, and they remained at the threshold of the bridge. "We know there are plans for an imminent coordinated attack. We just don't know when or where."

"Including me?"

"Everyone is until vetted," he said. "No offense. Our personal differences aren't a factor here."

"Commander, I think if you look at any of my communications—

private or public, you'd see that I have no love for the WM or extending this war." Demi forced movement now, walking onto the bridge.
This did open up a whole new set of variables, but it kept coming
back to the fact that aggressions and escalation between these two
sides didn't involve her.

She had a photonic species to rescue. That was what she could do.

She also had to keep Matthews away from Sadler's freighter. That
ship had to dock.

"What can I do to assure you of that?"

Matthews's chin wrinkled, as if he'd anticipated this question.
"It's simple. There's a security team waiting to question everyone as
they leave this ship. Go do that while I scan this mystery freighter.
And let the scanner team on board to do their job." Now he followed
her, eyes taking in the still-active stations. "It's the same reason why
they're checking the Horizon's transport shuttles. The cover story is
repair, the reality is they want to sweep them in a neutral environment. After Ark Getru, anything is possible."

While he looked, Demi realized he was temporarily distracted.
She scanned the bridge for options—chairs, stations, equipment.
None of that would really help. She had *words*, but she couldn't bring
him back down when Tanav might have still been discussing mutiny
with the crew.

Matthews turned to the status monitors on the far side of the
bridge, where a live feed from the docking bay sat adjacent to ongoing status updates. "It's getting closer. I don't like this. Captain." He
turned to Demi. "I'm giving you the benefit of the doubt here. Get
your crew, get off this station, prove your innocence. Help me find
this spy." He moved over to the helm station and tapped to activate
scanners. "These are standard scans. How fast is Commander Neera
with updates?"

Once Sadler landed, they'd need to take the Horizon immediately. That was the plan—catch security and everyone else off guard
for the fastest lead time possible. "He's fast. But this is also an old

ship," Demi said. Which ignored the fact that Neera was probably at the docking bay preparing for Sadler's arrival, but it *sounded* good. "You're right. I understand you're in a difficult position, and I want to get to the bottom of this too." Matthews continued looking at the scanner, and Demi checked from the space again for something that could hit everything that they needed right now. She needed a fast, easy solution, and it sure would have been nice if she could just snap her fingers to teleport Matthews over to Theta Seven. Bridge stations offered no support, and even if they could do something useful, she wouldn't have the time or excuse to operate them. Same thing with the emergency weapon stored beneath the captain's chair—shooting Matthews was out of the question, and she wouldn't have time to unlock all the security mechanisms anyways. "I'll gather the crew and make sure they all process through security."

"Appreciate it, Captain. That earns a lot of points in my book. Now, this freighter, it's angling its vector into a docking position." Matthews activated his comm link. "Transmission: Matthews to Neera. Neera?"

Demi turned, looking but not stepping toward the doors, and then she saw it:

The emergency medical kit adjacent to the bridge's entrance.

Neera didn't respond to Matthews, but that didn't matter because the chimes from the data table grabbed the commander's attention. "Proximity detection," he said, heavy boots clanking on the metal as he marched over. He stood over the glowing display, arms crossed in full focus. Demi's fingers fumbled through the kit's equipment until she felt the familiar cylindrical shape of a med injector sitting tightly in a foam casing. "It's not the freighter. Two new unidentified craft," Matthews said, arms now propped up on the table's edges. "Captain, come take a look at this." Just like that, mutual respect returned. Which was nice, though not enough to drop the injector in her hand. "Merchant ships. That's strange. There's a blockade." Matthews tapped the screen to project out a holographic profile of each ship in front of the bridge's window. "They used older clearance codes. And that freighter, it's closing in."

Unidentified ships and a warning that an attack was imminent *somewhere*? And a suspected spy among the crew, with an outgoing message today?

The plan was to steal the ship and fly off to the gravity well, yet her resolve wavered, old ingrained GCF feelings about duty surfacing for a moment.

At least until Matthews stepped over to the comm station. "That freighter's initiating dock. We can't let it land." He pulled a handheld comm link from his belt. "Emergency security team, this is Commander Matthews aboard the Horizon. We've got an active—"

As soon as Matthews initiated the call, Demi knew it was all over. He may have had the right reasons, but security teams interfering with Sadler would end their journey before they started. Matthews and GCF Intelligence dealt with factors in their control, the decisions made at the highest levels continuing the conflict and the death rather than reining it in.

But by getting to the Lumersians, Demi could take action *against* conflict and death, for a species that supported everyone on the Horizon when they needed it.

She didn't like leaving things this way. But she had to make a choice.

As Matthews spoke into his comm link, Demi jammed the injector into his neck. He collapsed to the floor immediately, eyes shut and completely frozen. She dashed back to the med kit and grabbed a scanner just to check . . .

All vital signs appeared normal, and the display indicated an estimated countdown for his unconscious state.

All those wakes. All those rescues. All those destroyed ships.

All in the well.

If Demi had to go to war, she would at least go to *her* war.

She turned her head to speak into the embedded comm link on her uniform. "Transmission: Kim to Neera."

"Neera here."

She'd already planned on begging forgiveness for stealing the Horizon. Now she'd really have to channel Grant on that speech. "It's just you and me right now. Give me an update."

"The docking sequence has been completed by Sadler. Equipment is being unloaded at the moment."

"Good work." Sadler was on board. Matthews couldn't get in the way. At Demi's feet, Matthews groaned, and the sight of the unconscious commander made her pause—what had she done? She'd thrown in a lot of trust to an engineer she barely knew, even if Neera vouched for him.

The answer came to her with obvious clarity: Sadler was the only way. No other choice existed.

Only one thing remained. Demi generally abstained from any religious beliefs, but right now she quietly manifested that Tanav's bond with the crew could get them through this.

"All right. Neera, get the ship ready to leave as soon as possible." Demi held up the injector and checked the device's usage history— she'd put a lot of sedative in there. "Matthews isn't going to be a problem for a while. So let's get things going."

"How long is 'for a while'?"

"Long enough. I'm going to plot a course," Demi said as she marched over to the navigation panel. "Kim out."

CHAPTER 16

*

TANAV

With Demi and Matthews disappearing into the elevator and Neera dealing with his friend's incoming craft, that left Tanav to explain what was about to happen to the remaining crew in the observation lounge. He should have been perfectly built for this moment. He'd trained his whole life to read people and find opportunity. So why did he feel so unprepared for this?

Unprepared may not have been the right word. Anxious? Guilty? Like filling two cups from a dry faucet?

This seemed like a hefty ask.

Tanav reminded himself: This wasn't a demand. Everyone had a choice.

As for the hangar bay on the front end of deck three? The corner display showed all icons flipping to blue, which meant one thing: Sadler had arrived.

That started the countdown to FTL launch. Tanav glanced at the different status display next to the lounge's window: instead of ship status updates, it flipped to a timer for FTL warm-up with different stages being highlighted.

The countdown started at twelve minutes and thirty seconds. Demi's orders were to go as soon as they could, so Tanav's window was clear. Too bad Thaddea wasn't here. She made being on time look so *easy*.

As if she heard his thoughts, Lynn looked his way, a flash of a reassuring smile—which also made the most uncomfortable juxtaposition to all of this. Or uncomfortable parallel, depending on how you looked at it.

"I'm going to be very direct with you," Tanav said, his words more curt than he intended, and confused looks formed across the group. "We've been through a lot together. And we all know that *they* want this ship to be part of the war. We all saw the footage. I don't think it sits well with anyone. And something has happened—something *outside* of the war." He scanned the room, gauging where this was going, what might come next. Lynn met his eyes with anticipation. Aurora scowled—slight, but present. Lindsay avoided talking to Demi after Ark Getru, but at least they appeared to listen here. Casey's face showed she was intrigued, though it sounded like she'd take any opportunity to spite her family line of GCF officers. And Karl, he'd expressed support for the Cluster before, but he nodded here.

Those represented the spectrum of first responses, with the others somewhere in between.

Tanav could work with that.

"Demi wants you to know," he said, "that the Horizon is not going there." He paused to let murmurs ripple around before quieting. "That countdown," he said, pointing at the display. "When it gets to zero, the captain is going to take this ship back to Lumersian space." Murmurs came again, this time louder—and Aurora wasn't the only one with a scowl. Normally Tanav worked to lead people to what they wanted, in a way that revealed what they needed. Except there wasn't time for that now.

"They need our help. Like we needed *their* help. The well has returned, and it's ripping their dimension apart." What was the phrase Demi used to describe this earlier? "Demi feels morally bound to offer them mutual aid."

Now he really had to choose his words carefully. "We weren't supposed to hear the details about Ark Getru. The cover story, the failed negotiations. To me, it sounds like the Cluster isn't even trying. But what we know is that the Lumersians need our help. That's a fight we can choose right now. Instead of a fight that I don't understand. I don't think anyone does."

Reactions splintered across the room, and Tanav's instincts pushed him to read through them, to pick up what they thought. But the countdown marched on.

"You say that," Aurora said, "but you're not from here. This *is* my fight. My family is at risk, just because of where their farm is." With everyone looking at her, she shrugged. "You all might as well know. I'm resigning my post. I'm going home. No one's looking out for my family, and they need help."

"She's not wrong." Material scientist Ali Kent stepped forward, and Tanav thought of Ali's darkest days in the well, when he found her alone in the med bay sitting silently in the corner. "We finally return home, and then I read about why the WM exists, and it made sense. Why *aren't* those systems getting more of a say? They do way more for the Cluster than my home system, that's for sure. The Cluster tried to *lie* to us about Ark Getru. What else are they lying about?"

Suddenly, everyone talked over one another, voices muddled together in emotions and arguments. Any goodwill from years of comradery seemingly evaporated, and Tanav put his hands up. "Hey!"

Lynn joined in too. "Please. We're all friends here. Look, we're running out of time, so just give Tanav a minute."

"Demi is offering everyone a choice. She got pulled away before she could tell you all herself. She believes this is the only way to help the Lumersians and potentially keep the Horizon as a research ship. But we have to decide now. I'm sure Demi's original speech was going to be more . . ." The words stopped, Tanav's mind searching for the right way to frame this. "More inspiring. But I'm making this up as I go." At least the sentiment earned warm laughter from the group. Ulpio, who started as a planetary scientist but wound up covering a range of atmospheric and even biological sciences. Macek, who actually talked about science more than Neera did. Lindsay, who started as the environmental operations officer but wound up spending half their time recruited into engineering.

And Lynn, of course. Who gave him a warm look that he took as "You're doing all right at this."

"I'm committed to going. We could use as much help as possible. The Horizon's a big ship. And I'm definitely not qualified to fly it." He tapped his chest with a laugh. "I imagine going back there is not something everyone will want to do."

Ulpio shook his head, an anguished grimace on his face. "I can't go back. I won't go back." He pressed his hands against his temples, fingers swept through wavy black locks. "Put a gun in my hand, put me on the battlefield. I'd rather do that. I'd rather have been on Ark Getru. I stayed on the Horizon because this promised to be better than the war, but the war is better than *that* place. I'm sorry."

He broke from the group, letting out one more "I can't go back" before storming into the docking tube.

"It's too much," Lindsay said. They shook their head, their thin face framed by lavender-tinted hair held back by a white headband. "I won't get stuck for another ten years. Plus, this is an act of treason, right? What happens to us after?"

A very sudden sinking feeling hit Tanav in the gut, a weighty realization that they'd banded together to survive—but now in the face of *choice*, everyone felt differently. Everyone had something different calling them. He wanted to go home. Demi wanted to rescue the Lumersians. Aurora wanted to help her family. Ulpio wanted a moment's peace. He tried to come up with a reasonable response to Lindsay's question—a very good, very justified question—but nothing came.

He just didn't know. And he really wished he'd realized that earlier.

Lynn took a step forward, noticing his hesitation. Her eyes locked onto his briefly, a sudden fierceness in everything from her look to her stance. "Look, Demi asked for volunteers. I've volunteered. Everyone makes their own choice, and soon, because we are out of time—"

The lounge's doors slid open, and everyone turned to see Ensign Diaz come in. He stopped in mid-stride and paused at the group. "Sorry I'm late. I was touring the ship since it's so empty and lost track of time. You never get to see ships this way." He craned his neck to take in the group. "I didn't miss Captain Kim, did I?"

Lynn ignored him and continued. "There's no time to debate. Anyone who does not feel one hundred percent comfortable should go. Like, right now. We won't blame you." No one moved, and an urgency took over Lynn's words. "Go, now. You have to." She glanced at Tanav. "Right?"

Pushing people out the door wasn't what Demi would have done. But one look at some of the faces and Tanav threw in with Lynn.

As loyal as Tanav felt to Demi—and as much as he wanted to have the largest support crew possible—they trusted him, relied on him. That created an internal paradox, a game of pry-apart wrapping all his sensibilities. He sensed their desire to leave despite loyalties and past experience. They just wanted a trusted friend to recognize that before taking that step.

Despite the tightness in his chest, he could accept that.

"We won't blame you." Tanav echoed her words, though he quietly wondered how Thaddea would have handled this, with her refusal to accept anything but her own firm stances.

Lindsay stepped back, offering quick hugs to those who chose to leave. Diaz stood with a confused look. Five others followed Lindsay out the docking tube. And while Macek offered an "I owe Demi" with a firm nod, the remaining others conferred in rushed debate. Hikaru tried humor to settle things, joking that he'd fly anyone back and forth. Aurora was clear, she was leaving but wanted a moment to say goodbye to her friends. The rest broke down in voices.

Diaz came up behind Tanav as the group talked in low tones. "I missed something, didn't I?"

"Yeah," Lynn said, "but you should—"

Out of nowhere, a jolt rocked the ship. Tanav reached out to steady himself, but nothing was in reach; instead, Lynn steadied him with a hand, looking around.

"Oh shit," she said. "Get to the docking tube now. Go!"

"Attention: This is the captain." Demi's voice came over the ship's public address. "Two Withdrawal Movement ships have arrived in disguise. They're firing on Theta Seven. Anyone who wants to leave this ship must do it—"

The Horizon shook again, and outside the large window the fiery glow of an explosion bloomed. Lynn ran over to the back window first, then everyone else quickly followed, with Tanav bringing up the end. Theta Seven began pulling away, a gradual shrink—

No—the Horizon itself pulled away, the docking tube that had connected the ship and the station now severed. Debris twisted in space, and ship systems clanged and groaned. The Horizon's automated systems jettisoned the mangled part of Theta Seven's docking tube and retracted its own part. Around them, displays flashed bright red letters: *AIR PRESSURE EMERGENCY PROTOCOLS ACTIVE*, and a large metal plate slid down in front of the docking tube door and the back exit.

They were trapped in the observation lounge.

The ship drifted, the low sounds of systems powering up as Theta Seven continued to recede.

Diaz stood without saying anything. So did Lynn, though she stepped back to interlock her fingers with his. Aurora muttered under her breath as she stormed between both sealed exits, a rapid-fire cursing probably on behalf of her family farm, targeting anyone and everyone in the galaxy.

As for Tanav, he braced himself as a burst of WM fire swirled past the observation lounge window, a horizontal phalanx of energy that missed its target and disappeared somewhere into the vacuum of space. A flash of translucent white wrapped over the window before breaking into tiny bubbles that disappeared from view.

Neera's voice broke over the ship's comm system. "The engine systems are entering power-up sequences. However, the ship is now protected by shields that have fully activated."

"Are they attacking us or are they attacking the base?" Aurora asked.

No one answered. Tanav supposed it was possible the WM found out about the photonic engine and was trying to capture it. Or the crew just happened to be at the wrong base at the wrong time—who knew what other resource craft docked on the far side of the station?

Either way, Tanav took a moment to say goodbye to all of this. Perhaps temporary; perhaps they'd go to the well, save the Lumersians, get to the precipice of sending him back, and he'd come rushing back into Lynn's arms, a swinging hug as her favorite Jenny Lewis song played in the background.

Or he'd head home and confront the people who made him want to run away in the first place.

Then two new thoughts dawned on him, clear choices that stunned in their simplicity.

First, he thought of Lynn—not Thaddea.

Second, he could ask Lynn to come with him.

He looked at her against the backdrop of debris and passing security craft, and wondered: How could he have never thought of this before?

CHAPTER 17

NEERA

Neera didn't have time to help Sadler unload after docking, instead sprinting to engineering to oversee the power-up sequence of the FTL engine. Still huffing from the sprint, Neera was peering over various monitors when Sadler's voice came over the small comm link in his ear, a different signal path than the intra-ship communication system. "You hear me, buddy?" Though he'd probably need a standard ID comm soon; that could wait until they pulled this off. "It's nice landing in an empty docking bay. Less nice when your friend doesn't help unload equipment," Sadler said with a laugh.

Neera still marveled at the way humans just let out casual quips like that under duress, without any need for lengthy explanation.

The FTL sequence was standardized and automated but not impervious to error. In circumstances as high stakes as this, Neera wanted to minimize risk. "In my experience," he said to Sadler, a conscious effort in his words to humanize a Dywen sentiment about safety and order, "the one time you don't keep an eye on it is the one time you'll need it."

That was when the first shake jarred the Horizon, with Demi's comm announcement coming shortly after, then followed by Neera powering up shields. Then the ship shook again. And from the live

external feed, the docking tube to Theta Seven disengaged and retracted, shrapnel and a large, severed piece floating away.

"Lexin to Neera." Tanav's voice spoke over the standard ship's
comms. "Neera, we're gonna have fewer people than we'd hoped for."

Neera switched off his private channel with Sadler to answer
with standard hardware. "Our crew will be how large, Tanav?"

"Only seven more are staying." From Tanav's pause, Neera knew
there was a caveat. "And not everyone's happy about it. Can you reset
the safety doors in the observation lounge?"

As Neera did that, news of those decisions to leave pulled Neera
the wrong way; such logic may as well have been gravity going up
instead of down. Everyone had their own situations and opinions,
but ultimately wasn't it something greater than that?

Where was their sense of *pack*?

The FTL status monitor beeped, interrupting Neera's thoughts
on the splintered crew. The noise marked a two-minute countdown
for active FTL engines. He watched as the clock appeared next to a
row of bar charts, each one gradually turning green to indicate ready-
to-launch status.

Another beep came through, this time a chime from the ship's
station-to-station conferencing. Neera activated it and watched both
the comm screen and the status monitor in view. The view of the
bridge appeared, though instead of Demi overseeing things from the
captain's chair, she sat far closer to the camera at the helm station—
enough to obscure the strange lump on the floor. Whatever it was,
it didn't seem to bother Lynn, who'd dashed through the bridge's
entrance and sat at the comm station. She'd carried an undercurrent
of uncertainty, possibly distress in her emotions over recent weeks,
yet Neera watched her as poised and ready as ever.

"Neera," Demi said without looking up. "I've set the destination.
Are we ready to go?"

Through his earpiece, Sadler's huffing and grunts came through,
a constant background noise reminding him that FTL marked only

the first step—they still needed to jump once they got there. "About fifteen seconds must pass until FTL is available."

A shock wave slapped Neera in the face. Or at least it felt that way. Yet he was certain that no WM attacks had just hit the ship. Sensor displays confirmed this; the Horizon continued to drift back from Theta Seven, with FTL systems nearly online.

No, this was not physical damage. This was psychic damage, a sudden loss of . . .

Neera looked down. Only for a moment. He still had duties to attend to. But just to confirm what his instincts told him.

A sudden loss of pack.

Ayenew. He was a new transfer, they'd only worked together for a short time, but they'd spent enough time in engineering for Neera's innate instincts to sense his presence, to welcome him in.

Ayenew had crossed to Theta Seven. Neera glanced at the live feed from the rear of the ship. Part of the comm tower at the top of the station showed damage, but otherwise the only signs of destruction came from the docking tube.

Ayenew must have lingered in the docking tube a little too long.

Did their plans to steal the ship cause this to happen?

Did Demi's *choice* cause this to happen? Different thoughts and options refused to consolidate, and a very quiet, very small part of Neera wanted to know more. But Neera pushed that aside, instead listening to the bridge feed where Demi spoke. "I need to know as soon as FTL goes online. Command will know something's up once we change our vector, so we'll have to move quick." Demi paused to say something to Lynn before facing the camera again. "Where's your friend?"

"Sadler's arrival will be imminent." The remaining status bars turned green, a status of *FTL ENGINE ONLINE* floating above them. "Demi, the most recent blast on Theta Seven has killed Ensign Ayenew." He spoke the words as if giving a report, and in a way, he was. He needed his captain to do something. Though he let himself slip out a suggestion. "Should we bring weapons online and engage?"

Few things visibly affected Demi. Her ability to compartmentalize and continue was admirable, and Neera wasn't surprised that she spoke with precision now. "This ship is not combat ready. GCF security craft is scrambling now. There's nothing we can do. And if we stay here, those ships could destroy us too. We need to stick with our original plan. Understood?"

A different rumble reverberated through the ship, along with the subtle g-forces of the Horizon beginning to angle into course. "FTL power consumptions are being calculated by ship systems for its target destination."

"I see it. Programming our launch vector," Demi said. "We're moving into position."

From behind, Neera heard doors slide open, and the grunts of someone pulling heavy equipment doubled in his earpiece and behind him. He turned to find Sadler walking in backward, each hand pulling two floating carts of equipment. "This ship has a different floorplan from the last one I served on."

"Is that our tech support I hear?" Demi asked.

"Yes." Neera projected his voice louder as he dashed over to grab one of the carts. They would have to do proper introductions later. "Captain Demora Kim, you should greet Lieutenant Colin Sadler."

"Thank you for risking everything for us," Demi said.

"Hi," Sadler said, waving vaguely at the screen as he moved the cart toward the synthetic energy generator. "I think the photonic engine is the future. I intend to see that through."

"Glad to have you on our side, Lieutenant," Demi said. "Trajectory is set. The Horizon is moving to a safe clearance distance before we hit FTL. Counting down, twenty seconds."

"Captain," Lynn said, "Theta Seven is hailing us."

"Fifteen seconds," Demi said. Neera looked back over at Sadler, who ignored the FTL business and was already hooking diagnostic equipment into the synth generator. "Leave it. They've got bigger issues right now. And they'll figure it out soon enough. If they don't, more power to us. We'll need all the surprise we can get."

A low boom shook the engineering walls, followed by a grinding buzz that reverberated throughout the ship. It grew in pitch and intensity, the noise of various systems coming to life before starting to work in unison.

"Launch sequence is being initiated," Neera said. Funny how this universe's FTL proved so much noisier than his own native FTL engine. He supposed he would have noticed earlier except he'd spent the bulk of his time either stuck in an energy well or in static space while experimenting on the photonic engine.

"Ten seconds," Demi said. "Nine ... eight ... seven ..."

"Captain, two GCF security fighters approaching with active weapons," Lynn said. Around Neera, the room's upper lighting shifted into an orange tint to indicate a proximity alert. "They're flying around us and engaging the WM ships."

"Five seconds," Demi said. "Everyone hold on. Two ... one. I'm taking us there."

On-screen, Demi tapped the helm controls to initiate FTL. The entire ship trembled, one sudden shake as the Horizon accelerated to maximum target speed. If Neera had a porthole view, he would have seen a starless expanse, light unable to catch up to the Horizon. The ship's rattling stopped, the outer plates and inner hull settling into the active inertial dampeners, and within seconds, the ship felt as calm as being stuck in the Lumersian energy well.

They'd escaped the war.

Just like that, a quiet took over Neera's mind, an air of the expected while surrounded by tools and systems and scientific possibilities.

If only he could keep things this way.

On the monitor, Demi settled into the captain's chair, and behind her, the elevator doors slid open to reveal Tanav. But instead of stepping in, Tanav looked down, and suddenly Neera remembered the biggest unexpected variable about their mission.

Demi had said that Matthews wasn't going to be a problem for a while. But she didn't say *why*. Now that Demi vacated the helm position, the camera held a much clearer view of the bridge, and with it, evidence about what she meant.

A stolen ship. A lost pack. An unhappy crew.

And now, clear evidence that Demi had *drugged* Matthews.

That newfound calm disintegrated, along with Neera's very essence of order and practicality. He'd rationalized stealing the ship as a form of roundabout journey, the Horizon as a means of helping the Lumersians before ultimately setting this right. But to attack one's own comrade? How would they even explain that to those that remained?

Breaking the rules in the Regent Empire meant imprisonment, enslavement, or death—or all of the above in one gradual, terrible sequence. And now that they'd actually pulled off stealing the ship, Neera stood very, very still, the totality of it all igniting his nerves in ways he hadn't felt in years.

Neera almost reached over to the drawer with his small fix-it projects, except he didn't have the immediate time to work on one. But it really would have helped.

Instead, his fingers fidgeted at air.

CHAPTER 18

※

DEMI

Demi had many, many reasons to second-guess her decision, and they all popped into her mind right after the FTL drive sent the Horizon on its way.

Should they have stayed at Theta Seven? Part of their crew had crossed that docking tube—the new transfers and some of the originals who chose to leave. Did she abandon them? Did she abandon the people in need at the station?

Ensign Ayenew counted on her to be a leader. Was he dead because of her? Or if they had all walked onto Theta Seven, would more have died? She intercepted a report that security ships fought off the WM attackers, with damage limited to the docking tube and comm tower.

But really, what difference would the Horizon have made? She made herself think this through in cold, practical terms—other than a distraction option, the ship had limited weapons and maneuverability. At best, they'd get in the way; at worst, the Horizon would have sustained damage as well, possibly been destroyed. And in the aftermath of an attack, they had an outdated med bay and no doctor or nurse on board.

On the other hand, they *could* help the Lumersians. One entire photonic species versus a localized attack where the Horizon could barely assist.

Demi was fully aware that even listing these things out side by side might simply be internal justification for her decisions. Or a subconscious preparing of talking points, because as she got Tanav's report, she was going to need to do some explaining—and convincing.

Plus, there were a whole other list of issues: Did GCF security think *they* were in on the attack? Would those ships pursue? How much of their trail and trajectory could be detected?

And then there was the whole issue of an unconscious Commander Matthews. For now, Tanav helped move him to the brig, where they planted him behind a force field and hooked him up to an IV for calories and nutrients.

Then Demi locked the room. No one really went to the brig anyways, and for the next while at least, she really wanted to keep it that way.

Perhaps it was more the morality than the specific choices that caused her to second-guess. Seeing how much this weighed Neera down certainly didn't help. He stayed quiet—of course he would. In different circumstances, she would have tried to break through those layers and layers of Dywen obedience and loyalty to pry it out of him.

Not right now, though. So much lay ahead of them, and getting the engine online was critical. She let Neera do his job. Sadler too, with his impressive bit of tinkering to tame the synth decay issues. They'd only met in passing, a brief flyby as she went down to engineering to check on progress before they all split up: Neera to the science lab to run power diagnostics, and Sadler to unpack some of the monitoring from equipment on his ship.

Only one thing mattered now: getting to the gravity well. And even if everything went as hoped, it still meant returning the ship to Cluster space. Which also meant court-martial.

Or she could never return from the gravity well. To die inside that place she'd tried so hard to escape . . .

Did it mean that nothing mattered? Their struggles, their losses?

That was ridiculous. Demi could count so many ways that their actions counted. Logic and numbers, though, didn't really apply here. The gravity well was calling her back. They'd barely escaped before. There were no guarantees now.

Court-martial or death. Facing such options could have sent Demi into a long spiral of "How the hell did I get here?"

But she couldn't give into that now, not when the crew needed addressing.

As for Matthews's claim of a spy aboard the Horizon, that created a whole new issue. She didn't know if the accusation carried weight, because most of the crew had departed. Would a spy play nice on a journey like this? That seemed like the most logical outcome, given how removed they'd be from the war, though the question remained: Could she tell *anyone* about that accusation?

Outside of Tanav and Lynn, seven crew members stayed. Diaz emerged with a stunned look, and as he took his seat at the helm station, Demi made sure to at least take a moment to put a hand on his shoulder and check in with him. Neera reported that Macek was already down in engineering. Hikaru ran diagnostics of the Horizon's transport shuttle in case they needed it.

Aurora sent her a message, though—she and three others wanted to talk. Immediately.

As the Horizon flew at FTL to the first convergence point, Demi considered all the different priorities facing her. Technical and navigational challenges for sure, yes, but crew morale and empathy had to be the top.

Demi walked into the observation lounge, where Aurora stood with three others behind her—Ali Kent, the Horizon's materials expert; Karl Buiter, who shifted between engineering and the science lab; and Casey Tarell, whose biology role forced her into being the closest thing they had to a doctor for stretches.

They could all be extremely helpful on this journey if she could just connect with them now.

"I was seconds from leaving," Aurora said.

Demi gave her a knowing nod and made eye contact with the rest of the group—particularly Ali, whose breath quickened as her knuckles pushed against her mouth. "Ali? Are you okay?"

"We can't escape it. It pulls us back."

"That's not true. Just breathe through this." Maybe she should get Tanav in here to help with this. Casey came over, and while Demi absorbed Casey's glare, the makeshift semi-doctor pulled Ali over to sit her on a stool.

"First things first. None of you are responsible for this," she said. "Regardless of the attack and what happened over there." She pointed out to the neutral black of FTL outside the window—which might have been the wrong direction, but it got the point across. "Being on this journey *right now* is my decision. You are welcome to help, and that would be appreciated. But I understand if you want to sit this one out. For now, it's the best I can do. I'll make it very clear to Command that whether you help or not, this was not your decision. Any assistance you provide is done purely to ensure our survival and safety."

"Assuming we make it back," Aurora said.

"Yes. Assuming that." Demi didn't want to be defeatist, but everyone knew the gravity well was dangerous. Whether or not it was more volatile than before remained unknown, but they couldn't assume things were safe.

"I told you I intended to resign once we got to Theta Seven." Aurora crossed her arms at that. "Guess that's not happening now. But I don't want to be here. None of us want to. We need to do something about that."

Demi had never felt physically threatened on her own ship, not even when raiders from neighboring crafts forcefully boarded to steal supplies. Here, she wasn't sure of everyone's intentions.

"So, where does that leave us?" Demi asked, her voice even as she noted their body language: clear eyes, stiff backs, chins out. "Are you looking at mutiny? I am still technically your commanding officer."

Aurora leaned forward. Demi wasn't even sure if that was a conscious choice, but Aurora stood with tilted weight, a posture showing just a hint of aggression.

"You stood right there. Several years ago," she said quietly, "right after the Crystal Dreams imploded. We were all worried the Horizon was next. I remember you stood right over there"—she pointed by the window—"and told us your priority was to protect the crew, no matter what. It was a pledge. And we trusted you. How are you going to do that now?"

Even the toughest negotiations in the well—or with Vice Admiral Krishna, for that matter—didn't match this discussion. Those were military or political.

This was personal.

"This was supposed to be a volunteer operation," Demi said, mind racing for some promise or guarantee she could use to protect anyone who didn't want to be there. Nothing came, and instead, she went for the next best thing. "I'm sorry. I really wanted to keep it that way. I didn't anticipate the attack, and it's unfair you are here."

"How do we know you weren't in on the attack?" Casey shot out, stepping back to the front.

Despite being at odds, Aurora still scoffed at that. "That makes no sense," she said. "Demi doesn't have anything to give the WM an advantage. We all know the Horizon's held together with staples and spare parts."

This got a laugh from the group, though Demi knew what this was actually about—and it had to be addressed.

"I understand things are uncertain, so your mind wants to fill in the blanks. Right now, the WM are the blanks. I'm asking you to trust me again. My only goal is to help the Lumersians. I don't want anything to do with the war. Everyone knows that." That was also her defense to Matthews about potential spy concerns. At least there was one constant for her reputation: Demora Kim, too tired and bitter to be a spy.

Aurora stared at Demi, though nothing in her gaze gave away her intent. "We could," she said after a few moments, "in theory, take you to the brig right now." She looked over her shoulder. "And take the ship home."

"We just left a civil war. I'm asking you to *not* start another one on the ship." Demi took in a breath. "I'm here, by myself. I'm not a threat. All I am asking for is patience."

"No, Demi. This isn't fair. You shouldn't do this to us and you *know* it," Karl said in a grizzled voice. "Turn the ship around right now. People are dying in the Cluster. My son just graduated the academy. I stayed here out of loyalty, but after Ark Getru, I'm not leaving him behind."

They all nodded in agreement, and the tension radiated off them, off her own frustrations. They needed an answer. They deserved one. But she needed a way around them. The Horizon could continue her mission if they acted as disgruntled bystanders. If they created active resistance, though, things could get ugly quick.

"Transmission: Kim to Neera," she said into her comm. "How much time until we photonic jump?"

"The jump will occur in nine minutes and thirty seconds. The engine processes are completing their final calibrations."

"Are we able to stop?"

"Stopping the engine would be very dangerous at this juncture."

"Okay. Thank you." Neera's response was unplanned, yet it proved helpful. They'd trust his assessment. Everyone knew deception was not his strong suit.

"All right." Demi chose her next words carefully. "You heard Neera. We can't stop."

"Give us a shuttle," Casey said. "We'll float back if we have to."

Demi chose *not* to address that—transport shuttles didn't have the range or speed to pull that off, even if they convinced Hikaru to pilot it. "I'm asking a lot from you. But we've been through hell together. You've trusted me before. I'm putting my trust in you now. Help us. Help us keep the Horizon going. That's the fastest way to get us to our goal and back.

"I understand the anxiety about the gravity well. I—" She took a steadying breath, forcing herself to release a full-body hesitation. "I feel that way myself. I wouldn't be doing this if the Lumersians didn't need our help. I'd like to offer a compromise. There will be time between jumps when we can check the engine for safety measures. Once we hit the final convergence point before the gravity well, we'll meet as a group and decide together if we go in. Your choice wasn't honored earlier," she said. "I'll make sure it is this time. Will you accept?"

For several seconds, no one spoke or moved. Demi half expected them to rush her and carry her mob-style to the brig—where maybe she would have even shared a cell with Matthews, which would have been *really* interesting. But then Aurora nodded. Then Casey and Karl followed suit.

Ali looked up. "I'll help," she said, her voice barely there. "I'll help with the engine. But only because making it run smooth is our best chance of leaving that place as fast as possible."

"Okay," she said, relief flooding her voice. "I'm glad to have you on board. Please check in with Neera. See what he needs. Once we have assignments for everyone, I'll piece together a schedule to make sure we all get rest. We do this together." So many thoughts swam through Demi's mind—logistics, hopes, fears, *Chuck.*

And the slightest acknowledgment that the exit ramp she'd presented, well, it made her feel better too. Facing that place again . . .

She still wasn't sure she could actually do it.

She couldn't give that away, though. Not right now.

"Dismissed."

Several minutes later, she was back on the bridge, staring at navigation charts and long-range scans, just her and Diaz, Lynn volunteering to help Neera in the engine room.

The photonic jump executed smoothly. The whole thing played out with anticlimactic precision, given the months of failed tests and reconfigurations. In one moment, they sat at the first convergence point, the ship rattling. The next, they jumped over to the second. Nausea hit, as expected, and Neera reported that he and Sadler would need some time to assess and tweak formulas before another jump. Shortly followed by a report from Lynn stating that some kind of pressure reset initiated for an unknown reason, an action that Neera estimated would cost at least a day, possibly two.

So they sat. At least they were out of Cluster reach.

Only in the post-jump calm did Demi allow a feeling so foreign it couldn't be identified to grow. The emotions stewed, different bits fighting to be heard if she would just let them through. Which she wouldn't—not as she left the bridge, not as she marched down the hallways of the Horizon.

Once she stepped through the doors to her quarters, the dam burst, like the act of exhaling tipped everything over. Her fingers curled into a tight fist, tension so taut that her knuckles hurt. Her hand shook, a gesture so real yet so undignified that she wouldn't even have let Tanav or Neera see it. Not exactly an angry fist, not exactly a fist pump—more just emotion that had to release *somewhere*.

She straightened up, sweeping her hands through her short hair. Indy looked at her, the dog's confused stare at her raw feelings. "You slept through the most exciting part," she said as she gave Indy a pet.

They'd done it. They got the photonic engine running. And it all happened like it was supposed to, like they'd discussed when Chuck and Neera initiated the first jump to return to Cluster space—all the way down to the sudden bout of nausea and dizziness that affected everyone but Neera and his two stomachs.

Demi considered what might be ahead.

She should have taken a moment for herself. A reset, an exhale, anything. But she couldn't. Maybe if it was a clean getaway, with no collateral damage and a united team. Right now, the science was the least of her concerns. Camaraderie held but remained tenuous; trust was even less so.

Trust between the crew. Trust from the crew to her. And trust from her to the crew.

In the well, they'd never doubted any of those things. Yet even though Matthews lay sedated in the brig, he succeeded in the one thing that no conflict possibly achieved before.

He sowed a seed of distrust in Demi. Of all the uncertainties ahead—would returning Chuck's spark actually work? What would happen to her when the Cluster inevitably arrested her? Could she shield her crew from the consequences of this choice?—the thought of a potential spy dug inside and gripped her.

She'd pressed forward on the notion that a WM spy would operate outside their journey; their mission didn't advance or detract anything from the Cluster's politics or capabilities. Months ago, they didn't even exist in the galaxy, and this achieved the same thing, like the Horizon got deleted from the galaxy.

Except Demi knew it wasn't that simple. For the very reasons she'd tried lobbying Krishna and the others. If a spy was on board the Horizon, they'd understand just how powerful the engine could be. The WM had sanctioned the destruction of Ark Getru. What could they possibly do with photonic technology? Photonic jumping covered too much ground for the WM to theoretically catch them, but their *return* might be an issue—if they survived. And Demi would need to get ahead of that.

Demi went through the list of remaining crew in her mind. They all had plenty of reasons to *not* be a spy: Tanav wanted to go home;

Neera probably couldn't have even acted like a spy if he wanted to; Aurora wouldn't resign if she intended to be one; Diaz was just out of the academy. And while Sadler came with his share of oddities—how did he have the time to learn so much about the photonic engine if he was supporting frontline duties?—he wasn't even on board the Horizon during the window of the supposed transmission.

And there was as much reason to think that the spy had departed the ship already—or that Matthews was wrong and the spy didn't even exist. But with everything in flux right now, Demi instead thought back to the moment she learned she was getting her own command.

"I have a rule that my mentor passed along to me," Captain Hayes had said as they talked in his brightly lit room quarters filled with xenoarcheological items. "It's kept me going as everything changes. And I'll tell it to you. You can choose to use it or not." Now he turned on his heel, presenting himself face-to-face with her. "Your crew has to rely on you. That's the only way you can rely on them. I have always found that means that none of them can ever really know you. And you should keep it that way.

"I think we're friends. And you're loyal, and I trust you. But there are facets of my life that I don't share with you. Things I worry about, things that I question. I have to keep those from you, from everyone. Everyone gets a very specific piece of me and that's it." He pointed beyond the dome, at the dark blanket of space. "Even your first officer. Because they are all counting on you. And the responsibility of a captain is that your crew can never lose that faith. It has to stay in a place where you can protect it, and only you can see it."

Outside circumstances had already dug cracks in their trust. As captain, Demi knew she had to do anything to preserve whatever remained.

She would not say anything. Not to Neera, not to Tanav, and certainly not to anyone else.

But Chuck?

"Can you believe this shit?" she asked the dormant spark. "Bringing you home is a real pain, you know that? What do I get in return for this?" She imagined Chuck's digitized laugh at that, which quickly led to thoughts of his robotic hand in hers. Her tone dropped, any lightness now stripped to weary, bare bones. "I don't know how we're gonna get through this."

She knew what Chuck would say in return. And for both of them, she said it aloud. "A puzzle to be solved." How he held such *joy* in the unknown. Perhaps that was what happened when pure science worked without the restrictions of bureaucracy. "I think I've had enough puzzles. I would like the—"

Before she could finish, Chuck's containment unit began playing a whirl of screeches and chimes, all ranges of pitches. The translation device next to it came to life, beeps and chirps of data flowing into its matrix.

The first few seconds were different from the previous message—longer, with a completely different series of pitches and beats. "Maybe you can duet with Tanav," Demi said as the transla- tion process bar filled up. Chuck remained excruciatingly static, a dot of purple floating against nothing, and though Demi knew why there was no response, she let herself pretend for a moment that he'd perfected a deadpan stare.

The translation matrix spoke through Chuck's synthesized voice, several monotone words slipping in between the digital noises: *ship* and *volatile*.

The message repeated two more times, and on the translation display, the processing icon popped up. It started a third time, and Demi tapped the screen to mute the noise. Only a handful of words—was that enough to send to Neera and Tanav for more in- vestigation? She looked at the various translation charts, different graphs inching toward completion, one even resetting backward from 10 percent to 3 percent.

This would take some time. And they had higher priorities right now.

Demi let it be for now. They could see it when the translation matrix made more progress.

Demi was already moving to get Indy that long-awaited kibble when a new sound came from Chuck's unit. Unlike the Lumersian message, this didn't arrive in digitized tones. Instead, she heard a very clear, very familiar voice.

"One plus one equals two."

Demi turned around.

The activation of the vocabulator didn't particularly shock her; that was the whole point of hooking up devices and monitors to it.

No, what caused her muscles to tense and her breath to stop came down to the actual words themselves.

One plus one equals two.

The simplest, most basic mathematical equation in existence. But for Chuck and Demi, it represented something far beyond the universal logic it defined. That phrase marked the foundation of their relationship, a path to understanding and an aspiration that they could get through anything thrown at them by the universe— by *any* universe.

The Lumersians wouldn't use it in a distress call. Not when they'd already built a form of translatable communication with Cluster technology. This was something different.

This was *Chuck.*

What form, she didn't know. But that thought came with a *certainty*. And that opened up so many more possibilities.

Something lay within that purple spark. The only way to know the how and why behind Chuck's voice lay with the Lumersians. And while she'd spent the last few hours dealing with distraught crew and the implications of a spy on board, she made a very deliberate promise to herself:

They were going to make it to the well. And before she turned over Chuck's spark, she was going to discover why he spoke.

CHAPTER 19

NEERA

Despite the circumstances, half of the Horizon's small crew sat in the mess hall, surrounding Neera with the most unexpected noise:

Laughter.

Joyful, uncontrolled laughter.

He'd spent nearly eight years with the Horizon, and even then, joyful laughter still took him by surprise. Another lifetime under Regent control caused laughter to mean something harsh and cold.

Life under the Regent Empire as a communications technician meant that Neera always knew what to do, where to go. No matter how absurd or illogical. It was the way things went. Even when things were unacceptable. Even when things were dangerous.

"Hefty," Konda said, and Neera nodded at his commanding officer. Regent Empire protocol very strictly emphasized respecting chain of command, and that meant ranks and names. Konda, however, claimed that the nickname "Hefty" was a sign of recognition for Dywen size and strength compared to most other species.

Neera didn't believe it. But as with all Dywens under Regent rule, his career could only advance so far. Questioning authority went against his natural instincts, but even more so when factoring in the penalties of insubordination within the Regent Empire. "Yes, sir," he said.

"I was up on the top platform," he said, pointing upward as lightning lit up large dim clouds above, "and the main encryptor circuit is just out of reach for us normal officers." He tapped his chest, then gestured at the other human maintenance teams around. "You're good with encryptors, right?"

Neera offered a silent nod.

"Hardware and software?"

Again, Neera nodded.

Konda clapped his hands, then slicked his rain-soaked hair back. "Good fortune for us, then. You go climb up there and fix it. I'll repair the hub down here." Neera had opened his mouth to respond, but Konda held up a hand. "Look, I know your kind love to give long explanations, but spare us and just go." Neera looked up, all the way at the tower's top plateau—and at the very long ladder alongside it. "No teleportation, either. That platform's tiny, accuracy is off. So," he said, kneeling down to look at the hub panel, "you better get moving. Rain's supposed to get worse in an hour. Don't want to get caught in it." Konda turned and walked slowly away, his laughter echoing as he spoke into a comm.

Neera saw what this was, exactly what this was. His left hand gripped into a fist, both thumbs pushing down on adjacent knuckles, and he told himself to push that laughter aside.

Unlike here. Where that laughter was frivolous, warm, joyous.

"I had this dream last night," Macek said. He leaned forward, elbows on the table, steam from his ramen bowl covering his face. "We did today's photonic jump. And then after that, the engine died, so I ate the synth, got out into space, and jumped the Horizon myself." He mimed two fingers as legs hopping across the table. "I mean, literally jumped."

The gesture prompted more raucous noise around the room.

"Well, we'll know in an hour or so if we'll need you. Would have been less but this reset malfunction keeps tripping," Sadler said. He now posed two fingers similar to Macek, except instead of hopping, they fell over. Macek put his hands up in defense, though his grin showed that this was friendly joshing, and probably their mutual acknowledgment that they couldn't figure out *why* that reset kept happening. "But hey, more time for ramen."

Sometimes it felt like the Horizon itself listened and reacted to its crew. Like here, Neera had just talked about this issue with Lynn during the space walk, and then it appeared after the first jump. They'd handled it, charged up the synth, and jumped again. And again the reset occurred. Something in the exhaust system wasn't working, but a diagnostic didn't turn up anything.

Sadler took the final bit of noodles from his bowl. "We're out of comm range after that jump. So everyone get your orders in for emergency ramen bar restock now."

More laughter. Neera sat on one end of two circular mess hall tables pushed together, and while Sadler sat next to him and even nudged him with his elbow, the level of laughter didn't seem to match the types of stories and jokes being told. Neera chose to sit back and observe the science of Sadler's magnetism on the rest of the crew.

Across from him, Hikaru tapped his chopsticks against his bowl. "It's funny, I joined the fleet just to eat the most exotic alien foods out there. Then we ration for ten years, and now I'm still sitting here eating ramen after a decade."

"And pie," Tanav yelled from the kitchen. He appeared from behind the counter carrying a tray with large mitts. Groans greeted him, to which he twisted his face.

"You always underbake things," Casey yelled, and then there it was again: more laughter. Neera appreciated the laughter from Casey in particular—her divide with the crew had gradually mended over these last days.

"My teacher is taking a nap. But I'll let her know what you all thought." He set the tray down on the counter and began cutting slices. Neera took in the ensuing reactions around the room. Not the sounds or physical gestures, but the feelings.

That was what was happening. The feelings.

The last ramen night didn't feel like this. Even during that time, a restlessness ran through the group, like tiny strings twisting them apart. Then after Ark Getru, after stealing the ship, his senses became blunted. He still had his intuitions, but the conflict between people filled the space, the tension putting up blockades and deviations that muted the weight of his pack.

However, the process of *work* seemed to be healing for them. Perhaps shared tasks reminded each of them of their common bonds. Of the Horizon crew, Neera's closest sense of pack was to Demi and Lynn; Demi from proximity and mentorship, while Lynn's eagerness and compassion drew him in fast. Yet Tanav remained a mystery to him.

They'd certainly worked together before and spoken socially at the mess hall, but Tanav's ability to put himself in front of people worked so counterintuitively to Dywen culture that a natural gap emerged between them. They were both strangers in this universe, but they acclimated so differently. Tanav blended in with every group, Neera struggled to discuss things beyond science. Tanav wanted to go home, Neera wanted to stay here.

Lynn, though, cared about Tanav. And that was okay, because human bonding did not make sense. It seemed many friendships thrived with the unknown.

"I expect full judgmental feedback—" Tanav started before pausing. His gaze fell to the other side of the mess hall; one by one, each person turned and looked at who had appeared: Aurora. And while she'd helped with technical needs, her divide with Demi also drove her away from what little social time they had. "You're welcome to join," Sadler said and stood, prompting nods across the room. "Take my seat, I have to get back to the engine."

Aurora stepped forward and held up a bottle. "Casey told me about this." Casey waved an arm at the mention. "Thought I'd bring a drink from my family farm." Tanav went to the counter for glasses, and they clinked on the table while she popped open the bottle. "It's not a lot," she said, "so hopefully the Lumersians learned how to brew."

Once again laughter filled the space. Yet what overwhelmed Neera wasn't the sound or the smell of alcohol, but the way his senses grasped pieces locking into place. This group was different now, even with the conflicts and losses. But for this sliver of time, they became cohesive again, a true pack.

Aurora poured a small amount in each glass, her nail tapping the bottle when empty. "You know, it's actually good that Demi's not here. Because here's a secret. I know I'm mad at her. But also, I think I understand her. Started to, anyway." She swirled the small amount of ale. "It's not like she had a bunch of easy choices in front of her. You put the ship, the war, the WM"—she counted with her fingers— "the engine, the distress call . . . what are the odds *anyone* gets it right and comes out happy? We're here now. We might as well enjoy one another's company." She held up the glass. "To survivors?"

Casey held up her glass and pointed at Neera. "Or, as Neera might say, to pack?"

Perhaps they all felt it too. Normally, Neera wouldn't partake in the dehydrating nature of alcoholic beverages. But this was a small amount to go with a nice moment. He held up a hand as everyone looked at him. "A moment has come to mind. Wakes for our fallen friends are typical for this crew. We have not had time to organize one for Ensign Ayenew." Silence now hit the group, though Neera could see thoughtful, wistful looks around. "Ayenew told me that his parents could not travel to space much because of an autoimmune condition. That is why he dreamed of a life in the stars." Neera chose not to mention that that desire was also probably why Ayenew lingered for a view from the docking tube when the WM ships attacked. "He achieved his dream, and that should be commended."

The table called out a round of "to Ayenew," and Neera swallowed the bitter drink, though he immediately followed it with a glass of water.

"I hope I'm not interrupting," a new voice said. Neera sensed the arrival a split second before it arrived.

Being around Demi since Ark Getru meant a constant emotional thrum, like shifting frequencies hitting Neera's senses. If he could communicate such a thing to Tanav, the former musician probably would have even been able to identify the consistent notes that reverberated.

They all watched as Demi waited politely with a tablet in hand, and Neera saw she met eyes with Aurora. Hikaru missed this unspoken communication and instead yelled a rowdy "Come join us!"

Demi waited for Aurora to nod, then came over. "I see you're all out of shots. But that's okay, because I have something here that needs some thinking. I was on my way to do final astrometrics calibration for this next jump when I saw this finished." She held up the device in her hands. "A new Lumersian transmission arrived a few days ago. The translation matrix was being stubborn with it." She pulled over an empty seat from an adjacent table and tapped the tablet to display the message's audio waveform as Tanav served pie slices.

It wasn't surprising that Demi ran the translation matrix privately. The engine and all its issues kept Neera busy enough, and he wouldn't have had time to examine the matrix processes regardless. But he had spoken to Demi quite regularly during that span, and she hadn't mentioned this at all. Information flowed freely between them, or it was supposed to.

The feeling marked the opposite of when people laughed at his joke. In fact, Neera battled that unsettling feeling several times over recent days, from the very decision to steal the Horizon to the sting of losing Ayenew to the way Demi simply did not mention Matthews in the brig. And the sense of pack that had appeared moments ago, Demi's hurricane of feelings set it all out of balance, even if no one realized it.

Neera's sense of stability built up over six months of working on the photonic engine in Cluster space, and though this was the only way to keep the engine going, everything else started to splinter.

A new voice played from the tablet. "The gravity well continues to increase in volatility. A new ship has become trapped. It belongs to one of the physical universes . . ." The word abruptly cut into several quick, varied pitches. Neera caught Tanav's look at that knowledge, a raised eyebrow in an otherwise calm expression. "It appears the paths to those other physical universes did not fully collapse."

"That's very . . . specific," Tanav said. He dashed back, his speed picking up as he grabbed utensils from the kitchen counter. "Lynn can help with the missing parts."

"There's one more thing," Demi said. "Something happened." Demi's eyes locked onto the fork in her hand. "It was just after the first jump. I had just gotten back to my quarters." The usual edge to her voice softened, and the rare appearance of vulnerability from their otherwise stoic captain needled at Neera's instincts. "I'm honestly still not sure what to make of it because it only happened once."

A beep from the ship's comm station interrupted Demi.

"Matthews to Kim. Answer your comm."

None of them spoke. None of them moved.

Any remaining sense of pack shredded away, leaving only a void. Neera looked at the slices of pie set up around the table, none of them being eaten.

"Matthews to Kim. I repeat: answer your comm."

"What the hell?" Casey yelled. She stood up, her knees banging on the table, and any jokes about Tanav's baking skills seemed like they came from a different lifetime. She looked at Aurora. Then Tanav. Then Macek, then Hikaru, then Neera before finally landing on Demi. And Demi, that familiar uncomfortable thrum now overflowed, spikes of emotions coming from behind her very still face. "What is this? Matthews is on board? *How?* Who knew about this?"

The comm system beeped. "Matthews to Kim," he said, a growing snarl in his words. "Somehow I am in the brig, there's no one here, and I am very, very angry. Answer your goddamn comm."

The word *brig* got an audible gasp from all around the table, and Demi stood up, all eyes trained on her.

How was Matthews awake? They'd given him sustained doses of triapdimone and a caloric IV to keep him stable while sedated, and yet here he was—not just awake, but with access to comms, no less. Demi had asked Neera to stay quiet about this, and with all the work on the photonic engine, his mind had plenty to occupy itself. His orders were to move forward. He followed that.

Now everyone knew. And getting them to follow additional orders would be very messy.

The softness that painted her brow and cheeks just moments earlier now shifted to stiff and cool. "He never left. I had to make a choice." She sat up, and Neera could practically see the change in her thinking, her internal operations. "It wasn't easy."

"Oh my god." Aurora's voice filled the mess hall. Neera never heard it hit that level of volume or force. "Is that all you have to say? 'It wasn't easy.' You've been lying about him the whole time? It's like, ever since we got back to the Cluster, you can't *stop* lying. Is that what it is?"

Casey shook her head continuously, her hands rubbing her close-cropped black hair. "You asked us to trust you. You had a whole big speech about it." She tapped her chest, then pointed to Aurora. "Should we go get Karl? He was there too, and he's, what, off doing whatever task in the science lab because you asked him to?"

"Sadler to Neera."

Sadler's voice stopped everyone, and now all the attention that *had* been on Demi turned to Neera. The action created a queasiness, much more than Aurora's family ale.

"Neera here," he finally said.

"Can you get back to engineering? Bring Macek and Aurora too. We're close to going online, I need the hands." Sadler laughed to himself. "And eyes. Probably ears too."

"Acknowledged," Neera said. He slowly stood up. "Macek. Aurora." The words came out quietly. "Your assistance in engineering would be—"

"Matthews to Kim. I'm just going to be repeating this until you show up," he said, a condescending singsong lilt carrying his words. "I wake up here behind a force field with a comm link at my feet. Which was helpful, because someone disabled the one in my uniform. So I got nothing better to do. Unless everyone is dead and it's just me."

"Who gave him the comm?" Hikaru asked, his normally boisterous voice now muted.

A sudden change fell over everyone. Seconds ago, attention was focused on Demi, and now everyone looked at one another. Neera did not need to activate any pack senses to feel the level of suspicion rise in the room. There were only so many of them on board. It wasn't him. It wasn't Demi.

But everyone else, half of whom weren't in the mess hall? Who could break past the brig's locks?

"Macek. Aurora. We should get to engineering. We still have a job—"

"No. You turn this ship around and jump right back." Aurora's eyes flared with each word. "You promised us a choice. Here is my choice. Turn. Around."

"A lot of things are happening at once right now," Demi said. "You can't just stop the photonic engine during its ramp-up process. But we all deserve a conversation about this. Matthews included. I will start with him. Then bring everyone into it. But after this next jump."

Demi was correct. She'd asked him that before, just a few days ago. "Aurora, you have seen how the engine works. I believe you will recall the details of energy storage and dissipation."

Aurora's breath was heavy enough to hear, a steady rhythm like a ticking clock. "Yeah," she finally said. "I have seen that."

"Demi," Neera said, "calibration must also complete at astrometrics prior to jumping."

"All right." Demi nodded. She stood and picked up the tablet off the table. "This still matters. Matthews matters. The jump matters."

"The comm matters," Hikaru said.

"That too," Demi said. Neera had seen her through all phases of the past several years, as neighboring ships imploded, as Chuck sacrificed himself, as she discovered the state of war. Somehow, none of those moments matched the way her cheeks drained of color and eyes glistened now. "I am asking everyone to be practical right now. There are always hours after a jump when processes restart. We will jump, I will talk to Matthews, and then I will call an all-hands right here." Demi curled up one side of her mouth and tapped the plate in front of her. "Tanav can bake pie."

No one laughed. No one even smiled at that.

"Macek, Aurora," Neera said.

"I don't trust you anymore," Aurora said.

Those words—five short, curt words said with flat venom—stopped Demi's emotional thrum. No, it was still there. It just changed, going from spikes of extremes to a dull, low hum.

"You two handle the engine. I'm going to my quarters." Aurora stomped out of the room.

"You think you can fix everything with a big speech about surviving and crew and trust and stuff," Casey said. "You know how I complain about my family? They say the same things about GCF duty. Same intent, different names, different nouns. It's always the excuse. It's always the cover-up. No. You cannot keep breaking this. At some point, it doesn't repair. At some point, things become permanent." She followed Aurora's actions, though she didn't say anything about where she was headed.

Macek walked over to Neera. "We still gotta science," he said quietly. He patted Neera on the back and motioned forward—though he didn't say anything to the rest of the crew.

Neera nodded and gave one last look at Hikaru and Tanav before landing on Demi. Her chin dipped as their eyes connected, and though Demi was the person he trusted most in this universe, he didn't know what to think about anything right now.

The only thing he could rely on was science.

"Yes we do," he said to Macek.

CHAPTER 20

TANAV

Hikaru excused himself from the mess hall shortly after Neera and Macek left. Tanav got the sense that the pilot didn't really know *what* to think, given the circumstances, and though he said he had to go repair a conduit outside of stellar cartography, that might have only been an excuse. And Demi didn't question him about the comm link, which meant that either she didn't think he did it or she didn't want to deal with that right now.

He did, though, pause for a bite of pie, followed by a "hmph" and a thumbs-up before leaving.

Now Tanav was alone with Demi. The Matthews situation wasn't new to him; he'd helped put the commander in the brig, and Demi's logic for doing so made sense in a desperate moment.

That still didn't ease things right now.

"I wonder," Demi said slowly, "if I got it all wrong." She didn't look at him; instead she stared across the mess hall at the dark blanket outside the window.

Tanav had asked Demi if she was all right several times recently, yet there was no need to here. Those cracks that he'd seen before, they finally broke.

"I don't blame them for feeling this way," she continued. "If I were in their boots, maybe I would too. I just wish there had been a way to do right by *everyone*. I don't think it's possible anymore." Tanav remained silent, allowing Demi to get these thoughts out before anything lured them back into hiding. "Maybe it's time I realized that."

Her comm came alive once more. "Matthews to Kim. You alive out there? Anyone?"

"Someone gave that to him. Someone is more loyal to the Cluster than to me." His voice triggered her sense of duty to kick in, a harder shell coming over the glimpse of vulnerability. "I need to deal with this. It's my responsibility."

She stood up, and though her face remained stiff and clear, her shoulders still slumped under the pressure of everything. "Astrometrics," Tanav said. That caused her to turn. "Neera said something needed to be done there."

"Yeah. Calibration before the jump." Each word built on the previous, reforming back to her usual self. "A captain needs to authorize the calibrations in astrometrics when jumping to uncharted coordinates."

"I just heard you tell everyone to focus on the jump. You should too. Get us going. I'll talk to Matthews." That last part came out unexpectedly. From what Tanav knew about Matthews, his experience wasn't exactly a match for the commander's way of thinking.

"I don't want you getting dragged into military politics. This is my responsibility—"

"You know what?" Tanav said. "Yes, it is. And I'm saying that to you as a friend. Not as your subordinate. But Matthews can wait, what, thirty minutes? You need to get that astrometrics thing done before the jump. Then have at it with him. Okay? I'll occupy him so he stops bugging you while you handle the science part."

Demi's eyes narrowed as several seconds passed. "I keep saying you're a good officer."

Tanav snorted at the comment, a reaction that surprised both of them. He turned to the exit, though she remained still. "This isn't an officer's duty," he said, and he left to give her a quiet moment alone.

A one-on-one discussion with Matthews should have intimidated Tanav. It didn't, though. Talking was much different than being at a bridge station or fixing busted ship hardware. Besides, Matthews didn't scare him as much as Thaddea.

Matthews was in the brig, behind a force field. Years ago, with Thaddea, there were no such protections. Back then, he'd walked slowly, stepping over waiting delivery parcels and forgotten children's toys lining the walls, toward their apartment door at the end of the hall.

Apartment was a bit of a misnomer. The space could barely contain all their musical gear *and* practical necessities like wearables and cookware. Sometimes it even felt like two people was too much, and that the very architecture wanted to spit something out, whether it was a guitar amp or bookshelf or one of them.

Thaddea stepped out, though her failure to notice him showed it was coincidental. She closed the door behind her, a manual lightweight metal panel that caused sound to reverb unnaturally off it. It clicked shut with an echo, and she faced him.

They locked eyes, and the way her jaw tensed and her shoulders slumped told him that she'd hoped to avoid him. Her broad cheeks flared, the cheap yellow tint of the building's lighting making her pale skin and black hair seem unnatural.

This stance proved different from their other recent arguments.

This looked like defeat.

Tanav walked slowly, reminding himself to stick to his prepared speech, to do *this*—not just for him, but for *them*. As a couple, as a musical duo, as working adults in an unfriendly caste-based society.

"You accepted without telling me." She didn't even say hello. Her words tightened, a sign that her anxieties tipped into anger. "How could you?"

He needed to respond constructively, to tamp down the emotions stirring within her. "If you've seen our funding account lately," Tanav said, "we're not exactly filled for spending."

"That is why we are *working* musicians," she said, flicking a finger upward to accentuate her metaphor. "We start from the streets. Because it matters to people like *us*."

People like us. Now she was really fighting dirty; Thaddea knew that *us* didn't always include Tanav, no matter how much he tried to distance himself from the Lexin Industries empire. "This contract is work."

"A Vicon Corporation cruise? They're the worst of the worst. Even your family hates them." *Exactly.* That was what he wanted to say to her. But he wouldn't. He *couldn't* give that thought life. And maybe he shouldn't have improvised. "The contract doesn't even pay that well." Thaddea's voice changed, every syllable enunciating perfectly for extra emphasis. "For the *same* amount of humiliation, you could get more funding from your parents in five minutes and be done with it."

"What does *that* mean?"

He shouldn't have said that. He knew it immediately, because it would lead to an argument they'd had for years—an argument that only grew in intensity. He probably could have predicted her words, the air, the very shape her breath would take before they even came out. "Once a month, they make a transmit. They make you feel bad, they justify doing stuff like, I don't know, deforesting an uninhabited planet. 'Sure, someone will figure out a replacement in a few centuries,' they'll say. It's a test to see if you're on their side. Then they go to 'There's a spot for you in Lexin Industries, but someone will eventually take it.' And repeat. They suck you into their game. You're so stubborn in your belief that they don't rule your life that you let them *rule your life*."

Thaddea had talked about how she didn't need a life anything close to the upper caste of Tanav's heritage. And for many years—

in fact, every time except for the last few weeks—Tanav believed that about himself too, that he saw things in ways that his family never might comprehend. But in that moment, he stuck to his script, eventually going to the backup plan of taking on the contract himself.

Landing him here. In this universe. With Demi and the Horizon and the Cluster. With *Lynn*. And a civil war and now a showdown with Commander Jonathan Matthews.

He supposed that moment felt easier than this showdown. Life with Thaddea hit a tipping point when a fracture felt inevitable. But here, he just had to tell an angry senior officer to wait a little bit for a photonic jump. Matthews might take it badly, but that's why the brig had a force field. Besides, Tanav was a field commission with a fake title, so Matthews wasn't technically his commanding officer. Tanav watched as the brig doors slid open. Even with a glowing force field separating Matthews, he gave a heavy stare as if they'd stood nose to nose.

"Finally," Matthews said. He sat up from the cell's small bed and held up his comm. "You leave this for me?"

Tanav half considered claiming that he did. It would have twisted the conversation, possibly gotten Matthews on his side. But instead, he played it straight. Antagonizing the commander right now wouldn't accomplish anything but make things worse for Demi.

Who did leave the comm for him? No one among the survivors was a military loyalist, especially with every revelation about the war. Karl probably came closest, but he'd talked about "doing something" to prevent things like Ark Getru. This didn't really seem to play into that.

"I didn't," Tanav said. "I just came with a message."

They'd never formally met before—Matthews *had* talked with quite a bit of the crew, but always at various stations. And since Tanav's job was a little more fluid than that, nothing ever pulled them together. Matthews seemed to recognize the same time.

Lynn, though, had said that Matthews was "a bit of a dick."

"A message. Right, right. You're the pop star, huh? You're not even on the official GCF crew roster. Just coming along for the ride? Got your free uniform and everything." Matthews chuckled, living up to Lynn's description. He held up the comm link. "So, where's Captain Kim? See, I still call her by her rank even though I know she's going to lose it."

"Her message is that she is making preparations for our next photonic jump." Tanav shifted his weight, and beneath him, the brig's deck plates creaked at the movement.

Matthews raised an eyebrow, nodding as his lips pursed. "The engine is online?"

That changed his attitude.

"It is. In fact"—Tanav went to the nearest monitor and cycled through the various department status screens until he got to engineering—"in ten, fifteen minutes? Maybe thirty."

"The long-range comm array. Have any of the engineers touched that?"

That was a weirdly specific question—and not something Tanav was prepared for. He went with sincerity rather than dodging or defense. "You'd have to ask Neera. Or Sadler."

"Who's Sadler? That name wasn't on the ship roster." His eyes scanned Tanav up and down. "You're the one from another universe. You want to go home."

"I don't see how that's important right now."

"Ah, something's *missing*," he said as he rubbed his face. "You're not the spy," he said, turning back to him.

That phrase made no sense to Tanav. "I told you I didn't give you the comm."

"Kim didn't tell you. Okay. I wonder if she told anyone on the crew. Where are we? Were there any recent WM attacks?" Tanav was kind of offended that Matthews didn't think he had the abilities to be a spy. But given his history, how he got on the Horizon, and his goal of returning to his home, he wasn't exactly the type to fit that niche. "The freighter at Theta Seven. The other ships that arrived."

"Security ships defended Theta Seven," Tanav explained. "Last we heard, the comm tower and docking tube were the only damage."

"Quick strikes. In and out. It's the WM's advanced FTL engine." Despite Matthews's very confrontational attitude to Demi, he seemed much more interested in the practicalities of this moment. Which Tanav was happy to oblige; he was just a stalling measure, after all.

Though his mind circled back to the *other* key point Matthews just made. Because if the whole spy thing had nothing to do with the comm, where did it come in? "What do you mean, the spy? As in, a WM spy?" Matthews nodded, and suddenly things tilted in a way that Tanav didn't fully understand. "Why are you telling me this?"

"Because I need some way to get some sense into Kim. She's so obsessed with getting to the Lumersians, she doesn't realize what else is at stake here."

That was a strange thing to say, given that Demi saw the Ark Getru footage and received regular war reports. But Tanav himself had seen it: too many demands, too many factors, not enough ways to wrap her arms around the Horizon when everything else disintegrated.

If Matthews was right, someone from the WM might have taken advantage of that.

But also, Matthews might be trying to manipulate him with half truths and rumors. Tanav could walk away now and let Demi take over later. Or he could retaliate and see what else Matthews revealed. "So you don't think I'm the spy?" he asked. "That's awfully generous."

Before Matthews could reply, a distinct chirp announced a ship-wide broadcast, followed by Demi's voice. "Attention crew. I've confirmed with engineering that we're ready for the next jump. We are ahead of schedule, so thank you for pulling together." Diaz, Sadler, and Karl didn't witness the mess hall incident. Had word spread to them about Matthews? And Lynn, she was probably still asleep, given her late shift—would he have to tell her when she woke up? "Countdown commencing from sixty seconds." Matthews absorbed this information, the lines on his face becoming deeper with each passing word. "Once we emerge from the jump, we will be out of communications range with the Cluster. I thank you all for taking this journey with me. And . . ." Her voice cracked, which caused Matthews to turn his head. "I know there are things to resolve." That pushed Matthews further, and his hand covered his snarky chuckle. "I promise we'll get to that as soon as we safely arrive at the next convergence point. I owe you that. Thirty seconds to jump. Kim out."

Matthews's expression shifted, and his hand rubbed over his close-cropped hair. "You might want to sit down," Tanav said, taking a chair at the nearest control console.

"I think I'll stand." Right when Matthews finished, the entire room shook, a single harsh jolt that the ship's dampeners couldn't overcome. Tanav watched as Matthews scanned the brig, first at his cell, then over at him. "That? That's why—" he started, before he fell to his knees, one hand on his stomach.

"We've found that photonic jumps induce dizziness and nausea. It's worse if you're standing," Tanav said, and while his own stomach rolled a bit from the jump, he masked it all by sitting up straighter and pushing a smile out for Matthews's sake. "Not as bad if you sit."

"Okay." Matthews took in a slow, even breath as he curled over. "A good commanding officer listens when crewmen offer advice."

"It'll pass. Give it a minute or two. But hey"—Tanav gestured at Matthews, arms up—"I'm just a pop star." Lynn had never used that term before, but he'd run with it. "You don't have to take my medical—"

The ship-wide channel beep came through again. Which Tanav expected—Demi usually followed any long-distance travel with arrival confirmations.

Her voice, though, came with a completely different tone, hurried words like her mouth couldn't keep up with her thoughts. "This is Kim. A Withdrawal Movement craft is on sensors. It appears to have been waiting for us." Despite Matthews's nausea, he looked up and he grunted a string of curse words under his breath. "They've got weapons trained on us. I'm trying to— What is this?"

That got Matthews to stand. So did Tanav. They met gazes. "The spy," Tanav said. "Who did you think it was? Who could—" Matthews shushed him and held a finger up as Demi continued.

"I'm locked out of security systems. Diaz, hard to port. Shields are down. Power systems are— Everyone, if you can hear me, get a weapon and lock down. Power is going offline system by system. The WM is closing in. I don't know if—"

The comms went silent.

Tanav looked at the monitors across the way, but instead of the usual windows of different department and system status, a flashing red list kept blinking with bold letters above it:

SYSTEM UNAVAILABLE

"What the hell did we get into?" Matthews asked, one arm out to hold himself steady. Before Tanav could respond, the lights around the room ticked off one by one, gradually darkening the brig. Shortly after, emergency power kicked in, a low level of illumination from around the floor's perimeter.

But in front of him, the semitransparent blue of Matthews's force field began to fade, and the hum of its generator went quiet. The same overwhelmed panic Tanav felt on the bridge returned— possibly even worse, and definitely faster, despite being near dark, as opposed to the endless flashing displays of Lynn's comm station. Now Matthews stood clear in front of him, the shimmer of the energy barrier completely gone, and to test it, Matthews put his hand through the empty space, waving it back and forth.

"I don't think you're the spy," Matthews said. "But if you are, you have a chance to get me out of your way right now." In the dim light, he turned and put both hands above his head. "If you're with the WM, then you would have prepared. You would have read my profile. You know I am far more capable than most of the scientists and engineers aboard this ship. The WM would have supplied you with a weapon. The brig also has a weapons locker for emergencies on the back corner. You'd know how to open it. Here is your chance to take me out."

Tanav stared at the silhouette in front of him. "What? Why are you doing this?"

"Because I was pretty sure you weren't the spy." Matthews stepped past him to unlock the weapons cabinet he just mentioned. "I needed proof. And since you're not, I need your help. Power's out, which means doors are locked, but we need to get to stellar cartography. Kim doesn't know the entire war depends on it."

CHAPTER 21

※

NEERA

Every monitor, every status, every graph simply vanished. Then the lights went out, leaving Neera, Sadler, and Macek with only the bright pink of contained synth. Emergency lighting activated, a row of dim yellow-white light circling the floor.

"What happens if the photonic engine loses power?" Sadler asked as he waved scanners over it.

A question only a true engineer would ask in the face of a disaster, Neera thought. Even with the WM doing *something* to the Horizon, the first thing Sadler focused on was the engine. A quick look at Sadler's scanner prompted a rush of relief, all numbers coming in as expected.

"The power levels are properly diminishing in the engine," Neera said, pointing to the scanner's holographic projection. "The power cycle will be stable once it completes, though the ship will remain static without any propulsion."

"Where can I help?" Macek asked as he came over.

Neera looked over to Sadler. "I think we'll need emergency supplies to start," Sadler said before gesturing at the synth generator, the pink glow casting all sorts of harsh lines over him. "And this?" Another set of numbers projected out of the tablet. "It's basically a containment unit right now?"

"The numbers appear to be that way." Neera looked around at the room, the creeping silence providing an engineer's worst fears. Normally, the rhythmic hums of power systems and the rattle of propulsion offered a soothing din of normalcy. Without that, a stark emptiness took over the entire ship. "Our own safety may be in question, but the equipment is stable for now, if nothing else."

His words were meant to bring levity to the situation. Sadler didn't respond, though across the space, Macek huffed a laugh while opening the back panel's emergency equipment hatch.

"Yeah," Sadler said, his tone tightening in ways that Neera had never heard before, a frigidity to Sadler's usual upbeat manner. The projected charts changed, now a bubble of blue-green glow as he held up a tablet. Through the semitransparent holograms, Neera saw him squint as his eyes darted back and forth before staying on a sudden flashing icon. Neera tried to decipher it, but the message blinked too quickly to be legible—though even from his angle, he could tell that the hologram showed a rotating ship rather than the photonic engine.

Was that Sadler's own light freighter?

Sadler's posture gave away that something was definitely wrong—even more wrong than just being in a silent engine room.

"Damn it. You gotta protect the engine and the generator at all costs. I need to—"

A blaring alarm cut him off, and Neera ran back to the engine, though its main control console remained dark. He grabbed a scanner off the equipment desk, knocking over *something* from the table that would require cleaning up once proper lighting returned, and he waved it over the different engine subsystems.

He'd spoken too soon. The conversion pressure chart showed too many bars over the acceptable safety limit. "The conversion pressure is at unexpected danger levels," Neera projected over the alarm's incessant buzzing. Sadler yelled something back, but when Neera faced him, Sadler's tablet went dark, and with it, Neera's poor low-light vision failed to track him. "Your words were not louder than the alarm. They require repeating." Neera's voice got lost in the warning noises, the engine's independent emergency system yelling that it needed immediate attention.

Through the dark, several clanging sounds squeezed between the alarm's rise and fall, and even if Neera could find Sadler, he likely would not have been able to convey exactly what to do in case of a conversion overpressure.

Chuck would have known what to do, though. The engine's failsafe containment was invented by Photonic Being #910047.

Now Neera had to remember.

He moved in quick, direct movements, tapping the scanner to project its findings. The results hovered, holographic digits and charts that offered some semblance of light—enough for Neera to find the different clasps on the engine's base. He opened a panel, then felt inside for the mechanical levers and buttons embedded in the hardware. A sharp heat singed the tip of his finger; confirming thermal overload in the system. The guts of the hardware flashed with a series of sparks and pops, and Neera shut his eyes, a desperate recall to pull up the manual exhaust reroute protocol.

He flipped switches and rotated levers when Macek arrived, the small cylindrical flashlight mounted on his shoulder shining a beam light. Though Neera was nearly done, he would take whatever help he could get. Macek took out another flashlight, compressing it from a handheld tube into a wearable form that he attached to Neera's shoulder. Neera flipped a final switch, and as it went, a chain of events started, groans and creaks from alloys responding to shifting heat. But most importantly, all the values on the display descended, text shifting from red to yellow until finally green.

The alarm finally went quiet.

The rest of the heat could naturally dissipate, allowing the engine to become nothing more than a meticulously crafted structure.

"Thank you for the light." Neera stood up, surrounded again by un-nerving silence—though strange creaks of metal echoed from the maintenance tubes.

"Conversion rate is stabilizing," Macek said, waving a scanner by the photonic engine's intake chamber. "I think we're in the clear."

"I am hopeful that the emergencies have passed," Neera said with a nod. "The engine has never undergone a test of power loss at the end of the cycle. I believe this is related to the excess synth energy requiring additional burn-off. More diagnostic data should help pre-vent this in the future, but—" He squinted, trying to see any move-ment in the dim space in front of him. "There are likely bigger issues we have right now. Sadler, can you access ship status?"

Sadler didn't respond.

Neera waited several seconds, then called out again.

Nothing.

He turned, the flashlight beam cutting through the darkness, catching bits of floating dust and particles. He scanned from left to right, then did a secondary sweep.

No sign of Sadler. Or a struggle, or anything unusual, for that matter, except now that he thought about it, his sense of Sadler diminished—though it faded so gradually that it was nothing like Ayenew's abrupt end. Sadler simply vanished, and outside of the last tablet he'd held, his equipment remained where it had been when the power cut out. Neera walked the perimeter of the engine room in measured steps, the Regent Empire's protocol for sweeping a space activating like muscle memory. This may have been the only time he was thankful for the rigidity his old life instilled in him, and halfway through his scan, he saw it:

An access panel for maintenance crawl spaces.

But only department heads had access to the tools that unlocked each section's panel. No one other than Neera could have opened that panel, and he usually only did so for authorized repair work.

Macek came up next to Neera, their intersecting flashlight beams lighting up the open hatch.

"Did Sadler go through there?" Macek asked.

"It appears to be so." Neera knelt down and peered inside. "I do not know why."

CHAPTER 22

DEMI

Matthews mentioned a spy. And she should have taken it much more seriously. So much more seriously. Instead, she had brushed those thoughts aside, focused on getting to the gravity well, and just assumed that any WM interference would come *after* they got back to Cluster space.

Or perhaps believing that was simply easier than acknowledging that she could have never kept the war away from the Horizon.

And because of her choice, everything around Demi died.

First, the data table went. Then status holograms on the captain's chair fizzled out, soon followed by display monitors at helm and comms. The ceiling lights were next, though emergency floor lighting activated to give what might have been mood lighting in other circumstances.

Finally, the small control panels on either side of the captain's chair blinked several times before fading, probably on a different power circuit than the rest of the bridge.

"Try to get something going," she said as she passed Ensign Diaz at the helm. She marched to the double doors between the bridge and the hall. The silence amplified every noise she made, from her palm slapping against the door to her fingers tapping the control panel next to it. "Come on," she whispered under her breath.

"I've checked each station," Diaz said. "Nothing."

"Ensign, I'm sorry to keep bringing you into unprecedented cir-cumstances." At the data table, his silhouette moved in response. Her head tilted to speak into her uniform's comm. "Transmission: Kim to Neera." No chirp of connection, no usual stilted reply from Neera. "Transmission: Kim for shipwide broadcast."

Every attempt failed. And she should know that. In situations of complete power failure, only emergency lighting and life support ac-tivated on a backup system. Everything else completely shut down. She began to pace at the back of the bridge, sifting through the de-tails of this catastrophe to find *some* way out.

They arrived at the fourth convergence point and immediately spotted a Withdrawal Movement ship—one far smaller than the Horizon, but much larger than an individual transport shuttle. A freighter of some kind, repurposed into a combat-ready vessel by the WM. This deep into space, this specific of a location, they had to have known where to go—more specifically, this jump point would have been a strategic choice, given the Horizon was not out of com-munication range.

Someone had given them a heads-up.

The WM's rumored FTL tech—Demi had heard about this in briefings, Matthews had mentioned it, but Command never con-firmed it. This far out? It had to be.

This spy knew enough to calculate the WM's travel time while syncing up the Horizon's jump schedule. Which wasn't set—they had minor delays and reset issues making the whole thing fluid.

The thoughts coalesced, forming into a single epiphany, the only logical cause behind all of this, an answer so *obvious*, and yet she'd refused to see it before, because its implications would mean so much more.

Someone betrayed her. Someone betrayed the *crew*, and she completely missed it. Worse, she knew this might happen.

"Captain?" Diaz asked.

If it was Diaz, she should access the emergency weapons stored beneath her chair right now. But as her eyes adjusted to the low light, subtle lines filled in his silhouette. His posture was tense, panicked, and his voice was vulnerable and questioning.

Had Diaz been the spy, his opportunity to capture her, threaten her, or do *something* came and went. She couldn't rule him out with absolute certainty, but enough that she'd take him at face value for now.

Demi pushed the whodunit aside; reasons and motives were secondary to security and safety. She refocused on the facts—they had no power, and the WM ship hadn't fired. Which meant they were possibly going to board.

Could she stop them?

Staying on the bridge wouldn't do anything; its open layout created minimal tactical cover. She had to assume that the rest of the crew faced similar problems with their doors. Neera might have access to equipment for emergency unlocks, but not the rest.

"Ensign Diaz," she started, when a noise interrupted her. With all systems down, the usual cadence of underlying rumbles and hums went away, though a rattle swept through the bridge. On a ship with power, a combination of shields and inertial dampeners mitigated impacts large and small. Here, the slightest of impacts caused movement in the smallest gaps between bolts and plate, displays and wiring.

"What was that?" Diaz asked, his voice a far distance from the bravado he'd displayed upon boarding.

"Something's bumped into the Horizon. A collision or force just enough to—" Demi quickly put the pieces together. "A docking tube." Which would require someone to manually churn the Horizon's mechanisms down in the observation lounge.

Someone was letting them in.

Names and faces flashed in front of her. Aurora's home sector aligned with the WM. Casey carried lifelong spite against the Cluster. Hikaru and Karl doubled as technicians over the last ten years, they'd know how to do it. So would Neera.

So would Sadler.

Demi fought to center herself, reminding herself that *who* didn't matter right now. They needed to buy time and try to thwart the invaders.

Especially if they were after the photonic engine.

Demi scanned the bridge, low lighting throwing the familiar into harsh shadows, a final sweep of any possible way to create localized power for the doors. Neera would have known—*Grant* did know, having done this trick once during a power outage in the well. But she didn't; her background in stellar cartography didn't apply here.

That left only one option.

"Diaz," Demi said, "we're going into the walls."

Demi knelt down behind the captain's chair and opened a back panel behind the base. From inside, she pulled out a brick-size box, a single blinking green light indicating that its independent battery remained active.

At least something still worked. She planted her hand flat over its side, a white line tracing down from her fingertips to wrist to verify her handprint. A small yellow square appeared on the box's surface, and Demi held it up to her eye to commence a retinal scan. Several more confirming chimes rang out, and the lid opened up.

Medical supplies. Emergency power packs. Access scanners for maintenance hatches. Utility backpack. She handed that to Diaz, who began packing, though she kept the last part for herself:

A gun—small, light power, limited ammunition. But a weapon, nonetheless.

Court-martial or death. She supposed she was still on that path, though she didn't expect it to go this particular way.

"Our goal," she said as she resealed the emergency case, "is to get to engineering to safeguard the photonic engine. We'll take a quick look at each deck to see if we can get any sense of head count. Ours or theirs." She slid it back into its original spot, everything restored to exactly the way it was.

"What about—" Diaz started, but she put up a finger as she marched over to a seamless panel by the doors.

"We don't know where anyone is right now," she said. "So, we work with known quantities." She held a scanner to the wall, running it over horizontally until she heard three consecutive beeps. The panel pressed in, then slid up, a battery-powered motor providing emergency entrance to the maintenance shafts between the ship's sections.

In that yawning metal tunnel lay her path to the rest of the ship—and the crew. But among the crew, a traitor. And *that* meant that this was no longer her ship.

The war had won. Maybe it always would have.

Demi ducked her head in, boots clacking on the grated metallic floor, and she squeezed in as best she could in a low crouch, Diaz in tow. The lack of power made for a frigid environment, and a shiver ran through her as she attached a flashlight to her shoulder. She tapped it on and the space ahead lit up. As her eyes adjusted, she noted the paths: one straight ahead, two shafts off to the left, one to the right, and a floor hatch for a ladder.

She turned, flashlight illuminating the metal-etched maintenance map on the crawl space wall. Which was better than nothing; at least she didn't struggle with folding it like she did as a kid with her parents' paper maps. She squinted at the details when a low thrum came from the distance. It grew louder and louder, combined with a vibration that soon rolled through the floor, and system lights returning to the maintenance ducts.

"Power's coming back," she said to Diaz. Within seconds, enough power surged through the Horizon's metallic veins to begin warming the environment. Beyond the adjacent wall, a grinding sound churned, followed by hydraulic bursts and a swift hiss that came from far below—but drawing nearer.

The elevator.

Seconds later, the sound of elevator doors sliding open. Then the low murmur of voices, followed by footsteps that got softer as they stepped onto the bridge.

"Captain," Diaz whispered. "I hear them."

Demi weighed her options—she counted three, possibly four voices. And per her emergency protocols, she left no visible trace of the maintenance equipment or her actions.

Demi clicked off her flashlight and readied the pistol before putting her ear up to the access panel.

A voice.

A *familiar* voice.

"Demi?" it called out.

Lynn. It was Lynn, though in what context, she wasn't sure.

"Demi? I need help," Lynn called out again.

"Where is your captain? You said she would be on the bridge," a different voice said.

"She should be . . ." Lynn's voice trailed off, though Demi knew her well enough to detect the tension in her brief words. Diaz inhaled to speak, though she shushed him with a finger. One breath came, then another, then another as she listened.

"This is a trick," the voice said.

"She should be here." Collectively, the voices dropped to murmurs, even Lynn's.

"We gave you a chance. You promised the captain, and she's not here. I don't have time to play around. I need results," the stranger's voice roared back, a yell loud enough to reverberate within the maintenance shaft. "Captain, if you're listening, I have a friend of yours. State your name."

"Lynn. Lieutenant Lynn Kohli, Communications Officer."

Hostage negotiation was part of GCF academy training, though their textbook lessons failed to match the intensity of the real thing. Hostages could come in many different forms—friends, crew, colleagues, family, even critical items and resources. With so few crew available, Lynn kind of checked all those boxes.

Demi would need to make some choices soon.

"I hear you've known Lieutenant Kohli for a long time. Seen some shit together. Well, she promised you'd be here, and I don't see you." Several footsteps echoed through the metal grating. "But in case you're hiding, you've got ten seconds to show yourself before I blast a hole in her chest. Got it? Ten."

This was a bluff. It had to be. The crew was small to begin with. Killing one now would severely limit their bargaining power. Demi handed Diaz her weapon and pointed deeper into the maintenance shaft. "Hide. That's an order," she whispered.

"Nine. Eight. Seven."

She *could* stay hidden as well, then try to track them. On the other hand, Lynn always proved capable and resourceful. If they're captured together, they may stand better odds.

"Six. Five. I'm losing patience here."

Resources. Everything in life always came down to resources. In this case, it was the engine versus Lynn, skilled comms specialist and survivor. She nudged Diaz to move, and he finally turned down the shaft.

"Four. Three."

Lynn. She would choose Lynn. A tactical move, yes, but also a reality check: this kept Lynn safe.

"Two."

She yelled loud enough to make sure it got through the metal plating. "Enough."

The panel slid, gradually revealing that most bridge stations were back online, including the overhead lighting. Demi counted three people in rugged dress, all with rifles—two pointed at her, and one pointed at Lynn, who stood with hands up. Demi stepped forward, arms out wide to provide Diaz as much cover as possible. It proved ineffective, though, and one trooper brushed past her quickly. Seconds later, he emerged with Diaz, now weaponless, with hands behind his head.

Demi looked Lynn over, checking for injuries. She paused, Lynn's emotions shifting too rapidly to reveal if everything was okay. "They're clean," the man said, then nodded for them to step away from the access panel.

"If you called ahead, we could have tidied the place up," Demi said.

Lynn took a heavy breath in, her eyes dropping to the ground. Her mouth opened, a small lip tremble before she bit down and looked Demi in the face again. Demi's tone softened. "It's all right. We'll figure something out."

"I'm really sorry, Demi."

"Don't be. This was my mission. I asked you to come along. I assume full responsibility." She straightened, nerves steeling up as she clenched her jaw. "That's something that everyone here has to understand." Her focus darted between the three different troops. "Everyone on this ship is my responsibility. You want a hostage for negotiations, you want to interrogate someone, take me." Their goal remained unclear, and they might not have needed her at all, but to start, she needed to claim whatever control she could. "I'll talk. Give you whatever information you want. Except I'm only doing it if the rest of my crew is safe. Otherwise, no deal."

"Captain!" Diaz started.

"Don't move, Ensign. That's an order."

"Demi," Lynn said. She gave another heavy sigh as her face fell. "We've been friends a long time. We've been through so much together."

"Stop apologizing, Lieutenant. That's also an order. This is not your fault."

"Yes, it is," Lynn said, her voice quiet. Demi watched as the next few seconds playing out in slow motion, a gradual realization of what was happening. First, the trooper behind Lynn set his rifle down to begin going through Diaz's backpack. As he did, he also reached behind his back and pulled out a pistol.

Which he handed to Lynn.

Who took it and armed it, bringing its charging phase to full with a thin, high-pitched squeal, then pointed it right at Demi.

"I've joined the Withdrawal Movement. I'm really sorry to do this to you. Please make it easy on all of us."

Demi had a rule, something that she started way back when she was a mere ensign specializing in navigation: always be professional on the bridge.

So many came and went alongside her, probably never knowing what thoughts lurked underneath the cool surface, or what her real personality actually sounded or looked like. After becoming captain, Hayes's advice pushed that dichotomy harder.

Demi's lips pursed, thoughts and emotions bubbling and mixing together, and she refused to look Lynn in the face as she let herself finally break that rule after twenty years in the Cluster fleet.

"Fuck."

CHAPTER 23

DEMI

Demi's reaction caused every one of the WM raiders to chuckle. And that created enough of a distraction that Diaz decided to dive for the rifle on the floor.

His element of surprise got him to the weapon, but not enough time for it to power up. A cry of "No!" came from both Demi and Lynn. Lynn may have been louder than Demi—maybe because Lynn understood exactly what would happen next.

Multiple rounds of energy bursts unloaded into Ensign Diaz.

"Let's go," said the leader, nudging Demi off the bridge before she could process the swift violence that ended Diaz. Lynn walked too, pacing directly next to her, but while Demi stayed quiet in her growing fury, Lynn seemed glazed over and stunned. Even when she spoke, her voice came out hoarse and cracked. They walked in silence to the captain's quarters. "They want all of you in the brig," Lynn finally said as they approached the doors to her quarters. "I lobbied to confine you to your quarters."

"Guess you didn't have a plan for Diaz."

Though the jab stemmed from her own impulse to lash out, she took that nugget of information. The brig meant they weren't killing the rest of the crew.

"He was supposed to go there," Lynn said quietly. "They go there, you stay here with Indy while we finish the job."

"What's the job?" Demi asked, hoping Lynn's vulnerability would reveal anything useful. The doors to her quarters slid open, and Indy, ever oblivious, got up from her bed and stretched before coming over.

Lynn and Demi stepped inside, leaving the WM soldiers in the hall. The doors slid closed behind them, and though Lynn kept the gun up, her posture relaxed. "Go ahead," Lynn said, and Demi greeted her dog. And while she gave Indy ear scratches and pets, she turned to Chuck's dim purple spark.

Indy and Chuck. Together, they offered Demi a sliver of very needed respite before she switched into tactical thinking. Demi got Indy's synthesized kibble and met Lynn's gaze.

There was something there. Perhaps enough to work with.

"You can put the weapon down," Demi said, mind racing as strategies formed. "I'm not going to try anything stupid."

Which was true. Items in her quarters that might have been turned into a weapon—trophies, books, kitchen knives, any sharp or blunt object—none of them would match the pistol in Lynn's hand. Plus, two guards stood outside, each armed with rifles.

Besides, information was the most valuable weapon right now.

"You owe me answers," Demi said. "That's the least you can do." Lynn bowed her head in a near apology before she powered down the pistol, its insistent high-pitched noise fading away. "We survived *everything* together. That should mean something."

"It does." A voice came through the door, and Lynn yelled, "We can spare five minutes," before turning back to Demi. "Five minutes. Ask anything."

"Okay. Is Tanav in on this?"

"No." Lynn spat the word out so quickly it felt defensive. But she followed it with softer words, clear regret in them. "Not yet. I plan to ask him. He can choose." She gave a small laugh, her mind veering off. "He's so innocent. Who knew corporate universes would be so peaceful?"

"All right." Demi told herself the ten years of friendship between them didn't exist. Everything was a verbal strategy, designed to exploit emotional opportunities. Tanav was one of those. But she'd selectively utilize that. "First, I'd like to know how. *How'd* you bring them on board my ship?"

"Nothing fancy. Their starship was waiting outside. I put primary power in a diagnostic cycle. Then I let them in." Lynn's words dragged with that last admission, like a child caught stealing candy. "Everyone was too distracted by Matthews to notice."

Matthews. Lynn must have planted the comm for him. Did she have help? Demi's tone sharpened. "Did you just decide to defect?"

"It's just me. I mean, Lindsay was in on it too." Lindsay refused to speak to Demi after Ark Getru, even before the ship heist. This must have come together quickly. "No one else. At least not here. But you'd be surprised. People are not happy with the Cluster. Ark Getru should have horrified people; it's turning people to the WM. I have a transmitter unit in my quarters. I send data to other moles within the Cluster. Coded language, standard channels."

That was what Matthews detected the morning of Theta Seven. What would have happened if security interrogated Lynn as he'd planned?

"I spacewalked for the WM," she said with a quick laugh. "That's how much I believe in the cause. Because when I tried to embed a message within secure protocols, it overloaded the array. This old ship couldn't handle it. I had to get out there myself to make sure no one saw the monitor on the external array."

The mysterious message during the space walk flashed in Demi's mind: *Data within embedded layer stuck in cache.* That was a leak. That was *Lynn.*

"I thought I cleared everything from my last transmission to the WM. I missed one," she said with a shrug. "When you found it, I had to cover it up. So I made a choice—tethered myself to the hull, overloaded a nearby circuit, and hoped for the best. Now we're here." Lynn's voice dropped. "You tried to keep the war outside the ship. That's impossible, Demi. It's not like it was in the well."

With those words, Lynn dismantled all outside context. The WM guards outside the door, the hijacking, Matthews, *Diaz*, those disappeared to leave only Lynn and Demi, like only they were on board.

"I made a promise to everyone," Demi said. "I tried my best to keep it." But her best wasn't sustainable. She knew it as soon as she let it slip that the Horizon was understaffed. She invited that in, and the very thought cut deep within her.

Which meant she could use that very same thought against Lynn right now.

"You invited it in," Demi said—strategic, but she also meant it. "And your decision killed Diaz."

Demi expected Lynn to crumble, but she replied with a fiery tone. "I didn't invite it in any more than you couldn't keep it out. It invaded the ship as soon as we got here," she said. "I didn't kill Diaz, the same way you didn't kill Ayenew. The war did that. This ship. They've wanted to get their hands on it ever since they heard about it. Their new FTL propulsion, it's good—but it's not this. They were lucky they had a ship within range. I had to cause delays for them to catch up. It was," she said with a weary smile, "kind of Neera's fault. He told me about it."

The engine's strangely resetting pressure cycle. It suddenly all made sense.

But then Lynn's eyes watered, a clear sign she wasn't fully prepared for this.

"It's so stupid. Why isn't the GCF pouring everything into the engine? It could win any war, and they don't even realize it." Her hands shook at this, tears leaking onto her cheeks. "They could have done that and saved so many people. But that's the problem with them, isn't it? They're just *stuck*. That sort of thinking is why systems want to leave." She leaned forward, her eyes getting sharper. "I agree with what they think. But not how they do it. I saw the casualties and thought, *If I could get in there, pull them back just a little bit, maybe I can save lives. Even just one.* Because the Cluster won't. We saw that at Ark Getru. *Someone* has to care."

Save lives. Such a phrase burned Demi deep in her gut. Saving lives was what happened in the well. The WM's actions seemed like plain and simple terrorism.

As if reading Demi's thoughts, Lynn's emotions calmed, her voice strengthening. "They originally wanted to take out Theta Seven. Ark Getru emboldened them. I spent days urging them to back off, told them that it's a transport hub, that civilians use it too. Two targets." She held up two fingers. "They agreed to two targets. Docking and comms. I did that. I did more for Theta Seven than anyone in Command." Now her eyes matched her voice in intensity. "Lindsay and I wanted as many crew safely on Theta Seven. I hoped to be the only one. So they wouldn't be in the line of fire." Suddenly, her voice softened, her sense of righteousness giving way. "The ships arrived too soon."

"Now Ayenew is dead. Now Diaz is dead. You've thrown me in here. This isn't about politics," Demi said. "Look at your body count."

"No, no, no, Demi, you don't get it." Lynn turned to her with a full glare. "That's the difference between you and me. You pretended this wasn't happening. I kept saying this—it's impossible. I knew when hostile GCF ships were the *first thing* we saw in Cluster space. I knew when my parents ranted about the WM instead of welcoming me home. It's so clear. I can make small differences, like at Theta Seven. But the only way to save people is to end the war as soon as possible. And that means giving this ship to the WM. The photonic engine is the key to saving lives."

Lynn was right. This stalemate grew more deadly with each passing day. Every single sign pointed to that: classified intelligence, resource reports, responses from Command. Demi had told Krishna, Cabell, and the others that photonic tech could win the war.

The WM recognized that. Why didn't the Cluster?

"I see you. Right now," Lynn said. "I see your face. I *know* you. You're thinking about this logic. You get it, don't you?" Tension melted from her shoulders, and her breath now came with a steady cool. "We don't have to be at odds. You've seen it. The Cluster is a single giant *thing* that operates without a compass." Her voice picked up pace with each passing word. "You built alliances out of nothing. Different cultures, different wants, different ways of communicating. *You* knew that if we were going to survive, that would need to change. It *changed* us. We can't go back, but the Cluster wants the status quo. This inertia, it's *maddening*, but it pushed the outer systems to do better. They build new ships, new fuels, but the Cluster still treats them like peasants. The Withdrawal Movement is *just*. You know this."

Lynn stepped forward, a brightness to her brown cheeks now, like the biggest idea simply appeared and might just manifest into reality if she chose the right words. "And since it's just," Lynn said in a slow, measured tone, "you would be welcome to join us. Along with the Horizon."

Join the Withdrawal Movement?

Lynn's points synthesized with her own emerging concerns about the Cluster—not just the uselessness of the war, but the morality of all the *churn* that she saw everywhere. She somehow took Demi's best reasoning for staying out of the war and inverted it into an invitation.

In principle, the Withdrawal Movement made sense. But the WM wasn't just about principles. If it were, the strikes on the Thexder supply lines wouldn't have taken place. Civilian shipping lanes wouldn't have been targeted. Ark Getru's mining station would still float.

The photonic engine *was* the key to saving lives. But by keeping it out of the hands of anyone who would recklessly use it. "Would you trust the WM to use the engine to strike only military targets? In a strategic way, in a way that forces negotiations? Could you guarantee that? Because from what I see, this isn't being considered in decisions. Civilians are dying. And just because they don't agree with you doesn't mean they deserve to be caught in a blast radius."

Lynn didn't answer. Seconds passed between them before a knock at the door interrupted.

"Kohli! We need to move!"

"I need a minute," she yelled, eyes still locked on Demi, though something behind them had changed. Demi just couldn't read what it was.

At Ark Getru, Demi saw the Cluster slipping even more, and the only path forward was what she could control. Then the Lumersian distress signal came, giving a clear beacon of what needed to be done.

In the face of everything Lynn just did and said, none of that changed. In fact, Demi's resolve rooted deeper.

"You were right when you said that I've changed. That *we've* changed. And I still may not know where that takes me. But I see a bigger issue. We could"—Demi waved a finger back and forth—"find a way out of this, in theory. The Cluster could better recognize what seceding systems want. WM strikes could be more surgical, less targeted. But that requires both sides to negotiate in good faith. And until that changes," Demi said, leaning back into her chair, "you're not on the right side. It's just a side. My focus has to be on getting to the Lumersians and preventing the collapse of their dimension. Because that's the one thing I know is right."

Another knock came at the door, and Lynn's head swiveled in uncertainty. "I don't agree with you, but I respect you. I always have. What do you think the Cluster plans to do to WM systems? They want everything back to normal, but too many people have seen the truth. Going back to normal is impossible."

Another knock came against the door, an intense pounding that echoed through the space and chipped away at any remaining time. Demi already lost Chuck. She nearly lost her command—and really, that was as good as gone once all of this finished. She would not let them take the engine.

"Listen to me," she said, a rare gravel to her voice. "You can't give them the engine. We have to help the Lumersians. They are innocent—they *helped* us."

"This isn't about them." Lynn glanced at the door again. "The engine—"

The doors slid open to the silhouette of a guard with a drawn rifle. "It's time," he said.

"I have to go. We're not going to kill you," Lynn said. "Or the crew. We'll figure out a way to get you home safe. I promise. But not with the photonic engine." She lingered for several seconds, though Demi refused to give her any response to work with. "It might be a while. But hey, at least you won't be fighting a war while you wait."

CHAPTER 24

*

TANAV

Matthews led Tanav through maintenance tunnels until getting to a hatch above a hallway. They'd dropped down and moved swiftly, the commander gesturing in precise hand signals: go, stop, hide, back away. The journey took them forward, more open hallways rather than maintenance ducts, and during this time, they saw neither WM soldiers nor Horizon crew. Nor did they hear any weapons fire or signs of violence.

"There," Matthews said, pointing to a Withdrawal Movement soldier. Unlike the clean uniforms of the GCF, all sleek lines and crisp folds, the soldier could have been mistaken for a technician at any base or station in the galaxy.

Except for the large rifle strapped to him.

"They still don't know about stellar cartography. Otherwise there'd be more of them here." The doors slid open, and the man spoke into a hand comm before stepping inside. "Go, now!"

"What?" But before Tanav got an answer, Matthews dashed forward. The commander twisted himself, sliding horizontally through the closing doors, though they shut before Tanav got through. First came several low grunts from beyond the wall, followed by indecipherable shouting. A loud thump slammed, causing vibrations to ripple through the paneling.

The wall absorbed an impact from either Matthews or the WM soldier. But which?

Tanav didn't have time to try to decipher, as more grunts came, along with a clang, and a shout—one that clearly came from Matthews.

Another new sound came: the familiar pulse of an energy weapon. Two more, in fact, one of the blasts impacting the door, causing a sizzle along with a dissipating heat across the wall.

Finally, silence.

Then the doors slid open with a full hydraulic puff.

Tanav started to twist into a hiding position when Matthews's low voice cut through.

"Get in here, quick."

Tanav stepped through the doorway, his view widening to the massive domed room that contained the GCF's most advanced mapping and charting tech in the fleet—even with the ten-year gap. All around them, projections of the galaxy floated, a mix of holographic imagery and continuous wall display to show an array of stellar bodies, lines and names zipping between them. Tanav spent so little time in this room that he needed a minute to take it all in: the length of the metal ramp, the maintenance floor some seven feet below them, and at the end of the ramp, a spiral staircase that led to a platform with a smaller spherical holo-map and a data table similar to the one on the bridge.

And below all that, the crumpled body of a WM soldier. But about halfway down the ramp, between Tanav and the WM soldier, two prone bodies in GCF uniforms.

Tanav took in a quick inhale and dashed over. He slammed a hand over his mouth when he realized who it was.

Karl had talked about wanting to do more after Ark Getru. Did he get reckless here? And Hikaru, they'd just seen each other in the mess hall. Tanav pictured his thumbs-up after trying his pie.

Matthews held up a tablet, presumably taken from the unconscious WM soldier. "Twelve soldiers occupying this ship. They're spread out. And this fellow"—he pointed over to the prone invader—"was apparently here to download intel from our stellar cartography repository." Matthews tapped a finger on a displayed list. "For these targets. Hey." His voice shifted, becoming softer, compassionate. "I understand if you need a moment. They were your colleagues. But we don't have a lot of time. We don't know if anyone else is heading this way."

In the well, death was a familiar companion—accidents, catastrophes, violence between neighboring ships, even the occasional suicide. But this felt so much heavier, like his body and mind couldn't shift back into the way it operated back then.

"Is that data why we're here?" Tanav asked, a conscious effort to push past his feelings.

"That's why *they* were here," Matthews explained, as Tanav examined the raider on the floor. Eyes closed. Lying still. But breathing. A quick look showed a rifle lying on a lower maintenance platform. It must have fallen during the struggle with Matthews.

At least one less needless death in this war.

"On the surface, it's star charts and trade routes. Geography. But the transport schedule? Density of traffic? Security measures? If you're going to scare people or disrupt a society, that's how you do it. Look at the highlights. These aren't military targets. They want to expose vulnerabilities. And they're right. The Cluster is losing." Matthews handed the list over to him, then peered over the side of the ramp, all sorts of half-exposed hardware tied into the guts of the Horizon.

In Tanav's universe, the course of history led to the gradual rise of capitalism and groupthink to rule over a firm caste system across forty-three regions. In Neera's, things moved to an authoritarian beat. This place, though, was much more complicated.

"I know you're hurting. I'm gonna let you in on a little secret." Matthews scanned upward, beyond the spiral staircase and its attached platform. "You can do right by your friends by helping me protect that. That is our best chance to make a difference. That's why the Horizon's so important. Their deaths can have meaning." Tanav's eyes tracked Matthews's scanner over to a large metal bubble at the roof of stellar cartography. "Inside there is ten-year-old communications hardware. The only active ship in the fleet *without* updated encryption protocols for classified materials. WM moles intercepted intelligence everywhere—at bases, on planetary stations, on ships. Because everything had been updated or built new. Except the Horizon. The Horizon uses a different protocol. No one can steal it."

The way Matthews laid it out, each point carried a practicality to it, answers snapping into place. But that didn't address Tanav's biggest question about the war:

Why did both sides let civilians get in the way?

"We couldn't bring old ships out of dry dock. It'd be too obvious. Same thing if we tried installing new protocols. A ten-year-old craft crashing into Cluster space out of nowhere? It's perfect. The Horizon will be the new hub, used to send out classified intel and orders to trusted individuals. Right now, all sorts of intelligence and orders leak. They anticipate our every move. It lets them strike when we're not looking—like Ark Getru. Command said the bureaucrats aren't negotiating until they can break the stalemate; *this* breaks the stalemate." He looked at the WM soldier. "I'm going to run a few more checks on this. Then we need to secure the ship. Find something to tie up that guy." Matthews said it as if spare parts for tying up captured raiders was an everyday occurrence on the Horizon.

Though, for a short period, it was—those weeks when raids took the life of Grant Singh. Tanav actually got involved in one of the captures, more by happenstance than anything else. But he knew that extra flexcables for ship power distribution also doubled as such. Trying to survive the well had forced that knowledge on him, yet this was different, like a wave trying to pull him under. Even as he stepped over the unconscious WM soldier, he wondered if others felt that way too.

Tanav paused at Karl and Hikaru. Had they been scared? Did they regret helping? He checked once more for life signs, tears stinging his eyes at their stillness. He wanted a moment. He wanted to *remember* them, but there would be time for that later. Tanav pushed himself forward, all the way to a small chest containing coiled flex-cables for the room's specialized maintenance.

"That'll work," he muttered to himself as he carried them over to the unconscious soldier. He strung it out for length, thoughts still weighing everything Matthews had just said. Lynn told him that Matthews kept looking at hardware schematics, but she'd figured he was considering how to upgrade things for the war effort.

She'd be amused to learn it was the opposite. Would he even be allowed to tell her? The question formed when suddenly everything went black.

Almost black. His vision blurred; what remained was a swirl of colors and a sting in his temple. A boot—or what he presumed was a boot—struck him square in the stomach, and momentum caused him to roll off the walkway, a loud impact as he landed on the lower maintenance deck. Seconds passed, and through the pain, he forced his eyes open; as his vision returned, he caught the WM soldier taking a step forward. Tanav tried standing but stumbled down, only focusing enough to see Matthews and the soldier struggling over the tablet near the door.

And then a shout of pain.

Followed by Matthews dropping to one knee, hand covering his upper thigh—and in between his fingers, blood oozed out, saturating his uniform. Matthews hopped up and swung an arm, missing completely and falling on his face. Tanav struggled to his feet, the world still swirling.

"Get the gun!" Matthews yelled.

"What? What gun?" Tanav called back, the very act of doing so caused his temple to burn. He tried to blink the blur out of his vision, at least enough to see several steps in front of him.

The rifle from earlier.

Matthews was still bent over, but where was the other guy? Tanav spun to the other side and spottend the WM soldier already up the circular stairs and at a station.

Tanav picked up the gun, putting the strap over his shoulder. The weight, the warmth from the discharge, they pulled him back into the bleakest days in the well and Grant's dying breaths, and he shook his head to snap out of the last time he held a weapon.

"Go! He's at the transmission console!"

Tanav headed to the access ladder, forcing himself up one step at a time until emerging to find the commander stumbling toward him. Matthews steadied himself on the railing, one hand putting pressure on a bleeding leg wound as he hobbled forward.

"Stop him before he sends over any data."

The commotion got the soldier's attention, though instead of confronting them, he refocused on the station, frantically typing like it was more important than his very survival.

Tanav found more steadiness in his footing, steps becoming lighter, and vision becoming clearer. Though his head spun when Matthews barked another order at him.

"What are you doing?" The commander's voice grew closer as he shuffled across the walkway. "Shoot him! You've got line of sight!"

Shoot him?

About five or six meters sat between Tanav and the winding staircase up to the transmission console. While they had a clear angle based on where the soldier stood, at least his upper half, Tanav wasn't sure he could make the shot. More importantly, he couldn't just *shoot* this person.

He'd shot one person before, during the incident that killed Grant, but that was with a weapon pointed directly back at him—

not to stop a data theft. And even then, Tanav only wounded the tall alien raider in the leg.

Behind Tanav, Matthews's irregular footsteps got nearer. He drew the weapon slowly, no muscle memory from the training Demi put him through several years ago, but hopefully he made it look good.

"Stand down!"

The man didn't react; instead he moved faster, attaching a device to the top of the console.

"He's transmitting now," Matthews yelled, nearly caught up. "You have to shoot him!"

"We can talk about this. No one has to—"

"Ah." Matthews yanked the rifle out of Tanav's hand. He leaned back against the guardrail, all his weight propped up by his good leg, his hand letting go of the bleeding thigh wound to hold the barrel of the rifle up. Two quick shots fired, so fast Tanav couldn't track them before he saw the man slump.

The rifle clanged as it hit the metal ramp. Matthews soon followed, both hands putting pressure on his wound.

"Go see if he finished his transmission."

Tanav took a shaky, steadying breath. "You didn't have to kill him." Tanav forced his way up each of the stellar cartography steps to the central station, making the full sweeping rotation until he arrived at the top level's consoles, where the soldier lay face up, eyes wide open.

With a massive, smoking wound burned through his chest.

"He wasn't threatening us!" Tanav screamed as he glanced at the displays, the stations, the attached device.

"He killed your friends. Their bodies are right there."

He squinted at the device's status and read it aloud for Matthews, each word filled with spite at the violence of it all. "'Stage three connection established. Press to initiate transmission.'" He wanted to yell about the pointlessness of it all. They had a chance, in this microcosm of violence. They could have taken this singular moment in a war spanning galaxies to shift something. Instead, Matthews killed him. Without any words being exchanged.

"It didn't finish. That's good." Matthews switched topics like he snapped his fingers. "Search the body."

That part, unfortunately, Tanav understood. More memories flooded him: the feel of lifeless weight and the *smell* of burnt flesh and blood mixing together as they scavenged Grant's killers for useful equipment. And while he did as requested now—followed *orders*—he stared at the burnt hole that ran from the man's front to his back. He forced each action, going through pockets and pouches until he headed back to Matthews with the few recovered items: the transmission device, another small data tablet, a data storage chip, a compressed ration pill.

And the knife that had plunged into Matthews's leg.

Along with a piece of long, thick fabric—a sleeve Tanav cut off the soldier's coat using that very same knife.

Matthews tied the fabric tight around his leg as he examined the device. "Transmission was set to an unknown vessel," he said, tapping through it to load up transmission targets. "We stopped it just in time."

Hikaru was dead. Karl was dead. Who knew what else had happened on the ship. But Tanav didn't seek *vengeance*, he just wanted everyone to pick a better way. "You think I'm some naïve pop star. I survived in that gravity well. I shot the invader who killed our first officer—my *friend*. I know how this works." For days after Ark Getru, the images of flung bodies would sear into his mind's eye. Now it had been replaced by the charred, exposed innards and smoking hole of the man on the upper platform. "That man did not have a gun pointed at us. Without weapons, there's always a chance to back down. To make a choice."

"He did have a weapon. He had data." Matthews grunted as he applied more pressure to his leg. "Data is how people make decisions. This is different from the gravity well. It's bigger. It's more sinister, because someone's decision can kill hundreds, thousands. They can deploy troops or plant bombs. Every moment that passes, when there's no true negotiations, this drags out. It makes it so people like him do things like this. He put aside his ego and believed in his cause. He didn't care if you pointed a rifle at him. Belief is a powerful thing. It makes people fearless." He stood up—or at least tried to.

"Your belief in the Cluster makes you fearless?"

Matthews shook his head at that question. "No. I don't believe *in* the Cluster. Not as it stands. I grew up in the colonies. I know how bad it can be. But I believe it can be better. I've seen that too. I fight to change it from the inside, however I can, with whatever I can. Command thinks I'm looking for ways to win the war. I'm looking for ways to *stop* the war. There's a difference." He put one hand on the ramp's guardrail and tilted back and forth, finding balance. "You're not fearless about killing yet. That's a good thing, though." Matthews tested his good leg with several hops. "As for our spy? They probably believe too. I just hope that belief hasn't hurt anyone on this ship."

The spy. Every moment since their escape from the brig had been about pushing forward, but now they had to deal with the spy. Matthews had an instinct about Tanav. Would he be able to assess the rest of the crew that way? The commander pointed down at the rifle, and Tanav handed it over. Though instead of holding it like a weapon, it became a makeshift crutch. "Come on. We gotta move."

Tanav didn't have that ability, and instead he forced himself to follow—left foot, then right foot, repeated over and over. Even then, he couldn't shake one quick phrase from Matthews, a passing phrase that carried far too much power:

It makes people fearless.

That drove Demi to go back to the well. It drove this spy, whoever it was. It drove the WM to wait out here in ambush. And it drove Matthews to kill the person that Tanav couldn't.

All these belief systems. All pulling in different directions, with the Horizon in the middle.

Matthews began explaining the best path to the bridge, with the goal of hopefully finding Demi. Halfway through his explanation, things suddenly went dark—first the outer hallway, then stellar cartography in a partial power outage, different from the whole-ship failure of before. This time the lights shut down, yet the star chart systems still hummed, and the floor groaned with the usual rumble of the Horizon's propulsion systems.

Before Tanav could consider what that meant, Matthews stumbled his way over, one arm on rails for support. "If I gotta use this," he said, holding up the rifle for a moment before setting it back down to lean on, "you'll have to prop me up." From outside the hallway, voices shouted, followed by the sounds of debris scattering. "Sounds like a firefight out there."

"Maybe it's one of our—" Tanav paused when all the noise went quiet. "What—"

Matthews shushed him, and even though the rifle still doubled as a cane for him, he flicked the power on. A new noise came, and Tanav leaned into the hallway to catch a silhouette that slowly backed in. Low lighting revealed it was an armed woman, though from her actions, she clearly didn't know about the room's occupants.

"Hey, Yellow," she called out. "What was that? Where'd you go?"

Tanav looked at Matthews, who nodded, which he took as at least some sort of permission to hold up this new invader. But before he managed to reply, a blinding white cocoon emerged around the person, quickly followed by the sound of her voice.

Or what Tanav assumed was her voice. It sounded like a cry of fear or desperation, yet it carried an electrical distortion that eventually meshed into a high-pitched wail.

The cocoon flashed, temporarily blinding Tanav. And when his vision restored, only an empty hallway remained. "Oh, it's you two," a voice said, and it took Tanav a moment to realize who it was.

Sadler walked into view. He looked at Tanav, then over at Matthews, then he glanced behind them.

"You two are a long way from the brig, aren't you?" he asked with a laugh.

CHAPTER 25

*

NEERA

In the engine room of the Horizon, though, every option now presented itself in the most petrifying way. Neera told Macek to find safety, and by sound, that put him somewhere on the opposite side of the space, probably behind spare equipment.

He hunkered down behind the engineering room's main workbench. Some cover was better than no cover, though his size likely meant the top of his head remained somewhat exposed. Still, he was at least on the opposite end of the double-door entrance.

More importantly, the workbench sat a level up from both the photonic engine and the synth generator, a perimeter of railing also providing some cover for that tech. Even the main FTL controls and propulsion core lay on the opposite side of the U-shaped level. Because if someone was going to try to shoot him down, at least he could spare the marvels of engineering in the room.

The double doors slid open, and he remained hidden as best he could while voices murmured. With other Dywens, his mind would have intuitively processed the interlink between his species. That could have estimated the number of approaching predators.

But on a starship in a different universe?

Five invaders, he guessed, as he tried to pick out voices and sounds and *presences*. Followed by the sound of hydraulics, then footsteps—first in a bunch, but then a set descending to inspect the photonic engine and synth generator. Something else tickled his instincts, though a practical realization grounded him first:

Blocked. Without weapons.

Without *options*.

What were the risks?

If he stayed hidden, he'd be considered a threat. If he waited for Macek to be discovered, they could target him. And while Macek proved to be an excellent engineer and an enthusiastic supporter, his naïve optimism here might be detrimental to his ability to stay hidden. Neera also didn't know their purpose, or their abilities. If they used thermal sensors or other scanners, hiding would be ineffective.

Footsteps spread out and he couldn't wait for orders. He outranked Macek, and while that only applied to engineering, it still created a hierarchy.

As uncomfortable—unnatural—as it was for him, Neera was responsible. Neera had to *choose*.

"I will stand up away from cover," Neera called out, his back still against the workbench. "Perhaps we may be encouraged to talk rather than fight."

No reply came, which he took as a positive, especially because he picked up on a latent undercurrent of anxiety. Not dread or anger, but the strange balance between all of those that often came with uncertainty.

He took that as a positive sign. If he was wrong, he would be dead in several seconds, so there wouldn't be much time to linger on mistakes. Though it did seem odd to pick up on this, and as he pondered that, a new idea emerged:

Perhaps the WM had a Dywen among its ranks?

Neera stood slowly, arms up. As the rest of the room came into view, he counted three WM soldiers, all with weapons trained on him.

Four, when he counted Lynn, who stood at the foot of the steps, the pink glow of the synth tinting her cheeks.

"Lynn," he said quietly. That must have been the anxiety he detected. "I was worried about you. They got—"

He paused, and his eyes focused on the short, quick movement of her hands.

Lynn held a weapon on him.

And her hands were trembling.

Everything clicked into place. Her constant feeling of discomfort. The strange flash of emotion during the space walk. It all made sense, and yet not at all.

Lynn was one of them. Survivor. Pack.

How could she do this?

"I'm sorry," she said with a quick glance to the WM soldiers above her. "You know, I said that a lot to Demi too. But it's true. I am sorry. This is not about us or the crew. Please make it easy. Where is Macek?"

The crew. But it was more than that. They were a pack. How could Lynn betray her pack? Neera's emotions whirled, his world shifting rapidly.

"Where is Demi?" Neera finally asked in response.

"In her quarters. She's safe. With Indy." She grimaced as she straightened the energy pistol in her hand. "I . . ." Her voice briefly trailed off. "Look, no one has to get hurt. We have one goal: dismantle the photonic engine. Break it down into components. We'll take the parts and download the schematics to rebuild it."

"The engine?" One of the soldiers peered at the tower of technology, eyes studying the control console and the adjacent synth generator, and a rare surge of rage coursed through Neera. Though he supposed that feeling was understandable. For the Dywen, the protective instinct only emerged over offspring. In a way, the photonic engine was the closest thing he had to that. "You cannot take that from here. The Lumersians require us to bring it—"

"I can't get into a philosophical debate right now," she said, her brow crinkling. "I know the engine is modular. Help us dismantle it."

Neera looked at the different faces surrounding him, most human and one nonhuman species that he didn't recognize. "I cannot. A promise was made to keep it safe," he said. Quick looks between the other soldiers showed that they grew impatient. "Dismantling and rebuilding will be a risky endeavor. It was built iteratively, and it may not work if pieces are tampered with."

A creak came from the far corner. Had this been any other situation, such a noise could be dismissed or ignored as the standard bumps and rumbles of the Horizon. But Lynn knew right away— though to her credit, she stopped mid-glance and focused on Neera.

"Go check it out," a soldier said.

Neera watched one of the WM soldiers break away, his rifle raised. He had to make a decision. They would discover Macek soon, and Neera didn't want his presence to lead to an accident. And maybe he could appeal to Lynn's own sense of pack.

"Wait, I am not alone," Neera said. "Macek, please stand up. Do not harm him."

The small man eased out from behind a cabinet, his hands raised. He glared fiercely at Lynn as he came slowly over to Neera's location. "Why are you doing this?" he asked Lynn directly, with more confusion than vitriol in his voice. Neera held up his hand to stop any additional commentary.

"Lynn, Macek can confirm the engine lacks the stability needed to dismantle and rebuild it." He reached out through their empathic imprint to gauge what she might be feeling.

"We're counting on breaking it apart," she said—honestly, based on Neera's senses. And she knew *he* told the truth. Yet something else lingered behind that truth.

Neera took another moment to ponder, then realized the outline of what she hid: she didn't trust her WM comrades. And that created a high level of risk for everyone.

"We have barely gotten it running as it is," Neera said. "For stability, it should stay on this ship—"

"It leaves this ship," one of the soldiers said. "Then we destroy the ship."

"Wait, no, you can't do that," Lynn said, her eyes widening. "These are good people."

"Lynn," Neera said, "the entire Lumersian species is at risk. If the WM truly cares about the freedom and safety of individuals, they should let us go."

"We don't have time for this," the nonhuman said in a growly voice, and as if on cue, a communicator on Lynn's belt beeped. Lynn's anxiety grew, and Neera's unease matched it, a feedback loop making a difficult situation that much worse. Next to him, beads of sweat formed on Macek's brow, and Neera's instincts were right— his friend's sunny, science-focused outlook was no match for violent threats.

They'd all experienced circumstances like this in the gravity well, yet Neera had seen being in Cluster space do *something* to this crew, as if the physical and temporal distance from that place made them forget how difficult it was. He could more easily return to emergency circumstances, possibly from the way of life forged in him by the Regent Empire.

Macek, though, showed neither stoic resolve nor calculated response.

"Macek, go to the brig." Lynn must have picked up on that too. "Someone bring him there. He's not a threat. You promised me we'd keep them safe during—"

Before she could finish, the nonhuman fired an energy blast at Macek. It bore a hole in his chest, a fist-size burn that ate through from front to back. Macek collapsed backward, a lifeless free fall ending in a thud on the deck plates, smoke wafting up from the wound.

Something in Neera wailed. He'd seen friends and allies fall in the well. But that was supposed to be behind them.

Lynn stood frozen, mouth agape, the emotions pouring out of her a storm, although in there came a sign that she had seen the WM murder a colleague before. She turned to him, a tremble that probably meant many different things, but none of that mattered. As he tried to weigh his options and their risks, everything changed.

First, a strange light emerged to his right, along with a high-pitched buzz mixed with a higher-pitched digital squeal. Neera turned—as did everyone else—to find a white blur of light, a cocoon that grew in intensity until he shielded his eyes. Voices clamored around him, disbelief and confusion about what was happening, and he eventually realized that *thing* surrounded one of the WM soldiers.

The light vanished, and the room looked exactly as it was prior to its strange appearance—except one less WM soldier stood in the room.

"What did you do?" the human in the back growled, gun raised. Neera's eyes darted, first at the man, then the rifle in his hands, then Lynn as her lips twisted in confusion. "Is this the engine?"

A sudden flash led to the next cocoon of light enveloping another WM soldier. The same spreading glow and sudden flash, though this time a distorted voice rippled through the strange energy, and suddenly, nothing was there.

"It's a weapon." The remaining soldier swept her rifle back and forth in a search for targets.

"We don't know that," Lynn retorted. Her sudden fear tied into his feelings, like power surging through wiring. "Neera, what is this?"

"We don't have time!" the soldier shouted. "If we can't take the engine, we have to destroy it."

She aimed her rifle, and Neera's eyes widened as he realized her target. The muzzle pointed directly at the photonic engine, and before Neera could offer any protest, a different kind of light flashed through the space:

The brilliance of a muzzle flash before launching a blast of heated plasma.

The photonic containment unit burst, sparks showering in every direction. Another blast came, this time hitting the control console and the connected thermal regulation system. More sparks flew, along with shards of metal and composites, and a glowing red whip tore out from the engine's base, a chain reaction of photonic energy mixing with electricity and oxygen and anything else in its path as it lashed out across the room. It died out, leaving only a burning line across the floor, the wall, and any fixtures in its path.

Then the blinding flash of white as the cocoon returned, soon followed by distorted screams. From the cocoon, a spread of energy fire fanned out. Neera ducked, one shot soaring over him as it absorbed harmlessly into the alloy plating of the engine room's wall. The rest of it moved in a constellation of blasts across the room. Right when the cocoon flashed, the plasma impacted, the sound of impact and explosion and twisted metal.

By the time Neera could see again, the soldier was gone. But two plumes of smoke bled into the space, the first from the photonic engine—and the second from the FTL control systems.

"Neera, what is happening? How are you doing this?" Lynn raised her gun with wide eyes, her voice shaking as she stared at him. Though the human heart was a physical organ, its pounding cadence in Lynn's chest overwhelmed her senses, and that made even *thinking* difficult, all of his own thought patterns overloaded with her panic. "Where are they?"

"That light is not from me," Neera said quickly. "It is unknown technology."

"How is this—" Her question cut off as the cocoon formed around her. "No. No, Neera, not like this." An electronic distortion took over her voice, gradually shifting its sound from Lynn's familiar tones into a garbled unintelligible mess.

The last thing Neera heard from Lynn was "Help me."

The silhouette of Lynn's hand reached out, fingers extended. As if the last few minutes of betrayal never existed, Neera reached over the guardrails to her, his own hand swiping through the edge of the cocoon.

The light disappeared.

Lynn was gone, and not just physically—the bond that wove into his senses, the weight of her presence, disappeared as well. No, it went beyond disappearance; this felt like a vacuum ignited in Neera's chest, imploding all his senses and stealing his ability to move. His hand remained outstretched, steadying breaths pacing through his body. A rush of hydraulics cut into the quiet, and the doors slid open to reveal Sadler. No weapons in hand, but holding a small module Neera had never seen before.

Sadler stepped inside, and shortly behind him trailed Matthews, with a clear limp and a bloodied bandage around his thigh, his weight supported by a rifle-turned-crutch. Sadler held up a small square device, and from the grin on his face, Neera knew that tech—whatever it was—did all *this*.

"Sadler, what did—" Neera stopped his question midway.

Because Tanav now came in as well.

And from the look on his face, he had no idea what just happened to Lynn.

CHAPTER 26

※

DEMI

Demi pulled back from the exposed wiring next to her door. No computer systems meant no schematics, which meant her non-engineer brain had to tread carefully over the past thirty minutes or so. She'd managed to pry the hand-size panel open with makeshift tools, but approached the wiring part a little more slowly. Hot-wiring the door's mechanism would be great; frying herself on live power would not.

She turned to the large square device next to Chuck—the translation matrix processing incoming Lumersian messages. It had a stand-alone power system, and if the door just needed a jolt, maybe connecting the two would do the trick.

"Not exactly date night, is it?" Demi asked as she glanced at Chuck's containment unit. "If I ever talk to Command again, remind me to request escape doors in the captain's quarters. Seems like a sensible design feature."

The purple spark twinkled, and while this was probably just a reflection from environmental shifts affecting light scattering, she chose to believe it was Chuck's way of responding to her jokes. She paused, a forced recall of his ridiculous stilted laughter.

But what came next from the containment unit wasn't a friendly mechanized chuckle. Instead, a harsh series of oscillating screeches and beeps arrived—similar to the last message received, but different in pitch and rhythm. Next to it, the makeshift translation unit refused to do its job, the display interface showing chaotic waveforms.

"Your people have either great timing or terrible timing," she said, stepping away from the door wiring for a closer look. She tapped on the translation matrix's different menus to load various language logs. The noises cycled through, Demi counting about a minute before repeating—shorter than last time, and definitely something different and new. But the previous message boosted the translation matrix's database, at least in theory. So this—and future messages—should hopefully translate faster. That thought led to other scientific questions—did each convergence point have its own message? Or was this a real-time transmission, with data originating from the folds between physical and photonic space?

Also, could the Lumersians help out right now? Because she sure could have used a boost.

Demi tapped the console again, cycling through different standards until bits of the message processed, though only a few synthesized words emerged from the vocabulator.

"*Trapped vessel.*"

"*Contact.*"

"*Different universe.*"

"*Parents.*"

The first few translated phrases made sense; they lined up with previously translated details. A starship was trapped in the new gravity well. Attempts at contact. Possibilities of different physical universes from the hub of photonic space.

But *parents*? The Lumersians didn't even understand that concept.

"Remember when I explained the whole 'birds and bees' thing to you?" Demi asked aloud. "Looks like your family was eavesdropping. I hope they weren't going to pressure us for grandkids."

Ever since Chuck's voice returned for that single moment, a flutter of hope had grown. Same with every cycle of transmission noise that came. The vocabulator stayed consistently quiet outside of translation work, yet even now that sliver of hope persisted. Immediately followed by a desperation to know *why* she'd heard *one plus one equals two.*

The unit remained quiet, but Chuck's spark twinkled again, and while she liked to think this was about everlasting love challenging the borders of space and time and dimensions, her rational mind gave a clearer scientific explanation: environmental changes affecting light scattering and particle reactions. The Horizon was a GCF starship with stable environmental controls, plus she'd spent plenty of time talking to Chuck's spark and had rarely received twinkles back. When it did, it usually came from some light source outside the window.

Demi glanced out the domed window of her quarters. The same scattering of white lay across a black canvas, the patterns and distances between the stars the same as it had been from the last time she looked. The only difference came from the port side of the docked WM craft, a freighter still barely visible from the angle of her quarters.

Then something flashed. Demi blinked several times just to make sure it wasn't a trick of her tired eyes. She squinted at the WM ship. A flash of light, and once again she wondered if her eyes deceived her. *Something* looked strange, like a gradual shift causing ever so slight color tweaks.

Another flash came, one directly within her field of vision. That was no trick; she saw it with certainty.

"Computer, run sensor scans off the stern of the ship, distance of five kilometers."

No voice came in return.

Of course. Other than the ability to synthesize dog food and water, Lynn's team had cut off all other functional access.

Demi went for something more old-fashioned—from the storage compartment beneath her bed, she grabbed a reliable pair of lens-based binoculars. Dirt still caked along the bottom edge from her last Earth-based hike some six months ago, when she'd used her only shore leave to take Chuck's spark to the California redwood trees.

Perhaps searching space for strange flashes was the intergalactic form of bird-watching.

With the eyepiece pressed against her skin, she scanned the space again. Even with a closer look, too few details were clear. *Something* was out there, and it appeared to be rotating slowly while drifting away. What it was, though, or how that related to the flashes, she wasn't sure. Perhaps pieces of the hull were burned off by the WM?

Another flash came, only partly visible in the far-right corner of the binoculars. Whatever it was, it lingered among the other debris.

"What the hell?" From across the room, Indy huffed, probably an exhale of deep sleep, but Demi took it as greyhound snark. "It's not food, Indy. Guess I'll—"

Another flash interrupted Demi's train of thought. Except this one arrived closer—close enough that she could clearly see that this *thing* was a body.

A human body. Or humanoid, at least. Was it alive when it shot out into space? That part remained unclear, but as her eyes adjusted to the contrast of hull lighting and black space, a clear silhouette formed: one arm extended, the other clutching its chest, legs tensed.

The body rotated, the extended arm clearly holding a pistol— and was that a GCF uniform under the crystalizing layer of ice?

Demi watched as details came into view. Right when she got a clear look at the uniform, its arm jolted, fingers releasing the pistol to drift away. And the face—Demi adjusted the focus for finer details, and despite the thin layer of frost and burst blood vessels, she knew exactly who it was.

Cheekbones. Lips. Long, curly black hair.

And indeed—a GCF uniform. With green trim for the communications division and two bands across the upper arm for the rank of lieutenant.

Lynn.

Lynn Kohli floated in ice-cold space.

And the others? Probably WM soldiers, judging by their lack of uniforms. Demi scanned around, counting at least four bodies floating into the nothingness.

But how?

Not that long ago, Demi had told herself to erase ten years of friendship and survival, to put herself into a strategic duel of words against Lynn.

Now the truth stared back at her, sinking in with every forming ice crystal over Lynn's face.

She could not erase their past. It *mattered*. It informed their decisions, defined how they got here. No matter what happened, those moments still existed and shaped their lives.

And that realization unleashed nausea in her gut, a weakness in her hands. Demi wanted to pull the binoculars away. But she forced herself to stay, to look at Lynn, to give her that moment. Despite their disagreements, they left things as a debate. Demi *almost* grasped Lynn's opinion. And Demi saw in Lynn's reaction—her hesitation, her eyes—that she'd edged toward grasping Demi's opinion too.

Now they wouldn't have that chance. And to die *this* way. Horrified. Cold.

Alone.

The thought *stayed*, its burrs digging deep inside.

The chime of the comm system shook her out of it—in fact, multiple chimes, as all the various blank status and communications displays came back to life. Someone, somewhere, must have flicked a switch to bring her quarters online.

"Neera to Captain Kim."

Neera? What was happening?

"I'm here. I'm not liking the vibes right now." Demi spoke slowly, the weight of the situation breaking past any of her usual masking of feelings. "I could really use some good news. Are we clear?"

"Our circumstances are stable. However, there are many issues for me to catch you up on." Neera's voice, usually filled with a steadiness that was equal parts physiological and cultural, now wavered. "We have problems."

Short, *forceful* wording. Demi knew the cadence was a choice from him, a muscle he had to exercise. He only did this when he needed to convey the absolute gravity of the moment. Demi waited, cautious and steady breaths as she listened to his next words.

"We are stranded."

OFFICIAL EVENT RECORD

Initial Contact Between GCF Intrepid 2 and GCF Horizon

GCF Intrepid 2: Command, we are on an imminent approach vector with the distress beacon. The message continues to repeat.

GCF Command: Proceed with caution. Defensive measures level two authorized.

Intrepid 2: Understood. We're now in sensor range. Ship specifications show . . . it's an old ship.

GCFC: How old?

Intrepid 2: Ten, maybe twelve years old? Weapons powering up. Decoding distress call now. It's taking a few moments, the transmission protocols are all outdated. Command, please advise.

GCFC: This is a common WM ploy—take an older craft, disguise it as a distress call, and arm it. Confirm the location?

Intrepid: Sector SDF7. Well past the cease-fire barrier.

GCFC: And in a trade route too. Patch the audio through.

Kim: Mayday, mayday. This is an emergency distress call from Captain Demora Kim of the GCF Starship Horizon. We are damaged, lacking basic resources, and carrying refugees.

Intrepid 2: Preliminary lifesign scans show ninety-three on board. Forty-four identify as human. Eight other species that do not match anything in the Cluster database.

GCFC: Demora Kim and the Horizon crew were declared dead nine years ago. We can't afford to lose more war assets. Two other GCF ships are within FTL range. Wait there for thirty minutes. Do not answer any hails. Do not engage. When the other ships arrive, approach in coordinated flanking positions with full weapons and await further instructions.

Intrepid 2: Understood. If they move?

GCFC: Shoot them down. It's not worth the risk. We can salvage the hardware later.

CHAPTER 27

DEMI

"Within these walls, the war doesn't exist."

Since arriving in Cluster space, Demi uttered those words so many times—in a public address to the entire crew, in personal discussions with worried individuals, to herself when she doubted herself.

She probably said it to Indy at one point or another too.

Most times, she didn't believe it. Maybe she never did. But at the very least, it set a goal, something to strive for as long as she captained the Horizon.

She'd tried. And during everything with Lynn, she realized it was a delusion or a fallacy.

But now, she realized it was even worse than that. It was a *mistake*.

Adapting was how they survived in the well. She, of all the members of the Horizon, failed to adapt to life after that. The fallout of this war affected anyone within the Cluster and beyond, a chain reaction that wove through the walls of a single ship.

Because they were stranded.

Stranded.

This marked the second time Demi had heard that as captain of the Horizon. Was that two more times than most captains got?

When the Horizon set out ten years ago, it was her dream assignment—to explore the unexplored, forging paths that made the galaxy seem a little smaller, a little more accessible. Ever since her first visit to the enormous holographic stellar cartography chart at the academy, she simply *knew*. Talking about trade routes might have bored most people, but the actual purpose of the paths didn't matter. What mattered was the discovery process, identifying safe and clear travel lanes free of asteroid fields, star radiation, or unexplained phenomena.

The Horizon had been commissioned to chart into the unknown and beyond, and Demi stood at the helm.

Demi still recalled the excitement rippling through the ship's science lab when scanners picked up something strange—so different and unexplainable and completely *invisible* to anyone staring outside the bridge's large front window.

And, unfortunately for their science team, something with measurements that didn't repeat or follow any patterns.

Speculation turned to panic when the ship's thrusters failed to respond.

"Maximum thrust is not enough, Captain!" Followed by, "What is that?"

That—as in the glowing pink blanket of the gravity well.

And then the sobering words from the seat next to her as Grant—the steadiest person Demi had ever flown with—spoke with a very uncharacteristic waver in his voice.

"Captain, our navigational readings show that we're . . . a hundred sixty thousand light-years from our last known location?" Controls chirped as the different stations updated systems and sensor outputs. "Propulsion is active, but we're unable to move."

Silence cascaded over the bridge, and Demi knew her next choice of words and actions would define the tone of this catastrophe.

"Commander, go oversee a diagnostic of our scanning systems, then run those scans again when ready."

Grant nodded as he stood up, the steadiness back in his voice. "Helm, load an extended database of reference points to triangulate. We need as many ways to verify this as possible—"

"Captain, we're being hailed. A vessel, about two hundred thousand kilometers away. According to the ship's registry . . ." Lynn had said at the time, her voice so much more frantic than the sardonic woman she'd become. "The registry says it's a supply ship reported missing seven months ago?"

Demi had stolen a second to absorb how two, maybe three minutes might have changed *everything* for them. But then she responded, establishing a different kind of first contact.

Not with a new species or culture, but with the first ship to get lost in the Lumersian energy well. And the first steps to forming a colony of some sort.

Just like ten years ago, the Horizon was stranded, and the means to get out of this situation were murky at best. Unlike then, Demi did not have a full crew for repairs and scans. She didn't have Grant Singh to lean on. Nor did she have the gradual arrival of other ships to exchange ideas and resources.

Instead, she had dead invaders. And dead crew—at least Diaz, possibly more. And the Horizon itself was damaged. She supposed the one asset she had was Neera's friend Sadler, whose expertise on both systems might have rivaled Neera's. In fact, Sadler might have been even more helpful, given his longer span in working with Cluster engine technology.

She stood, poised over the large display on her desk. Only a minute or two had passed since speaking to Neera, with systems still booting up. "Computer, give me the location of all crew members with life signs and their locations on this ship." At least that worked. The display showed a two-dimensional cross-section of the Horizon, soon populated with dots attached to floating names, a comprehensive view only accessed by senior officers. Neera, Matthews, and Sadler were in engineering. Tanav's icon blinked several times

before locking onto his comm-boosted signal, putting him in engineering as well.

"Tarell to Kim."

Casey's hushed voice came over the comm, and Demi saw her
icon moving slowly through the crew deck. "Casey," Demi said. "We
seem to be all clear. Are you all right?"

"I dented my door pretty good with my chair." The WM must
have locked all crew quarter doors, not just Demi's. "So that needs
repairs."

"The map shows Aurora's still in her quarters. Can you check on
her and then stay there until further orders?" Demi scanned the map
again, and though she did see those two, too many names simply
didn't appear. Her nails dug into her palm, a quiet, desperate hope
that sensors just hadn't fully reactivated yet. "I need to assess damage
and . . ." Her voice trailed off, unsure if she should say "casualties" just
yet. "Damage and impact first."

"Understood." The reply came prompt and clipped, a clear wall
against more things to be said. There would be a lot of that coming
very soon.

"I just need a few minutes," she said. "But I owe everyone an
apology."

Casey took several seconds before speaking again. "Yeah, you do."

Demi stole a moment with Indy, who lay blissfully unaware. As
she felt the warmth of a snoring greyhound next to her, her eyes
stayed on the display, a silent urge for more names to appear. She
allowed herself sixty seconds before accepting the reality that they
were all dead, and the Horizon's skeleton crew was as damaged as its
propulsion.

The Horizon had lost crew before. To raiders, to accidents, to
suicide.

This was different.

Previous deaths came in the grips of surviving the well and
everything with it. Here, Demi made the choices. She'd pushed to

keep the Horizon out of the war. She'd argued that her crew needed time and space.

She chose to steal the ship.

Her mind raced with theoreticals: What if they'd crossed to Theta Seven instead? What if she'd worked with Matthews? What if she'd hunted for the spy herself?

She shut that down fast. She'd been through enough to realize that what-ifs didn't matter. The only thing that mattered was what existed.

Sixty seconds came and went, a hard stop for introspection. She had to pull everyone together. That was what she did, what she always did. But how? That question defied an answer as Demi kissed her fingers and tapped Chuck's containment unit, rerouted the translation matrix output to the engine room, and leaned to quickly scratch Indy's ear.

Then she set off.

Demi walked with tablet in hand, a short summary from Neera about the extent of the damage. None of that detailed *how* the WM threat was handled, or who handled it.

Nor did it say anything about how Lynn was left floating in space.

Neera had pointed out that he had only told Tanav that Lynn was "missing." Perhaps that was how he understood it as well. *Something* needed to bridge that assessment and the strange flashes Demi saw through her window.

Lynn's open-mouthed, wide-eyed look, a layer of crystalized ice over her skin—the image stayed present. Plenty of research examined the human body in space, yet the abject horror of such an experience made Demi push those lessons deep into her memory for now.

Spy or not, Demi hoped that Lynn was spared that.

Demi stepped into the elevator and waited while the lift accelerated. Usually, these quiet moments in between choices and confrontations helped her stay grounded—a time-honored survival mechanism that leveraged context. Like when an entire crew needed *someone* to put a brave face on. Or when she was alone, a smart-ass quip in her mind to center herself.

The elevator's location blinked on the lit display, descending from the bridge past the mess hall, then the science lab, before slowing to a halt on deck four. The doors opened, and Demi took one more glance at the damage assessment, a report that updated in real time, with Sadler adding additional notes.

Details indicated some kind of shoot-out between the WM soldiers and her crew. Which made this even more curious—who among the crew would have been able to outgun them? Neera and Sadler were engineers; Tanav's baking skills were probably better than his shooting abilities.

That left Matthews.

Demi braced for his inevitable *I told you so*. Probably loaded with a whole lot of anger.

All of that would need addressing.

The entrance to engineering sat adjacent to the elevator bay, yet the walk seemed a mile long. She stopped just outside the doors' activation sensor range. Instead of moving forward, she told herself to take a few breaths for herself and only for herself.

This might be her only foreseeable chance to do so.

CHAPTER 28

TANAV

When Tanav was eight, his parents took him to the Lexin Industries year-end gala for the first time, a one-day cruise ship similar to the Crystal Dreams but on a much smaller scale. Its tinted open dome allowed for a view of a nearby nebula as donors and sponsors celebrated annual accomplishments, with his parents, Nova and Rolf Lexin, playing the gracious hosts. He'd heard about these events his entire childhood, marveling at the way his parents dressed for it. Yet when experienced firsthand, the whole thing was really, really boring.

Except for the band. A six-piece band playing a variety of the era's popular songs—a glorified cover-song band at best, but his first real exposure to live music, and it wove differently into his young body than simply listening to a recording.

"Well?" Nova Lexin asked, snapping him to attention. "Tanav, is there anything you'd like to say?"

"Thank you for being part of the Lexin family."

He'd said that from table to table as directed, but no one seemed satisfied with it. An assistant followed Tanav's mother, and they spoke quickly. Tanav looked up at his father and asked something that came from a mix of curiosity, boredom, and fatigue:

"Why are we doing this?"

Rather than get mad or show irritation, his father knelt down on his level and said something that burned into Tanav's psyche. Probably not the way Nova and Rolf intended, but those very words tinted Tanav's understanding of how people operated. "If you're ever going to make a mark in the galaxy, you need to learn to ask questions that find opportunities," he said, like this was normal parent-child conversation.

Though for Rolf Lexin, it might have been the only way he knew how to connect with an eight-year-old. Especially after several drinks.

"You can get what you need by giving people what they want—especially if they don't know it," he continued. "Every discussion is like . . ." His voice trailed off, his eyes watering for a moment before snapping back into focus. "Every discussion is like a hostage negotiation. Each side wants something. And that means there's always a resolution." Tanav nodded at this, unsure as to what that meant. Instead, he kept glancing at the band—which his father noticed. "Here's what we need. Say your line as happy, as *fun* as you can. Then you can go listen to the music. You understand? If you do it wrong, no music." Tanav nodded again, but this time the very idea of being close to the music drove his enthusiasm.

At the rest of the tables, Tanav glanced at the band before saying his line. And every time, his parents approved.

Two things stayed with Tanav for the rest of his life: the way people were so malleable that the smallest changes in phrasing lulled them to vulnerability.

That, and the experience of music.

He hated the former. And he loved the latter.

Ironically, the music alienated him from his family but brought him here—and the way his parents taught him to think, it could be inverted for something much better.

It could bring people together in dire circumstances. Like when a neighboring ship traversed the gravity well to raid the Horizon for supplies, he could talk them down and turn an act of aggression into a mutual understanding of needs.

Yet as he stood unsure in engineering, none of those skills worked. No one talked. Nothing had gone as planned and no one had next steps. After Neera spoke to Demi, he moved straight to Macek, moving the body to the far corner of the room before kneeling next to him; the Dywen placed both of his hands on Macek's cheeks and bowed his head. Near the main doors, he watching Sadler hunch over smoking pieces of propulsion technology and remove damaged pieces from the base of the control console, a steady rhythm to his actions: scan, tinker, remove, and repeat, all with precise, intense movements.

Then there was Matthews. He carried the highest rank here, though he didn't give anyone orders. He simply stood, his injured leg propped up against a makeshift crutch. Matthews wanted to protect the Horizon's comm hardware, which they had. And since the WM was no longer on the ship, that mission was successful.

Now what did he want? To get the Horizon operational again? Or something else? Matthews wasn't exactly subtle, and his quiet observations may have been just that—information gathering to understand the current landscape.

In this room stood Neera, Sadler, and Matthews.

But what about everyone else? Hikaru and Karl remained in stellar cartography, but so many others were unaccounted for. Wasn't there still a spy on board?

And where was Lynn?

Tanav managed to get that particular question out, to which Sadler quickly replied, "We should wait until Captain Kim arrives to debrief."

Neera broke from his ritual for a moment, and while he still knelt still with one hand on Macek's forehead, he paused only to say that a full assessment must be made. But Neera's low voice told him that something was really wrong with Tanav's . . .

Tanav's what?

In his universe, relationships didn't use titles like *girlfriend* or *wife* or *partner*. They existed as states: enjoyment, companionship, committed, long-committed. Thaddea was on the cusp of committed and long-committed. With Lynn, they'd never really talked about it, though the way they'd confided hopes and fears with each other, well, that marked the companionship stage.

And now *unavailable*.

"Transmission," Tanav said, hitting his communicator. "Lexin to Kohli."

Nothing. Neera shot him a quick glance before he resumed bowing his head.

Behind Tanav, the familiar hydraulic sound of sliding double doors came, and he turned to see Demi stepping in.

Since coming to the Horizon four years ago, Tanav recognized Demi's different modes of operation. If he ever called that out, she'd deny it—perhaps half jokingly, but she'd still stick to it. Demi wore an inscrutable look on her face: lines of concern, a narrow gaze of suspicion, and tense, pursed lips. Yet her shoulders carried a barely visible slump, signs that even with her businesslike facade, uncertainty weighed her down.

None of that was comforting.

"Is this still the latest?" she asked, holding up a tablet of multiple charts and tables. No jokes, no greetings. The dynamics all carved different lines of tension between Demi and the other people in the room. Matthews sent her an unblinking glare. And while Sadler kept working on the engine, he spoke up.

"It is. It's bad. But it could be worse. I have ideas, though." He tapped the outer shell of the engine's frame. "I have some resources in my ship. I brought some supplies, figured we'd be tinkering with stuff. Didn't expect it to be after battle damage, though."

Neera simply nodded, continuing his work, and Tanav knew he'd shut down. There would be no getting through to him.

"How are you, Tanav?" Demi said, her soft tone surprising him. Which, at first, he appreciated. But immediately his mind turned to Lynn.

What did Demi know? Was that why Neera refused to say anything, because he deferred to his commanding officer?

"I followed Commander Matthews," he said quietly. Though he could feel Matthews's anger at Demi, the commander seemed *military* enough to know to save that. Ranks, secrets, strategy, those types of things likely held him back for now. "He got us through it." He glanced over at Neera still standing over Macek, like he was on guard watch. "Hikaru and Karl are dead. We found them in stellar cartography."

Her lack of reaction proved surprising. In the well, she'd held things tight during acute situations, but the ship was safe and stable, her grieving surfaced in palpable ways. Yet right now her face remained cold, almost like a mask over her true self. Tanav glanced at everyone in the room, all eyes still on Demi. "Is there any word on Lynn yet?" he asked. "Where is she?"

Demi's eyes searched his own for . . . something. But whatever it was, she appeared unable to find it, and she finally broke, softer creases around her mouth and eyes. "I need one moment on that. I promise. Commander Matthews?" She turned to him. "I owe you a discussion. But not right now. Do you require medical assistance? Our med bay isn't the most stocked, but it has supplies."

"At some point, yeah," he said, his weight still supported by his rifle. He groaned as he straightened out. "And at some point, we need to talk." The word *talk* caused a rare flush to Demi's cheeks. "But I think we really need to understand what just happened. Don't you?" He turned to Sadler, who ignored him and stayed working on the engine. "Don't you? In fact, I'd like to know what's going on with that device of yours." Demi was all business. Sadler's full-speed-ahead mentality didn't fit this situation. And Matthews, he was on the offensive. Three different strategies, but Tanav still struggled with *why* they were at odds.

"I think that's an explanation you owe all of us, Sadler," Demi said. "What is this mystery tech? How does it work? Why are there bodies floating in space?"

Mystery tech?

Macek's body lay by Neera. They found Hikaru and Karl. But bodies floating in *space*?

That couldn't mean . . .

"Where's Lynn?" Tanav stepped forward, his voice uncharacteristically sharp, drawing *everyone's* attention. Soon followed by a rapid-fire exchange of glances, a sequence that made it feel like something was very, very wrong.

Demi held a hand up, pursed lips and crinkled brow that came far more loaded than she probably intended.

"I'm sorry, Tanav. Lynn was the spy on our crew."

For several seconds before Demi spoke, Tanav knew something was clearly wrong, and those thoughts started to creep in as soon as Sadler dodged questions.

But a spy?

That couldn't be true. That didn't make any sense. She'd committed to the photonic engine. She wanted to help the Lumersians.

She told Tanav he should have a *choice* about going home.

"What . . ." he started, though words failed as the truth of the moment sunk in. His fingers curled, tightened knuckles echoing the stiffness that suddenly pulled him from the inside. His entire sense of being crushed from the outside in, like so many of the ships that got stuck in the gravity well.

Like the Crystal Dreams. "Where is she now? Is she in the brig?"

"She's dead," Demi said. "I'm sorry."

"That can't be true," Tanav whispered through forced breaths.

"I'm very—"

"That can't be true." He spun on his heel and stormed over to Neera. "And you knew?" He turned to Sadler. "You knew?" Then back to Demi. "How did everyone know? No, we can't—"

Tanav's mind had moved so quickly that it had skipped over the very information that got them here. Sadler had a *device*. He saw Sadler use it on a WM raider. He saw the aftermath of pure, sudden disappearance.

Bodies in space.

"You killed her!" Tanav's voice echoed off engineering's walls.

"She was a spy," Sadler said coldly, and Tanav felt a sudden urge to hit him for every single clinical science statement he'd ever said, every single stupid grin he'd ever flashed.

"That doesn't matter." His words seethed through his teeth, and from behind, Demi's hand landed on his upper arm. He threw it off and turned back around. "In space? She was floating in *space*?"

Neera took a slow step forward. "The group that shot Macek included Lynn." His voice came out heavy, at a far lower register than Tanav had ever heard from him. "However, it should be noted that Lynn did not want to hurt any of us. Lynn wanted to protect Macek. Our safety was her goal. She was my friend." Neera's hands pressed against the angles of his head, a gesture that Tanav did not fully understand, though it must have gone with the Dywen's visible distress. "She was my friend. She was my friend."

"I spoke with Lynn shortly before she went to engineering." Demi broke off for a moment, and as she did, Matthews hobble-stepped forward. "She let the WM on board. But . . ." Tanav struggled against the weight of air coming in and out of his lungs and turned to Demi to hear this. "It's not that simple." She looked at Sadler. "None of it is, is it?"

Sadler set down his tools and plucked a small control device from his belt. "This tech is something I've been working on. It targets matter and moves it to a localized spot."

"'Moves it to a localized spot.' Do you mean . . ." Demi squinted at the small gray rectangle in his hand, like such a little device might have all the answers to the galaxy in them. "Teleportation?" Matthews's face twisted in ways that Tanav couldn't read, but the commander definitely didn't expect that.

"Not technically. But functionally, yes." Sadler held up an arm and pulled down his sleeve to reveal a small white cuff. "With this cuff, you can target an exit point. Within a reasonable distance, of course. Without one"—he pointed out toward the south wall of the engine room—"you just kind of get moved in a general direction. Which can break apart the atoms in the same way as if you hit a tree or a wall or something like that. Unless you send them into space. Space is pretty empty."

Space.

Bodies floating in space.

It all went back to Lynn, freezing to death in space.

All the things he was going to tell her, to ask her, things for her to consider as they got closer to a potential way home for him, their *next steps* . . .

Gone. Lost to a cold vacuum of nothing. Lost to the *war*.

"Lieutenant Sadler, I'd like a word with you in private," Demi said, shaking Tanav back into the moment.

"I think we've got pressing matters here?" Sadler asked. He tapped the open panels of the photonic engine.

"Yeah, about that," Matthews said. "Captain Kim, one quick word first."

"Commander, I owe you time, but I—"

The floor clinked as his rifle-cane moved. "Just for a moment."

Demi's gaze swept the entire space, first looking at Matthews before meeting Tanav's eyes. And Neera. Lingering on Macek's still body. Then at Sadler, before returning to Matthews. She nodded at him, and the two moved to the foot of the entry ramp. They only spoke for several seconds.

In that span, however, Tanav felt a weight land on his shoulder. He looked up to see Neera staring straight ahead. They waited together, quiet, as their own tiny fragment of the galaxy continued to churn.

Matthews turned and hobbled back down the ramp. "I'm familiar with the ship schematics and crew roster. I'll do a full assessment."

"Get in touch with Aurora Sterling and Casey Tarell. I asked them to stay in Aurora's quarters until further notice," Demi said, and despite her short stature, she suddenly loomed over everyone in the space. "Sadler, you're with me."

He moved first, and once he passed Demi, she turned as well.

For the first time since she came into engineering, Tanav noticed a lump tucked into the waist of her uniform.

Was Demi hiding a *gun*?

CHAPTER 29

NEERA

The *athkowa* was the Dywen mourning ritual, a way to honor the fallen from the pack. It called for the mourner to kneel next to the deceased with bowed head while placing hands on each side of their face. This physical action was done in conjunction with an internal calling out, a search for the pack member's presence—and when that pack member could not be detected after twelve such calls, the mourner would focus on the strongest memory between them to forever tie their bond.

Neera had done it whenever possible for the Horizon's fallen.

And he had done what he could for Macek. He told himself that he would for Hikaru and Karl as well.

Since Demi left, Matthews used the engineering display to check hardware status and station operation. But he used a different type of scan to search for body locations, a trick he said he'd picked up during active combat situations. It confirmed their fears—Ali was also dead, and her body lay in the science lab.

Neera would perform the *athkowa* for her too.

But Lynn?

He didn't have the luxury of *belief* under the Regent Empire. Yet here, he found himself reaching out, empathic senses grasping for *something*. Despite seeing her disappear. Despite feeling her presence evaporate.

Nothing. Over and over again. Nothing—no emotional connection floated on the other side, no tangible feeling to provide hope out of disaster.

Nothing. Nothing could be done for Lynn. Though Neera performed an empathic search, the *athkowa* ritual required a body to make that forever bond. With Lynn, all they could do was *remember* her.

Strangely, even though their connection via Lynn had severed, Neera still intuitively received Tanav's deep turmoil. He supposed that was how packs should work. Even with non-Dywens.

"I get it," Matthews said on his comm, to either Aurora or Casey. Neera missed which one he had spoken to first. "I'm pissed off too. Take a moment if you need it."

Matthews had been the only one to speak since Demi and Sadler left, though he'd only used comms with Aurora and Casey. Tanav withdrew, staring at a scanner that he likely did not know how to use. Neera considered finding a sheet to place over Macek's body, when Tanav finally broke. "I don't . . ." Tanav said, his words coming slow as if he waited for breath to form before he might be able to express himself. "I can't . . . a spy? She was a spy? I've known her for years. But we just got . . ." He glanced down at the blinking *OFFLINE* message on the adjacent display. "We got close only in the past year. I just wonder if she was using me."

The gradual revelation of Tanav's relationship with Lynn marked a surprising turn over recent weeks, and Neera hadn't asked her about it—mostly because the intense complexity of those types of human relationships still failed to make sense to him compared to Dywen pack units. Right after Demi discovered it, she told him, "They'll talk to us about it when they're ready," and then . . .

To use a human phrase, all hell broke loose.

For now, Neera tried his best to convert feelings into words, a map of cause and effect laying out in his mind. "Your relationship with Lynn began when?"

Tanav cracked a smile. "It was just one night, a few months before we escaped the well. The night the Hallidar imploded next to us. Listening to archival music and wondering if we would be next. There's this historic band she loves called Rilo Kiley." Tanav caught himself, a shadow falling across his expression. "Loved, I suppose. She wanted to play me their entire catalog. We put on these songs about longing and hopelessness. It fit, you know? One minute we're talking about the lyrics, and the next minute it just kind of happened. I remember it so specifically. It was a song called 'Silver Lining.' She said I was that to her, and I didn't know what it meant. I still don't know, honestly. We don't have that term."

Neera watched as Tanav's demeanor gradually lifted, the power of release through the spoken word.

"Our time together wasn't supposed to mean anything. We just needed it then. Because our situation was horrifying if you stopped to look at it. I think we both felt like, if the engine didn't work, if the gravity well imploded, if the Horizon itself imploded, we could at least exist outside of all that for a little while. We kept it private, though. You know, our group had been through so much and had gotten so small, we thought it might feel weird to someone. But something changed after the jump." Tanav's face turned upward, his gaze locked to a very benign, very blank bit of wall paneling in the engine room. "A few weeks after we landed here, we were talking about the miracle of making it out of the well. She said she knew she could never be Thaddea or the home that I miss. She got that. And she said that despite that, maybe *we* could be something new and different. Not better or worse. Just different, like we were in that moment. No gravity well. No Thaddea. No Lexin Industries. Only us, right there. It took a while to accept that." His shoulders fell. "Now I just keep wondering if it was a game, a way for her to get intel."

The most obvious, simplest point of deduction appeared in Neera's engineer brain, a reality of math that Tanav somehow missed in his grief. Perhaps that realization was a victim of the suddenness of events, and Neera took it upon himself to make the connection that Tanav's emotions missed. "Truth can exist in several different ways at once. The Withdrawal Movement is a political movement that called to Lynn. At the same time, her feelings for you were clearly natural. All evidence leads to that conclusion."

"You think so?" Tanav asked. "Is that what your pack . . . thing . . . tells you?"

"A simpler explanation exists. Lieutenant was Lynn's rank, and communications officer was her role." Neera pointed at his rank bars on his uniform. "Lynn did not need you to provide intel to the WM. Your rank was too low to be of importance."

An unexpected laugh came from Tanav, and he mirrored Neera's movement by tapping on his own rank bars. "That makes perfect sense." Matthews, of all of them, did not laugh, though he appeared to be biting down on his bottom lip. "Thanks. That makes me feel so much better."

"Is that sarcasm? It is difficult for me to detect."

"There's always a little truth in sarcasm," Tanav said. "You know, I was torn. With us going back to the well. The possibilities . . ." He turned to the wall's navigation chart, the same one that seemed to occupy Matthews. A blinking triangle showed the Horizon and a spread of dots and icons, scaled far enough back to show the eventual estimated path to the Lumersian well far beyond the Cluster's borders. "She knew I was committed to going home. But what she didn't know was that I wanted her to come with me. Regardless of Thaddea. I guess it's not an issue anymore." Tanav's last sentence came out low and dry, a crackle to his voice that told Neera that much lay underneath that glib sentiment. He chose to stay quiet, though based on what he'd intuited from Lynn, Neera felt certain she would have said yes—had things been different.

Her feelings were that strong. When Tanav was ready, Neera would tell him that.

Tanav took in a long, slow breath. "I still don't know what's worse," he finally said, his voice barely above the thrum of the diagnostic equipment. "The fact that she's gone or the fact that she betrayed us." Now his eyebrows angled, and gritted teeth formed visible lumps on his cheeks. "We just got here. How could she throw in with them so quickly? I don't even understand all of this."

Neera considered the question and thought through it with the same analysis he would use on a circuit that needed rewiring. "I suppose I did not discuss politics with anyone. The differences in perspectives were very confusing. Our constant state of survival in the well was likely the reason for this. However, in my universe, the Regent Empire eliminated any voices of dissent. Conscious dissent was not possible," Neera said. "Dissent is evidence of a functioning society. It has not had the idea of action scared out of it yet." It was strange, talking about Lynn like this. Not that long ago, they'd been caught on the outside of the Horizon together, magnetic boots clamping down for repairs as she made jokes to Demi over the comm. He pictured her now, her half-conscious face as he pulled on her tether.

Yet his mind pivoted quickly, the sheen of the white cocoon and the panic in her voice as she cried for him to help her.

"It is possible for Lynn to have pushed her empathy for those ideals into actions that we both do not understand, all while having feelings for you or being friends with me. The complexity of the individual means that many truths exist at once. She was my friend, and I trusted her." *Strange.* The word repeated over and over in his head. Perhaps not for humans, but the way that she toed the line, being close with Neera and Demi and even closer to Tanav. How did they live these separate lives? From the Dywen pack to the forceful nature of the Regent Empire, Neera's life had played out in such a straight line. Even with their time in the gravity well, everything focused on survival, resources, science, *knowledge* of the most impossible situation.

Lynn's choices only reinforced Neera's fundamental understanding of the chaotic nature of humans.

And yet, she was still his friend. He still mourned her.

Clearly, Tanav did too. While Demi put up a stoic front, he imagined that deep inside, she did as well.

"And though she chose to join something responsible for a violence that I do not agree with," Neera said, "I shall miss her."

Matthews approached, a repeating cadence of metallic clamp followed by a footstep, though instead of stopping at Tanav, he approached Neera. "Need any help with repairs?" he said, his voice with less of its usual gruff edge. "I still got two good arms and a working head."

Neera angled at Tanav, the glow from the engineering console now casting an orange hue across his brown cheeks. "There are tasks where you may be of assistance if you wish, at least until the others return."

"One way or another, these systems need repairing," Tanav said. "How can I help?"

Matthews tilted his chin up at that, though Tanav didn't respond. Something existed between the two of them, though what exactly that was, Neera couldn't tell.

Strange. More of that strangeness, that balance between two different states of mind.

Neera started to respond when a high-pitched squeal came from a side engineering console, a frequency piercing enough that both Tanav and Matthews winced. Neera understood what it meant, and he quickly stepped over and began tapping at the screen. One look confirmed the two parts of his hunch:

First, Demi must have output the Lumersian translation matrix over to engineering. Second, they'd just received a new transmission.

The display changed to a combination of audio waveforms and

text as it processed the incoming data. The words filled in gradually, and while coherent sentences would likely take time to sort out previously unknown language elements, a phrase came through. Tanav gasped, Matthews squinted, and Neera considered *why* that specificity would be in the translation matrix.

Then he realized it: part of the translation matrix was based on Chuck's logs. And Chuck considered Tanav Lexin a friend. Chuck *knew* his history.

"A spacecraft from Lexin Industries."

CHAPTER 30

DEMI

Weeks ago, Demi wondered how Colin Sadler had the time and energy to know so *much* about the photonic engine, the synth generator, and their journey out of the gravity well—all while helping the war effort on the front lines. His answers, his data, they seemed *miraculous*. And while it was authentic and verified on a scientific level by Neera, Demi let her desperation for success overlook one very obvious point.

The miracle was not in the numbers. The miracle was in the fact that a support engineer dealing with the daily impacts of brutal conflict could somehow calculate those numbers.

Sadler's hiding something.

Matthews whispered that to her when he pulled her aside. Not a word about how he awoke drugged or how a member of the Horizon was a spy or the fact that the WM invaded the ship. Of all the commander's concerns, he led with that—and only that.

Before they'd jumped, Demi thanked Sadler for risking everything for a captain he'd never met, a species he didn't know. "I think the photonic engine is the future," he'd said. That took on a completely different weight now. And now that they were alone together, she intended to find out what lay underneath his bold claim.

"My guess is," Demi said, breaking the silence, "that teleportation tech is not something left over from your high school science fair."

Sadler's laugh bounced off the hallway walls, a casual friendliness to it that seemed both charming and off-putting given the situation.

"Not exactly." Several seconds passed between them before he picked up on Demi's cue. "I've been studying the intricacies of photonic science since the Horizon returned. Its potential and the applications are boundless. Photons and matter and energy working interchangeably. Consider that. If only the powers that be would let *us* use it. Wouldn't you agree?"

"Is that why you're here? The pursuit of science?" Demi gestured at the Horizon's hallway. "The 'potential' of this ship?"

"I don't see why it matters. The bottom line is that this tech saved us. We were in an extreme circumstance. I chose to use it." Sadler paused, and Demi let him wait this out, a forceful steering of the conversation. "You sound doubtful."

Demi looked at the contradictions in front of her. Neera trusted him, but did he really know him? They'd collaborated for months, but that didn't necessarily mean that Sadler underwent proper vetting.

Sadler's hiding something.

"Who are you?" Demi asked. "We're in life-and-death circumstances. Halfway to a photonic gravity well, outside of Cluster communications range. In that room, I know my crew. I may not like Matthews, but I know people like him. I don't know you, though."

Sadler raised an eyebrow. "Are you curious about my parents, my brother, our family cats? You didn't have an issue trusting me when you wanted to steal the Horizon."

Valid, almost enough reason to *not* say anything more. Still, Sadler could use his device on any of them, at any time, for any reason.

"No one got teleported into space back then. When you no longer have the power to turn any of us into a Popsicle, I'll stop asking for transparency."

"Fair enough." Sadler nodded as he reached behind him. Demi heard something unlatch, then his hands came up quick. She remained still, bracing herself not to flinch at his sudden gesture—one hand empty, but the teleportation control in the other.

"Do you want to inspect this up close?"

Strapped to Demi's back belt sat a small energy pistol, a safeguard she'd grabbed on the way. She felt its weight there, the way the metal dug into the small of her back. Did Sadler know it was there? The only time he might have possibly seen was when he passed her on the way out of the engine room.

"I wouldn't know what to do with it," she said, waving her hand.

"How about this?" Sadler reached into his back pocket and held out another cuff. "Watch this." She took it, though she didn't put it on yet. Instead, she watched as Sadler tapped on his own to bring status lights to life. The control device in his other hand beeped in sync, and he pointed down the hallway. "Precision targeting. I'm just going right down there." Before Demi could respond, the lights on his cuff shifted to a blinking blue, then a cocoon of white light enveloped him, and while her eyes adjusted to the sudden intense flash, the same thing brought him back by the doors. "You see?" Sadler called out as he walked back. "It doesn't have to leave people floating in space. Wanna give it a try?"

He made it look simple, benign. Perhaps one day this technology would be. But right now, hedging her bets felt much smarter.

"I'm good for now. But you can tell me why the GCF funds that project yet doesn't want the Horizon's engine running."

"Ah. The bureaucrat concerns. Captain, you outrank me, but that's classified."

That word was *not* what she expected. Classified did not always mean justified. Ark Getru proved that. Matthews suspected him quickly; Demi kicked herself for being too blind to match the commander's insight. "Not good enough, Lieutenant."

"What *is* good enough?" Sadler's tone shifted, picking up a flat seriousness that wasn't there before, "I am committed to making the photonic engine work. Does that meet your standard? I thought you were trying to keep the war out of the Horizon."

Several dots connected rapidly for Demi. She *should* have inspected the module—in fact, she should have opened it up. Because if she had, she was certain she knew what powered such a device.

It needed photonic energy. That was the throughline with all of this. Demi now understood why he felt it was limitless.

Sadler had found a way to weaponize photonic energy.

But how? And who was he loyal to?

Matthews was here at the behest of Command. He wanted to put the photonic engine in storage and bring the Horizon to the war. But who pulled Sadler's strings?

"No, Lieutenant. It doesn't meet my standards. I need more. You have unknown, untested, undocumented technology that I haven't heard about. Commander Matthews clearly hasn't heard about it. So, if you get some sort of reprimand for divulging classified material, you can blame me." The urge to smirk pulsed through her body, and Demi made a calculated choice to let it through and see how he might react. "I'm already in enough hot water." What she left unsaid was that that inevitability created a freedom to face Sadler head-on.

"I'm telling you," he said in a teasing tone, "it's classified. As in a 'I could tell you but then I'd have to kill you' kind of way." The playfulness remained, but a much sharper edge crept in, and in doing so, another epiphany came to Demi.

During her years at the academy, rumors swirled of a black ops team known as Oversight—whether that was an official name or a nickname, no one knew. They were a punch line within the fleet, often a joking threat: "Oversight will come for you if you don't pass your final exam" or "Watch out for any Oversight stowaways before you leave spacedock."

No single piece of evidence ever proved their existence.

Until now. Who else could drive this type of research?

Demi kept her eyes trained on him while speaking into her comm link. She didn't have Grant with her, but someone else came with that level of expertise.

And in this moment, Demi chose to trust him.

"Transmission: Kim to Matthews."

Matthews's voice cut into the hallway. "I'm listening, Captain."

"Commander, I am standing in the hallway just beyond the deck four elevator with Commander Sadler. Mark the time. One or both of us will be back in shortly."

Several seconds passed, yet Demi didn't check for a stable connection. She knew that Matthews would be interpreting what that meant. "I get you, Captain. Matthews out."

"Lieutenant, I need to know what that tech is and why it's on my ship," Demi said, resisting the urge to blink as she stared Sadler in the face. "That has nothing to do with fixing the engine."

Demi had her own suspicions, but she wanted *him* to say that his interest in the Lumersions was not magnanimous.

"That is where you're wrong, Captain." Sadler ran his free hand over the layer of dark scruff on his chin. "It does have everything to do with the engine. We've been trying to crack safe teleportation for years. But we only had a breakthrough when the Horizon returned. The photonic effect, the way matter pulls into the photonic dimension and uses it as a conduit—on a small, localized scale, you don't need convergence points. You just need the right way to connect the physical and the photonic. Like a drip of water through cracks in a wall."

"Oversight wants to exploit this for their own purposes." There. She named it. And he didn't even react.

"It's a tool. Just like starships are a tool. The conflict between the Cluster and the Withdrawal Movement will end at some point. And what you don't know, what none of you know," Sadler said, gesturing in a wide circle, "is that there are threats far beyond some guerrilla groups who are mad about FTL fuel. We need all the tools we can get. This tool"—he tapped the cuff—"got me undetected to the WM ship, handled their remaining crew, and back here so I could safeguard the Horizon. It's useful and it's powerful."

Demi considered reaching for the pistol right now and taking Sadler out. She *could* get away with this—if she was fast enough.

Right when she considered that, the elevator behind her chimed and opened. Sadler turned and looked.

Demi took a step back to create some space between them.

Out stepped Aurora and Casey, every line and angle on their faces heavier and harsher than before. Matthews must have talked to them, but Demi wasn't sure what they knew. Sadler nodded in acknowledgment at them, and Demi considered all the different scenarios here.

If what he said about the WM ship was true, Sadler had the tech to take them all out now, and quite easily. So he wasn't an immediate threat. Matthews, as angry as he might be, seemed to be on her side. She just owed him one massive apology later.

Casey stared forward. Aurora looked at the floor. Neither of them probably knew the scope of what had happened just yet.

They were stranded. Sadler was capable of fixing the photonic engine. They also had an empty WM ship with experimental FTL tech.

She couldn't let her focus drift from Sadler here. But she released just enough to address the incoming pair. "Neera and Tanav are in engineering. They could use your help while we finish debriefing."

Both walked right past her.

Facing the loss of command caused Demi to panic. Facing Lynn's betrayal caused her to be furious—and facing the death of so many crew members burrowed grief deep into that fury. And the reactions from Casey and Aurora, they showed that conflicts aboard the Horizon continued to fester.

One time in the well, right after the Crystal Dreams imploded, Demi and Grant stood alone in the observation lounge, staring at the floating remains of the massive cruise ship. Grant turned to her and asked, "Can I be honest for a second?" Demi nodded and Grant followed with, "I don't know how the hell we're getting out of this one."

Followed by a headshake and a laugh. To which she'd said, "My friend, it can always be worse."

Did this count as worse? Because it definitely inched toward that. She heard Matthews's voice welcome the two into engineering before the doors shut, leaving only Demi and Sadler again.

"What do you want?" she asked. Clean and simple.

"Our goal is the same: get to the Lumersian well. Now, we have a very simple choice. That WM ship floating next to us? We've been wanting to get our hands on their drive for months. Their surgical strikes are all based on that engine. We need to get that back to Cluster space. By my estimates, it's a three- or four-week journey using that propulsion. About half that to get into communications range." He thumbed toward engineering. "I think the remaining crew should leave in that craft while I fix this ship with Neera." Sadler softened for a moment with a chuckle. "We'd talk a lot about math. He loves that."

Sadler showed he understood one of the underlying facts about GCF starships—even older ones like the Horizon basically ran themselves if they just had to go from point A to point B. Autopilot, continuous self-diagnostics, and balanced power systems all operated smoothly as long as someone watched over the whole thing for emergencies and instructions.

This was no longer a discussion. Sadler turned it into a hostage negotiation, with his demands being the ship and Neera. "No." Demi shook her head right away. "I'm not leaving Neera."

"All right. Fair enough. *You* and Neera remain. The rest go."

Sadler had his teleportation tech and he had knowledge to fix the engine, both of which he weaponized to take the Horizon by quiet force. Demi took this sliver of a moment to reach behind her, and her fingers just wrapped around the pistol's grip when Sadler spoke up. "I wouldn't do that. At least"—he tapped the module in his hand, and its holographic display switched—"not until you consider this."

Instead of power metrics, the silhouettes of six figures showed—five human and one distinctly not.

And above those figures, the words *Targets Locked* hovered.

"I'll be honest with you, Captain. This thing can only teleport one person at a time. I've calibrated it to the exact biometrics of everyone on this ship, but it can only do so much. When you lock onto multiples like this, it does a calculation by proximity. You'd be first. Then whoever's standing closest to the door. And so on. One by one, teleporting a hundred feet or so that way," he said, pointing outward. "You can try the cuff now if you want, but it won't help you much if the destination is somewhere in space."

Despite that, Demi still pulled the pistol out and aimed it squarely at Sadler's head, its power cell coming to life with a low hum. "You're bluffing. You need us."

"No, I need Neera. And I'll use you to establish communications with the Lumersians. The others need to go. Either they leave on the other ship—and deliver that WM tech—or they get sent out into space." Sadler angled the module, his thumb hovering over a flashing green button on its top side. "Your call."

Demi considered her options. The photonic engine, the synth generator, both needed time. In the Horizon's hangar bay, Sadler's light freighter. The WM craft floated, connected via docking tube and waited to be taken. Beyond that, a photonic convergence point, part of the way to the gravity well.

"I said it before, we want the same thing. This *conflict* between us, all these threats? That's on you. So," he said, "are we working together or are people dying?"

Demi did not want to let him win. Part of her *refused*. After everything they'd been through, to have the Horizon and her crew pulled into Sadler's purpose.

It really pissed her off.

But it came down to the crew. It always did. She'd lost too many.

"We all have choices to make," Demi finally said. "Unless the engine is repaired, none of it really matters. Now, those people are confused, hurt, mourning. Aurora also knows the engine too. Here is my offer to you—we give them some time to grieve while they assist in engine repairs. I won't say a thing to anyone. To protect them."

"You're not in a position to bargain." Sadler looked back at the doors to engineering. "But I'm not evil. I'm not malicious. Those are reasonable asks. If anything happens, if anyone slips, they go into space. No second chances. It's really easy to make things look like an accident. And when the engine is ready, your time is over, and they get off this ship. Either they set off or I take care of them myself. You understand?"

Time. She'd bought them time. To repair the engine. To find a way around this. And if possible, repair any fractures among the crew while they mourned the dead.

That last part was just for her.

"Agreed." Demi's thumb flicked the side power switch on the pistol, and its hum evaporated into nothing. "I appreciate you not killing me, Lieutenant."

Demi took one step back, and whether intentional or not, Sadler mirrored the action. "Likewise. Now," he said, "shall we go fix the engine? Clock's ticking."

They worked as a team to sweep through the Horizon for bodies before bringing them down to the med bay, where the back wall panel slid open for an emergency morgue. Later, Demi planned to lead a proper send-off for each of them. "Ali always thought she would die in the well. Even when we were just sitting in Cluster space," Demi said, arms folded in front of the morgue. "She didn't leave specifics. But she wouldn't want to go back. We will leave her here, on the edge of Cluster space. And far from the well."

Hikaru's last will recorded his desire to use the standard coffin launched into space—appropriate for a lifelong pilot like him. Diaz hadn't filled that out, leaving him with that same standard plan. Karl requested cremation, with his remains brought to his son in the colonies.

Macek, though, asked for something unique: to be cremated and blended with photonic energy and left in space. Demi wasn't sure if it was even feasible, but Neera insisted he could make it work. "I *will* make it work," he said, and then described how he would spend his off-hours looking for a smaller containment unit that could double as an urn.

As for Lynn, Demi wasn't sure. There was no body, but the hurt ran deep and refused to let go. They'd responded to many different catastrophes in the well, but "beloved turncoat" wasn't one of them.

Her mind shifted so many times in the past hours, and while she still felt the weight of those deaths—most of those caused by *loyalty* of all things—she still had pressing matters to attend to.

Matthews didn't participate in the sweep for dead crew members. He probably wanted to, but given his injury, he stayed in the med bay for different reasons. Demi found him down there still, post-injury IV to help with blood loss.

She brought him something else, though. "I thought you could use this," she said, carrying a tray from the cafeteria. He set it on his lap and stared at the chicken club sandwich made from a combination of synthetically generated meat and stored produce. "I imagine your body is craving real food after getting IV calories."

Matthews tapped the bruise from his previous IV insertion. "Thanks for not letting me starve to death while drugged."

"It was never my intent to do you harm. You have incredibly bad timing."

"Or incredibly good timing." He stopped to take a huge bite out of the sandwich. "Given the attack on Theta Seven. I could have died if things were different."

Despite his mouth being full, Demi understood every word he said. "That is true." Her shoulders rose in a steadying breath, and she decided to offer one new piece of information for him. "Lynn knew. For what it's worth. She knew the attack was imminent. She convinced the WM to *not* destroy the entire station."

Matthews set the sandwich down on the tray and glared at her. "That makes it okay? Is that enough for you to forgive her? She could have warned our security team. She could have done more." Demi saw the truth in what he said, but also the fallacy. *Everyone* could have done something different, something more, an endless ripple effect of which bad decision tipped into other bad decisions. "If you'd let me do my job, we would have all gone to Theta Seven. Lynn would have been interrogated. Hopefully apprehended. She'd be *alive*. How many people died because of your decision?"

"The WM would have gotten the engine. How many civilians would have died because of that?"

"You don't know that," he said in a louder voice. "Security ships arrived right away."

"Okay, then let's play this out." She stayed calm, steady against his rising temper. "The WM ships arrive. Lynn has convinced them to back off. They want the engine. Security ships interfere. They fight back. This escalates and then they destroy Theta Seven to get the Horizon." She gave him a half shrug and said, "Just as plausible."

"You're saying you did the right thing?" His scoff filled the med bay. "Things turned out better this way?"

"I did the right thing for the Lumersians." Saying their name grounded her resolve. In the end, it was what mattered. "That's the only part I know to be true. Everything else? It's theoretical. It's philosophical. It doesn't change anything."

"I'm—" He stopped himself. "I really think you deserve every single bit of my rage right now. But I am going to not do it. Because there are bigger things than us yelling at each other. So we're at a stalemate then."

"Yes we are." Demi pointed at the tray in his lap. "Even though I brought you a sandwich."

That caught Matthews off guard enough to break his momentum. He paused, rubbing his face and blowing air into his palms, a noise that evolved into a low, quick laugh. "You know what? You drugged me. You stole this ship. You will face consequences for that." His hands swept down, and he looked directly at her. "But there's one thing I need to own. In that meeting with Krishna and the war council . . . I brought up the photonic being strategically. It was over the line, but that was on purpose. This ship is important. Rattling you could have influenced their decision. It's not something I personally believe."

The photonic being.

Many, many responses flew through Demi's mind. But within all the chaos of recent days, one thing that lurked, a quick, almost incidental singular moment that centered her. Even now, it remained the thing she held on to.

Chuck spoke. Only once, but Chuck spoke.

Hearing that phrase. Hearing Chuck's voice. It was days ago, and yet everything changed since then. How it happened, why it happened, they didn't have the time or resources to solve it, but it *had* to tie into the engine, photonic jumps, and everything at play.

She understood that solving that mystery wasn't a priority, given Sadler's control over the ship and crew. But finding a way through that, *maybe* Chuck would be the prize at the end.

She sure could use one.

Demi watched as the med bay stations continued their quiet, steady monitoring. Matthews stayed focused on her but kept eating. Perhaps if she'd brought chips as well, he'd be more amenable.

"There's a reason I came here. Besides the sandwich." As if on cue, Matthews picked it up and took a bite. "Surviving in that gravity well, I learned the most important thing in uncontrolled situations is adaptability. I am adapting to circumstances." With a sword above all their necks, she needed to tread carefully. Neera's earnestness would put him at risk if she spoke to him. Tanav didn't have the military discipline. Aurora and Casey carried a bitterness that made them vulnerable. "I need your help."

Matthews swallowed his bite and eyed her up and down. Though they'd had their share of standoffs, this felt a little different. "I have," he started slowly, "adapted every day of my life. It's how we work in the colonies. Instability is a terrible way to live. But it's the only way I know. Adaptability through chaos makes me good at my job. We're in something much deeper than any animosity between us. I get that. That does not absolve you of anything. What do you need?"

"I can't say." His face tightened at that: lips thinning, eyes narrowing, jaw tensing.

Despite their rocky relationship, he'd clearly seen enough to know the seriousness of the unspoken.

"Is this," he said slowly, "regarding my suspicions earlier?"

Was Sadler monitoring things? She wouldn't put it past him—it made strategic sense and he'd had access to everything since he'd boarded. Her promise to him was one thing; how he planned to track that, exact punishment if necessary, she wasn't sure.

She needed to stay within boundaries here.

Demi dipped her head in a subtle nod. "I see," Matthews said.

"Right now, I am asking you to put our recent differences aside, use your instincts, watch closely, and follow my lead."

Seconds ticked away as Matthews absorbed the meaning of this. "Is there a timeline?"

"In a way." Demi considered all the ways to strategically speak. Sadler marked the finish line. Sadler also had the ability to *change* the finish line—and who survived long enough to make it. "Like I said, use your instincts and follow my lead."

So many parts of Matthews's face stayed static at this, but the glint in his eye changed. "I don't forgive you. And I don't think you were right at Theta Seven. You should know that," he said, squaring his shoulders. "But I will work with you. Because I would rather us get through this pissed off at each other than not get through it at all."

"All right. We understand each other." Demi took a half step to leave, but stopped to address the final unresolved matter between them. "Commander, one last thing," she said with arms crossed. "I still don't know what your interest in the Horizon is."

"Yeah, that." A thoughtful look arrived as his eyes turned up. "Given everything, I'd rather not say just yet," he said. "If you'll excuse me, I'm hungry."

That was as good as it was going to get. For now, Demi would take any victory that came her way. "Enjoy your sandwich. There's more in the mess hall."

CHAPTER 31

*

TANAV

With this latest batch of cookies, Tanav took a test bite and realized that Lynn was still right. Those extra five minutes worked wonders.

That thought orbited his mind as he brought the tray up to Demi's quarters. Despite the revelation that she was spying for the WM, Lynn's voice filtered into each of his thoughts. Even now—especially now, a day after the most recent message from the Lumersians.

Because that stranded mystery craft stuck was sent by his parents. His parents might even be on it. They would do something like that for headlines like **Moguls Search for Their Lost Musician Son on Experimental Spacecraft**. And Lynn would have laughed hard at that.

His return wouldn't have been about publicity. It would show his parents, his extended family, his relatives, everyone who constantly doubted and mocked his life choices, that all of this *meant* something. The connections between people, the art of communication, they would lead him to the Crystal Dreams. Which put him on a collision course with Demi on the Horizon. It would be the reason he survived and got home.

He wondered about Thaddea, given that several years had passed since their hallway argument. Knowing her, there were equal chances that she'd want to give things another chance or that she'd moved on, happily and healthily.

Either way, she'd appreciate his journey. She might have even liked Lynn.

What might have happened if they'd met? Now he'd never know.

One day after the massacre by the WM, they held a ceremony in the docking bay to honor their fallen. And now, one day after those ceremonies, they staged something smaller, more private, and not everyone showed up.

Plus, there was no body.

It was fitting, though. Tanav set the tray of cookies on Demi's small, empty dining table. Lynn wouldn't want décor or long speeches, just a good soundtrack.

The doors opened and everyone turned to see Aurora. "I don't know how to feel," she said as she stepped in. "Lynn put us in danger. You"—she pointed at Demi—"put us in danger. Everything complicates everything. I just want to help my family. But I can't right now." Tanav offered her a cookie, which she took with both hands and held tight. "So I'm here instead. Because I figured I would regret it more if I didn't come. Casey felt otherwise."

Neera stood up from the small corner station that held Chuck's containment unit and its translation matrix. At his feet, Indy got up as well, giving a big stretch while looking at him the entire time. "You're allowed to take a break," Tanav said, bringing over a cookie for him and a bone-shaped one for the dog.

"Ample time has not existed to process yesterday's message from the Lumersians," Neera said. "Eleven days is Sadler's estimate for getting the engine back online. If the Lumersians are transmitting a new message at each convergence point, a full understanding of each one should be established before moving forward." Neera gave Indy a pet, and his textured black eyes squinted thoughtfully. "Macek would have been a great support during this time."

The translation matrix beeped, prompting Neera to keep working. And, Tanav supposed, Sadler might call them for engineering support. Or Casey might have a change of heart. Matthews declined to come, a polite "I don't share enough history with her to warrant this" from him.

Tanav wasn't sure he could forgive Lynn, and he hadn't felt ready to ask anyone else. They'd all avoided the topic, talking more about the wake's logistics than the actual person. Though the fact that they were all here, even with cookies, probably meant enough.

Tanav took a cookie and stepped forward to face the large clear dome window, unsure of what he wanted to find there. Demi said all the bodies floated away some time ago, the ceaseless movement of an object drifting through the vacuum of space. Did he want to see her again, even in that horrific condition? Or was the absolute emptiness more comforting?

He didn't know. Maybe he'd never know.

"I'll go first." Demi inhaled, a deep breath that ultimately produced no words. Instead, she stood in the middle of the room, petting the dog, who chomped the final bits of the cookie by her side. "Goddamn it, Lynn. I don't know. You were the best. You were the worst. You were going to leave us for them. But you didn't want to hurt us." Demi squeezed her eyes shut as she spoke, and a waver snuck into her voice. "You challenged me. And while there's merit to those ideas, I can't fully forgive you for putting us in this situation. For selling us out. But I can recognize that through each of those steps, you viewed us as your friends. You wanted to keep us safe. You tried to shield us, to stand in front of us. I understand that. God, I get that." Demi's quiet laugh grew infectious, and everyone joined in, even Aurora. "We might all be dead without Lynn. So, am I mad? Yes, Lynn, I am fucking mad at you." Tanav had never seen Demi cry and had rarely seen her furious. She didn't give into tears, but her voice was laced with anger, the kind that could only be born out of love. "But I also love you and miss you, and you did not deserve to die that way."

Tanav held up a chocolate chip cookie, one that was baked exactly to her specifications. He took one bite, then another, then another, chewing the whole thing as he remembered *her*: her voice, her scent, her laugh, her list of bands that she wanted him to hear, all of the times she went off about how Jenny Lewis wrote the best lyrics.

His palm flattened against the cold glass, and his weight leaned into it.

Or rather, that structure propped him up in this moment.

"Demi," Neera said, a hesitant waver in his voice. "There is something urgent from the translation matrix despite the possibly inappropriate timing."

"That's the way it goes with us. You see," she said, "Lynn would appreciate 'possibly inappropriate timing.' Wouldn't she?"

The beeps from Neera's tablet stopped as he paused and looked up. His massive shoulders somehow seemed as fragile now as a human child's, and his voice took on the most unfamiliar tone. "She would."

Two short words from Neera. With effort.

They all nodded at Neera, who pulled up the text. The bulk of it was now complete, and as Tanav read the words, he considered the opportunities.

So many opportunities presented themselves in a short paragraph.

It wasn't just a Lexin Industries ship. His parents were indeed on board. And as for the Lumersians? They confirmed an energy tether between Tanav's universe and the gravity well.

Tanav didn't understand the science behind it. All he needed to know was that a path home really existed. His fervent hope had shifted from mere conjecture to something very, very real.

Tanav looked at the vastness of space, strangely calm at how this night dedicated to Lynn fit together with what might have been. Now he would move forward without her. But if his entire purpose for going home was to show his parents who he had become, then Lynn was absolutely part of that.

CHAPTER 32

DEMI

Ten days had passed since the WM's attempt on the Horizon. Ten days since Lynn was teleported out into space.

Ten days since Sadler held the Horizon hostage for whatever Oversight's end goal was.

She'd negotiated space for the crew to adapt, to mourn. And time for herself to figure out a strategy. Hopefully time for Matthews to gain some insight into the situation.

And now she had to make a choice.

Demi wasn't sure how Aurora and Casey would react—chances are, they'd be happy to get home. And even without Sadler, it was a much safer bet than staying here; there was a certain relief in severing them from the growing uncertainty of what lay ahead for the Horizon. They didn't want to be here in the first place, and while it took the long way around, ultimately Demi delivered.

But Tanav, he'd be unhappy with this. Possibly furious. He was already fragile without Lynn, and this would push him further. He'd likely see this decision as an act of cruelty, and there was a good chance he may never discover what really played out.

Either they set off or I take care of them myself.

Neera had wondered if the Lumersian transmissions were

recordings planted at each convergence point, like messages waiting to be played. Demi now knew that they were not. Another one has arrived about two hours ago. The translation matrix improved, as it processed without any additional tweaking—either that, or it grew a sense of humor and wanted to scare the hell out of her.

Because as bad as things had been, they were about to get much worse.

Demi squinted at the text output from the translation, reading it for the fourth or fifth time:

Our latest calculations confirmed suspicions that the well is expanding. This energy is leaking into convergence points within physical space. The well's expansion also increases its photonic density to create a gravimetric effect on matter to create compression on an atomic level. If this expansion is not stopped, this implosion will encapsulate this universe and others intersecting our dimension. The immediate return of 910047 is required.

She stared at the text on the translation matrix display.

She could have output it to engineering for Neera to see. Or she could have called him for a discussion. She weighed these, considering the ways that Sadler might respond to it, or how this information might impact decisions—by her, by Sadler, by Matthews.

The well was a threat to them. To the Cluster. To everything beyond the Cluster, to Tanav's universe and the Regent Empire in Neera's, and everything else—all of physical existence bled into implosion, courtesy of photonic science gone wrong.

Grant would have known how to handle this information, whether to parse it out or hold it for now—and if he thought Demi's instincts were wrong, he'd provide a very detailed explanation why. Without that sounding board to brainstorm, she sat on this catastrophe with only her thoughts and Indy's background snoring. Different paths played out, but the most important thing came down to this:

She needed to get to the Lumersians. And before she committed Chuck's spark to the gravity well, she needed an explanation from them on how Chuck's true voice had come back.

It still had only been that lone time, a miraculous several seconds of his voice for her to hear. Between repairs, Lynn, Sadler, and so many possibilities and choices, she'd kept it to herself.

She told herself it was to keep Neera on task, to give Tanav space to mourn, to respect how Aurora and Casey felt, given how everything unraveled. Yet during those quiet moments, when she sat facing the purple dot, she let herself wonder if he might be in there, if there might be some possible way between the Lumersian existence and the photonic dimension to forge a way back.

If there wasn't, if the Lumersians simply used his spark to seal the well and stop its expansion—the whole "saving all of existence" bit—then that was that. But until they gave her a definitive answer, she kept a tiny bit of unbottled hope, as dim and present as Chuck's spark.

For now, there were consequences to face.

The console on her desk chimed as she activated a shipwide address. "Attention, crew," she said, "with the photonic engine repairs nearing completion, we need to discuss upcoming possibilities."

Demi continued, an intentional steadiness in her voice. "We'll assemble in one hour at engineering. Kim out."

One hour. Within that span, Demi gave herself half of it to stop strategizing, stop thinking, stop *captaining*. She kicked off her boots and felt the chair beneath her, like if she just let go a little bit, she might actually sink away into it.

She had priorities—both within the ship and outside of it. But for a sliver in time, she wanted to simply be.

An hour later, Demi stood in front of the photonic engine and the synth generator, hands clasped behind her and spine straight. Though she'd often felt like her life would inevitably lead her back to the well, she realized now that such fatalism wasn't true. Ali's fears weren't true either. They had a choice. *She* had a choice with all of this, but the one area that she absolutely could not escape or dress up or ignore was how everyone else got *here*.

In the past ten days, Demi watched Sadler closely. But as far as she could see, he'd stayed strictly on technical duties, delegating orders and instructions. Aurora knuckled down, working task by task, scan by scan. As gradual progress pushed the engine to a state of readiness, her defense lowered in kind. Whether the passage of time or the growing inevitability of *something* ending, Aurora finally cracked one night after a shift and said, "It's going to be good to get back to the farm."

"I'd like to see it someday," Demi had replied, ready to take what little wins arrived. This counted as one. Especially because Casey essentially worked by herself in the science lab, talking with Neera or Aurora but never to Demi.

Matthews assisted as well, his hands-on repair experience proving helpful at areas damaged during the WM invasion. Demi kept her distance from him, a quiet understanding that they both watched but never disclosed things.

Neera stayed the most quiet. He worked, and though Demi tried to find a way through his shell, she knew that his sense of pack had shattered. Death and betrayal created shock waves, and whenever she even asked about repair progress, he simply said, "Sadler would know the answer to that question."

Tanav offered to help, but his lack of technical skills meant he spent most of his time in the mess hall attempting meals for the small crew. Perhaps the isolation gave him the space to grieve; when he spoke, he mostly talked about Lynn, each word seeming to sink in the reality of her loss and the memory of her life.

As for Chuck, he remained silent. Because of that, Demi stayed on mission.

None of the crew realized what would happen when time ran out. And Demi steeled herself for their reactions, particularly Tanav.

Now she looked at them, including Sadler, who had the tele-portation control module attached to his belt. Was it active? She couldn't see if its status lights glowed under his palm.

"Thank you for coming," Demi said, a conscious channeling of Grant Singh over the tone and cadence of her words. "We've all worked hard in recent days to get the engine and the generator back online. They're nearly operational. Lieutenant Sadler projects that it'll be one more day before we can proceed with a photonic jump.

"Because of that, I've had to make some hard decisions about next steps. My responsibility has always been to this crew—you. To that end, here are the facts: the Horizon needs to make the journey to Lumersian space. Immediately. Because"—she took in a breath and looked at Sadler—"I've received a new transmission from them, just a few hours ago." Sadler narrowed his eyes at this. "The gravity well has not only returned. It is expanding. Expanding at an alarm-ing rate, and the Lumersians believe that if it is not contained soon, it may be impossible to do so."

"What does that expansion lead to?" Matthews said, his eyes alert, clear tension in his face.

"Given enough time? The well will encompass all physical space. And because photonic space is a gateway to other universes, it may leak there as well. All of physical space, across all physical realities, stuck within this well until the gravitational forces cause implosion." Demi nodded to Neera and Tanav. "Just like the ships we saw years ago."

Everything shifted in Tanav, his eyes sharpening. "We'd better hurry."

"I've thought this through." Demi paused to give herself a frac-tion of a second to consider what she was about to commit to. Sadler held all the cards, and Demi had to accept that. He may have wanted people off the ship to reduce threats, but that did offer something in return.

Without them, Demi would have fewer people at risk.

"We have dual responsibilities here. The goal is to get to the Lumersians and repair the fissure between dimensions. All of reality is at stake." Demi looked up at the towering cylinder that made up the photonic engine. "No pressure, right?" This got a reaction from the group, and even Casey cracked a smile. "At the same time, we have the WM ship. It has their secret FTL engine. This is critical for Cluster R&D teams to examine. By understanding its capabilities, it can save lives. It can end the war faster.

"There's only so many of us to do the work. And to be honest, we don't totally know what's at the well. It might be more volatile than before. There are no guarantees of coming back." Demi paused for a moment, thinking back to her epiphany about choice.

She could have gone back to the Cluster. She didn't have to do this. Sadler gave her a way out.

The gravity well didn't pull her back. She forged a path herself.

"To accomplish this, we'll split up into two teams. Tanav, Aurora, Casey, and Commander Matthews will take the WM ship back to Cluster space. The estimate is that you'll be within communications range in one to two weeks. Neera will stay on board with Sadler to assist with final engineering issues. And I will stay to lead discussions with the Lumersians." She met Matthews's eyes for just a second with a knowing look.

Tanav, however, wasn't going to go so cleanly. "Demi . . ." he started, before clearing his throat. "*Captain*. The Lumersians well may be my chance to go home. I'd like to stay."

Demi shook her head, thinking through the different excuses she'd prepared in advance. "Matthews has a severe leg injury. The WM ship has a small medical bay with a diagnostic scanner and treatment systems. He'll need help to get through the journey. It's too important to leave to chance." Tanav shot her a look that she'd never seen, despite so many years together—a sheer disbelief written through lines and wrinkles across his face. "I'm sorry, Tanav."

"Wait. No . . . I—"

"She's right," Matthews jumped in, cutting Tanav off. "Getting that ship to Cluster scientists is an immediate priority. I'm going to need all of you."

"He doesn't need me to fly a ship! And he's not going to take medical advice from me."

"I've examined the flight systems," Matthews said. "I'm gonna need all of you. It's a complicated hardware with advanced stations. Every set of hands counts. Like the captain said, this will save lives."

Demi told herself to treat Tanav's ire as white noise. She tried, at least. But Tanav recognized the weaknesses in her defenses. A single look told her that he'd caught that.

It didn't matter. She was protecting them from the vacuum of space. Only one solution existed. "Tanav, you're going," she said with cold precision. "Captain's orders."

Her tone shocked everyone. Neera even took a step back. He must have heard far worse during his time with the Regent Empire, but in his years with Demi and informal approach, such militariness must have seemed beyond foreign.

Except Tanav didn't back down. He may have seen right through it. "I told you before—I'm not an officer."

"This is bullshit," Casey said. "He's not even from here. You're taking away the thing he's talked about for years, for what? To be a set of hands on an experimental ship?"

"If you close the well, then that might seal off my way home," Tanav said. "My parents' ship is there. There's a path. They said that in the transmission."

"I need you to listen to me right now." She'd mentally prepared for this protest. Of course he'd want to stay. She'd made a promise. Her focus shifted. She stared at Sadler as he stood quietly, hands at his side and a thin line across his lips, and new ideas popped into her head. They were all here. Could they take him down? Neera would know how to fix the final stages of the engine and the generator.

She'd considered as such when he slept, but given possible security traps with his teleportation device, it felt too risky. But right here?

Except . . . who knew what else Sadler was capable of? Oversight agents were black ops for a reason. It wasn't like they'd go through all the secrecy and advanced tech to be unprepared.

No, she had to stick to the script.

"There is nothing else I can do. You must go."

"Demi—"

"That's it, *Counselor Lexin*." She had to cut him off before this spiraled out of control, before Sadler sensed any doubt in her. "This isn't up for debate. Lieutenant Sadler, let's go over the remaining checklist for the engine. Everyone else, prepare for departure tomorrow. Dismissed."

Demi turned before anyone could speak, then moved over to the large star chart on the far wall. She pretended to be focused on map details—their current location, distance from Cluster communication range, known location of other convergence points.

But in reality, she tracked the crew's reactions from her peripheral vision.

Neera immediately went back to work. Aurora stepped forward, and Demi prepared herself when she broke off after Neera. But Tanav hesitated—first watching Demi cross the room, then opening his mouth to say something. It never came out, though, and after several seconds, Casey joined them with another gripe about how "this is bullshit."

Then Matthews hobbled behind him. "Let me tell you something, pop star," he said as they left. "I'm not such bad company." As they moved, Matthews turned and met her gaze, just long enough to show he understood.

Sadler came up alongside Demi. "Sounds like everyone's on board," he said. Demi let herself have a small sigh, one step closer to whatever fate awaited her.

CHAPTER 33

NEERA

Anticipation. Or anxiety. Weren't they the same thing? It felt that way as Neera stood next to Demi. While Sadler remained in engineering to work on the final test of the synth generator, the time had come for the rest of the crew to depart. Neera muted his tablet's alerts, setting a break of eight minutes to say farewell. He got to the observation lounge, where Tanav stayed quiet. Strangely, Demi hadn't tried to smooth things over. Aurora seemed excited to finally leave, and Casey softened in this final moment, possibly with the realization that Demi and Neera may not return from the well.

In engineering, Neera and Aurora had their own moment of quiet too. Sadler assigned them to spend the last few days fine-tuning the engine while he'd worked exclusively on the synth generator's calibrations. And that morning, she'd paused one set of final checks to remember Macek:

"He was always so happy to be scanning things, huh?" she'd asked. Then she laughed, which prompted his laughter in response. Her observation was correct, and those qualities made him an exceptional engineer. That loss made him wonder how much responsibility he bore over his death, over everyone's death, as if quantifying it could precisely define how much guilt he should feel. "This is some scary shit, isn't it?"

For that, he actually didn't reply, too focused on determining whether the question was a joke or a confession. It did, though, set off a chain reaction of thoughts, examining the different choices that ultimately led here.

What could they have changed? Did Neera make a mistake by not saying anything after Theta Seven? They had chances to go back, to abandon this plan, or at least slow down and evaluate things. Yet he had agreed to work with urgency above all else instead of saying something.

It was too late now. They were here, perhaps past the point of no return.

He didn't answer Aurora, and perhaps she didn't seek one. Instead, she hugged him. "You visit me at the farm, okay?"

And Demi, she'd stopped him in the hallway too right before this moment. "I'm sorry we're here together. But I'm very grateful it's you by my side."

Now they stood just outside the docking tube. Beyond the massive doors lay the airlock section, green status lights showing a secure connection with the Withdrawal Movement ship. Not that long ago, the docking bay serviced the ship's crew to depart for Base Theta Seven.

That was when and where Ayenew died.

Finally, Demi spoke.

"Commander Matthews. I know we've butted heads a little since you've arrived. I'd say my head still hurts a bit from it." Matthews chuckled at this, then Tanav's head tilted, and without a word, Tanav finally let the hint of a smile through. That very reaction seemed enough to pull Demi forward into a different, lighter place. "We clearly have differences of opinion about many things. But you have put yourself in danger for all of us, and for that, I am indebted. And grateful."

"We committed to trusting each other," Matthews said, hand snapping up in a salute. "I'm certain we'll both fulfill our ends of the bargain."

"I hope you're right," Demi said. She turned to Casey. "Our makeshift doctor. Casey, you don't have to tell me again that biology is different from medicine. You got us through it. And Aurora—"

Aurora interrupted her with one hand up. Then the other came up, holding several glowing hot peppers. "Last ones in this corner of the universe. If you ever want to try them," she said.

"Ramen night won't be the same without you," Demi said as she took them. "I might put them to good use. *Might*." She paused, then turned to Tanav. "Tanav . . ."

He shook his head, causing Demi to pause. "You don't have to say anything," he said before straightening up. "We're good."

"We are?" Demi's response was laced with surprise.

"We are. There are bigger things at stake here." He put his arms on Demi's shoulders, his brown eyes locked on hers. "We'll see each other again. Just be careful."

Demi failed to react, and knowing her, she'd probably prepared for every other possible statement from Tanav except this one. "I'm going to be with two engineers. You can't get more careful than that," she finally said. "There are no guarantees about how this will play out. But if we are successful, I'll find out whatever I can about getting you home."

Matthews tapped Tanav on the shoulder and motioned to the docking tube door. Some final words passed between Tanav and Demi, but Neera's attention changed as his tablet beeped, its eight-minute time-out over. He skimmed through the different status notifications—the synth containment issue still existed, but he knew this already. Sadler had instructed him to focus on the main engine, and despite Neera's instincts to review the data, he complied with Sadler, saying he'd apply the fix right before launch.

That notification was anticipated. Everything else . . .

Strange.

Pre-jump sequences had started. But why? They still had another few cycles of calibrations to finish, and it wasn't like Sadler to skip necessary steps. His engineering approach mirrored Neera's in its methodical nature.

Despite the ongoing farewell, Neera decided to speak up. "This data is unexpected," he said quickly. "An investigation is necessary."

Just like that, Demi snapped back into being herself. "Okay, sentimentality is over. Science awaits." The docking bay doors slid open, and without another word, the crew started down. The doors closed after the last of them entered, leaving only pressurized alloy in front of Demi and Neera. "They're off," Demi said, a rare solemnity in her voice. "Part of me really can't believe we're going back there. Can you?"

"I cannot judge that until we determine the status of the engine," Neera said.

"Is this a big problem?"

"Two issues are showing up on the status notifications. Synth containment stability is the first. Several other functions appear to be powering up, which is unexpected for a dry run." Neera turned to the comm link in his shoulder. "Transmission: Neera to Sadler."

No response came. They waited as the grinding mechanisms of the Horizon's docking tube collapsed into its full stowed position. From the observation lounge's large windows, the WM ship separated and tilted before its propulsion system came to life, four bright white circles igniting to push the ship away.

"Transmission," Neera said again. "Neera to Sadler." Once again, no response arrived, and Neera began tapping through his tablet for updates.

"We better get to engineering," Demi said, setting Aurora's glowing peppers on the nearest table. "I have my suspicions about what's happening."

"Do you think perhaps Sadler is injured?" Neera asked, cycling through the status charts one more time. The good news was that the engine's metrics looked on target; though that still didn't explain *why* things powered up.

"I'll explain later," Demi said as she shook her head. "Transmission: Kim to Sadler." She pushed the pace despite his taller body and longer stride. "I knew it. I shouldn't have waited."

Waited for what?

"Demi," Neera said, and though this circumstance required clear lines of communication, the natural verbose impulses failed to consolidate his racing thoughts. "Demi," he said again, trying to sum up his confusion and questions.

"You deserve a full explanation," she said. "But we need to focus first." They stepped out into the long hallway, Demi moving with a bold intention, her body tilting as if she couldn't contain it.

Except halfway through, she stopped abruptly. Demi took an open palm and tapped it against the air, a shimmer of light crackling upon impact. Neera did the same, his larger hand hitting against the same vertical plane.

It pulsed back on him with a surprising weight, like two magnets repelling each other. The same crackle of light appeared, and Neera tried it again.

A force field. Blocking their way to the elevator.

"What is this?" Demi asked under her breath. "Transmission," she said. "Kim to Sadler. What the hell are you doing?"

Neera pulled out a scanner and pointed it up to the ceiling. The scanner's display lit up with detailed numbers showing power being funneled to the emergency security field generator. "The ESF generator has been activated by someone and—"

"By someone—you mean Sadler." Demi's words now came with a clear venom. "Short version: your friend's been holding us hostage. Ever since the WM attack."

Hostage?

"I am not . . ." Neera said, and though he continued staring at the scanner's display, his mind raced through all the times he'd discussed the engine, the Horizon, his *friendship* with Sadler. "I am not understanding the meaning of this."

What was happening? Had Neera led them to all of this?

Was he the weak link?

"He offered a deal. To keep everyone safe. I took it. And now he doesn't have them"—she thumbed back at the observation lounge—"to worry about. I know this: he wants the engine online. I know his teleportation tech is based on that. It's all driven by a black ops group called Oversight." Demi glanced at Neera's scanner before smacking the force field again. "How do we override those?"

"I am . . ." Neera started, and though his pack instincts *should* have kicked in, his thoughts centered on all the ways weak links were handled in his previous life.

"Neera. Look at me. Focus. This is not the Regent Empire. This is not your fault. Sadler was going to find a way to the engine one way or another. Either through you or me or anyone else on this crew. What we need to do right now," Demi said, the force of her words sounding as if they could puncture the barrier in front of them, "is find a way through this. Understood?"

Neera had *trusted* Sadler. And hadn't Sadler been honest? His data was correct. His engineering theories were correct. He solved the decay issue, he got the engine to go.

Suddenly, Neera grasped the very human behavior that he simply hadn't seen coming. In his old life, it was obvious when situations were crafted with disingenuous purposes. In the well, their crew worked with overwhelming honesty, sometimes emotions being too visible for calm discussion. And with Lynn, their friendship remained true to the very end.

But Sadler's words did not match up with his actions, subverting all flow of decisions and communication. This changed something in Neera's mind, branching off into new examinations previously impossible, like being able to see a new color for the first time.

Neera understood so much more now, and yet he felt so much worse for it.

The scanner's display changed as he tapped on it, switching out from generator power levels to hallway schematics, a flow of data showing him the problem's initial conditions. "Power conduits are flowing through this entire area. It is possible to deactivate a certain portion of them with the right access."

"You figure that out. I'll be pacing. Pacing helps me think." With that, Demi did exactly as she claimed, a forceful walk up and down the hallway with hands on hips. Neera didn't have to see her to know what expression she would have had on her face.

Sadler locked all of the direct power controls. Which meant that Neera would need to get creative to shut down this barrier. He started to examine ways to bypass power maintenance access methods when, beyond the force field, the elevator chimed, followed by a familiar hydraulic whoosh.

"Oh, I am going to—" Demi started. But she paused, squinting down the hall, and Neera saw her face change: her mouth opened, her brow softened, and *something* caused her to inhale sharply.

Neera waited for his vision to adjust and come into focus. But he paused a few extra seconds because what he saw didn't make sense.

Tanav turned the corner and stepped into view. Wearing a plain gray shirt instead of his uniform, and with a cuff around his wrist.

And as he slowed in front of the force field's plane, he did the same thing Neera and Demi did: he slapped the air, feeling out the vertical slice creating an invisible barrier.

"Demi," he said breathlessly. "Something is very wrong. Sadler's stolen Chuck."

CHAPTER 34

TANAV

That morning, Tanav considered storming through to Demi one last time. She promised him. And she broke it. She should know that.

He almost did it.

Almost. Until he realized that it wouldn't do any good. Because in the end, she was military.

And he was not.

They both treaded toward the boundaries of that at times, but they never fully crossed it. And it served them well. Demi's training and experience got them through *everything*. And Tanav's background gave an outside perspective when she needed it the most.

This circumstance wasn't about feelings or family. Demi looked at resources, practicalities, life and death on many different fronts. She wouldn't budge.

Funny how he'd provided Demi with perspective so many times, and thinking through this offered the same to him. He was still mad, hurt, and resentful for the sudden collapse. But he understood. And that led to a quiet resignation—that he'd spend the next few weeks with awkward silences on the WM ship. At least it was big enough to claim a spot to hide out, relax, maybe even write a song or two.

It'd been a long time since he'd done that.

Lynn had, of course, suggested he try. He always said that he didn't feel inspired or didn't have the time or something like that. But recent days had taken away the very things that carried him forward: the thought of going home.

The thought of bringing Lynn.

Songwriting seemed to be the only way to consolidate those two things. He even began assembling rough lyrics in his head to capture the limbo he felt.

Then Matthews surprised him.

"Meet me at the docking tube," Matthews had said in his doorway. "0800 hours. By yourself."

Curiosity and the desire to do *something* drove Tanav to obey. And when Tanav got there, Matthews made a big show of contacting Demi and Sadler to say they were going over to the WM ship for safety checks before the afternoon flight. Matthews remained quiet as they walked, only the clink of his rifle-crutch on the docking tube's metal floor and hydraulic bursts as doors pressurized.

Once they stepped on board, his demeanor changed, a brightness coming to his eyes. "I think we're clear," he said. Matthews pulled out a scanner. "Yeah. No active transmitters. It's funny, this ship. All the records show it's called the 'Silver Lining.' I'll take it at this stage."

"I still haven't figured out what that means," Tanav said. "Other than it's an old song that Lynn liked."

"It means that something good might come out of something bad." That made no sense to Tanav, but Lynn often said that his universe's sayings didn't make sense either, so this was fair. "Whoever named it had a sense of humor about the WM. But it works for us now. They can't listen to us here."

"Who's 'they'?" A legitimate question with too many plausible answers, given the circumstances.

Three deep lines formed on Matthews's forehead as he squinted and leaned forward. "Sadler," he said quietly. Which was not what he expected. The commander glanced around, then rubbed a hand over his mouth. "Sadler's ship—we have to check it out before taking *this* ship back to Cluster space. Something stinks about him, and it's not in the ventilation system. Kim and I have come to a bit of an understanding." He angled his look, as if he could see through the docking bay doors. "Sadler's watching her, so we're being careful. I don't know what she knows. She doesn't know what I know. We've had to keep our distance."

"If he's the problem, then why not just take the ship by force?" Tanav asked. "We outnumber him."

Matthews inhaled as he looked over the Silver Lining's walls. "The GCF needs the Horizon. They also need this ship. Sadler's got some mystery tech. Not to mention your light being's in danger. And a gravity well expanding out of control. I wish a good punch could fix this, but it's much more complicated now. Let me ask you something, you really think Kim wants you off this ship?"

It was a good question. Demi's orders had jolted him at first, a betrayal of her sense of loyalty. He'd justified it in his head as her military sensibilities overtaking everything. And while that might be true, Matthews's question gave him the permission to push that just a little bit more.

Because even with all that, she still would have tried to do *something* to find a way. The fact that he didn't recognize that or question it . . .

That might have been Tanav's own fear that she didn't really care after everything they'd been through.

"It's not like her," he said. "When they talked at the engine, she was controlling the discussion. She was thinking about next steps."

"Sadler is making a play." Matthews pointed beyond the docking tube. "What do you know about him?"

"He's an engineer. He's Neera's friend," Tanav said. "His experimental tech saved us."

"I'm deeply involved with wartime discussions. Strategy, resources, weapons. No one has ever brought up teleportation tech."

Matthews's eyes narrowed. "Rumors of a black ops division have existed forever. And there's always some truth to rumors. The fact that he wants all of us off this ship? That's something. But you see, we have the advantage. We have *you*."

"Me?"

"He's watching Kim, he's working with Neera and Sterling, he knows my background. You, he treats you as just kind of there." Matthews gave a quick chuckle. "You're not military. You're not an engineer. You're not a scientist or a pilot. You're not even on the official crew roster. You're the pop star who organizes noodle night."

Several weeks ago, Matthews would have had said those things in a demeaning way. Today, though, his tone wrapped each point with optimism.

"Ramen night," Tanav said. "There's a difference."

Matthews dipped his head in acknowledgment. "There's also a difference with *you*," he said. "I spent the last few days reviewing all of Kim's notes about the crew. Your quantum signature. And *that*." He pointed to Tanav's communicator clipped to his uniform. "They're just footnotes in her debrief. She called it 'an annoying technical hiccup.' But we can do something with that.

"GCF biometric sensors can't detect you without the signal enhancer in your comm. And since Sadler doesn't see you as a threat, he's not tracking you as much as everyone else." Matthews took on a grim, serious tone with his words. "You're the only one who can break into his freighter undetected."

Breaking into any standard GCF vessel meant overriding varying levels of physical and electronic security. But Sadler's ship came with additional layers, all meticulously detailed by Matthews, who had apparently surveyed the possibilities the day prior. The only path lay so outside of common sense that Matthews swore that it wasn't even documented in any maintenance manual.

Two hours later, Tanav was in the Horizon's docking bay in civilian clothes while his uniform and its clipped comm stayed in his quarters, pinging away a false location. He crawled under the light freighter, first shuffling underneath the landing skid on his back, then using whatever pressure and handholds he found to slide himself along.

"If one of these landing skids gives out, I'm going to be completely flattened," Tanav said over the private comm in his ear.

"Don't think about it. Just look for the hatch. It's hexagon-shaped, about three feet in diameter. Center starboard underneath any carrier-class light freighter," Matthews said. "And don't damage the RSAI. That's our lifeline."

Matthews pronounced the term as *are sigh*, his shorthand for the remote secure access interface, some sort of military tech for hacking into systems. And apparently, their best chance at doing something—as long as Tanav could squish in under the ship. He angled as he could, the flashlight on his shoulder casting shadows at all sorts of angles. "I don't know which way starboard is," Tanav said, half to irk Matthews and half because it was true.

Right on cue, Matthews sighed. "This isn't a game."

"I didn't say it was." Tanav *thought* he saw it—an elevated lip on the otherwise flat middle section of the freighter. He scooted over that way, his joints aching in ways he'd never considered before. "'The execution of all things,'" he sang quietly to himself, the words coming out almost more as instinct than anything else. "'The execution of all things.'"

"What was that?"

"Nothing," Tanav said, immediately pushing away thoughts of Lynn. "Just a song. Okay, I'm here. Hexagon. About a meter in diameter. Now what?" Matthews provided detailed steps to the panel, a combination of pressing in or twisting specific regions to open up sensor-based locks. After several minutes, the hatch slid open and Tanav turned his light straight up at a maintenance duct of some kind.

"You see it?" Matthews asked. "There should be some wiring going through there."

"Um . . ." Tanav started. "Some wiring" was a bit of an understatement. All sorts of colored and glowing cables wove through the cylinder, along with several lengths of stiff composite tubing.

"That's a combination of power lines, propulsion lines, and EM waveguide. As long as the engines aren't running, you'll be fine. Climb up. That stuff is sturdy, you can use it to pull yourself up. Halfway through, there will be a gap. Pause there."

Tanav did as requested, his body contorting to the different cables and tubes that blocked the path. Sweat formed over his brow, and though Matthews claimed the shaft only ascended twelve feet, the journey upward might as well have been from a planet's surface to the upper atmosphere. His fingers felt for holds, his shoulders burned as he pulled himself up, and his heels searched for places to grip and steady himself, all until he got to the break point, where over several minutes Matthews attempted to walk Tanav step-by-step into wiring the remote secure access interface into the ship's . . . something.

The RSAI came alive, now a solid green light on its side.

"I can't believe that worked."

"RSAIs are easy to wire in. They're made for spying. Even easier when you're spying on your own side. I know exactly where this goes. Head on up," Matthews said, with an almost teacher-like pride in his voice.

Seconds later, he emerged in the near dark of the ship's cargo hold. "How did you know this was there?" he asked Matthews through groans as he pulled himself.

"I was in one of these freighters. Got shot down over a colony called Genesis Climber. All power drained. Pilot dead. Only a maintenance tech aboard. Backside was crushed, side door jammed." Tanav wiped the sweat out of his eyes and took in a deep, cooling breath. "She mentioned the prop line shaft—those are the longest energy lines in the craft. You need to access it at different points for maintenance. We didn't think it went through, but it did. You just need to know where to look." Matthews's voice changed, words coming out clipped now. "Don't take too much time in there. What do you see?"

Tanav angled the shoulder lamp with his hand and swung around slowly. "A lot of large crates. About twice my height. All the way to the top of the storage bay. They've all got blinking status lights on them."

"No signs of what they're for?"

"If you're asking me for labels and instructions," Tanav said, inspecting one up close, "you're out of luck."

"Okay. Leave them. They might have alarms. See what else is there."

"Easy for you to say." Tanav moved in tentative steps to the back of the storage bay, where a workstation sat in the corner. "You're not here breaking into someone else's—" He paused, squinting for a closer look.

Was that . . .

Sadler kept the teleportation control device closely clipped to his belt. It had a distinct pattern of status lights, though: two green across the top, one yellow on the bottom.

The same as he saw here, sitting on some sort of dock. But no cuffs or any other associated tech to go with it. "I think I found a teleportation thing."

"Thing. Define 'thing.'"

"The control device. Same type that Sadler has hooked to his belt. Looks like," he said, searching all around it, "it's plugged into a station. Probably charging." He knelt down for a closer look. "The station's wired into the ship."

"That station may be the base of the teleportation tech. Or a more powerful version. We don't know how it works, though. Leave it for now, it might be handy later." Matthews paused, and Tanav could practically see his crooked "I'm thinking" expression. "Keep searching. Scout before touching anything."

Tanav searched elsewhere, though the only other thing left was the hallway deeper into the ship. Tanav approached, though energy repelled him. "I can't get out of the storage bay, though. Force fields. Looks like the cockpit's at the end of the hall. And there's some sort of . . ." He squinted, trying to make out the details. "It's a console of some sort. Doesn't look like it belongs there. Maybe it's the only place he could wire it in."

"Hmph." The comm popped with that noise. "You know what? Grab the smaller teleportation device and get out of there. We've seen that one in action, we can work with it. Two hours 'til we leave the Horizon. It's just enough time."

Grab it? The power cable unplugged like any standard device, but beyond that, was it wired to any security or anything? Once again, Tanav felt the urge to blurt out "easy for you to say," but that already played out. Instead, he looked closer and wished he knew how to inspect for traps. "Time for what?"

"I'm thinking. I'm thinking. Sadler's clearly up to something. We need an ace in the hole." Through the comm, his words came out with a slow, even seriousness. "I got an idea."

The white that surrounded Tanav proved intense enough that he wanted to close his eyes. Except . . . he couldn't. And he couldn't move his limbs or yell, despite the feel of electricity rippling through his body. Everything jolted him forward, and while he remained still, unknown g-forces fought against the entirety of his body.

Then it suddenly stopped.

Time returned. Inhale. Exhale. The simple act of breathing. And feeling activated all the way down to his fingers and toes. Tanav patted himself up and down just to confirm: yes, it worked.

He had teleported.

The execution of all things, indeed.

Several minutes prior, he'd said goodbye to Demi and Neera, then walked onto the Silver Lining. Even before that ship's navigation had fully gone online, Matthews pulled out the teleportation device from his bag, plugged it into the nearest power portal, and scanned Tanav's biometrics into its targeting system. A holographic silhouette of Tanav appeared, and Matthews showed him the most logical, sensible, and likeliest-not-to-die landing point on the Horizon.

Demi's quarters.

Because Sadler had given her a cuff, one that she'd left on a desk in her quarters. The cuff pinged out a connection to the controller, some sort of amplification of the target signal. Or consolidation. Or whatever it did to it. Matthews tried to explain that it ideally worked with the cuff *on* a person, but from all of the basic metrics he could find, it at least brought in a general location. Tanav half suspected he made it up just to assuage his fears.

Either way, they only had one path forward. Matthews didn't bother explaining what was happening to Aurora and Casey, instead starting teleportation preparations while Tanav changed out of his GCF uniform with its augmented comm chip.

Tanav put on a tech-free shirt, walked to the corner of the Silver Lining's main cargo hold deemed closest to the Horizon, stood *extremely* still, then waited for Matthews to nod.

He arrived. About two feet away from a wall—and farther away from the cuff than he would have liked. But at least not half in the floor or with a table slicing through his midsection. Feet on ground, body in tact, private comm still in his ear.

"I made it," Tanav said. He grabbed the cuff and examined it closer. "I'm in one piece. I never want to do that again." The cuff snapped around his wrist, an ironic action given what he had just said. Still, some equipment was better than no equipment, even though he had no idea what he might use it for.

"Okay, pop star." Matthews cleared his throat. "I'm taking the Silver Lining. And I have to explain all this to Sterling and Tarell. If

I don't make it back to Cluster space, you know they didn't take it well. You're a good officer, Counselor Lexin."

"I'm not an officer."

"Yes, you are," Matthews said. "Go save the day. Good luck."

Without any more ceremony, the line clicked dead. Soon followed by a familiar confused whine from the floor next to him.

"Indy," Tanav said. "Sorry to just arrive like this. I have to—"

Something was different about Demi's quarters. It took a few seconds for Tanav to realize it, and the disorientation from the photonic teleportation still made his thoughts go a little slower than he would have liked. He blinked several times, first quickly to center his thoughts, then slowly to focus his vision because the room seemed *darker* than usual.

Chuck's containment unit wasn't there.

The translation matrix was. Along with the various cables and pieces previously connected to it—processors, interpretation output, and other stuff that Neera had set up to translate the interdimensional transponder/photonic urn.

Did Demi take him?

No, because he just saw her at the docking tube. He glanced at the clock, and by his check, only a few minutes had passed since they parted. There was no way for her to get over here, unhook Chuck, and go lug him somewhere in that span. And she wouldn't have left him in engineering or any other location.

That only led to one possible outcome:

Sadler stole Chuck.

Despite the fear rolling in his gut, maybe he had learned something from Matthews after all. Because even in the face of that, he saw the next step so clearly that he started his sprint out of the room without even saying bye to Indy, a hurried journey eventually bringing him to a hallway with Neera and Demi.

CHAPTER 35

✳

DEMI

On their trip back to Cluster space, Chuck had counted off the jumps one by one, his mechanized voice going in sequence starting from "jump one."

Except it never got to "jump thirteen."

"What's happening?" Demi asked, loading up status holograms. Chuck stood up from the first officer's chair, the servos from his mechanical legs grinding with the motion. In front of the bridge's window, a holographic viewscreen projected an image of Neera, Macek, and Aurora dashing between engineering stations.

"A stall has occurred in the engine."

"I see it," Chuck said, a data tablet in his mechanical hand chirping as updated numbers and graphs scrolled by. "The engine has initiated a connection with photonic space but can't complete the jump cycle. We are too heavy."

The entire ship shook, enough that Lynn steadied herself at the comm station as it swayed back and forth. "Heavy?" Demi asked. "What does that mean?"

Chuck's glow twinkled, a move that Demi had come to recognize as the equivalent of a human's furrowed brow. He was *thinking*.

Though the ship rattled again, and Demi stifled a scream of disbelief at how things went wrong at the very last possible moment.

"Our energy calculations were based on the Horizon's maximum capacity. Due to accumulated refugees, the ship is over capacity and the engine is stalling. This should not have been an issue, and it's possible that the energy source became extra volatile from the collapsing well. That may have impacted its efficacy. We're like," he said, "the Earth saying of 'one foot out the door.' Photonic and physical space are pulling on the Horizon." That probably wasn't the right saying for the situation. But Demi gave Chuck points for trying, and later on—*after* they survived this—she'd correct him.

Being pulled apart by opposing dimensional forces—that wasn't something GCF engineers planned for when they designed the ship. Before Demi could say anything, Chuck handed over the tablet and walked across the bridge. An alarm chime came from her chair's console, prompting a hologram of data showing fractures in the starboard hull. By the time she managed to send more to structural integrity fields, Chuck had left the bridge.

"Where are you going?" she yelled over another shake. But she knew the answer to that question—he was going to engineering, where Neera and his team kept scrambling.

But why?

"I know what the engine needs," he said.

She *should* stay on the bridge and trust Chuck and the engineering team. But something tore at her gut, a firm intuition that knew this went beyond tools and scanners.

"Keep me posted," she shouted as she started toward the exit. "Tell the science lab to shift as much power as needed to maintain structural integrity. We're keeping the Horizon together." As she moved, she spoke directly into her comm. "Transmission, Kim to Chuck." Chuck didn't answer, and after two more hails, she patched through to Neera.

Neera answered as she stepped into the elevator, another rattle hitting the ship right as she descended. "Chuck's containment unit now has cables attached to it," Neera said. He continued explaining, but those words slipped into white noise as Demi arrived. The doors to engineering opened, and another rumble tore through the ship as she met Neera and Macek on the lower level.

As for Chuck? His mech legs folded under his cubic body, like a twisted kind of kneeling. Several cables were plugged into the side of the containment unit, a thing he'd done before for maintenance.

The issue came from the cables connecting with the *intake* chamber of the photonic engine.

"Wait," she yelled, slipping between Neera and Macek to kneel in front of him. "What are you doing?"

Chuck's plane of light glowed with a brightness that forced her to squint, the pink now intensifying into a blinding white. "More stable photonic energy is needed to complete this final jump. This will get both feet out the door."

"That's not totally what it means," Demi said, desperation lacing her words. "We have other options."

"We do not. Without this, the Horizon will be pulled apart in six minutes. Either everyone dies or I die. It is a simple case of mathematics." Demi reached over toward the locking mechanism of the plugged-in cable, but Chuck's robotic hand grabbed hers—first blocking her, then interlocking their fingers. "Please don't," he said, his robotic voice laced with a softer effect. "Neera, run the sequence again."

The entire photonic engine groaned, a rattle like the extinction burst of a dying beast. "No," Demi said. "No, we're so close. This isn't how it's supposed to end for us."

The torsion of dimensional pulling shook the Horizon again, tools and tablets flying off the engine room's workbench.

"There are ninety-four beings aboard the Horizon. You are one of them. I am another. Ninety-three will survive. Ninety-three is better than zero."

"Damn it, stop with the stupid numbers, that's Neera's thing," she said, emotions breaking past her defenses to glisten her eyes. "We'll find a way. We always have. Every single time *something* happened to us, we—"

"I cannot," he said, and his plane of light flashed, a palpable heat coming from it. "I cannot stop with the 'stupid numbers.' It is how I operate. But"—a series of clicks and low thunks came from the engine—"the physical realm has taught me of *purpose* behind the numbers. Of beauty in that purpose. The only way it works is if I get you home."

"What if we stay here? It's modular. We could break apart the engine, right?" Demi asked, the questions coming out fast, and without any sense except for being *ideas* that offered a chance. "We could power it down. Dismantle it. We might even be in communications range of the Cluster—"

"Demi," he said. "I am going to get you home. Just promise me one thing." She didn't respond, her wide eyes now unable to comprehend anything in this moment, let alone speak. "When you get there, get that dog you always wanted. Like when you were a child. They sound like wonderful companions."

Chuck's robotic hand went limp. His plane flashed again, then compressed down into a piercing white that siphoned into the cable, all the way into the engine intake. He sat there, a glowing ball of energy different from the pink swirl he used to be, and a flash came. Then another flash. Then two rapid flashes.

One plus one equals two.

Chuck's brilliance melded with the rest of the energy within the intake, and within seconds, the entire system huffed and groaned. The Horizon shook again, then the whole thing shut down.

"We're in Cluster space," Macek said quietly.

Demi blinked, then blinked again. She kept blinking, trying to make sure what she saw in front of her was true.

Within the empty intake chamber floated a muted purple spark—immobile, without sparkle, without *life*.

Since then, she'd kept Chuck in her quarters, her most private confidant next to a greyhound who preferred naps. Other than the occasional maintenance for the containment unit or to interface with the translation matrix, Chuck stayed put.

Until now.

She'd lost him once. She refused to let it happen again.

Tanav sprinted through an explanation about his past few hours—and how *Matthews* of all people was the one who snuck him back on board the Horizon. How his own background as both non-military and a visitor from another universe kept him safe. How he'd experienced teleportation and lived to tell the tale.

Why Matthews really needed the Horizon. And it made sense, including his level of secrecy given the issues with spies. But then everything went to hell.

While Demi quietly nodded through each passing revelation, her body fought *everything*. Her pulse raced. Her breath quickened. Her cheeks flushed, and her entire body tensed.

She needed a *release*. Somehow.

But that wouldn't come. That couldn't come now. The fear, rage, confusion, love, hate, *panic*, they all bubbled under the surface, but she held tight to an absolute shell of calm. Her breath remained steady, her posture stayed stiff and professional, her face never revealing any of those emotions.

She couldn't let any of that out. No, her brain needed to focus on a plan.

"Neera, what can we do about these force fields?" She stepped back and squinted at the row of small generators in the ceiling panels.

"An analysis of their schematics is imminent, and it will provide some options."

"I need an assessment *now*." She gave into her impulse to pace as she thought through options. She could try raising Sadler one more time—he might answer and they could stall. Tanav had the teleportation cuff, and that *seemed* like it might give them some possibilities as well. Or perhaps Neera could hack through one of the data lines to see what Sadler was really up to. Or—

"Demi," Tanav said, "are you all right?"

"Of course," she snapped immediately. "Our first priority should be—"

"Demi," Tanav said again, his voice slow and deliberate, "are you all right?"

Her response came with reflexive speed. "I will be once we recover Chuck and stop Sadler."

"Well," he said, glancing back over his shoulder. "That's going to take a minute, so . . ." His words faded out, a glint of compassion shining in his eyes. "Someone once told me, 'You gotta slow down. Don't rush the bake. Don't jump to the next step.'"

"The bake." Tanav was correct. *Lynn* was correct. Correct enough that Demi paused and told herself to feel the ground beneath her feet, like she was in her quarters with boots kicked off. "I guess that means you forgive me for kicking you off the ship?" she finally asked.

"I mean, I figure it has something to do with this." Tanav gestured around them. "Unless you're just being a jerk."

"This was my secret plan for a private ramen night," she said, prompting a wry grin from him—and *that* provided more comfort than Demi would admit to herself. "That, and Sadler sure knows how to apply pressure." Demi tried to not ramp her thoughts back up to full speed. Nothing had conceivably happened just yet, not to Chuck or the Horizon or the engine.

"Neera?" she asked, turning to her chief engineer. He replied by holding up his scanner, its display showing various bars and lines growing and shrinking. None of it meant anything to her other than that things processed, and processing was better than doing nothing.

"There appears to be a solution, though it provides further complications." Both Tanav and Demi groaned at the last part of the statement, yet Neera seemed to miss their very *human* reactions. He stepped past Demi to open up a small panel on the side of the wall, revealing several layers of tubes and cables. "This line," he said, pointing at a cable near the top of the bundle, "can disrupt power to the ESF generators in the ceiling. A power disruption leads to the generators halting in sequence from start to finish until a redundant circuit restores that line." He tilted the scanner so the display presented clearly to Demi and Tanav, and on it, a schematic showed eight ESF generators along the length of the ceiling. Neera tapped the screen and the display changed, the green generator icons starting to gray out from left to right until they restored and switched to blue.

"That's our window to leave," Demi said as she glanced up. "How wide will it be?"

"The distance of clearance may only be half of the ESF generators at best," Neera said, matching her look before pointing at an angle to the left side of the ceiling panel. "The power switch will start with the farthest one, then in sequence."

"And how long will it be open?"

"A fraction of a second at best," Neera said. "Several variables affect the time between the primary and redundant power swap, including the current state of ship power usage, the distance—"

"All right," Demi said. "I'm taking that as there are limitations to this strategy."

"I would not recommend trying to get us both out. Redundant power will be reactivating the force field, and ill timing may lead to it cutting through a body—human or Dywen." Neera glanced up at the ceiling. "This process cannot be repeated until the system recalibrates itself to baseline. That will take an hour."

"Are you sure?" Tanav asked.

"Numbers never lie. These calculations are set without any new variables to disrupt the power."

Demi's eyes scanned the area, looking for *something* that might be a "new variable" so a force field wouldn't slice her in half. Her eyes went wide as she realized that the solution might not be part of the power systems.

It might come from a farm.

"Neera," Demi said slowly, "do you remember the last ramen night? Aurora said her family peppers were hot enough to disrupt the power lines. She said, 'Don't ask me how I know.' But if anyone would have asked her, it would have been you."

Neera's demeanor had switched from grim to curious. "I did ask. I had asked about the properties that made the peppers glow. We did an analysis. A low-level natural current runs through them, causing an exothermic chemical reaction. The heat and the glow are created by this reaction. A temporary shutdown happened when Aurora did not fully wash her hands and opened a conduit. The action pulled the power levels outside of acceptable ranges."

Even before Neera finished his sentence, Demi was sprinting over to where she'd left Aurora's glowing hot peppers in the observation lounge. She came back and handed them to the Dywen. "These will buy us more time?"

"It should increase the window of safety. Possibly up to three seconds." Neera looked closer at the peppers. "Possibly."

"All right. We'll thank Aurora the next time we see her. Don't touch your eyes after handling them." That prompted a laugh from Tanav, though they all quickly returned to the seriousness of the situation. Demi moved to the tangible edge of the force field. "I'll go this time. Tanav and I will find Sadler." Her nerves came alive, a rolling momentum as plans formulated. "And Chuck." She pointed down the hallway. "You'll need to find a way to take the force field down permanently. Then go to the hangar bay and see if you can pull any information about what Sadler's doing. Find us an advantage. And remember, we don't know how or where he's listening. Even right now."

"Are you sure?" Tanav asked. "There might be—"

Demi shook her head. Was this the best choice? It made for the logical one, given Sadler's position and current status and the unknowns about his goals. And while something might have worked better, they didn't exactly have time to deliberate. Anything messing with ship's power lines and force fields deserved more of a thoughtful approach, sanity checks for holes in their logic or missed variables. But the luxury of double-checking their work, well . . .

That wasn't exactly available to them right now.

"I cannot guarantee anything," Neera said. "Casualties have occurred because of my recent decisions."

Demi understood that all too well. But sometimes, choice was a luxury. "Decisions have consequences. We can't know with every decision. But we have a responsibility to deal with the consequences." She pressed her hand on the force field, the magnetic-like pushback temporarily numbing her palm. "We have to go. Now." Her legs tensed, muscles ready to spring forward before any second-guessing might occur. "That's an order, Commander. I'm the test run. If it works for me, you find another way out. And if it kills me," Demi said with an exhale longer than she would have liked, "can one of you feed Indy dinner tonight?"

A quiet laugh came from Tanav, though Neera stayed quiet, Demi's levity in the moment probably clashing with Neera's sense of duty. He wouldn't stay irritated at her—either he'd learn to laugh at the situation or she wouldn't be around to teach him further. "You will need to move swiftly when you hear the generator shut off. That is your cue," he said. Neera spent the next few minutes poised over a console, his fingers dancing over a display of the wall's power schematic until the lines between units crossed in different patterns. He held up one glowing pepper. "A temporary overload has been prepared. Listen for the generator."

Demi shut her eyes and let herself have a flash of a thought: Grant would have really loved how ramen night saved the ship.

From above came several clicks, so close to each other that they rattled like echoes.

Demi jumped.

CHAPTER 36

NEERA

Neera watched Demi leap through the deactivated ESF. She landed with enough momentum for her feet to stumble another step forward. She paused, checking herself up and down before standing tall. She turned to Neera, who met her gaze. "Your turn. Go find out what Sadler's up to." Before he could respond, she turned and left with Tanav down the hall and toward the deck's elevator.

Leaving Neera in a dangerous place:

Alone.

No matter what he did, what technical task lay at his fingertips or fixes bubbling in his brain, Neera's thoughts moved beyond risk analysis; this was more like *blame* analysis, and the pattern repeated with relentless force.

Seven years in the Lumersian well with Demi and the Horizon should have taught him about the consequences of choice—they all made mistakes during that time. Yet none created the level of havoc caused by his own decisions with Sadler.

He owned this.

He let Sadler into the photonic engine project. That was the initial condition. He gave Sadler direct access to the Horizon's network.

He lobbied for Sadler to come aboard, to help them steal the ship. All of those were objectives. All accomplished.

The best-laid plans, indeed.

Just days ago, his mind had lit up with limitless possibilities— saving the Lumersians, breaking boundaries with the photonic engine, stabilizing synthetic photons.

Crew members had died. Macek had died. Lynn had died, in the worst way possible. Sadler was some sort of secret operative. Chuck was at risk, the Lumersians were at risk, *all of reality* was at risk, and the probability that Demi and Tanav could stop an Oversight agent with a teleportation weapon . . .

Neera needed a way out of this. He needed to escape the upstream battle in his mind and help his *pack*. His fingers stopped, his breath slowed, his feet grounded.

He began again, trying to find some way to fix what he'd created. He started by doing what his captain ordered: find a way to dig up Sadler's true motive. A few power reroute cycles bought him enough time to escape the force field. Minutes ticked away as he dashed out of the elevator bay and science lab toward the front of the Horizon.

Until something else stopped him. This time in the form of large doors that protected the hangar bay. Sadler must have shut down all power to the entire section's door systems.

"Transmission," he said into his uniform's shoulder comm, "Neera to Kim."

Nothing.

Which meant either something deactivated Demi's comms or she wasn't in a position to answer. Which also meant that he owned his next decisions completely. He needed a way through. Or possibly . . .

A way around.

Neera's thoughts rolled as he moved aft, standing in the middle of the large storage hangar that also acted as a junction point.

Behind him sat the inaccessible docking bay. Ahead of him gave three options: a side hall returning to the observation lounge, two elevators to go elsewhere in the ship, or another door for the Horizon's science lab.

The observation lounge was inaccessible. Other decks might offer tools to help, but they might also be dead ends—either with disabled doors or additional ESF fields.

Neera angled his head, bringing into focus the third option. He moved forward, each step echoing against the floor, and he approached the science lab until he got close to trigger the doors' sensors.

A hydraulic *whoosh* sound came as the doors slid open to reveal a fully operational space.

The science lab acted as a secondary engineering station when needed, with displays and controls fed by different operational stations—including communications. In most circumstances, that wouldn't prove particularly helpful. Neera recognized the key to it now—when they'd first discussed moving beyond official work on the photonic engine, Sadler secured their transmission. That must have been Oversight tech to prevent detection by the GCF. He'd sent a patch to Neera's account, a secured tunnel just between the two of them.

Sadler had used that to protect their conversations. But for someone with experience as a communications engineer for the Regent Empire?

Neera could find a way. He focused, connecting the science lab's comm station into a portal for his own account. From there, time melted away as he moved data through different paths, inverting or circumventing security until . . .

There it was.

Though Sadler's ship sat behind locked doors, Neera may as well have been inside it. Thanks to Sadler directing his ship's communications through the Horizon's network, Neera found back door after back door using Sadler's own security patch. This digital tunnel wasn't powerful enough to activate the ship or disable its functions or anything of that nature, but for now, it offered something more powerful:

Information.

And truth.

Neera scrolled through the archives, a complete history of Sadler's transmitted texts and transcriptions of conversations using this secure channel. Including his own—a stack of discussions that he skipped, the guilt inside burning deeper as each message came by.

Guilt, though, dissolved into curiosity. And panic, as everything came together.

Messages between Sadler and an Oversight supervisor named Warston. Too many messages to read; he skimmed enough and downloaded the rest as copies for later, but even that revealed an overwhelming amount of details:

Since the Horizon returned to Cluster space, Oversight had taken a keen interest in the possibilities of photonic tech. Sadler's primary task was to learn everything about the engine. In the early days of generating synth from matter-based energy, Neera had thought that Sadler's suggestions came from enthusiasm about this new type of science. There may have been some truth in that, but also Sadler had a team of fifteen Oversight scientists building prototypes and running experiments in parallel to his operations, everything from failed attempts at replicating the engine to the synth generation project to smaller-scale experiments in photonic energy. This included experimental long-range communication, using the photonic dimension to carry digital communications to standard transceivers, even all the way out here.

And one more project: teleportation.

All of this bypassed GCF Command, with Warston dealing with the admirals and vice admirals and government officials as they moaned about war resources. And when people like Matthews pushed for the Horizon to be recalled to the front line?

Warston ordered Sadler to get involved.

Someone in Oversight brass thought the Horizon and its mash-up of tech gave them an advantage against something only identified as Threat Z. The messages showed an argument about whether Threat Z was a greater issue than the gradually expanding well. Ironically, Sadler proved a measured weighing of evidence of both, but it didn't matter—Warston identified a successful photonic engine as a priority, with its fallout being a new range of technology that could also stomp out the WM.

Then they would focus the next phase of their operations—though Neera couldn't find those details. In the latest messages, Sadler detailed the unexpected damage from the WM boarding party, along with pessimistic estimates of repairing the synth generator.

His final message: *An alternative power source is needed to get the engine online.*

In recent days, Sadler insisted that he focus on the synth generator. "You're needed on the engine's final checks. Let me handle this."

Neera's instincts told him something was off. He'd spent much more hands-on time over recent months with the generator, and yet he deferred to Sadler's direction.

He now understood: his instinct was right and deferring to Sadler was wrong.

Neera should have trusted himself.

"Transmission," Neera said as he took in the information, "Neera to Kim." He looked around, half expecting some sort of trap or security to come after him. He remembered to choose his words very carefully. "I have procured relevant data."

The Colin Sadler who was his friend, fellow scientist, and fellow engineering enthusiast wouldn't have done that. But the Colin Sadler in these messages, *that* person was more than capable of such things.

Again, Demi didn't answer. He tried not to worry. Multiple reasons could cause his hail to be ignored.

Neera had fulfilled his orders. He'd learned the how and why behind Sadler. Now, with Demi and Tanav still as unknowns and Matthews on his way back to Cluster space, Neera looked at the range of
consoles within the science lab.

The Neera of the Regent Empire would see everything in front
of him as technology to be harnessed within guidelines and parameters. But as he considered the circumstances, synthesized the waves
of guilt and anger and commitment pushing inside of him, he made
a decision.

Six science consoles, three lab stations, and a workbench. Those
were not just pieces of technology.

No, Neera now saw them for what they truly were, for how Demi
would see them:

Possibilities.

CHAPTER 37

TANAV

As they stepped out of the elevator, Demi signaled him to pause. She put a hand out, waving it in front of her, scanning around, from the closed double doors in front of them to the hallway's walls to the far side of the deck lined with empty crew quarters.

It took several seconds, but Tanav soon understood Demi's deliberative movements—they led to smart questions. Like why weren't other force fields set up? Why weren't any drones or other automated security in their path?

Why was it so easy?

If the answers stumped Demi, she didn't give it away. She pushed onward, and they quietly arrived at the entrance for engineering. Neera had hailed moments earlier, which Demi waved away. If there was a time to return the call, they had a moment—but Demi didn't do that.

"Could he be expecting us?" Tanav asked.

"Might have even baked pie. Trying to outdo your recipe." Demi turned his way. "Just keep an eye out for things, all right? Let me do the talking." A hum activated, its tone quickly going from low to high, and Tanav looked down to see her handing him a pistol. "Take this just in case. I trust you. Though try not to shoot me, please."

A weapon. Next steps would really need careful consideration from here on out. "I'm not the best with these things."

"You don't need to be," Demi said. "Just get a lucky shot."

With that, she stepped to trigger the doors' sensors, and the doors slid open to a surprisingly calm view: the Horizon's FTL engine, the photonic engine now repaired and online, and the synthetic generator.

And in the middle, Colin Sadler with tools in hand.

In front of Sadler, though, sat eight containment units, all tied together into one long snake of glowing photonic energy. Except for the front one. That one lay mostly dark, except for a glowing purple spark in the middle of it, like the head of the snake.

Tanav caught Demi's gasp as she recognized Chuck, though she quickly straightened up and smothered her feelings. They stepped in, footsteps announcing their presence. Sadler didn't move, though. He didn't even react. Instead, he continued tapping away at the various displays in front of him while moving around the setup, the glowing pink of the synth casting shadows in many directions. Demi took a measured step with a hand out, only for a flash of energy to strike her palm.

A force field.

"If you're expecting some sort of grand speech, you got the wrong type of Oversight agent," Sadler said. "I like math. I'm more of a 'calculate the time I need to finish' type of guy."

"That explains the barrier. You mind telling me why you're doing this?" Demi asked. She moved back and forth across the small entranceway, and while the limited space prevented her usual wide pacing, it probably let her at least gauge different angles to Sadler's specific actions. "I'm failing to see why you're separating us. We both want the engine working. We both know that it's critical to deliver Chuck to the Lumersians. Other than the GCF divisions we work for, we're really on the same side. Kind of makes your dramatic setup a little silly."

Sadler squinted at Tanav. "Guess you didn't leave? Your captain and I had an agreement about that."

"I hid," Tanav said. "You didn't look."

Sadler tapped at a tablet. "You kept your word otherwise," he said to Demi. "Appreciate it. A B-plus grade." He turned back to the hardware, moving from station to station—with occasional stops at the hovering workbench where Chuck remained.

Tanav squinted at Chuck's containment unit; no data holograms hovered, no abnormal status lights blinked, and Chuck's spark came with the same hue it always had. Beyond that, a screen with ship status showed something that *was* abnormal—various systems were offline, including weapons.

That probably wasn't because of Neera.

"I see you," Demi said again. "You're trying to do this all on your own. There are two stations there. The engine and the synth generator. Neera always had a second set of hands. Aurora, Macek, Lynn, me, whoever was available. You worked with him, you know this." She stood at the center of the invisible wall between them. "Let me help you. Drop this force field. We'll do it together."

"You're right. We're both trying to get this engine to jump. We both want to go *there*," Sadler said in a surprisingly contrite tone. Tanav narrowed his eyes, suspicious. Given how he held the advantage over everything, that shift exposed a possibility.

Tanav kept his hands behind his back, the pistol primed in his hand. If Sadler *did* drop the force field, should he shoot him right away? Demi stayed trained on the Oversight operative, no signal one way or another to Tanav.

"Good, we agree. So, people who agree shouldn't be separated by force fields. That's not how collaboration works." Now she looked up at the ceiling, probably to assess the generators embedded in the panels above them. She gave Tanav a sharp look, then nodded again above—a gesture he took as her request for doing the same.

Shoot a series of ESF generators in the ceiling? What would

happen if he missed? Was there a right spot or wrong spot to blast? And would it completely shut down the field?

Tanav figured that doing so would *not* set off a catastrophic chain reaction, despite his own misgivings. Demi wouldn't hint at it otherwise. So the biggest issue would probably be missing and making Sadler mad.

Sadler paused in his actions, hunched shoulders rising and falling in breaths. Finally, he faced them, hands on hips and a sour look across his lips.

"I can't fix the synth generator."

That caught Demi by surprise, enough that she took a step back and fired another glance at Tanav. Tanav certainly wasn't expecting it either. Was Sadler lying?

Demi must have considered the same thing. "What proof do you have of that?" she asked. "Neera would have caught that."

Sadler grabbed the last of the synth containment units and hit the unit's repulsors, causing it to lift several inches off the ground. "Neera never saw it. I had him work on the engine once we restored generator activity." Several cables detached with clicks, allowing him to push it close enough that the energy's sheen cast a hue over all of them.

"Look at the readings," he said, tapping on the unit's small display.

"Photonic density is down to fifty-two percent," Demi said, leaning close enough that the faintest of glows showed up in the force field's response.

"Same issue Neera was having before with synth efficiency. Except this time, it's not the engine's environment causing the decay. It's the generator itself. It took a blast from the WM. There's only so much I can do." His hand rubbed over the dark stubble on his cheeks. "Believe me, I've tried."

"Bring Neera in. There's gotta be something you two can do together," Demi said, her tone taking on a strategic lightness. "We'll find a way. Look, if all of this was a misunderstanding, a lack of trust, that's something we can build." Both of her hands went up. "We've clearly got off on the wrong foot—"

"I plan to get the engine working. I absolutely do." Sadler pushed the synth unit back toward his workspace and quickly followed it, like he was doing simple maintenance on a shuttle rather than using experimental technology that tapped into another dimension. "I realized shortly after I started repairs that I need an alternative power source. I don't think the WM meant to cause this. But they did."

"'An alternative power source' . . ." Demi said, her voice trailing off. She looked at Tanav again, and though she snuck another glance above at the force-field generators, one raised eyebrow was enough to tell him to hold off. "Except," Demi said. "If the Horizon was truly stranded, why send the WM ship away? That could have taken all of us back to the Cluster?" Sadler returned the synth units into place, forming them in a straight line parallel to the generator and the engine itself, a runway of pink glowing with cables connecting each of them. "Unless you sabotaged the ship."

Tanav stayed as quiet and still as possible. If Matthews was right and Sadler *did* overlook him, then remaining inconspicuous gave him the best advantage for whatever opportunity might lie ahead.

Sadler's voice came between the various clicks and pops of his handiwork. "I'm still very aware of the Cluster's needs. They need that for the war. *This* is so much bigger than the war. I don't think any of you realize this."

"Transmission," Demi said, activating her communicator. "Kim to Neera."

"Demi." Neera's voice came through loud enough that it caused Sadler to turn for a moment.

"Sadler is doing something here. He's got eight containment units of synth all wired up together. They're all tied to the engine's intake. And he says that he needs—"

"An alternative power source," they said in unison.

Strange that Neera knew that. Dywen empathic abilities couldn't have detected that, could they?

"I am asking," Demi said, projecting her voice loud enough to make her intentions clear, "Lieutenant Sadler to stand down and let us help. So we can work together. We want to get this online."

"That is not an advisable course of action based on what I believe the alternative power source to be," Neera said.

Lynn would have been able to decipher Neera's twisty language, but Tanav couldn't quite grasp it—other than the fact that Neera disagreed. Sadler seemed to get it, an eyebrow raised in realization.

As for Demi, she remained still for a moment, only her eyes darting back and forth in thought. Then a sharp inhale came and she pressed forward, one hand up against the force field. It sizzled with a flash, probably numbing her hand for several seconds, yet she held it up.

"Chuck."

Tanav saw Demi's reaction shift toward a panic she never revealed. That told him everything about what was at stake—but he didn't quite grasp the how or why. That didn't matter because Sadler's reaction gave it away. Click by click, he attached more cables to Chuck to go directly in line with the photonic engine's intake module.

"Sadler," she called out, with the closest Tanav had ever heard to a crack in her voice. "Colin. Don't do this."

"Captain Kim, you don't understand what's at stake. There is a big, big universe out here." He turned and stared at Demi, their eyes locking together.

"You can't put Chuck in there," Demi said. Her words quickened, the desperation wrapping them so unlike her usual controlled manner. "You can't. He needs to go to the Lumersians. They need him to close the well. You don't understand, it's expanding. All of us, across galaxies, across universes. In nine hundred forty-five years—"

"In nine hundred forty-five years, it will expand large enough to reach the Cluster. Oh I know. I've done the calculations myself." As if he were a student proving a theory to a professor, Sadler tapped the module closest to him, and a nearby wall display switched to a simulation of gravity well expansion, its reach growing larger as the projected year ticked up on a corner counter. "I get it. *They* get it. But that's not my concern. They have centuries to figure that out."

They have centuries to figure that out.

Tanav had heard that before, said often with a dismissive wave of the hand. His parents had said it at one time or another, often about complaints regarding how Lexin Industries stripped natural materials across planets into assets.

Though spoken in different contexts, the overlap between the words shook Tanav, splitting him between past and present. "This is why people join the Withdrawal Movement." He spoke slowly, choosing his words deliberately, an epiphany used as bait to slow Sadler down. "These shortsighted decisions."

Sadler continued plugging away like he didn't hear Tanav at all. "I have orders. I have a job to do." Across the status display, a spread of charts and notices all activated, bars gradually rising into ready position. "Captain, your personal feelings about the Lumersians can't get in the way. That's why you're behind a force field. Countless people in thousands of systems live in the Cluster. In all of that, only a few make the hard decisions to maintain their way of life." He paused, and for a split second, weary lines etched across his face, vanishing as quickly as they arrived. "I'm one of them."

"At what cost?" Demi asked, slamming the force field again. "You're sentencing all of reality to destruction."

"It's not just here." Tanav wasn't a scientist, but he understood what "across universes" meant. "It's my life, in my universe. Other universes—what if they don't have the technology to seal off the well? We can't make these choices for them."

Mechanisms locked into place with clicks. Status panels chirped, and the engine itself came alive with a constant thrum.

"If you have faith in science," he said as he stared at an engineering module, "then you have faith that the problem will eventually be solved."

Demi's brow angled in defiant lines, though still no signs of orders to Tanav. Tension in his arm caused a twitch, and he held the weapon still and began looking at specific feasible targets.

"You say you have a job to do. But your duty is more than just a specific task. Judgment, forethought, context. They train us to apply those things. Look at what's happening here. You have a choice," Demi said.

Tanav stood, existing almost outside of time. More activity came from the engine, clicks and rattles and thunks as mechanisms came alive, the mix of technologies straining to work together. Several chimes rang out from the engine's console. Next to it, blank displays came to life, like switches all flicking to the on position.

Adjacent to that, the wall displaying the Cluster star chart changed; instead of systems and waypoints, it scaled out before a series of jagged yellow lines mapped a course, angles breaking at specific points.

Convergence points.

On the map, more lines drew in, this time starting from the final destination of the Lumersian gravity well. It moved in blue, going from convergence point to convergence point—then it bypassed the location where they were *right now* to finally return to the initial jump point in the heart of Cluster space. Tanav counted the points on the screen, then realized that the number of synth units matched.

The ship was going to the well and then immediately home. The engine shook, enough force causing the deck plates beneath them to rattle.

"I suggest you sit down. You know how photonic jumps induce nausea," Sadler said, holding up one hand to reveal a teleportation cuff. "We're going to the well, then you're heading home."

"Tanav," Demi whispered. She put her hands behind her back, though one of them formed into the shape of a pistol. He nodded, just subtle enough for her to see, and her voice returned to normal volume. "Why's that?"

"Once we get to the well, I'm teleporting to my freighter and setting out. I've programmed an autopilot to jump back to Cluster space once my ship clears. You'll be sent back to the start of this journey"—he pointed at the star chart—"where Oversight is ready to take over the Horizon and prepare the engine."

"Prepare the engine?" Demi asked. "For what?"

"For all the photonic energy we're going to mine." Sadler tapped the cuff, then the teleportation device. A small holographic silhouette of himself appeared over it. He stopped for a moment, then focused on Tanav. "Oh, interesting."

Which got Demi to look at him as well. Their eyes connected, and he finally snapped his arm out to aim the pistol above them. He squeezed the trigger—

Or at least, his brain told his body to do that. But nothing happened. Time slowed, everything becoming completely still except for Demi's voice. "The cuff," he heard her say, right when he noticed his cuff started blinking blue. After that, electricity spidered up and down his limbs before a cocoon of white enveloped him and everything disappeared.

CHAPTER 38

DEMI

Tanav was gone.

Probably not to the depths of space, like Lynn and the other WM invaders. He had a cuff—and Sadler detected that. Sadler saw some sort of potential in that, a last-moment realization that prompted the action. Tanav became an asset in *something*, but what? And where?

Before she could derive an answer, the panels in front of Sadler beeped, and his attention shifted, now turning to . . .

Chuck's containment unit.

"Don't worry, Tanav's not dead. I borrowed him, just in case he comes in handy. Gotta think ahead." Sadler tapped the side of his temple. "You're not here to just stop the well," he said while continuing to work on the unit. "This is personal. There's something else involved. You're unflappable." He patted the metal frame of the containment unit. "Except for this."

Demi considered the possibilities in front of her. Only one remained, a path that she rarely went down in circumstances like these.

"You're right," she finally said. In return, Sadler paused, and he looked down at Chuck's spark. Perhaps despite all training and subterfuge, an actual person lay at his core after all. Demi chose to give into vulnerability. "There is something else. About him. About Chuck."

"Photonic Being Number 910047." Sadler knelt down and looked directly at the floating spark. "I've read about how you called it—*him*—Chuck." He looked over his shoulder, meeting her gaze. "Did your crew know about this 'something else'?"

"Some. I didn't want it to be a distraction." Sadler wasn't exactly a heartstrings type of guy; she chose to appeal to what she *did* know about him. "It's unexplained."

Sadler's lips pursed before he silently nodded and stood. "Okay, Captain. I'll give you one minute to state your case." He stepped away from Chuck, from the line of containment units, from the engine itself, and took a breath. "Why should I *not* activate this engine using these remains? How does this unexplained event push photonic science forward?"

A force field stayed up, and Tanav was no longer around to shoot out its generators. Time was the only thing she could claw back—for her and Neera. That commodity perhaps more valuable than anything else at this point.

"He talked," Demi said. "About two weeks ago. He said something, something only he and I would know." She swallowed hard, and beyond all the strategizing, a strange feeling fluttered in her chest, a certain catharsis formed by finally speaking these things. "It only came once. He's in there, somewhere."

"So you don't want me to load him into the engine. But," he said, "what about the Lumersians? You need him to collapse the well, right?"

"That is their working theory. But there might be another way. I need to establish communications with the Lumersians. We've only gotten bits and pieces in these transmissions. There might be some way to collapse the well while finding out what's going on with him. For you, this means a different form of photonic energy. We unlock what happened to him, then we unlock more." She leaned in, a rhythm to her words. "A gap exists between us and them, and it seems reasonable—scientific—that something valuable might be in there. Maybe," she said, her tone turning brighter, "there's a way for us to all get what we want. You want to mine the gravity well; there might be a way to tap into that while we prevent it from expanding. I want to see if Chuck's words mean something. And the Lumersians, they need stability in their dimension, they need to stop the bleed from photonic into physical. If we"—her hands emphasized each word with a shake—"if we just slow down, take a moment, we can see the possibilities."

"You know," Sadler said as his words drew out, "if things were different, I'd agree with you. But you're forgetting one thing." He stood up and his hand slammed down on the controls lining Chuck's unit. A cold, empty beep started, a mechanical drone that marched with quiet churn. "The WM—led by *your* officer—damaged the synth generator. The synth it's producing can't get the engine to fire off. The only way—the *only* way—it works is mixing the synth with a natural spark."

"GCF officers have a code of ethics," Demi said quickly. But now everything tipped, her statements becoming shouts against everything unfolding. Her hands balled into fists, and if she could punch through the force field, she would. "If you let this happen, the engine will burn up what is left of him. You could be murdering him. You could be dooming his kind, their dimension, *all* of it."

"I'm Oversight," Sadler said dryly. "Those ethics don't apply to me. And murder is the least of what I've done."

With that, Sadler hit a flashing button on the console.

"Stop!" Demi said. "Don't do—"

Her pleas came too late. The photonic engine groaned, gears churned, and new notifications flashed across the display. Demi slammed the force field, as if she hit it just right, it might disintegrate. Energy blinked in response, pins and needles across her palm, but no changes to the force field itself. She looked up, only to see Chuck's purple spark *move*—after months of perfect stasis, Chuck's only remaining piece floated from the very center of the unit toward the back, where a clear tube connected it to the engine.

The spark trickled upward to make its way farther, and as it did, light intersected it at all different angles and sides, a spectrum of bright hues dancing within her vision. Demi forced herself to watch, like her intensity might be enough to reverse everything underway. The single brilliant dot failed to respond, though, and it emerged into the intake chamber, surrounded in a sea of pink synth. For several seconds, Chuck's purple remained distinct against all of that.

Then it disappeared.

Demi fell to her knees.

She wanted to fight her emotions. To push them back, shove them down. Be a *captain*, unshakable and stoic.

She couldn't. Everything sank as the containment units drained into the engine chamber, one by one fading in intensity until they all sat half-dimmed. The Horizon shook and rattled with each progressive jump, her ability to keep *everything* at bay finally loosened. Chuck's spark represented their whole purpose. Getting the engine online, saving the Lumersians, collapsing the well. Finding a way to bring him back—or at least understand how his essence somehow continued.

All of that gone.

And from the engine itself, the tint of the energy in the chamber changed ever so slightly, the mixing of Chuck's spark with the incoming synth created . . . something. Not necessarily a color shift, but like someone turned the intensity and contrast of a display all gradually up.

How many minutes passed? Demi wasn't sure. Photonic jumps executed near instantaneously, only the mechanics of the engine requiring time. Sadler's tweaks clearly did something to make this happen, and the usual ramp-up/ramp-down times weren't needed. Or maybe Sadler just didn't care about operating within safety protocols.

Either way, the ship finally settled down after twelve successive jumps.

Nausea rolled through Demi's gut, and in front of her, Sadler held himself up, likely dealing with the same post-jump sensation. The star chart on the wall changed, the first line now completely gone. In its place, the icon for the Horizon sat blinking at the apex of the course, the blue line ready to return to Cluster space. On the corner of the display, something new:

A countdown timer appeared, starting at 00:30:00 and ticking downward. Neera's voice came over the comms again, though this time Demi answered.

"I'm here, Neera." Saying simple facts suddenly felt impossible, each breath and syllable refusing to budge despite the most intentional of forces. "We've just jumped. We're at the Lumersian well."

Sadler looked at the screen as well, glancing just long enough to confirm their destination. From his belt, he pulled out the teleportation device. Different colors on his cuff started to glow as it synced up, and he gave one final look.

"Tell Neera," he said, his voice calm, "I'm sorry for the trouble."

With that, a white cocoon enveloped him, leaving Demi alone in the engine room.

ARCHIVE OF ENCRYPTED REPORT

Colin Sadler
Oversight Operative / Galactic Cluster Fleet—Research Engineer

In conclusion, despite the many setbacks and unexpected complications, it appears this initiative's goal is within reach. Four of the
GCF officers on the Horizon (Lexin, Sterling, Tarell, Matthews) are
about to fly back to Cluster space with new WM technology. Given
the extraneous factors involved with entities beyond publicly known
threats and issues, I understand the time-sensitive nature of orders.
I will likely have to improvise some tactics once the other ship de-
parts, as damage to the synth generator is more extensive than expected and I am running out of options.

It is my understanding that most of GCF Command and Cluster governmental leadership do not know about the true potential
of photonic technology. Given the imminent potential return of the
Horizon and the start of our long-term operations, it seems very
practical to provide some cursory knowledge. Of the proposed cover
stories discussed, I recommend going with option 3. Option 1 (recruit Captain Kim to cooperate with Oversight) seems very unlikely,
though depending on how the next few hours unfold, I would keep
it as a remote possibility. Option 2 (recruit WM support) remains
unfeasible and more dangerous.

On a personal note, I should note that the Dywen refugee known
as Neera (see previous notes on unknown species from the gravity
well) is an incredible engineer and has deep knowledge of the photonic engine. Captain Kim appears to be extremely protective of
him, but I feel that he would make an excellent Oversight engineer,
with the potential to lead in the area of photonic research.

CHAPTER 39

✳

TANAV

Tanav was alive. Which was surprising. And most welcome.

When the wall of light began to encapsulate him, he figured that would be the end of things. Strange that rather than dread, resignation set in, even a sliver of peace. When he teleported into Demi's quarters, anxiety stretched out the process of emerging, all sorts of panicked thoughts telling him to check that he didn't re-form halfway through a wall or a table.

Here, things simply . . . happened.

Like before, white bled through everything he saw, *felt*, as if the energy itself soaked through his pores down to nerves and tissue. Air stood still, yet pressure threatened to crush him, sound simply disappeared.

Then it all inverted. Feeling returned, from toes to fingers to blinking eyes.

Maybe Tanav was getting used to this.

Except this time, he materialized in darkness, though not quite silence. Instead, a rhythmic electronic chirp greeted him, and as his eyes adjusted, tiny dots of glowing blue lights came into view.

The disorienting flush of the process meant that he needed a few moments to put it all together, along with the fact that he *wasn't* freezing to death in the vacuum of space. No, he'd re-formed with feet on the ground, limbs ready, a standard comfortable environment, and then it hit him:

He'd been here before. In fact, just a few hours ago, he had crawled up through the guts of a maintenance shaft—and halfway through, learned how to wire a RSAI into a secondary power line.

This was Sadler's ship. Sadler had targeted him to appear *behind* the force fields he had seen earlier; in fact, he materialized between two columns of the massive crates, the cuff's precise teleportation placing him safely—even with a small radius of clearance. Tanav waved his hand ahead, the flash and sparkle of a force field briefly illuminating the space, though it also made his hand numb for several seconds.

Whether Sadler intended to use this small space as an emergency brig or if it was just a convenient spot in his ship, Tanav didn't know. But he did appreciate the precision—he only had an arm's length around him. Even sitting down would be difficult, given the space. But priorities first: a quick tap on his feet and legs and waist ensured that yes, everything arrived in one piece.

Except, now what? Survival was great, but what played out on the Horizon? And why take *him*? Sadler clearly acted with intention and strategy. He wouldn't take Tanav as a trophy—not even as a hostage. The Lumersians weren't going to barter for him, and Sadler had already gotten what he wanted from Demi and Neera.

Tanav leaned against the storage bay's cold wall, and though he might have best used that time trying to figure out an escape plan, the quiet provided ample space to actually *stew* with his thoughts. Sort of. He probably should have reviewed previous military advice from Matthews, or any technical steps remembered from Neera about force fields. Hell, he probably should have been banging the metal walls or searching the containers on either side for some hole in the force field.

Yet he just kept thinking about Lynn. Not the questions about their future or Thaddea or journeys to other universes. Or choices to join a secessionist group.

Just her. Her attitude, her spirit, her endless baking experiments. And the way she always sang songs under her breath.

A moment like that existed several weeks ago, early morning while he made them coffee. She rolled over in bed and told him about the theory of the multiverse, that every possible decision from anyone *ever* spawned off a new and distinct universe. Somehow, that theory didn't exist in the popular culture of his universe, and no one mentioned it during their time in the well, but right then and there, Lynn did. She wondered about all of the slight variants of their situation. There must have been versions of themselves who escaped the well, maybe settling down somewhere as farmers. And another version who lived in a stable colony until they got old. Even one where they found a time machine to go back to the early 2000s to see Rilo Kiley live in concert. "2001," she'd said specifically. "To see the *Take Offs and Landings* tour. Or their reunion shows. Or maybe when Jenny Lewis played solo. Maybe the shows with the Watson Twins. That would have been an experience."

But in *this* universe, they were together. And she had been secretly informing the Withdrawal Movement while she'd said that. While he'd obsessed about how to get back home.

He thought of that now, the wisdom of hindsight presenting itself: Knowing what would happen with the WM, Lynn had wished for a different ending. Not necessarily a happily ever after.

More like a *simpler* ever after.

And some version of them in the multiverse got that.

Take Offs and Landings.

Tanav breathed, his mind flooded with images and memories and singsong voices, breaking only when the entire ship rattled. He steadied himself, then looked up to make sure that the massive crates weren't going to fall on him. A wave of nausea came, causing him to buckle over for a moment. He knew what happened. Successive jolts hit at a regular cadence, and Tanav lost count of the times the ship shook.

After that, everything stopped. The craft settled, floor plating and walls creaking to a perfect silence until a new noise arrived— a high-pitched electric buzz that grew in both volume and intensity, followed by a blinding flash.

When that went away, Sadler stood on the other side of the force field, just as they had in the Horizon's engine room. Except here, hums and chirps ramped up, the gradual din of the freighter coming to life, followed by the sound of something powering *down*.

Sadler lowered the force field—though he also pulled out a gun.

A gun—didn't Tanav have one? The last few minutes proved so dizzying that he'd forgotten about it, and as his fingers flexed to search, Sadler cocked his head.

"Oh," he said, "I added a weapons filter on the teleporter. It identifies the shape and circuitry of known weapons and scatters their particles." He held up his own pistol and then pointed it at Tanav. "Unless you're me, of course. Let's move."

They stepped from the storage bay to a hallway where a makeshift console jutted out. Just to the left sat a smaller storage room; Tanav's quick glance showed that space didn't have any consoles or systems—no tech of any kind, or storage, for that matter, though the room had a wide bench along the back. He recognized it, as every universe had one: the industrial type, the kind that led to uncomfortable naps and aching joints.

Sadler gestured to that room with purpose. Tanav stepped in, another force field activated at the doorway, leaving Tanav with nothing but hard seating and a partial view of Sadler's actions at the cockpit, if not his intentions. From the front window, he saw the shuttle lift off and exit the Horizon's long runway. And from the eerie pink glow outside, their location was clear.

They were at the final convergence point—the new gravity well.

Which, based on the color, was roughly the same as the original gravity well, though it lacked the complete and solid density of the previous well. Now its expanse appeared more like a thick nebula, gradients weaving together with a wispy cloudiness. The Lumersian transmission had talked about instability and rapid expansion, and this looked like the difference between a solid wall and a patchy, degrading one.

So, there was that.

Sadler angled the ship around slowly, the pitch and yaw on the central console tilting against a calibrated line. In front of them, the Horizon came into view, now sitting idly below them. Somewhere inside, Demi and Neera were trying to gain some control over the large craft. Sadler didn't pay attention to the Horizon. Screens came alive on his console, and if Tanav interpreted the information correctly, then the freighter's back storage door was opening.

And those crates? Those activated as well, based on the flashing diagrams on the display—eight of them, one for each crate. *Why* had they activated? The screen showed a grid that tracked metrics like *energy storage* and *engine capability*, but all sat at zero.

On the display above the window, the image flipped to a live feed broadcasting the storage bay, its wide door rolling upward and a shimmering force field keeping the pull of space from dragging everything out of there. The first crate elevated, a bottom propulsion that lifted the cube before corner thrusters pushed it through the force field and into space. It hit the glowing cloud of the well, and as it pushed deeper away from the ship, square arrays unfurled from either side of it, like historic satellites from the dawn of space exploration.

The other crates followed, one by one, and on the display grid, the drone status shifted, the words *Mining arrays active* popping up in each box.

But beneath that status, new words flashed—words that didn't make sense:

No photonic energy detected.

How could the drones not detect any photonic energy while traveling through an entire sea of it?

Sadler stared ahead with an unblinking look as he assessed everything in front of him. He groaned with a "Hmph," then tapped at buttons and icons. Nothing changed, and as he rubbed his chin, he shot a look at Tanav. Their eyes met for a moment, and Tanav considered what he could actually do in this situation.

He had no weapons—and really, he'd be useless with that anyway. But he did have a lifetime of understanding how people operated and the importance of parsing out information, asking questions, taking advantage of what was presented.

Of thinking about next steps.

"I think you got the wrong guy," Tanav started, his mind firing off ways to draw out what Sadler actually wanted—and needed. "I don't know if you realized this, but there's a reason why I'm not on the official crew roster."

Sadler punched several more keys on the screen before flipping switches on another console. "This isn't part of some elaborate scheme. You had a cuff," he said, staying completely focused on his displays. "You have a history with the Lumersians. You're a tool in my toolbox. I may or may not need you. We'll find out."

Another rumble shook the floor beneath Tanav, though this felt different from a photonic jump. It came with the groan of engines, and in the cockpit, the Horizon pulled gradually closer. In front of them, the drones moved in formation, individual status showing matching speeds and angles before they began to scatter.

Only seven months had passed since Tanav had lived in the original gravity well, yet his mind seemingly buried all these details away. Seeing everything ahead of him gradually surfaced them, like buttons pushed to activate the elements of that life. Memories, sensations, movements, the way that massive ships sat like city centers but smaller crafts crawled through it.

And even smaller crafts—shuttles, fighters, or in this case, drones—their ability to cut through the photonic web still came with some drag to their speed and turns, like trying to walk through a body of water.

Also, apparently, none of them were immune to the volatility of this new well. In front of them, a cloud swirled to life, some type of photonic energy storm bubbling until it burst out. Despite the distance, Tanav saw the storm whip outward, a ripple rushing toward them. It clipped one of the drones, causing the array to buckle and tear into the side of the cube. Bits of debris scattered in every direction, though their view got interrupted by the ripple hitting Sadler's ship, and a violent jolt caused Tanav to lose his balance enough that he had to brace himself—only for his hand to bounce and sting off the force field ahead of him.

"I'm guessing you didn't deal with that before," Sadler said.

"Only at the very end," Tanav said as he grounded himself. "When we knew we had to go."

On the grid display, one of the drone slots blanked out. In front of Sadler, the ship's largest console display switched from operational data to a large view of the local navigation map. It started with a bright circle in the middle, then gradually built out with an expanding radius, icons for the Horizon and the remaining drones sitting within textured colors representing the patches of clouds among the well. A new line appeared to map the trajectory of the lashing ripple of energy, followed by numbers calculating *something*. Sadler tapped away at his console, a frenetic energy to each action, and for the first time since they'd met, Tanav got the impression that things weren't going the way Sadler wanted—or needed.

In the middle, a new icon appeared. Text floated next to it, and while the Horizon's icon listed its ship name and registry number, this one stated *UNIDENTIFIED CRAFT*. Tanav squinted as he looked out the front window. It took him several seconds to focus against the brightness of the well, but the details eventually registered for him.

An elongated tube, all plated in shiny alloys, with propulsion units formed as large, curved brackets on the back side. In between those sat a tall spire for observation and elegance and nothing else.

A Lexin Industries cruiser.

"It's no good," Sadler said under his breath, and Tanav wondered if Neera ever heard him utter similar words when they tackled the synth generator together, or if he shielded his frustrations from someone he respected. He turned to Tanav, studying him much longer than expected. "I called you an asset before. Your experience in the well is just that. Why are my drones unable to detect photonic energy to mine?"

"Well, the problem is..." Tanav said, letting a pause draw out. "One, I'm not a scientist. Two, we didn't try mining the gravity well before."

"But you sourced energy from it. You had to." Now he stood up, arms folded and eyes glaring. "Neera oversaw the journey back to Cluster space. That energy came from *somewhere*."

"You're missing a key point." Though he certainly didn't match Sadler's intensity, Tanav tried his best to mirror that. "They *gave* us that energy. They wanted to help us."

"They gave it to you . . ." Sadler broke his gaze, nodding as he talked through his thoughts. "They gave you the energy that worked. It's not random. It's not what is just sitting here in space. Just like on Earth, how there's a difference between the combustibility of elements and natural resources." Sadler rattled off a rolling theory of ideas, and Tanav realized that Neera worked thoughts out this way too. Tanav didn't know if Sadler's friendship with Neera was authentic in any way, but they certainly *thought* similarly. Sadler finished, a fist now up against his lips as his eyes narrowed. "They know how to identify it. They know what to do with it. There must be stable pockets to mine." His hands planted on the cockpit console as he stared at the map of local space. "Sure would be nice if the Lumersians could just *tell* us where these pockets are. You've talked with them before. Maybe we should try reaching out?"

Before Tanav could answer, a bubble of white surrounded the Horizon for a flash—just like the teleportation cocoon. Bright pink energy danced over the ship, crawling up and down it before the whole thing became a single intense ball of *bright*.

With a flash, the Horizon was gone.

He put it together: teleportation, photonic jumps, all of it was the same thing, just at scale.

Despite Sadler standing next to him, Tanav was very much alone. Caught somewhere between Demi's universe and his own. Leaving the gravity well didn't feel this way, even when neighboring ships imploded and the Horizon shook. The only time he probably felt this way was that moment onstage on board the Crystal Dreams. This marked a stark contrast, a void compared to the chaos and screams of back then.

Tanav quelled the growing panic and forced himself to look at the map, now without the Horizon's icon. But his eyes tracked to the other ship, the *UNIDENTIFIED CRAFT* still planted next to it. Sadler followed his look, then his eyebrows raised. "You see that too. That's your family, right? You wanted to make it back home?" Sadler tapped on a different window to activate a scan, bringing a detailed mock-up of the ship.

The schematics detailed every curve and ridge of the vessel, to confirm his hunch. No one else in the universe—in any universe—would prioritize aesthetics as much as a Lexin craft.

"I'll level with you." Sadler sighed with arms stretched overhead, a casualness that felt more disconcerting than it should have. "The Lumersians claim to know how to open a portal to your home universe. The sooner I get what I need, the sooner I can try to make that happen. In fact, I could even hail that ship now. Your parents are on board, aren't they? We could all work together." Another rumble rolled through the ship, this time causing the ship's power systems to flash. "I heard you don't quite get along with them." Where did Sadler get that information? Sadler must have dug deep on him and likely the rest of the Horizon crew. Except, with the Horizon gone, maybe none of that mattered and all Tanav could do was consider surviving this. "How fitting that after all these years, all the grief they gave you, you could blaze in to rescue them from another universe. So if there was ever a time to help me out, it would be now. Think about that." The ripple fired away, a blend of light and dark, and this one brushed by the Lexin ship. Even from this distance, Tanav saw it tilt in distress. "Before their ship implodes."

CHAPTER 40

※

NEERA

They had spent months and months trying to get the photonic engine to work. And when it finally, finally worked, Neera only had minutes to *stop* it.

In the end, he wasn't quite fast enough, and the Horizon jumped.

Part of the solution was down to dumb luck—the docking bay was on the same deck as the science lab, and the science lab had secondary access to all ship systems. Thus, accessing the ship's operational controls typically found on consoles within engineering, well...

It took the long way around, but he was almost there. He'd established extended access to four of the seven major operational systems before the entire ship rattled.

They'd completed the journey to the Lumersian well.

Everything settled. One spare coffee mug, probably left out by Demi at some point over the past day, tilted back and forth until eventually coming to a calm rest.

As silence returned, Neera realized he'd been so focused on connecting systems and controls on the far terminal that he'd missed the complete change of view from the wall display's live external feed. It took the reflection off the smaller terminal's screen for it all to register—instead of the empty black of space leaving the screen's details clear and distinct, a pink hue tinted the display.

Neera stepped forward, focusing on the live feed.

They were *there*. Yet, looking into the swirling pink cloud, Neera finally understood what humans meant when they said they had a sinking feeling.

He understood the commitment to this mission. He knew what was involved, how the engineering would unfold, and what the goal was. He still would rather have undergone this journey to ensure a life of science. Yet seeing the endless walls of the gravity well, however, proved equally overwhelming and jarring.

The Horizon sat absolutely still within the gravity well. Propulsion would not work. FTL would not work. The logic of engineering and chain of command, that would not work here.

The gravity well looked off. As he took it in, Neera questioned whether the strangeness came from the colors detected by his compound vision and natural sensitivity to contrasting light. When his eyes adjusted, the gradations of color within the well stood out— clouds of dark and peaks of red weaving in and out of the blank brightness.

Demi's voice interrupted his observations, bringing him back to the moment. And while her words offered the ship's standard transmission protocol of sender and receiver, it was Demi's *tone* that snapped him out of his stupor. A waver, a crack—a *desperation*.

"There's a force field blocking off engineering," Demi said. He could practically see her tightened jaw muscles and furrowed brow. "You need to take it down now. We've got . . ." She paused briefly, Neera's keen hearing picking up a slight tremble. "Twenty-eight minutes."

Neera was curious about what bothered Demi, but he knew an order when he heard it. His curiosity dispersed, every action zeroing in on fixing the problems ahead in as efficient a way as possible.

He had two choices: He could go to engineering and try to take down whatever barrier Sadler erected, the same way he did with the ESFs on this deck. That carried many unknowns. With time ticking away, the smarter, better chance came from taking down ESFs on a systemic level. That meant finishing the extension of the final three engineering systems to the science lab.

"Control of engineering is being rerouted to my location," Neera said as he tapped access and override codes. The next few minutes passed with Demi staying silent while Neera gave running updates. She only spoke to announce time remaining as he worked a make-shift operations console. "System control is becoming active," he said. "I am being granted operational access of key systems. The force fields set up by Sadler are being taken down."

"I see it," Demi said. "We're through. Get down here."

Neera took off. His long legs pounded, echoing footsteps across the hall. Demi continued her countdown over comms, minute-by-minute updates as he waited for the elevator, rode it down to the engine deck, and burst through the double doors.

Awaiting him was the most unexplainable of sights: photonic energy, yes, but contained in a serial chain of units, all of them glowing at about half intensity and hooked up to the engine's intake. And *that* chamber seemed different somehow. Neera couldn't quite pinpoint it. It might have been a trick of the room's lighting or even the stress of the situation.

"A difference seems to exist with the intake chamber."

Demi spun on her heel and approached Neera. "We'll get to that later. You must stop the engine. Like, right now. Before it goes again."

He stifled the impulses to provide the detailed options that could guide a sound decision, and instead assessed what lay ahead:

Eight containment units sat in a straight line, cables chaining them together, and it seemed reasonable that they moved systemi-cally into the intake. Some sat with a low glow, and the front one was completely empty. The Horizon powered its way to the gravity well, but the state of the remaining synth showed that Sadler had a clear plan to go beyond that. Some of it still sat within the intake engine, ready to fire off.

And that first, empty one: Neera recognized the unit's additional sensors and connection ports.

He would sort out his feelings on that later.

Eleven minutes and twenty-six seconds remained.

The thing was, photonic energy didn't naturally *exist* in this space. That was the whole reason why they needed containment units. It had to go somewhere—either in specialized storage or processed by the engine to fold back into photonic space.

Turning the engine *off* before this jump completed? Stopping power flow to the whole system would cause a catastrophic failure, the kind of which Neera wasn't prepared to explore. With the containment units tied to the intake, severing the connection would create potentially disastrous volatility.

He identified two safe options.

One: He could siphon energy from the engine's intake *backward* and fill up the containment units. With that empty, the energy would be stable—safe. And nothing would happen to the engine. Problem was, it would take time—most likely, more than the time remaining on the countdown clock. Any leftover energy would process and burn off, with the risk that *that* would take the Horizon across into however many jump points necessary to finish.

Two: He could push the remaining energy forward *into* the intake chamber. That would burn things off, just like it did during diagnostic cycles, with the excess energy converted into thermal energy to dissipate into space. This was faster than the previous option. But Sadler had locked in a jump cycle, and they'd never tried a burn-off in parallel with an actual jump cycle.

And unlike the first option, such a process would consume all of their synth. They'd be stranded until they could generate more, and even then, Neera wasn't sure if he could replicate Sadler's techniques to get the engine going.

Safer, worse results. Or riskier, yet better results.

Neera lived pretty much his whole life playing it safe and achieving worse results. Now seemed like as good a time as any to break that streak.

He moved swiftly and precisely, first commencing the burn-off process, then recalibrating the intake sequence to simply *move it faster*. Several minutes passed, Neera danced from control to control, unit to unit, adjusting settings and tapping confirmations until no tasks remained.

On the engine's main console, one side ticked down to the inevitable jump. The other showed an empty bar filling up as photonic energy burned off.

"You're not doing anything," Demi said quietly as the timer flipped to four minutes remaining.

"There is nothing to be done." Neera pointed to the burn-off bar. "If this one finishes before the other one, then I believe we will remain here."

"And then we can reach out to the Lumersians." Demi's shoulders fell, like whatever kept them tense and propped up couldn't pull them anymore. "I know I can be tough. And cold. Thank you for being there for me. Ever since we met."

"This life of science has been made possible by you. I am not ready to give it up," Neera said. Such *weight* in his words, speaking with an authentic emotion so rare for his people. "Demi?"

"Yes, Neera?"

"Your trust in me is appreciated." Suddenly, Neera's fingers twitched, itching to *fix* something. Instead, he forced himself to remain still and pushed the words out. "There were several times in recent weeks when I disagreed with you. I feel you should know that."

Neera braced himself for frustration, some scolding, either in a professional capacity or a personal one. Perhaps both. Demi, however, reacted in the most unexpected way.

She laughed.

"Well," she finally said, "why didn't you say anything?"

No good answer formed in Neera's mind. Seconds ticked by, and they would soon need to track the energy burn-off. Neera decided on the most obvious truth. "I have said something now."

"You should do it more." She put a hand on his tall shoulder. "You make good decisions. They're worthy of being heard."

She had talked about such a thing before. Their circumstance necessitated both of them to make more decisions, but he realized that she spoke of something greater. He saw the role of first officer framed by position and rank. Her words here built a simpler idea:

All this time, Demi trusted him more than he trusted himself. Yet she was referencing evidence, data points that proved he could do just that.

Numbers. Everything always came down to numbers. And numbers never lied.

They waited and watched together, Demi and Neera silently awaiting the outcome of two processes involving the same mystery energy. Without it, Neera would not be in this universe. Without it, Demi might have moved on to another ship.

Without it, they never would have become friends.

This substance, an energy too raw and immaterial to naturally exist in physical space, carried the power to steal their destinies and forge another one. And now it had that chance again.

The density of the intake's pink glow shifted between dissipating and solidifying, a push-pull combination as the ship fought between leaving and staying. However, the latter seemed to be winning. The glow began withering, its complete, shiny, thick soup of bright breaking down into gradual opacity.

It was working.

Clearer and clearer, sometimes stepping back but then surging forward, the remaining energy became more and more transparent. On-screen, the numbers backed it up, the burn-off rate staying at a steady high velocity while the synth finished feeding in.

But as the timer hit the one-minute mark, Neera knew. With thirty seconds left, Demi seemed to know too.

The burn-off wouldn't finish in time.

A hand came to her mouth, an obvious resignation to what lay ahead:

They were going to jump. How many convergence points, how far away from here, that remained to be seen. Even still, a single jump put weeks away from this point via FTL—and still an impossible distance back to Cluster space.

"I'm sorry, Captain," Neera said, an intentional use of both syntax and title.

The numbers ticked down. Fifteen seconds left. Then ten.

Nine. Eight. Seven.

Neera's face dropped, taking his eyes off the numbers for a moment. It didn't matter. Whatever came next would require a solution of some sort, even with the despair gnawing away at him.

Two. One.

The photonic engine hummed to life, and Neera looked to see how much energy remained in the intake chamber. His mind immediately tried to calculate an estimate, but it didn't matter. The cycle finished, the Horizon shook, and they jumped to the first convergence point. The engine ramped up again, all hums rising in frequency and speed, but not enough remained, leading to a natural power-down sequence.

Demi and Neera stared at the impossible problem in front of them.

"When Sadler teleported away," she said slowly, "I told myself that I didn't have time to mourn Chuck. Things needed to be done. We had to stop the engine." She pointed at the nearly empty, colorless intake chamber, now only a thin haze of purple and pink remaining in it. "I guess we have time now. Time to mourn. Time to tell you what Sadler is planning. Time to tell you what the hell happened here. To Tanav." She pointed again, this time turning her finger to the empty containment unit sitting at the front of the line, the only one with additional modules lining its frame. "To Chuck."

Demi collapsed on the hard floor, hands planted out behind her. And though she bore the uniform of a GCF captain, she looked as ordinary and tired as Neera had ever seen.

Neera knelt down next to her and stared at the remaining photonic energy, a veil of color awaiting . . . something.

Except . . .

Neera's head tilted and eyes focused. His compound vision picked up details and shifts that humans couldn't detect, and he focused, making sure that this wasn't just a tint from the display's changing colors.

Because he was fairly certain that the veil of color grew stronger. More solid.

And more purple.

A purple, like Chuck's spark.

"The intake chamber was injected with Chuck's spark?"

Demi gave a quiet "mmm-hmmm" with a nod.

Organic mixed with synthetic. The very last bit of Chuck's organic body, living in the intake chamber mixed with volume after volume of synth.

So much remained a mystery about photonic energy. But now one of those mysteries appeared to be resolving itself. Neera got back on his feet, then stepped toward the intake, getting close enough that his face remained inches away. Had the chamber been full, the intensity of the glow might have proved blinding. But here, the view offered a level of detail that confirmed his hunch. It *was* growing more dense. And the color *was* changing. Not quite the pink standard photonic energy, and not the purple of Chuck's spark, but a hue in between.

Demi's human eyes must have caught it too. "That's not . . ." She moved to Neera's side. The two of them watched as this newfound energy, whatever it was, coalesced. Then it jumped, collapsing into a thin beam that moved through connected cables until emerging in the first containment unit in the chain.

Chuck's containment unit.

The beam hit the center of the unit, and soon after, the rest of it began coiling around, row after row growing until a bright square floated whole and independent within it. The corner of the unit's frame lit up with status indicators all showing full activity. When it finished, the vocabulator popped, as if it cleared its throat.

And then a voice spoke:

"One plus one equals two."

Demi had told Neera that Chuck's voice spoke before—those words, and *only* those words. Neera's mind raced, a scientific list of what might possibly trigger such an event. Energy combined with latent memory, something along those lines?

But then the voice spoke again, and this time, no doubt remained: *"Hello, Demi. I've missed you."*

The words came with the clear diction of intentional thought. Demi pulled forward at it, her weight angled ahead, like a single thread held her from breaking away.

Except no other words came.

As they stared, the plane of energy remained, but the unit's status lights went out.

CHAPTER 41

✴

DEMI

Before Neera had arrived, Demi did a very un-Demi thing, a decision that she only could make in isolation.

She pulled up a live outside feed from the ship's bow camera. Any external view would have worked, because it was everywhere:

The gravity well.

The place that had taken so much from her. Ten years of her life. So many of her crew. Where she'd lost Chuck, her career, her *innocence*, all traded for a future ruined by a war she never chose.

She only stared at the feed for ten, maybe twenty seconds. But every single pixel in the image pierced into her bones. This wasn't just the massive silent blanket of glowing pink from the years they'd forged a community out of nothing. The vision in front of her filled with deep red lashing tendrils and glowing bursts of blood clouds, just like the last few months when the well imploded ship upon ship. Even though the Horizon sat static, the chaos felt like it beckoned her back. She sat with that feeling, stewing in it, like it formed the soul and bones of who she really was, a view accessible only from the inside.

Then Neera arrived and she became Captain Demora Kim again. Now she focused, telling herself to ignore *that* voice. She repeated that to herself over and over. She could not get lost in those possibilities, not when the navigation map on the far wall showed that they'd made one photonic jump away from the Lumersian well.

"Demi," Neera said. "That—"

"I need you to get us back to the well. Immediately." She pointed to the synth generator. "Sadler said the synth wouldn't do it alone. That it lacked the density. We need to find a way to make it work."

Neera faced the synth generator. But then he turned in the opposite angle at Chuck. No, not Chuck—she wouldn't dare speak that name right now. Whatever floated within the containment unit, whatever temporarily activated the vocabulator, whatever conjured up *those words*, that wouldn't solve their current problems. Neera's whole body tremored, like he was caught between what to do, where to go.

"Get us moving." Demi spun, now with her back to Neera, the engine, the glowing plane of energy—all of it. "That's our priority."

The thrum of the synth generator wove through the space, and it barely registered that Neera didn't move. Instead, Demi fought the mounting anxiety clawing away inside her, and all she really wanted was to sit down and hug her dog *right now*.

"Demi," he said purposefully, "I need you to listen to me."

"I am disagreeing with you."

Demi caught him flexing his long fingers, stretching them out before curling them to a fist and then back again. "I should examine Chuck," he said.

The mere mention of the name sent a ripple through her entire body, and she focused on the navigation map. One jump. They were one jump away.

They still had FTL. Demi considered the distance—a rough estimate of between three or four weeks would cover the trip. Thoughts pulsed through her mind, weighing the consequences of burning off that much time versus staying at this convergence point, hoping to bring the engine online.

Several electronic chimes rang out behind her. She didn't move though, and knowing Neera, this was not a gesture done to bait or motivate her. Neera would do what he always did: gather information and present it.

Several seconds later, Neera spoke.

"This is data you should see."

Demi's eyes opened and the world snapped back into view. She balanced herself, the weight firm between her heels and her toes, and she turned to find Neera holding a tablet.

With a lot of numbers. Two of the same multidigit number, then a whole lot of different numbers.

"I hope you're not expecting me to memorize that," Demi said.

Neera was locked in. She knew that because he completely ignored the quip.

"The photonic wavelengths of that energy plane in the containment cube are listed here." He pointed to the last number on the screen, then the bottom left corner of the glowing square. "Distance from the center is how I have taken the readings." He moved up, number by number, each correspondingly getting closer from the farthest corner to the center. "The center point is this value," he said, tapping the second number on the screen.

Which was identical to the number above it.

"What's the first value?"

"The photonic wavelength of Chuck's spark is that number."

Neera really could have said anything because his *look* mattered more, his expression bypassing the captain-minded, mission-oriented defenses she *knew* she always put up.

"What does," she paused, her voice dry. She cleared her throat and tried again. "What does that mean?"

"The spark at the center of the plane is still Chuck. Yet a new type of existence seems to have formed." Neera stepped over to the synth generator and peered at its configuration module, graphs and numbers glowing in its display. "A new possibility is happening outside of expectations. As a scientist, it would be foolish to ignore"—he took a breath and looked at her—"*possibilities*."

The word sank in, more than she would normally allow herself in this moment. Neera awaited an answer, his pause a little different than usual. Rather than deference, she recognized that the emptiness was an act of caring.

"What do you suggest?" she finally asked, and she realized that her continued questioning was almost like a challenge, throwing a gauntlet to fate and testing to see if she would lose everything again.

"Every incident of Chuck's voice was precipitated by a photonic jump."

Demi considered the different moments, and while so much had happened since the first time, Neera was right. He parsed things together, his voice gaining confidence toward a conclusion.

"Different laws of physics apply to the Lumersians compared to corporeal beings such as you or I. There may be a difference in their notion of death. Deactivation may be the more appropriate definition of being. The engine used Chuck's spark, but it did not disappear completely." Neera paused as he pulled up a graph of data on his tablet. "My hypothesis has evolved: The use of Chuck's spark in combination with synth may have introduced a new variable into the Lumersian way of being. The spark, the synth, the engine's combustible environment, I am considering the different options presented by that combination.

"Something new may have been created during this process."

Demi looked at the glowing square, and her mind flashed to the sequence of frequencies Neera had just shown—and suddenly, things didn't seem as impossible as before.

"Chuck had often talked about how his life was supposed to exist for a specific function across a specific time," Demi said. "And lucky him, meeting me changed that."

"Destinies tend to be altered by meeting you," Neera said, the corners of his wide mouth angling into a grin. He peered at the silent square of glowing energy. "Something remarkable may be within our grasp if we decide to explore it."

This wasn't just hope. It made *sense*, at least with what little they understood of Lumersian existence. But enough sense that Demi's internal balance turned, her entire decision-making process tilting in ways she wouldn't have ever considered before. Finally, a logical path to overcome the impossible, yet she knew—she *knew*—the danger of the emotions tied into that.

And if she let them surface, they may never go back. Terrible things, those emotions, always getting in the way of work.

She chose a very measured question as a response, a completely noncommittal way of committing. "You have an experiment in mind?"

Neera nodded. "The result may provide a way to return the engine to full acting status."

"How much time do you need?"

Neera loaded up another set of numbers and graphs, and once more, Demi didn't bother to take in the details. "My best instinct is to project several hours for this experiment."

"And the spark," she said, purposefully leaving Chuck's name out of it. "Will mixing it with synth do anything more to it?" More questions arrived, captain instinct returning to her sensibilities. "The Lumersians still think they need it."

"No signs of deterioration from the spark at the center are presented within the wavelength data. As with other photonic energy, existence is simply its state." Neera looked down at the tablet, though he accessed further information. In fact, Demi guessed that maybe he didn't even read it. He just used the gesture to mask the fact that he was *thinking* about something.

So he did learn from her after all.

"Perhaps that span is a good time for you to recuperate and assess larger situations." Neera offered a rare gesture, his mouth curling upward in as close to a smirk as a Dywen could make. "Indy's hunger probably needs to be addressed. A reasonable reminder at this time would be that the development of the photonic engine was a joint venture between myself and Chuck. Should this work in any capacity, our goals with the engine would likely be supported."

Neera dressed up his intentions with layers of words, enough that it took a little too long for Demi to realize what he meant. "You're telling me to get the hell out and take a nap."

"And to feed your dog."

Finally—finally—Demi let herself exhale completely enough to transform her entire sense of being. "It's not easy for me to let this go."

"I know. My friend."

"Well then," she said, giving Neera one final pat on the shoulder. "Take us there."

CHAPTER 42

TANAV

In the past few hours, Tanav did as Demi would: pace back and forth. Except in his case, he only had about ten feet of space to do it. Since Tanav got locked in the room, Sadler mostly left him alone to focus on whatever he was doing with his drones. Because based on the dashboard display, they sure weren't mining—everything stayed at 0 percent of mining capacity. Sadler did, however, update the label on the navigation display from *UNIDENTIFIED CRAFT* to *Lexin Industries*.

His body language showed a visible frustration, the increasing intensity of his actions giving it away. Switches, buttons, screen icons, everything pressed or flipped or tapped harder, sometimes with sighs and grunts. He even set aside the teleportation module to grab a gun from a small locker underneath the console, like the very presence of a deadly weapon helped him channel his frustrations.

Tanav at least had an educated guess at that move. That tease about the Lexin ship, it was an attempt to draw out Tanav's own experiences in communicating with the Lumersians. But Sadler didn't want to rely on him. Relying on him created a liability, and Sadler seemed to want as little of that as possible. Tanav made the blanket assumption that all Oversight agents were kind of loner jerks in that fashion, and that probably suited them best for the job.

Finally, Sadler tried something different after so many minutes of getting nothing out of scans. He punched an unused button on the console, and the display switched to a spectrum of communications frequencies—and a status of *Communications Channel Active.*

"This is Galactic Cluster Fleet spacecraft Safe Passage. We have come to communicate with the Lumersian species on behalf of Captain Demora Kim and the starship Horizon. Please respond."

Demi wasn't going to like that part.

It didn't really matter because nothing came back. And though Sadler couldn't figure out why, Tanav knew. And it was just like his dad had told him:

"If you're ever going to make a mark in the galaxy, you need to learn to ask questions that find opportunities."

This moment might have been just that. Problem was, Tanav didn't know too many of the specifics behind communication with the Lumersians. Their first encounter needed time and technology—time for the different species to understand *how* each other communicated, and technology to act as a translator between them. Because while the Lumersians had a reasonable vocabulary of the human language by now, it didn't matter if they couldn't connect to it.

Sending hails wouldn't work. They needed a message in *their* language. And somehow, Sadler wasn't getting that.

Tanav turned to the cockpit and took in the different displays and charts—plenty of information, plenty of *data,* but none of it producing what Sadler actually wanted. Sadler's next best thing would be someone who *could* achieve that. Or at least claimed to.

This was an opportunity.

"I might be able to help."

Sadler's chair squeaked as he spun it around. His lips pursed in thin pensiveness, and for the first time, Tanav noticed lines of fatigue across the operative's face. He may have been Oversight, but even they needed sleep, or at least the comfort of results.

"You're right." Tanav stepped forward. "No matter what, there's only so much time, and there's only one way for any of us to get out of this." He tapped the force field, only for his finger to bounce off it with a shimmer of light. "Wanna drop this? We can work together."

"You really are new to this bit, aren't you?" Sadler got up, arms stretching overhead. "That's not how hostage negotiations work. I could put you anywhere I want."

"I'm a hostage? I thought we were partners." Tanav tried to line the words with humor, though his own nerves failed to fully land it, and his laugh came out as a stifled chuckle. No performer's experience could hit that properly. He slid his hands behind his back, fingers beginning to unlock the cuff's clasp.

"You're free to remove that if you want." Sadler held up the teleportation control. "I can still target you. Especially this close. I just have less precision with where you land. So, taking it off is probably only a good strategy if you want to wind up in space or merged into the floor or something."

"Actually," he said, holding both hands up, "just scratching an itch."

"Fair enough." Sadler set the teleportation control on the ship's console, then pointed at the myriad controls and displays. "So, you've decided to help?"

"I might be able to. I did live here for a while, you know."

"All right." Sadler came face-to-face, only an invisible barrier between them. "Why can't my drones lock onto any photonic energy for mining? Is there something else you're not telling me about that?"

Tanav steeled himself with a moment to pull in any technical jargon floating around his memories. Making it sound good was never more important. "I told you, they gave it to us. But"—Tanav paused, trying his best to match the tone Neera would have during an explanation—"photonic space is made up of three things— Lumersian beings, the environment they exist in, and the raw energy itself. We see it all as the same glowing cloud. From their perspective, they can see the differences between them." He stood taller now, as if that would make for more believability. "Look, I'm not a scientist. I'll admit that part. But my best guess is that you need to be able to tell those apart."

"And you can do that?"

"Neera would probably know." Tanav wasn't quite sure why his gut told him to say that. Everything told him that Sadler moved strategically, but his friendship with Neera seemed genuine, or as genuine as it could be. If nothing else, such a statement might chip away at Sadler's equilibrium. "I could, though, sing you a song about it." That crack didn't elicit a laugh, so humor wouldn't work right now. "You know one type of energy—synth. Synth was based on the energy given to us to escape the well. You know that whatever you're scanning right now isn't right. If you have any data on Chuck, that's another form. It's like, if you wanted to understand how a song was composed, you take away each track—the vocals, the drums, each instrument," he said, peeling off a finger for each. "Now, I could tell you how to do that with a song. I *can't* help you on the science part."

Sadler finally moved, first craning his neck to look out the window, then glancing down at the area map.

Then he grabbed the teleportation control.

Sadler stared at it, as if he looked hard enough, the microcosm of photonic tech in the device might unlock the secrets of the entire well. His finger flicked the side switch, igniting several confirming chimes and lights.

Tanav braced himself for the inevitable cocoon and reminded himself *not* to try jokes with secret agents who had clearly snapped and fell crooked.

Yet, instead of any flashes of light, Sadler turned and opened up an interface on the side of the cockpit console. He plugged the device in before cycling through various options on the holographic settings that popped up.

"Neera did say that before. I'd just focused so much on *our* tech that I didn't think about it," he said. "Thank you. Some of the data collected during teleportation processes may help the system identify the differences between those energy states. Let's see what this recalibration process uncovers."

Tanav tried *not* to let his relief be too obvious. And through all of it, he told himself that Sadler viewed him as an asset—something to be discarded, sure, but also something with knowledge.

"It might just be easier to *ask* the Lumersians."

Sadler's sigh filled the cockpit, though it quickly shifted as he realized that Tanav's suggestion was serious. "I've tried. They're not very talky."

Tanav realized the opening created by Sadler's fatal flaw: He really was an engineer through and through, despite his role as an operative. That made Tanav's experience and knowledge a point of barter in exchange for a deeper in. "They exist in light. That is how you have to hail them. They don't understand sound waves, at least not without translation."

"Light." Sadler's head angled at this explanation. "The records showed that they boarded the Horizon."

"That's right. Audio hails are as effective as, I don't know . . ." Tanav searched for the right analogy, *something* that had nothing to do with light. "They don't understand because it doesn't even exist in their realm." He looked out the cockpit as much as he could. "We built up a very basic understanding through the use of numbers. Once we took that first step, that was when we could upload things like dictionaries and encyclopedias, and eventually their containment suits had translation tools for them."

"You remember how to reach out to them?"

Tanav weighed how much to reveal—too much and he might give away his leverage. Not enough and he'd be deemed useless, or worse, disposable. "Neera made a system. He called it 'hexadecimal,' though that oversimplifies it a bit. It's very . . . mathy."

"I know what hexadecimal is." Sadler's fingers punched against the console before a flash of numbers came up. "So, what, do you just spell out 'hello'?"

"In a way." Sadler really didn't know. He really didn't read up on the first-contact details. All that *technology* consumed him and blinded him to the fact that two civilizations needed to overcome a language barrier. "You want to know how we established communication, let down this barrier and give me access."

"You're not exactly in a position to bargain." Sadler took a very long, very purposeful, very *unsubtle* look at the teleportation module. "Don't you think?"

"It's one thing to understand the concept. It's another to know how to actually do it. Timing is kind of a factor." Which wasn't necessarily true, though Sadler had no way to disprove that. At this point, he just had to commit to the semi-truths he said. "Or," Tanav said with a larger-than-needed sigh, "you can try one of your mining drones again. You've got, what, seven left? Go ahead, give it another shot while I take a nap."

Sadler kept staring at Tanav, a wide-eyed glare probably meant to intimidate. But the fact that he didn't just send Tanav out into space meant that things gradually moved in Tanav's favor. Without a word, Tanav turned and lay down on the uncomfortable metal bench.

About a minute passed in total silence before Tanav heard the sounds of buttons tapping. He braced himself.

Several clicks came from the doorway, followed by the fading hum of an electrical surge as the force field dropped. "All right," Sadler said. "You're up."

CHAPTER 43

·⁕·

DEMI

"Several hours" proved to be the right estimate. Two hours and thirty-eight minutes, to be precise. Demi fully acknowledged that she counted. Instead of resting, she paced. And while she sometimes paced to clear her mind, this action was designed to accelerate solutions.

Because she had failed Tanav. He'd found a way back onto the Horizon, only to get back in Sadler's clutches. There had to be *something* she could do.

Logically, she knew that everything depended on the engine, which meant it depended on what Neera could accomplish. Her brain refused to accept this, instead stewing on all the ways she'd failed people over the past weeks. So many things fell out of her control, yet ideas churned in her, like if she could come up with the most unlikely, most magical solution, she could bring everything back through her own force of will.

It wasn't that simple, though. So she continued pacing, feeling the carpeted floor beneath her bare feet as she moved back and forth, occasionally looking out the dome window long enough for dim dots to become bright stars against a canvas of black.

Despite the emptiness, the black made it feel safe to look outside. She wasn't sure if she'd able to do so when they got back to the well.

"Neera to Kim. We are ready."

The time had come. No brilliant solution came for Tanav or anything else she wanted to undo, which meant that it was all up to Neera. Demi took a moment to gather herself, tugging slowly on the seal of her officer boots, a small piece of the GCF uniform that sometimes acted as the single difference for her mind to shift between acting in an official capacity or just being Demi.

She made a conscious choice to be somewhere in between. She grabbed Indy's lead from the small end table and called the greyhound over.

"Big stretch," she said as Indy set her front paws out and leaned so hard into the move she trembled. The dog shook her whole body, her black tail whipping against the side of the wall like it didn't matter.

Demi noted Neera's surprise the instant she appeared. It wasn't everyday that a dog visited restricted areas. Indy noticed too, immediately pulling in different directions to sniff, which probably wasn't a good idea at the heart of the ship's propulsion. "FTL is not powered by kibble—" she started to say, until a new sight caught her attention.

The containment unit—*Chuck's* containment unit—was standing. Two legs flanked by two arms, though a mess of cables still tied into the frame's left and top connectors. Neera must have caught Demi's hesitation, and he stood up from the synth generator's main console.

"Restorative actions seemed prudent," he said, nodding to the mechanical limbs, "should this experiment be successful."

The FTL engine groaned and depressurized before mechanisms clicked and locked into place—a standard maintenance cycle that came every four hours for the massive propulsion system. Indy, however, had never witnessed it before, and the whole thing caused her left ear to stick straight up with curiosity at the newest of new things.

Demi supposed she marveled at that too. The idea that she

might actually have a future of some sort proved to be quite the novel concept.

As if Indy could sense the change within her, the dog stopped pulling to sniff all the strange scents about and simply leaned against Demi's thigh.

"Some thoughts have stayed with me as I have prepared this," Neera said. Next to him, the generator's console noted a status of maximum capacity. "We use synthetic chemicals and parts to heal us. The idea of synthetic photons never occurred to the Lumersians. The concept of natural photons and synthetic photons intertwining is beyond impossible from their perspective for them. Which means its outcome is unknown." Neera tapped the edge of the synth control screen. "On your order, Captain."

Demi put her hand on Indy's broad shoulder, feeling the soft fur beneath her palm. "Okay," she whispered.

In between all of the graphs and numbers on the synth's control panel, one single button flashed on the digital display, the word *EXPORT* nested within a green icon. Neera took a breath, looked at Demi and Chuck, then pressed it.

Mechanisms groaned, pieces knocked and clicked, the whole thing coming to life. The synth began draining out, the color of the generator's storage compartment gradually thinning. In return, the colors in Chuck's unit fluctuated, beams of white light weaving in and out and through the square of energy. Brilliant shades flashed and flourished, like light itself was fighting to find a way into every possible photonic orifice and crevice within the energy.

Then it all settled.

The synth generator sat empty, only a quiet ticking noise as it cooled down from its process. In Chuck's unit, all of the shimmering flattened into a single consistent plane of light—brighter than before, denser than before, and a shade more purple than before.

One by one, the status lights on the upper frame of the unit ticked on: power, processing, vocabulator, and movement control.

Neera raised a scanner, diagnostic chirps and beeps studying . . . something. Indy let out a huff, then a high-pitched whine, as if the dog picked up on something that they couldn't.

That was enough to make Demi believe.

"Chuck," she said with a tentative ripple through her voice. "Are you in there?"

Neera continued scanning, the engine room continued thrumming, and while Indy started a relaxed pant, Demi's own breath held, waiting for what was next. Even if that "next" turned out to be nothing.

Nothing would be closure.

But then Demi heard it. One very tiny, almost inaudible click. Followed by a whir, a noise just as quiet. Her chest fluttered, her stomach leapt, and all of a sudden . . .

She *knew*.

Those sounds came from the directional servos of Chuck's sensors.

Which meant that Chuck had *conscious thought*.

Demi leaned forward, eyes focused on the row of sensors lining the top of the frame. Though they sat protected within a metal frame, she saw reflections dance as they moved back and forth, small cameras and microphones working through data and technology to replicate the organic experience for Chuck.

Tanav might have had a more dramatic, more appropriate way to express the moment. Demi didn't. Her emotions weren't wired that way. Beneath the years of GCF training and experience lay the pragmatism of her family line, a commitment to near-obsessive constructiveness—but at least Demi grew enough self-awareness to recognize it. Tears of grief, that sometimes happened. Yet relief, joy, exhilaration, she simply didn't know how to process them.

She stepped toward the containment mech, toward *Chuck*.

As she did, a mechanized voice spoke over the din of the engine room:

"Is that your dog? You finally got one."

Embraces between humans, hugging dogs, even Dywens and other species, all of those came with a softness and warmth. That didn't exist with Chuck's mech body or robotic arms. But it didn't matter; it was still the best embrace of Demi's life. Her cheek pressed against the upper edge of the containment unit, a familiar cold smoothness to the spot that felt just like coming home.

No. It was better than that.

"She's a very good girl," Demi managed to get out. "Her name is Indy."

More servos whirred as Chuck's arms folded over Demi, pulling her in close. "I look forward to getting to know her."

He spoke. He *understood*. Damn it, Chuck even hugged.

He really was back. It actually worked.

And Neera—Demi told herself to remember to commend him later. Because he knew to give them space despite the mission at hand. Jokes and empathy; her friend really had been working on his emotional capacity.

Demi relaxed her hold on Chuck and pulled back, looking directly at the small ridge where his audio and visual sensors lay. Chuck reacted in kind, straightening up and now placing his arms atop her shoulders.

"I am assuming my captain would not resurrect me just for a hug."

There still was a mission. There was *always* a mission. Maybe someday there wouldn't be, but for now, Chuck offered intrinsic knowledge as a Lumersian.

"When you see the mess we've gotten into, you may wish you remained a spark." Duty pulled at Demi, and it won—the whole "being stranded, plus implosion of all known realities" thing kind of gave it a cheat. But she felt the inner resistance, a stronger and deeper kickback than usual, before she switched back to being a GCF captain. "Neera, can you upload to Chuck?"

"That is possible." Neera walked over to engineering's primary console and brought various statuses onto the display: navigation map, automated security log, photonic engine status, and all the other things that might comprise a mission briefing.

Or a reunion with a recently resurrected photonic boyfriend.

"The good news is that we got back to Cluster space. The bad news"—she pointed at the navigation display—"is we decided to return to the well."

"What happened?"

War. The Withdrawal Movement. The return of the gravity well. Krishna's orders, Matthews's command. Sadler. So many crew members. *Lynn.*

And Tanav, hostage on Sadler's ship.

"A lot." Demi tapped the side of her hip, prompting Indy to follow. "How about you assess this data upload while my dog decides if you're good enough for me?"

Chuck reached out, all fingers extended, and Indy sniffed the mechanical hand. The greyhound even gave it a little lick.

CHAPTER 44

※

TANAV

During those early days on the Horizon, Tanav often spent his time resolving crew tensions or greeting guests from visiting ships; interactions with the Lumersions were far less frequent and often involved explaining why they had customs like dinner. Of the ones he actually got to know, only Chuck showed interest in life beyond the logistics of daily life. If it hadn't been for Chuck's curiosity about music, they may have never bonded.

So he wasn't exactly an expert. But he put on his best front to act like one.

"The Lumersians exist in photonic space," he said slowly. He stared ahead, the glowing pink clouds of the gravity well filling up the entire cockpit's field of view—though for Tanav, the more helpful part of the view was Sadler's reflection. Tanav took in the image, trying to guess if any danger lurked as Sadler stood behind him. "On the Horizon, we debated between flashing the ship's navigation lights, firing emergency flares, or concentrating low-energy weapons. Demi was very concerned about appearing hostile."

As he spoke, his eyes scanned the various screen metrics in front of him: power status, propulsion speed, course heading. Thankfully, the mining drones' status remained at zero.

"She also didn't want to burn off flares. We had a limited supply. Fabrication took time." Now he entered bullshitting mode. Demi chose concentrated bursts of energy, mostly because it offered the best combination of visibility and control. "The nav lights were a concern as well. Too dim. She wasn't sure that they could detect light shifts from that, especially because"—Tanav sucked in a breath and tried to remember which side was starboard or stern or whatever those were called—"the back lights blink regularly anyways."

"But they must recognize a GCF ship at this point," Sadler said as he crossed his arms. "Kim knew they sent out transmissions at each convergence point."

Tanav wondered how much of that was revealed by Neera during their idle conversations. So much of surveillance came from simply being friendly and letting people unburden their own concerns.

That was how Lynn did it.

"Demi started cautiously. She went with the nav lights." Tanav nodded to the back of the ship.

"And how did you know they replied?"

That part, Tanav knew. Everyone on the Horizon knew, because they all saw it, the initial rhythmic flashes of white bursts within the glowing well, like an all-encompassing lightning. "I think," Tanav said, "their ability to control light within the well is the equivalent of a human knocking on a door."

"All right, then." Sadler patted Tanav on the back, a gesture that might have been equal parts threat and encouragement. "Let's start knocking."

It started with a flash.

One flash. Then a pause. Then a second. And another pause.

Finally, two flashes in succession.

After that, Tanav and Sadler waited. And Tanav wondered if this would even work, given that the Horizon used energy bursts instead of the ship's lights. The answer came quickly, though; about thirty seconds later, the clouds in front of the cockpit brightened, like lightning illuminating from within. Two in succession, then a pause, then another pair in succession, before finally finishing with four rapid flashes.

"It's funny, music is all math. But I'm still terrible at math," Tanav said. "I can figure that out, though."

"One plus one equals two. Two plus two equals four. Simple, yet similar equations." Sadler tapped on the thick glass protecting them from the volatile expanse. "So, we've established contact. How do we get them to tell us mining coordinates? All I need is one that works."

Chuck never explained how the passage of time or even basic memory worked in the photonic dimension. Teaching them about physical cause and effect was a gradual process. But the experience of it, whether it had felt like ten seconds or ten thousand years since the Horizon left, he wasn't sure.

"Once we established the basics of our language, we used hex code to flash messages to them. It wasn't perfect, but it—"

A loud alarm interrupted, and soon several other chirps layered over it. Tanav scanned the different displays across the console, but couldn't decipher the unfamiliar layout. He could, however, read Sadler as he approached the glass, close enough that his breath formed a disappearing bubble of fog on it. "Oh, you are good," Sadler muttered before he deactivated the noises. The cockpit fell back into the regular comfortable drudgery of occasional status chirps. Sadler didn't change his focus, though, and Tanav tracked his gaze to a long, slender shape cutting through the gradients of colors and clouds.

The Horizon.

"You are good," Sadler said again, this time with his fingernail tapping against the glass. "Neera, you are one hell of an engineer." He leaned over Tanav, his fingers flying over the console until a table showing hex code and the standard alphabet appeared. "Start communicating," Sadler ordered. "I need coordinates."

"I'm not sure how easy that will be." That was an honest assessment, no stalling required. Not only did the Lumersians need to communicate, they had to understand the type of energy required. More importantly, *why*. But built into that, Tanav saw the opportunity to intervene to lead Sadler on for as long as possible.

Because if Neera and Demi made it this far, they had to have something else ready for this situation.

Ahead of them, the clouds flared in flashes again. The ship's computer picked up on the patterns, enough to generate an output character by character—all of them rammed together, without spacing or punctuation. The translation formed, and Tanav understood it right away.

Where is 910047?

Sadler grunted, clearly irritated at where the conversation was headed. "At least they're talking," he said. "Tell them we need to identify energy variances. Get me coordinates."

Tanav flashed the message using a simple toggle of the nav lights. On the Horizon, this process automated through the ship's computer, but Sadler didn't bother with the necessary software/hardware connections and Tanav didn't complain. This method was manual, a methodical on/off tap of hex code numbering to identify alphabetic characters, but it also bought time.

Sadler stepped into the short hallway, but instead of going into the storage room–turned-brig, he faced the makeshift console that barely fit into a side alcove, its footprint sticking out enough to cause a tripping hazard. Sadler didn't catch his toe on it, but working the console meant that he took up most of the space.

Sadler also, however, got a clear view of the storage bay.

Specifically, the teleportation module set up in the corner of the space. The very same one where Tanav took the control device that ultimately teleported him from the Silver Lining back to the Horizon.

During the chaos of their arrival in the gravity well, Sadler had other things to worry about. Now he looked directly at the module, and from the way that Sadler lingered on it, Tanav knew he'd caught it.

Yet rather than face him or accuse him, Sadler pulled over a data tablet and skimmed its display. He finally turned to Tanav, though his expression bore amusement rather than fury. "I said Neera was good," he said. "Captain Kim is good too. Did you know she broke in here?"

She broke in?

Demi knew Sadler watched her on the Horizon. If she'd successfully raided *this* ship, she would have told him in those final few minutes leading up to their engineering confrontation, when every single detail marked a potential advantage.

No, Demi didn't break in. Sadler just missed that Tanav had— and if he ever spoke to Matthews again, he'd let the commander know about his astute choices in infiltration.

Before Tanav could answer, Sadler waved a finger. "Apparently not. You look too confused to know. She probably did it all on her own. Didn't want to implicate anyone else. Even the ones waiting to defect or resign. She's a leader that way."

Tanav chose to stay very silent, focusing his gaze on the cockpit's front view. He did *not* give away that Matthews had him plant a RSAI within the maintenance hatch.

"Clever. I bet she thinks she can teleport over here with that. And," Sadler said, pulling up a holographic display on his own teleportation control, "she could have. Except I'm locking her biometrics out. And Neera's."

As he cycled through the teleportation system's logs, Tanav realized a rare opportunity had just presented itself.

A window of a minute? Maybe thirty seconds. And the more time he spent pondering this, the shorter it would be. He needed something clear enough to subtly warn the Lumersians, any way to slow them down until whatever happened on the Horizon might kick in.

Sadler cursed to himself, probably at the fact that the teleportation systems showed zero signs of tampering—Tanav made a mental note that Matthews made the right call with that.

For now, a short message:

DANGER. DO NOT LISTEN.

Given the differences in vocabulary, grammar, and all the nuances of communication, the four words offered the best bit of on-the-spot thinking Tanav could muster. At the very least, it would confuse the Lumersians for a beat.

"Are they?" Sadler asked.

Tanav started. "What's that?" Tanav knew what Sadler asked and why, but playing dumb stretched a single moment into something longer.

"Are they listening now?" Sadler said, an irritated bite to his words. "They've *stopped*."

"We'll find out." Every moment that passed without a response produced relief, though a single flash finally arrived after several minutes. Others in succession; as the seconds ticked by, the clouds of the gravity well intensified. The ship's display captured the hexadecimal numbers, displaying those in a row up top before translated words began underneath letter by letter.

Five words.

Five words in response to his cautionary message, and someone like Sadler might see it as a response about processes or logistics, Tanav read them and knew right away that something had changed.

Something was brewing on the Horizon. Neera must have connected to the Lumersians.

Only Neera and Demi would understand how that phrase carried a depth and power over Tanav. Because they knew how, spy or not, Lynn was a part of him—his past and his present. No other possible motive would produce this message:

THE EXECUTION OF ALL THINGS.

CHAPTER 45

✳

CHUCK

When Chuck first encountered Demi, he wasn't Chuck yet, neither in name nor spirit. He was an it, a series of digits known as 910047 that spoke via the translation matrix and its digitized voice. Demi would later describe their initial conversations as similar to talking through calculations with the Horizon's computer. Thus, when Neera completed the mech suit and it approached the Horizon's mess hall, Demi's look of surprise said a lot about the human experience in the moment.

910047 walked into the space, sensors picking up turned heads with each step, the intense pink of the Lumersian glow casting a tint like a halo effect. As if she anticipated his arrival, Demi got up and waved it over.

"Glad to see you on the Horizon." She raised a hand, and the expression on her face read as uncertainty until she offered a quick smile. "I guess we're officially meeting now. Captain Demora Kim."

910047 weighed various responses. "I am aware of that. We have spoken several times already."

Captain Kim paused enough to show that was not the appropriate response before asking, "Sorry, social customs. Commander Neera has treated you well?"

"He has. I have started to acclimate myself to this space"—a robotic arm waved back and forth—"and I am trying to understand both the scientific and cultural nuances of your dimension."

"There's much more to our dimension than just me, I can tell you that," Captain Kim said with a laugh.

"I see that. But you are where I prefer to start." Her face angled slightly and her mouth trembled in a way that made it seem like potential muscle twitching. "I have downloaded a history of the Galactic Cluster. I am trying to consolidate that with each individual's purpose aboard this ship."

"Purpose?" As if Captain Kim suddenly understood the construction of the mech body, her eyes flipped upward, shifting from the main glowing torso to the row of sensors atop the frame.

Now they looked at each other.

"My species are assigned an individual purpose and length of existence," it said. "When both are fulfilled, a being's energy folds back into the collective." Now 910047's cameras—its *eyes*—broke from Demi's and dropped to the floor for a brief moment, a gesture that seemed strangely intuitive as a response. "My purpose is to understand how your physical engineering can interface with our dimension."

Captain Kim leaned forward, an inquisitiveness in her eyes that 910047 had not experienced in any other conversation. "Your purpose is engineering. But while you're here, is there anything else you'd wish to explore?"

910047 met her eyes again, and her expression, the way she propped her chin on her hands, the way she leaned forward, it created the strangest . . .

The strangest *feeling*?

"I don't understand what that means."

"When I was young," Captain Kim began, "they taught me to focus on our natural home rather than the stars. I made maps of the forest around us, I charted each tree and shrub—height, age, type, color. And one night, standing in a circle of trees, I looked straight up. It was like I never noticed the stars until that moment. All these brilliant dots against a sea of nothing. My purpose evolved. My curiosity started at one thing and became another." Her head had naturally tilted up at this, and he watched her face as her lips turned, pushing her cheeks up. "This is an entirely new state of being for you. Are you curious about anything else?"

"I have never considered the possibility before."

Captain Kim broadened her expression. A quick search of the historical database of human expression showed that this particular smile translated to something called *empathy*. "Well, 910047, you are always welcome to join me for a meal to discuss." Captain Kim took a quick slurp of the noodles, which still steamed despite the drop in temperature due to time. "And we're not formal aboard the Horizon. Call me Demi."

"Demi?"

"Short for Demora."

"Yes. That makes sense." 910047 made note of this new human tendency for shortening names—but was this a stylistic choice or for convenience? The mech body rotated on its hip joints, though its feet remained planted, pausing before taking a step. "I have a thought, Demi. I have noticed that my identifier is difficult for the crew to say and I am seeking a more convenient alternative."

It took several breaths for her to grasp what he meant, though her eyebrows raised with understanding. "You're picking a name?"

"In human culture, the most common name on record is Charles, with a masculine pronoun." The entire robotic unit now stood up. "You may use that as my identifier if it is easier."

"I appreciate the gesture. Though," she said with a laugh, "the more casual form is 'Chuck.' Do you like that?"

910047 considered a gesture of affirmation he saw from a duo in the science lab and held a hand up. Demi gave a quizzical look until she seemed to grasp the cultural context.

She returned the high five. "I will use Chuck from now on," *he* said.

Such a strange moment, trying to interpret human behavior and words and syntax, just as he did right now, standing on the bridge of the Horizon. However, this time, the stakes were much different than a first date in the mess hall.

To make one jump back to the well, Chuck and Neera identified the minimal ratio of synth with a small amount of his own self to blend with the synth. Further jumps would need different solutions. For this purpose, it worked—and now their challenge evolved from engineering to communication.

"The message says, 'Danger. Do not listen,'" Chuck read aloud.

"That's Tanav. It has to be. Sadler wouldn't do that," Demi said. Her voice sped up, a fascinating quirk of hers that popped up in unique combinations of stress and inspiration.

"Nothing else has come. He must be awaiting an answer." His visual sensors—his *eyes*, for lack of a better term—focused on the holographic map projected across the front of the bridge, seven dots representing the mining drones from the ship. "The Lumersians must not know how to respond."

"Chuck's response abilities to the Lumersians require thirty more seconds before reactivation," Neera said, tapping through configuration settings on Lynn's communications console.

"Good. Let's get to them first." Demi put her hand on the corner of Chuck's metallic body, and though that part of him did not support heat or pressure sensors, the very act of doing so impacted the balance of his legs and his stance on a fractional level, with equally fractional compensation.

He missed that sensation. In his strange existence as a lone spark without consciousness or energy, time passed as it did for Lumersians when they were outside of their active, aware state. Except, instead of being part of the photonic dimension, he remained in a limbo next to Indy's bed. The experience should have been many things: isolating, terrifying, empty. Yet even though that time lacked the consciousness of material beings, somewhere deep in his thoughts he felt comfort.

He supposed it had been akin to humans sleeping, yet getting some sort of sensory feedback that wove into dreams. And in his "dreams," his underlying state missed being connected to Demi, in any way.

"Is Lynn unavailable to assist with the transmission?" Chuck asked. The Horizon did seem strangely empty. They rushed from engineering to the bridge in the short period—perhaps an hour—since his revival, and outside of Chuck's brief reunion with Demi, every moment filled with steps, plans, options.

"She is not," Demi said, a complete shift in her tone and presentation over three short words.

"Did she remain in Cluster space?"

"The Withdrawal Movement is where Lynn gave her allegiances," Neera said. As he did, Demi uncharacteristically looked away.

The internal computer in Chuck's body suit silently processed a query. "What is the Withdrawal Movement? I show no references to it in my previous archives of Cluster history."

Chuck's question prompted Demi's expression to change again, creases forming deep, telling lines around her face. First, she turned to Neera. "You see? It kinda worked. 'Within these walls' and all that." Then she focused on Chuck. "The Cluster is in a state of civil war. I'm sure your downloaded archives have many examples of that," Demi said. "It's a big, relentless *thing*. It's invasive. It's taken too much from *everyone*. For now, we're working around that." Her hands rubbed against her temples, a gesture that caught Indy's reaction as the dog napped in the first officer's chair. "Let's get through this, and I promise you can ask as many questions as you want."

"Full activity has resumed with the Lumersian communication interface." Neera stood up from Lynn's station on the bridge and uncoiled a long cable. He walked it over to Demi and plugged it into the data access port in Chuck's side.

Everything snapped into view for Chuck. In the same way technology-driven sensors translated visual, audio, and environmental data for him, interfacing with the Horizon's external sensors unlocked photonic space. No metrics appeared in his technology-powered field of vision, and instead the connection simply created a greater sense of *awareness*. He likely couldn't describe it if Demi had asked.

Within that awareness came messages, direct from the photonic beings dedicated to external communications.

"They are trying to understand what is going on with the other ship," Chuck said. "You were correct. They are unsure of how to respond. Sadler's ship has asked for energy coordinates. He says it is necessary. However, they fear any disruption to the gravity well will cause it to surge and expand more."

"The act of mining may make the instability worse," Neera said.

"It caused the drone to implode," Chuck said. That got both Demi and Neera to turn his way.

"That's what they're telling you?" Demi asked. Chuck gave a silent thumbs-up before going deeper into the current situation. Her voice became quieter, more focused, producing audio of lower-band frequencies than her typical voice. "We have the advantage. We can whisper in their ear." She turned to Neera. "We have to assume that Sadler is watching all communications from his ship. But we have to let Tanav know that it's us talking to him by proxy. What could we say does that safely?"

"Did Lynn leave any notes on cryptographic communications?" Chuck asked. Instead of Demi answering, Neera turned, a rare brightness to his expression as he held a finger up.

"Lynn," Neera said. "Yes, Chuck's question brings up an interesting purpose. A phrase would be used by Lynn on occasion that made little sense to anyone except Tanav. Recognition feels natural for him, given their relationship." He tapped on the console, holographic words coming letter by letter over the bridge's wide window. "This message should be used in their reply."

"Of course," Demi said. "Of course. Tell the Lumersians to start with that and run all communications by us before responding." She reached over, though instead of merely tapping Chuck on the shoulder, her fingers wrapped around his mechanical hand.

Her hand's surface temperature was 35.4 degrees Celsius.

The pressure she exerted was almost indistinguishable, fractions of measurable pascals.

And this very action caused her heart rate to raise by half a beat per minute.

"Very well," Chuck said, and through the myriad of ship sensors, all he had to do was *think* his next message—no flashing lights or bursts of energy required.

The execution of all things.

As they awaited a response, Demi cycled through ship functions. "Sadler's ship is small enough to get some movement through the well. Any chance weapons could be repaired in time to disable it? Or shoot down those drones before they get out of range?"

Neera shook his head silently.

Demi moved forward, seemingly appreciative of the economy of this newer, evolved Neera. "So . . ." she said. "We're unable to move. Our weapons are down. And it's just the three of us on this ship." A finger raised with each item as she spoke it.

"Are you going to ironically say that you like our odds?" Chuck asked, trying to gauge her tone.

"What? No. These odds are terrible," she said with a laugh. "I would like to take it easy for once."

"The Lumersians are passing along a new message from Tanav," Chuck said. "'Will exhaust in the propulsion maintenance shaft cause instability?'" The question caused both Demi and Neera to pause. "That is an oddly specific question."

"Especially for Tanav," Demi said, standing up quick enough to cause Indy to raise her drowsy head. "He's not exactly a technician. It's a clue." The front holographic projection changed, now displaying a schematic of Sadler's light freighter. Demi began to pace in front of the captain's chair. "Okay, so the propulsion maintenance shaft. Is anything strange there?"

The Horizon pulsed out scan after scan, and as it did, Neera activated a highlight of the maintenance shaft underneath the freighter's storage bay. Power, propulsion, exhaust, all of those appeared to be running nominally.

Except for a telemetry scan. That created a single orange dot highlighted in the middle of the shaft.

"That location should not have telemetry data," Neera said. Demi examined the hologram, finger poking into it.

"What is that?" Demi asked. "Who put it there? And what the hell does that *thing* do?"

Chuck was not sure if Demi wanted all of those questions answered, though Neera attempted to be trying. The Dywen walked to the holographic image, his tablet showing the schematic of a small boxlike device. "Cabling and waveguide are contained in this maintenance passage." He raised a finger and traced it through the floating image until he stopped at a hardware junction. "Visually, a planted item could be obscured by the various hardware. My best guess is that the placement was strategically made by Commander Matthews."

"Matthews," Demi said quietly. "He'd said he'd do some digging of his own."

Neera turned, his large compound eyes piercing through the hologram. "Exhaust and propulsion are the primary purpose of this shaft. A power terminal at this junction shares some sort of beacon with the ship's primary data processor."

Chuck ran what details he could find against his downloaded GCF database. "It appears to be a device called a remote secure access interface."

"RSAI. I've heard of them. Never actually seen one. And a data processor," Demi said under her breath. "So we've got an RSAI plugged into a data processor. Neera, you've also found a back channel into Sadler's private communications." Now it was Demi's turn to point, a quick item-by-item gesture as she noted each detail. "And we have Tanav over there with some measure of control. What can we do with all this?"

"The list of subsystems should be considered," Neera said. "Propulsion, communication, tactical. Drone control is a possibility as well, depending on how Sadler configured it."

"I wonder . . ." Demi stopped pacing and folded her arms, eyes drawn to the floor instead of the schematic. "There are several reasons why we're here, and none of them matter if we can't stop Sadler and his mining operation first." She snapped a look at Neera. "Easiest way to do that is to capture Sadler, sedate him, and put him in the brig. Like I did with Matthews." This caught Chuck's attention enough that his sensors audibly swiveled. "I'll tell you later. I like to think it was pretty badass."

"Is this how you channeled your grief?" Chuck asked. "I have studied human psychology about how emotions project to other actions."

"It didn't hurt." Next to them, Neera let out a laugh—a rare event during their previous time together. "If we could access that system, maybe I could sneak on board. The Horizon is stuck, but one of our shuttles could dock through that same maintenance hatch." She pointed at both Chuck and Neera. "Neither of you would fit, and I'm not sending my dog. We just need a distraction."

"His arrival was due to my . . ." Neera paused, eyes narrowing in thought. "My *willingness* to find any help in the name of science." The tone of his gray skin darkened, making the crevices around his eyes lodge deeper into creases. "I was responsible for Sadler's effect on this ship.

"I will be responsible for occupying him now."

CHAPTER 46

NEERA

The default communications screen appeared in front of Neera, and he wondered how many times Lynn saw this very same display over the years. Monitoring communications, attempting communications, understanding and translating communications, it all started with this screen and the written text on the comm station's display:

Communication established. Awaiting response . . .

The final ellipses animated, one period growing to two and then three before repeating itself.

"He's not biting," Demi said. She stood by the data table, arms propped on its glowing edges while the gravity well's glow cast her silhouette—a strategic spot, and one Demi used before to remain hidden from incoming transmissions at the comm station.

Chuck had gone down to the science lab, where the broader range of capable systems lay within his grasp. Demi could have gone there too, a way to assist Chuck while monitoring the transmission remotely. Neera, however, figured that Demi wanted proximity, to "check the vibes" as she liked to say.

"Three minutes and eleven seconds have passed," Neera said.

Over the ship's comm system, Chuck's voice came through. "I've identified the RSAI signal. It must have been wired directly to receive power, though data is not connected. Tanav needs to grant access before I can use it."

"Time for a backup plan," Demi said, turning to look out the large bridge window. "Anyone got—"

At that moment, the display changed in front of Neera, the words *Awaiting response* now replaced with *Transmission initiated* just long enough to read it before Sadler's face appeared.

Neera had talked with Sadler at many different hours and in many circumstances. This marked the only time Sadler's face carried so many lines. Fatigue, stress, or other feelings, Sadler projected some or all of those. At least for the initial few seconds. After that, something flipped, and Sadler adjusted with tight lips and neutral gaze.

"You got control of the engine?" he asked.

Neera saw his goals: keep the discussion going, distract Sadler as long as possible, all without giving too much information away. On the display adjacent to the transmission, a window of text appeared, real-time input from Demi and Chuck.

Demi wrote only one line: *Keep him talking.*

Chuck's input contained rolling updates about ongoing communication between him, the Lumersians, and Tanav. With Tanav now flashing messages under less scrutiny, Chuck was able to convey a simple series of directions with the goal of activating access to the beacon. Which would have been easy for Neera—or Demi, or Chuck, with his downloaded knowledge of ship schematics.

Tanav would require a bit of time. Chuck relayed to the Lumersians that they should provide false mining coordinates. But that strategy might only work so long—one more imploded drone could easily test Sadler's patience.

And unlike with the WM, Lynn wasn't here to protect any of them.

Neera reminded himself to follow Demi's direction and keep drawing things out. "The engine did work using a compound of synth and remainder energy. An engineering explanation might take more time than either of us would allow," Neera said, though it would require creative deception. Making plausible explanations did not come easily to most Dywen. However, proximity to humans did provide some applicable lessons.

Sadler glanced to the side at Tanav. "How's it working there?" he asked. Tanav replied about incoming coordinates, which meant at least one part of Demi's plan succeeded. "Look." Sadler thumbed over at Tanav, who sat just out of view. "Proof of life." On the screen, Neera spied the corner of their navigational map, including the new icon that appeared as Sadler input coordinates. "We have a few minutes before the drone gets to its target. So you can tell me, I'm curious how you got the engine going."

Logic. Cause and effect. Those were the basics of engineering— a start-to-finish built upon a flow of decisions among variables. Surely with all his time around the photonic engine, Neera could come up with something?

"You see?" Sadler asked. "You give it away. I know you're stalling, Neera. Because you *love* talking about engineering. Normally, I wouldn't be able to stop you from telling me this." Sadler leaned in, his face coming closer to the camera. "There's something else going on in there." From off-screen, a high-pitched whirr came alive, one that Neera had come to recognize as the power cell of a gun ramping up in activation.

As if he wanted to really reinforce the point, Sadler held up a gun, a green status light showing full charge and a red status light showing full lethality.

"Why would you stall?" he asked as he pointed the gun at Tanav.

New text popped up from Demi in the message window: *Don't look at me. Stay focused.*

Could Sadler be bluffing? Neera weighed this as he replied. "I am telling the truth. You understand how communication works in my brain."

Sadler looked again at Tanav, whose left arm popped into view as it tapped over the control panel. From the hint of the ship's cockpit window, the outside area flashed with a Lumersian message.

"All right. Let's run with that," he said. "We'll skip the fun part and get to what really matters. You got the engine running again, why come here?"

Chuck now sent over a new status: *RSAI activated. List of immediate system access: propulsion, shields, communications. Secondary systems integrated: long-range scanners, landing control, solar power capture, teleportation unit.*

No docking control or other mechanisms. No drone control, for that matter.

Demi's next message arrived: *Can we activate the docking or maintenance hatches by overloading a full circuit?*

Neera locked eyes with Sadler while Demi and Chuck continued exploring options. The flow of text continued, and Neera made the assumption that as long as it did, no solid plan existed yet.

"Our return is necessitated by returning Chuck's spark to the Lumersians," Neera said. "Its reabsorption into photonic space should seal the fissure."

"Did they promise you a way to get back to the Cluster? A farewell gift of several units of photonic energy?" Sadler asked, waving the gun to emphasize the point.

"Our arrival was recent," Neera said. "Those discussions have not taken place yet."

All of that was true.

"Regardless, you should have gone to the Cluster with the rest of the crew," Sadler said, and Neera tried to ascertain the tone in his voice. He recognized it before—from Tanav, from Demi.

From Lynn.

Though he couldn't completely confirm, his understanding was that the monotone gravel, combined with the angle of Sadler's eyebrows and pursed lips, all lined up to a singular emotion. If

Neera's previous experiences proved accurate, then Sadler felt *regret* as he spoke.

"I came from a perpetual state of war," Neera said. "I did not want to return to the same."

"Wars end. Every single one does, eventually. You could have had the life you wanted," he continued. "Once all this was said and done. We'd have all this photonic science to explore. It could have just been your imagination pushing the boundaries of it all."

That part sounded like it came from Sadler the engineer rather than the operative.

"There is truth in your statement. However, I am deciding for myself. If it is inevitable for me to return to a state of war, then I will delay that for as long as possible. And in the time that I delay, perhaps my actions will create a greater impact," Neera said. "This explains why my focus belongs on the Horizon." The text continued to scroll from Demi and Chuck. No solution yet. "The Regent Empire had taught me that leaving a species or civilization behind can create an empty peace. The Lumersians offered kindness, science, and strategic action to all of us. That debt must be repaid."

Sadler's eyes trailed off camera, everything on his face stuck halfway between emotions. That in itself might have been the most honest look Neera had ever seen on Sadler.

"You sound like your captain," he said. "She gave a nice impassioned speech too."

So much of Dywen communication focused on unfiltered passing of information. Word choice, grammar, structure; switching away from the default of Neera's brain required so much more effort, and in that moment, it took all of his mental capacity to dam up his impulses and speak with human eloquence. "Yes, but Colin—" Neera paused and counted three breaths to pass before continuing. "The key differentiator here is that I am speaking to you as a friend."

On-screen, Sadler shook—Tanav did too, his hand reaching out across the console to stabilize himself. The Horizon got a jolt as well, though their impact only caused Demi to balance herself. Neera didn't react.

Sadler turned and looked at the mining displays, with a second drone now darkened out from the grid.

"Damn it." His chin angled up as he took in the expanse of colors outside the ship. "Those coordinates didn't work," he said to Tanav. "Get the right ones. If we lose another drone, I will no longer have patience for you." Sadler returned to Neera, a steely fire now under his glare. "Here's the bottom line: I need photonic energy. A few handouts from the Lumersians isn't going to do it. Right now, there's a dock in Cluster space with the next photonic ship. It needs this energy. Synth does not come close. Once the drones jump back there, then *that* ship can come here. And the real mining operation begins. And everything changes. The Cluster, the war, exploration, *science*. And the things that go so far beyond what people think they know. This can't fail."

The drones making photonic jumps? That explained the research team from Sadler's secret discussions. They enabled the Horizon's ongoing science experiment despite people like Matthews wanting more ships and more resources. Up until this moment, Neera knew that Sadler had used him for the engine—but the fact it went into a full fleet of size and scale surprised him—and made things worse.

The speed of Sadler's mining operation would accelerate the well's descent into instability; fixing it would still belong to future generations, but that deadline would come years, possibly decades sooner thanks to the sheer efficiency of what Oversight planned.

Neera tried to find a response. Something that might steer the discussion away from a premature end. In the face of that, focusing his thoughts became difficult, let alone articulating them. Sadler seemed to recognize this, and to his credit, he gave appropriate pause, first waiting patiently before turning to check on Tanav. *That* part, though, caused his attitude to flip.

"What is this?" he asked, pointing at a display just out of Neera's view.

"It's the Lumersian responses. It's a conversation."

Sadler planted his hands on the console, the weight causing a squeak. "These numbers don't make sense. Is that what you're dealing with?" Tanav didn't say anything, though Neera assumed he nodded enough to draw further reaction. "Did you hear what I told Neera? I need this to work. I've seen transcription logs with their species. They don't just sit around and brainstorm." That must have been the result of Chuck's misdirection. Which meant that *that* particular option had evaporated.

Neera glanced at the message log between Demi and Chuck. And while he hoped he would see a plan on the screen, what he got looked more like an argument.

One that kept going.

Demi: You can't do that. We can have other ideas.

Chuck: This is the only way. He does not know about me. We don't have time to debate.

Demi: If we're within range of the teleportation system, why don't we just bring him here?

Chuck: From this distance, I can't get a lock on him. It detects my photonic body, though.

Demi: Too much of a risk. We'll find another way. That's an order.

Chuck: I am not GCF.

Demi: I can't lose you right after getting you back.

Chuck: Do not worry. I didn't return just to die again. Besides, I still
have many questions you need to answer. You promised.

"All right. This is for both of you." The barrel of Sadler's gun first
pointed at Tanav, then at the camera. "I need working coordinates,
otherwise I'm finding another way. Maybe," he said, "on the Horizon.
I have weapons. You don't. Understood?" While he spoke, activity
fluttered behind Sadler on the small white teleportation control. Status lights flickered to life on it before a hologram appeared, various
metrics tracking the unit's subsystem power and activation status.

Suddenly, Neera understood Chuck and Demi's argument. His
long fingers typed out text to Chuck, swift orders that communicated much more efficiently than verbal messages, at least by his
standards. *Distraction: tell the Lumersians to give Sadler real coordinates now.*

OK.

Several seconds later, the gravity well flashed again. "Colin,"
Neera said, and he leaned forward to hold Sadler's attention. "Don't
hurt Tanav. Some options have yet to be explored."

On the teleportation unit, the status holograms faded out as start-
up checks completed, changing out for a more subtle series of lights
lay across the controls: two green dots across the top, one yellow on
the bottom. Neera assumed it indicated a power-up sequence.

One more message appeared from Chuck: *Meet me in the science
lab immediately. I will need your help.*

From across the bridge, Neera caught Demi's heavy sigh, and
they glanced at each other before she dashed off. From the comm
screen, Tanav spoke. "More coordinates incoming."

"You were talking about options, Neera," Sadler said. "Here's
one now. I've got one more set of coordinates here. Which means

your friend here has one more chance to play Cultural Counselor with the photonic species before I take more drastic measures. You understand?" His left arm whipped out, pistol aimed at Tanav, while his eyes stayed on Neera through the comms.

"Nice talking to you, friend."

It took Neera a second to process the bite in his words, and at that moment, the screen went blank.

CHAPTER 47

※

TANAV

Tanav stared straight ahead at the glowing field of photonic energy in front of him. Not at the log of translated messages. Not at the status grid for each drone, now six of them with two darkened slots. Not at the navigational map, where his parents' research ship and the Horizon lay marked.

Just straight ahead. With red whips lashing through glowing pink clouds and patches, causing a tint from every reflective surface within the ship.

Nothing new to see, really. He'd been here before. Which meant that all of his other senses could attune to the fact that Sadler was very, very unhappy. And if Sadler looked in the right configuration settings in his ship's computer, he'd discover that a RSAI wired directly into a power junction deep in the maintenance shaft now had direct access to a handful of systems.

Sadler watched too, though he tracked the drone moving slowly through the well. He stepped closer, and the distinctive hum of an armed weapon grew more and more present.

When a cocoon of light teleported Tanav off the Horizon, he'd stayed calm, almost serene. Yet here, a gradual sense of panic wormed its way into Tanav's thoughts. His breath quickened, seconds stretched into minutes, and his heart pounded so intensely it felt like it might shatter his bones. Whatever Demi concocted, every passing second would help. And that meant Tanav *could* affect things from his end, even as Sadler now used this new set of coordinates.

"It's almost there," Tanav said, pointing out the window.

The drone maneuvered farther until gradually halting.

"Mining systems are activating," Sadler said. "We'll see what happens." As he stood, he propped one arm against the top displays. The other arm, though—the one holding the very active and very armed gun—that hung at his side, and Tanav considered what lay before him *without* giving himself away.

It seemed very possible that Sadler left a deliberate opening as a way of testing Tanav, or at least tempting him. And it worked well enough for him to consider things. Tanav tensed his legs and gave his fingers a quick flex, mind stuck in a rapid debate with all questions, no answers. Go now? Wait for movement? Slam a button first?

Tanav bit down on his lip, pain registering but not fully processing in the moment. These weren't the types of next steps he was prepared for.

A chime broke his concentration, combined with a flashing status from above.

"Finally," Sadler said, hitting the cockpit chassis with a startling slap of celebration.

Right when he did that, another noise came from behind. It wasn't nearly as loud as Sadler's gesture, and if Sadler hadn't let a rare bit of emotion slip into his demeanor, maybe he would have noticed it too. It might have been nothing, the usual rumbles and bumps of a starship—except Demi wouldn't have stood pat on this. That meant an opportunity presented itself:

If there was a time to rush Sadler, now would be it. He could put up his best fight, maybe even catch him off guard and wrestle the gun away from him.

But that type of physical heroism wasn't in him. He wasn't a soldier or a spy. He could not be the guy who fired easily at his enemy. No, Tanav Lexin was a product of his environment and upbringing— a pop star, as Matthews said, one who struggled to break free from the molds of upper-class expectation. Which he did—by writing music, by being with Thaddea, by surviving the well, by finding something with Lynn.

And here, fighting Sadler would be a losing prospect. He needed something better, more attuned to himself. What did Matthews tell him? "I fight to change it from the inside, however I can, with whatever I can." Tanav found himself both appreciative and slightly irked at how much the commander was right. But also, he realized something more from Lynn.

"Don't rush the bake."

If that noise was caused by whatever Demi planned, then Tanav wouldn't help by pushing buttons on the ship's console. No, he just needed to forget all he *wasn't* and focus on what he actually was, as a means to buy time.

Tanav needed to slow Sadler down, yet it couldn't be obvious— it had to be authentic to the moment, to suck Sadler in.

"Can I ask you a question about all this?" He gestured in front of them.

Sadler met his gaze, a thin line of curiosity across his lips. "Sure."

One breath. Two breaths. A genuine pause, given the weight of the question, yet doing so helped whatever brewed in the back of the ship. "Do you see anything here that leads to my home?"

That prompted a smile in return, the type of expression that meant Sadler understood the authenticity of such a question.

He also, though, wanted to stall. Both of those things could be true.

"It's possible," Sadler said. He tapped the console, and some of the displays changed to different readings. He pointed in front of them. "I've got scanners checking for all types of things. I don't think the tunnels that pull in from other universes are visible, if that's what you mean. But within the well, you might be able to detect them with quantum vibrational frequency. Like a trail of crumbs." He turned to Tanav, looked at his gun, then back at him. "Still worried about that, huh? Lighten up. We're one step closer to getting you home. And—" Sadler stopped.

Neera traced his eyes to the teleportation control unit. Then back to him.

"This," Sadler said, "came to life. See, you can tell because it's in cool-down mode. That little blinking blue. Computer, scan the entire ship for life-forms."

A console display changed to a schematic of the ship, though it only showed two blinking dots in the cockpit, nothing else. They watched as the blinking blue light eventually finished, returning to a static green.

"Did you invite Captain Kim over here? Pretty sure she stole one of my controllers."

"You've been here the entire time." Tanav tapped on the display. "Looks like it's just us. I don't see Demi. Do you?"

Sadler's head swiveled, a full view all the way across from the cockpit to the small room-turned-brig to the outer hallway that led to the storage bay. "I don't. But"—he tapped a button on the console and a force field flashed to formation at the end of the hallway—"can't be too cautious."

What *did* Demi have in mind? He supposed he held an advantage if Sadler used some sort of invasive interrogation procedure; Tanav legitimately did not know the answer to that question.

"Stand up," Sadler said.

"What?"

Sadler turned the gun to him. He tilted his head. "I said, stand up. Your job's done, so you wait over there. I've got some data to analyze. But I'll do you a favor and let you know if I see a clear path of quantum frequencies. Fair enough?" Tanav nodded, his boots scuffing against the cockpit chair as he followed Sadler's orders.

"Look at that," he said, nodding outside, "drone hasn't imploded. No shock wave shaking us." The heat from the gun's muzzle radiated enough that Tanav felt it on his neck. Sadler nudged him with it, pushing Tanav to return to the storage room. The now-familiar sound of force-field generation came. Rather than sit, Tanav watched Sadler, who now sat tapping away at scanners. "Strange," Sadler said to himself. "Still no life signs back there. Maybe Kim *tried* to teleport and got the target wrong. Computer, one more full craft scan for life signs, increase organic material density check by fifty percent."

The top display flipped to a full-ship schematic, though only two blinking dots appeared on it—one in the cockpit and one in the brig. Sadler began to speak when another chime interrupted him.

On the ship's main console, a screen flashed a message of *ANALYSIS COMPLETE*. Sadler tapped through the obscure numbers and graphs until the display changed again, layer by layer. First came a local map of the region, with the center as Sadler's ship. Next, icons placed the Horizon and the Lexin Industries ship, along with a different set for the mining drones. Finally, a wave of triangles dotted the map, spread out without any pattern or reason, and as Tanav stared at the icons, a certain logic came together: one of the triangles sat directly underneath the icon of the currently mining drone. Each of those other triangles meant mining locations.

Tanav blinked as his eyes adjusted at the sight in front of him. Had something changed in the blanket of the well? As the mining operation continued, the tint of color around it darkened and swirled— a subtle change first before a swift clouding eventually producing a shock wave. The shuttle rattled again, this time more of a rolling wave rather than a jolt, but the drone remained steady and safe.

Sadler tapped more buttons on the display, and a new window popped up, this time with the words *Long-Range Communications Secured—Channel Active*.

"This is Agent Sadler. Sending a confirmation message to Oversight operations. Mining operations have begun. Anticipate drone returns in one Earth-standard day. Over."

A squawk came over the comms, followed by a new voice, the Oversight tech somehow able to carry transmissions far beyond standard Cluster means. But as they talked, Tanav found himself drawn to the hallway leading toward the storage bay—where a strange hue tinted the hall's metal plating.

CHAPTER 48

·······✳·······

DEMI

Demi and Chuck rarely argued. She'd often wondered the reason for it—was it because they were both too pragmatic, too driven by solutions? Or were they still in the honeymoon phase when he sacrificed himself to the photonic engine? Maybe Lumersians didn't know how to argue, and conflict was simply something that Chuck had to absorb through experience with humans, Dywens, and other species.

Whatever the case, their text-based tiff proved as infuriating as it was off-putting, and only afterward did Demi concede that their fight was not about any sort of tactical strategy. In fact, part of her temporarily lost military sensibility, and instead, the mindset of a GCF Captain dissolved into a stereotype of begging someone not to go.

But Chuck, to his credit, saw right through that. Maybe he didn't know anyway else to see her. And she agreed, which led her to the science lab with open panel and a bunch of wires plugged into a waist-high terminal. "This will boost the signal detected by the teleportation controls—" Chuck started, but Demi waved him off.

"I don't need to know the details," she said.

"All right. Then I need you to go to the far panel and push the flashing blue button when I am in position." Chuck moved over to the device and checked its display, then walked to the center of the room. "We should move quickly. Do it now."

"Now?" Demi asked. Chuck clearly still lacked the dramatic cadences of human conversational patterns.

"Yes. I am in position. Do it before Sadler discovers what Tanav has installed."

Demi looked at the station's display: a schematic that showed various RSAI controls mapped to icons, along with status bars showing signal detection strength. "There has to be another way," she said, her finger hovering over the icon. "It's too risky."

"I do not deny that," Chuck said.

Her gaze broke from the display to connect with the two notches on the top of his frame. "There has to be another way," she repeated.

"There likely is. But we do not have time to discover it. Our recent events have taught me the temporal fragility of good things."

"That's one way to put it," she said.

"Tanav has put us in a position to succeed if we act now. And I have come to understand one consistent thing across my experiences:

"The greatest goals require risk." Chuck broke free from his position, crossing the lab's open floor to come Demi's way. "I have seen you be bold in this choice before," he said, standing only inches from her. "It is required again. You must send me over."

Demi knew he was right. She knew that Sadler was smart enough, aware enough to pick up on the hacked hardware within his ship. She knew that so much was at stake.

She just didn't *want* any of that. She wanted an easy, safe, clear solution, one without collateral damage or complications. For *once*.

But that was the fallacy of it all. Easy, safe, clear, that didn't exist. Maybe it never did. "Grant would have been proud of that speech," she said. She squeezed his hand twice. "Get ready."

"Grant was wise," Chuck said, squaring into position. "We shall toast to him when I get back."

———

Demi dashed back to the bridge immediately after and made it into the captain's seat as Neera tapped the configuration at the data table. "We are receiving the data feed transmitted by Chuck's visual sensors," Neera said. At the front of the bridge, a hologram appeared, a floating display showing exactly what Chuck saw—which, in this moment, was the wall of an empty storage bay.

"Chuck, we're here. And I want you to keep one thing in mind," she said aloud, a direct audio-video connection to the sensors in his body. "I plan on taking a long vacation when this is all done. So you better not ruin that for me."

He replied with a silent thumbs-up placed directly in front of his visual sensors. No dramatic goodbye or tearful parting. They simply didn't have the time for it.

"Sadler's cargo bay looks empty," she said as she watched the live feed projected as a hologram above the bridge's data table. "That must have been where the drones were stored. He brought them aboard the Horizon. I thought he was just a heavy packer."

Chuck's fingers came into view as they flexed, though his communication appeared as direct text on the screen. *My weapon did not materialize.*

"A possibility is that Sadler has filtered out incoming threats," Neera said, now standing at the data table.

"Switch your vision to infrared sensors," Demi said. "You'll be able to detect the heat signatures of any power going to security systems." A layer of thermal imaging came over the view, the muted blues of cool metal walls broken by several pops of orange and yellow.

"That signature appears to be standard ESF generators," Neera said. "The exit for the storage bay is likely blocked by a force field."

"You'll have to deactivate them to get to the cockpit. But, you know," Demi said, "quietly."

Understood came across the screen, but then the view took a stumble—a shake, a crooked angle, and the clear sight of Chuck planting a hand on the floor.

"Chuck? What's wrong?" Demi asked.

Is this what pain feels like?

Demi and Neera looked at each before the Horizon shook with a sudden jolt.

"The mining operation," Neera said. "The act of mining photonic energy must be detectable by a Lumersian in physical space."

"Oh no you don't," Demi said through gritted teeth. A new window appeared and floated over Chuck's field of vision, this one a direct feed from the Lumersians.

The rate of the gravity well expansion has increased by 74% since the mining operation began. It must be stopped.

Chuck got back on his feet and held up one arm. From within the mechanized wrist joint, a single red light appeared before extending outward in a lined, retractable cable. *You see? I am good for more than just repairs in the science lab.* He paused just adjacent to the hallway entrance; a finger tapped the air, and a repulsive flash gave away the presence of an active force field. Chuck opened up a side panel, then the cable snaked its way into the guts within the wall until it interfaced with a power cell.

The force field flashed again, except this time the light came from the act of powering down. The interface cable retracted into his wrist, and Chuck angled for a look at the now-accessible hallway when he paused.

About thirty feet away lay another doorway, but just inside of it stood someone else.

That is Tanav, Chuck said at the exact same time that Demi thought it. *He appears to have seen me.*

"Don't approach yet," Demi said. "Look in the cockpit. What's Sadler doing?"

Unclear. He is working with various consoles.

The view collapsed again, except this time a clear *clang* rang out as Chuck fell to a knee. Before Demi could get a word out, the view shook in a different way—an empathic jolt that rattled the environment around Chuck, his camera swaying with the movement. Several seconds later, the Horizon shook too.

A new chime came over the system. "Damage has been detected by scanners on the other ship."

"Sadler's ship?" Demi asked.

"No, the one farther into the well." On the nav chart, the icon for that craft highlighted and zoomed in. "Structural integrity appears to be collapsing from pressure."

"That's the one sent by Tanav's family," Demi said. "They're not ready for this." Of course they weren't—years ago, those first few startling weeks in the gravity well, every creak and groan of the ship triggered panic about what lay ahead. Except in this case, the destructive capabilities were very real and much worse. "I'm opening a channel," she said, stepping over to Lynn's comm station. "Attention, unidentified vessel. This is Captain Demora Kim of the Galactic Cluster Fleet Starship Horizon. Have you sustained damage?"

Two people appeared on the comm screen.

Two people who were *definitely* Tanav's parents, from skin tone to hair texture to the fact that the man's eyes and ears directly matched Tanav's, while the woman's mouth and nose did the same.

Despite their calm appearance, though, they bore the worried lines of controlled anxiety. And when they spoke, they carried Tanav's strange accent from another universe.

"We have. We saw that another ship arrived earlier, but it has not responded. Our engineering team has been cut off, our propulsion is dead. Your repair team can dock when ready."

Tanav had talked a little about his parents, enough to get a sense of what they were like, though Demi realized that he'd never mentioned their names. This level of presumptuousness lived up to all expectations. Demi chose *not* to mention Tanav; they had enough to deal with.

"Is your damage getting worse, or is it stable?"

"I would think the damage level is obvious if your scanners were worth anything," he said with a tilted smile. "It's progressing. Our ship computer estimates structural failure in twenty hours. But another one of those shock waves might take us out."

Neera tapped Demi on the shoulder, and she turned as he leaned in slowly, an audible breath as he said a single word. "Pack."

Demi understood.

Neera certainly had the engineering knowledge to provide assistance. His experience in the well, dealing with photonic energy, that applied too. Demi knew that his intention, his *choice* was more than that.

He was volunteering because he knew that this mattered to Tanav.

"Prepare your docking bay." One look at Neera showed that he understood what had to happen next, and as she turned back to her display, Demi saw that *something* was happening with Chuck, enough that the view moved too quickly to grasp. "I'm sending my chief engineer."

"Your ship has propulsion?" asked Tanav's father as he raised an eyebrow.

"We do not. But shuttles can move through this."

"How do you know?"

Demi couldn't hold back the bemused grin tugging at her. "We have experience here." More movement came from the main display, drawing Demi's attention. Chuck swiveled and swerved, the exact movements remaining unclear. "Stand by. Expect him shortly. Kim out." She ended the transmission and intercepted Neera on his way to the bridge's back exit. Demi took Neera's hand to give it one large squeeze. "I'll let Tanav know."

The sound of a weapon discharge grabbed their attention, and on the holographic broadcast, she saw a first-person view of Chuck ducking down. "Go," Demi said, dashing back to the captain's chair, and as Neera departed, she watched Sadler approach, one plasma bolt singed into Chuck's robotic left hand, melting pieces away from its alloy plating. Chuck ran through the damage, a focus that startled Demi with each step. Bolt after bolt flew toward Chuck, one of them directly absorbing into his cubic torso.

Even still, he got close and swung his damaged arm—

And the metallic knuckles smashed directly into Sadler's jaw. He winced and stumbled back, the gun dropping from his hand, and when his eyes opened again, they lacked focus and direction. Chuck angled to the side, then plowed one metallic foot into Sadler's chest.

Demi knew their relationship was built on intellectual connection and discovery rather than any sort of natural physical intimacy. That part was kind of impossible.

And yet, this was really sexy.

Over the display, text appeared: *Do I apprehend him?*

All sorts of GCF regulations went through Demi's head, except she knew—she *knew*—the nature of Oversight would not hesitate to kill her or any of her crew. Matthews might have even gone for the finality of death too in this particular situation.

But even outside the ethical quandary, a tactical decision still had to be made. Next to Neera, Sadler knew the most about the engine, the synth generator, and whatever secret fleet the Cluster planned.

If Grant were here, he'd tell her that wherever they were in space, they still represented the GCF and its core species. "Don't think about what the bureaucracy would want us to do; think about what the people we represent would want us to do."

When he said things like that, Grant left the ultimate call up to his captain—but his logic always provided the types of guardrails she needed. And here, the situation wasn't exactly binary; all sorts of risk factors came into play.

With that, no single choice proved feasible. Instead, Demi went with an option that scaled. "If possible."

Sadler crawled on the floor, the force of impact too much for him to center himself. With his good hand, Chuck reached over to grab Sadler by the collar, when the entire view shook again.

Chuck collapsed to one knee. Followed by a massive jolt that sent Sadler flying several feet off the floor.

This really hurts.

Sadler landed with a thud, and an instant later, so did his dropped pistol. Another rumble clattered the space before the shock wave hit the Horizon. Demi gripped the chair's arms for support, and when she turned back to the holographic screen at the front of the bridge, the gun clearly slid close to Sadler's grasp. He rolled onto his belly and his fingers searched until they found the pistol's grip, slipping on the lined texture before finding traction and pulling it into his hand.

Sadler stood up, a marked stumble to his gait to go along with the blood oozing from his mouth. Yet he maintained enough control to aim the weapon and fire direct shots. Eight of them in total, two each into each limb, all at close range and maximum power.

Chuck tried to push himself up, but the damage seared through his arms, the integrity of his forearm pieces snapping from the weight. The remaining pieces of his arms rotated, finding the right angle where his legs might be able to get him upright. Except when he did, his left leg completely buckled, sending Chuck flat onto his back. Sadler came into view, and Demi gasped as he kicked Chuck's right leg hard enough to snap most of it off.

"I always wanted to meet you," Sadler said. "And in most cases,

I'd love to stop and talk. But not now." He peered over the side of the containment unit before disappearing out of view. "You're organic and synthetic combined," he said as his voice faded. He returned into view, this time holding two metallic cables in hand. "And that needs to be studied."

"Chuck," Demi said, "can you move in any way? Can you communicate?"

No text appeared on the screen. Instead, the view stared straight up at the ceiling, though the sound of cables clicked as they locked into his body.

CHAPTER 49

※

TANAV

With Tanav stuck within the confines of the storage room, the last few minutes played out nearly out of view. He twisted to see as much as he could from his doorway, interpreting glimpses and sounds to try and confirm things.

Because it didn't make sense. It sure looked like Chuck had somehow returned and was sneaking around the back bay.

But then Sadler noticed and burst out of the cockpit, weapon in hand. Then *something* happened: pistol discharges, impact sounds, scuffling and footsteps, and further discharges—eight methodical blasts, followed by Sadler's low voice. It got closer, and he came into full view while ignoring Tanav, instead stepping over to the large console that took up hallway space. From there, two cables uncoiled and Sadler dragged them back before finally returning. As he passed close, Tanav caught the blood smeared across the side of his mouth, staining his dark chin stubble a deep red.

"What happened?" Tanav asked while the console chirped and trilled with inputs and processes.

"You don't know?" he answered without looking up. "They didn't key you into the plan?"

"If you hadn't noticed, you kind of captured me."

"Your captain stole one of my teleportation modules. And somehow used the synth to revive her photonic boyfriend. She's resourceful, I'll give her that." Sadler glanced back down the hallway. "Most GCF captains are bureaucrats. Either too excited about fighting in an actual war or so embedded in the chain of command that they might as well be a computer program. Kim at least thinks for herself."

He blamed everything on Demi, yet apparently without malice. So many contradictions came from Sadler, though it *seemed* like some consistent guiding principle existed for it all. Which made sense for all these GCF types. Matthews had one. Demi had one. He supposed, in a way, he had one too, and like Demi, his changed over time. "Surviving here for a decade will do that to you."

"I like to think there's a chance for anyone to work together if their goals align." Sadler said something more, but Tanav only caught part of it. Instead, his attention drew to the teleportation cuff on Sadler's wrist.

Because a blue light started to flash.

But how?

Suddenly, the force field ahead of Tanav flashed and hummed down, deactivating to a gradual silence. This also caught Sadler's attention, who squinted as he quickly scanned the space. He took a step over, pausing at the doorway before sticking his arm through and waving.

His eyes widened. But rather than address any threat from Tanav, he looked down the hall. "You're still in there, aren't you? The one time I didn't keep an eye on things . . ."

Over the ship's comm system, a voice came through. But it wasn't Demi. Or Neera.

It was Chuck.

"Tanav. Back away."

Though he wasn't sure exactly what that meant or why, given the circumstances, it seemed like good advice. Sadler now looked at him, and the floor echoed as Tanav took quick, even steps back. Sadler's eyes widened as an intense light grew out of nowhere, along with a high-pitched buzz that intertwined with a higher-pitched squeal. It wove through Sadler, and he looked down at his wrist. Though his movements slowed, Tanav saw him reach for the cuff on his arm before the cocoon overtook *everything*.

Several seconds later, the light stopped. The noises stopped. Everything stopped.

Sadler was gone.

Tanav stared ahead, unsure of what to do next, what was even safe to touch or examine.

"Chuck?" he asked tentatively.

"Go to the cockpit. My containment unit's systems are interfaced with this ship's systems through Sadler's data analyzer."

Tanav did as directed, still moving slow enough in case Sadler left any booby traps. "Guess he didn't account for that part, huh?"

"He did not."

Tanav settled into the same chair he sat in minutes ago, though new systems activated even though he hadn't touched a thing. "Okay. I'm here." He scanned the controls, only now parsing out that some remained idle among all the activity. And outside the cockpit, another flash—not a flare of unstable energy or the glimmer of a teleportation cycle, but rather something much more practical: a shuttle bursting out of the Horizon's docking bay. It tore through the gravity well, intense white propulsion blasting a wake of eddy swirls among the photonic backdrop. Tanav tracked the trajectory of the small ship and lined it up, the craft pushing farther toward the Lexin Industries ship.

As if Chuck could see him—and maybe he could via the ship's internal sensors and cameras—he responded, *"Neera is on that shuttle. He will repair your parents' ship."*

They really came. Not just a research ship but his parents themselves. Tanav felt an instinctive tension grip his chest at the very thought of it, like he was ten years old being scolded for noodling on his guitar instead of studying the supply chain of the family business. And Demi, did she deal with them?

As he pondered that, the view in front of him changed again, a sudden shower of bright white fluttering into existence. The gravity well ignited in return, sparks twinkling like stars against an inverted sky. "What was that? Are things getting more unstable?"

"*On the contrary. Demi gave me permission for what to do with Sadler. His teleportation process required finishing. Instead of materializing him into physical form somewhere, I deemed that he was needed most in the well.*"

Tanav blinked at Chuck's words. Did something get lost in translation? "*In* the well?"

"*The law of conservation of energy states that energy can never be created or destroyed. It transforms.*" Chuck spoke like a teacher explaining core concepts to a child. "*Sadler's teleportation process brings matter into photonic space. Pushed further and it begins* converting *matter to photonic energy.*" The sparks flashed again, a wave of light passing through before they were pulled one by one into darker clouds and disappeared.

"He's become . . ." Tanav gulped as he tried to absorb the whole concept. ". . . synth?"

"*The mining operation was making the well increasingly unstable. It posed a threat to all of us. I needed to see if injecting synth into the well might heal the fracture in the photonic dimension. As synth healed me.*"

Charts and numbers flashed a dizzying level of information, and the fact that Chuck wasn't freaking out had to be a good sign. Several more seconds passed before he continued. "*It has worked. This will be a process. And now we must make the Lumersians whole. First by reversing the mining operation. And then analyzing how the synth stabilizes the gravity well. I believe it may be possible to seal the well without returning my own essence to it.*"

"That simple, huh?" Tanav asked.

"*Processes are often simple once we know what to do. Or—*" Chuck paused to let out a few of his mechanized laughs. *"As you often say, 'gravity-easy.'"*

More data flooded the screen, first on an isolated portion of the display before eventually taking over the entire thing, even the secondary displays at the top of the cockpit. "I probably can't help you with the analysis part."

"I wouldn't expect you to," Chuck said. *"But while we work?"*

"Yeah?" Tanav asked.

Chuck paused. Given the circumstances, Tanav wondered if that was a glitch in his connection to ship systems or if something more difficult simply came to mind.

Probably the latter.

"Perhaps," Chuck said, *"you can tell me what happened to Lynn."*

CHAPTER 50

✴

NEERA

The Sadler situation is resolved.

Neera wasn't exactly sure what that meant. Under the Regent Empire, "resolved" could mean anything, though it almost always meant the mission reached its primary objective. That was the only resolution that mattered to the Regent Empire. But who died, what was lost, what the fallout might be, that created a spectrum of uncertainty.

But in this universe, under Demi's command, Neera saw the message indicate a satisfactory conclusion. Those simple words carried such power, an ability to sooth the anxieties in his mind for a complete focus on his immediate task: flying his shuttle into the docking bay of a starship from a foreign universe.

Some measure of overlap existed between this universe and Tanav's, just as it did with Neera's. His own personal theory about this came from the fact that venturing to a location tied to the gravity well required space travel on at least an FTL level, so origin universes having comparable technology and designs made sense. He was, however, surprised at how human primary language seemed to be the same in the three universes.

Culture and custom, though, were not.

As his craft dropped landing skids and touched down with the usual bump of contact, he considered how to approach this, weighing whether it was worth it to connect briefly with Tanav. Except given Tanav's family history, Neera chose *not* to do that to his friend.

Instead, he'd approach this strictly as a chief engineer under Captain Demora Kim. Not the Cluster, and certainly not the Regent Empire, but the individual who shaped him the most over the last few years.

The shuttle's loading ramp lowered, various hydraulic bursts depressurizing excess steam and exhaust as ship systems powered down. Neera tapped the side of a storage bin filled with a standard maintenance loadout; the unit lifted into a hover, and he grabbed a set of handles to tow his tools into the large Lexin Industries craft.

Most starship docking bays carried a utilitarian design. Lexin Industries seemed to go for a different objective—the cargo bay had plenty of space for incoming craft, but the lighting offered much warmer glows, and while the flooring remained rugged, a wood-like siding lined the walls. Blue plant life adorned the top of it, decorative lights weaving in and out.

It was the strangest docking environment he had ever seen.

When he got back, he'd have to look at the Horizon's cultural archives to identify this aesthetic.

As Neera disembarked, he caught sight of an older couple standing in the middle of the docking bay. Despite the ornate décor of the docking bay, they dressed in contrast: simple muted tones and clean lines of shirt and trousers, cut to a slim fit. Whether the simplicity of their outfits was due to their current circumstances or their society's standards, Neera didn't know.

The most surprising part, though, came from their expressions. Neera had encountered his own form of trepidation about his size, his skin color, his compound eyes. Plenty of people within the Regent Empire viewed Dywens as a fixture of something lesser, and life within the gravity well wasn't always welcoming or friendly.

Those came with a sneer, though. This, however, felt different. Rather than a visceral shock at seeing something new, Neera picked up on the inaudible but present human signals: the narrowing of eyes, the parting of lips, the hushed whispers.

Risks presented themselves, along with options. He recognized both, but at the same time, they came with the realization that in the end, these people needed *his* help. He ultimately controlled how it all played out. He could even leave if he wanted to.

"I am Commander Neera." He patted the floating storage unit in front of him. "Scans of the structural damage have been reviewed during my flight over. A temporary fix should stabilize things until your own engineering team can generate permanent repairs."

"You speak our language," the woman said.

Neera noticed several other people, fanned out at different angles with circular drones following them. Were they security? It did seem prudent to initiate first contact with some level of skepticism. Except security teams usually faced potential threats; in this case, all but one of the people watched the couple.

"There are commonalities between the cultures we are from," he said, tapping the GCF rank stripes on his arm. "Integration was accelerated due to this convenience."

"You don't look like your captain," Tanav's mother said with a scowl.

Neera found himself unable to respond to that statement for a moment. "Dywen is the name of my species."

The couple looked at each other, then back at Neera—specifically, his hands and their extra thumbs.

"I believe," he continued, "a path back to your universe is feasible based on detectable quantum vibrational frequencies. The goal for now is to stabilize your vessel until that time."

"That is good to hear." Tanav's father squared his shoulders, like he could squeeze some spare inches of height with the gesture. "We're needed back where we are from."

Once again, Neera considered his response. This was not exactly the same thing as discussing technical ship specifications. "Yes, the prominence and impact of Lexin Industries is something I am aware of."

That brought a large grin to Tanav's father's face, and he tapped his chest with a closed fist. "You see? Our reputation precedes us." One of the nearby people approached the couple, the drone elevating several feet, and Neera realized something: Those people weren't security at all. They were directing drone cameras to document the expedition.

Neera didn't need his empathic senses to tell him that these people judged him. Though his instincts told him to quietly go about his business, a different kind of emotional memory kicked in, feelings that stirred his own experiences of distorted hierarchy and what he knew of Tanav's life.

Neera made a decision.

Clasps unlocked on the toolkit unit, and he took out several basic scanners. He clipped them to his belt, one by one, and he closed the lid. "The assessment should be started as quickly as possible." He stepped forward, and his wide field of vision caught even more camera operators standing by large storage crates in the bay. Their drones soared to about ten feet above the floor, angling down and tracking him as he moved. "My understanding is that you are here searching for your son."

"You know him?" Tanav's father asked.

Neera continued walking, still pushing the floating box of tools until he triggered the exit door. "Yes," he said with a pause. He turned and considered his words—his *syntax*—as thoughtfully as possible. "Tanav is an invaluable member of the ship's crew. We would not have survived without him." He pictured Tanav's expression when Sadler took over the Horizon, the moment he faced Neera and Demi with a force field separating them. "My native culture has a term for someone like him:

"*Pack.*"

CHAPTER 51

DEMI

The crew assembled on the bridge of the Horizon, starting with Demi in the captain's chair. Chuck's rebuilt mechanical body stood next to her, a cable running from his side output to the comm station. Tanav oversaw the updated translation matrix where Lynn used to sit. And Neera took the helm to make sure ship operations remained steady.

One week had passed since the incident with Sadler. Despite everyone's individual experiences creating an overlapping confusion over what *really* happened, they pieced it all together—scientifically, strategically, and with just plain old common sense.

Which brought them all onto the same page. As for what came next, though, that needed additional input.

"Incoming transmission from the Lumersians." Chuck tapped a module on the shoulder of his square frame, which prompted Neera to activate several controls on the comm console.

Demi looked over at Indy, who seemed to enjoy her new semi-permanent spot in the first officer's chair. They'd have to see how long that lasted, given what awaited them in Cluster space. For now, she figured Grant would be okay with sharing his old seat.

"Time for diplomacy. Open the channel," Demi said. "This is

Captain Demora Kim. Hello, my friends. To whom do I have the pleasure of speaking?"

"*This is Photonic Being Number 620199,*" a synthesized voice said over the comms. Demi stared at the blanket of energy in front of her and wondered if the very person who currently spoke lay somewhere directly ahead of her.

"I understand that our initial experiments to repair the gravity well have shown marked improvement." Neera broadcast a set of holographic metrics over the bridge's data table. "Can you confirm?"

"*That is confirmed. Please continue with this process.*"

Demi sent Neera a look. He nodded in return, tapped several buttons on the adjacent weapons display. "Torpedo bays are fully loaded with synth projectiles," he said. "They are ready to launch on your command."

"Fire," Demi said, and five glowing cases soared into view, zooming quickly at high velocity until they became dots in the distance— dots that exploded in a spiderweb of white-hot energy before reabsorbing into the pink canvas. "Photonic Being 620199, further synth has been dispatched into the gravity well. What are you seeing?"

"*Integrity of the well has increased by four percent. Expansion is slowing.*"

"Good. We'll generate more synth."

"*Your fleet has stopped its previous operation?*"

Previous operation. That was one way to sum up Sadler's plans. So much of Demi's headspace was spent on trying to explain Sadler's motives to the Lumersians; this was a species that lacked the very concepts of emotions or gain or borders. How could they possibly grasp an Oversight agent with his own agenda?

Before she could easily summarize things, Chuck spoke. "This is Photonic Being 910047. I have been compiling a summary of what transpired, along with the proper cultural context for it."

"As we say here, it's a bit of a long story," Demi said.

"'*The cultural context of this.*' *We are curious,*" 620199 said. "*Perhaps it is more accurate to say that I am curious.*"

"How so?" Demi asked as Chuck gave a very "hmm" of interest.

"*Something is different now. Our initial analysis shows that integration of synthetic energy provides our kind with greater control over any intersection in physical space. We believe that is due to this energy originating from matter. With time and practice, we may be able to open and close the well, or even open up direct portals to other . . .*"

Its voice trailed off, and Demi glanced at Neera, who confirmed the connection held.

"Direct portals to other what?"

"*I believe your species calls them 'universes.'*"

Now it was Tanav's turn. His gaze bounced from Demi to Chuck to Neera before settling on Demi.

"You think you can create a . . ." Demi paused to search for the right word. "A hub of sorts? All under your jurisdiction?"

"*That is our going assumption.*"

A regulated supply of photonic energy. A working engine. From Sadler's ship, a teleportation system and extended-range communications. And on the WM ship that carried Matthews home, a completely different type of engine that far exceeded FTL travel.

For months, Demi had told herself that within the Horizon's walls, the war didn't exist. And for months, she tried to make that true, even when it proved to be impossible. Such a goal proved to be idealistic, and while ideals were built from past experiences, they didn't necessarily translate to what actually unfolded.

They could, though, form the outlines of possibilities, marking the fine differences between hope and reality. Because the Horizon, with its skeleton crew, now held the knowledge to change *everything* for the Cluster and the Withdrawal Movement. Possibly any other government, organization, or species beyond even those.

How to do it, though, remained a mystery. She'd have to figure that part out. She looked over at Neera—though he'd sat at the helm, a small toolkit lay at his feet. In between tests and scans, he'd reached into it, pulling out tools to tinker with the module he'd kept by his side:

A long-range comm system recovered from Sadler's ship. And soon, Neera claimed he'd be able to integrate it into the Horizon's own hardware.

However, one question remained: Who to contact with it?

"Captain Kim, I must ask something," 620199 said.

"Go ahead," Demi said, one hand reaching out to take Chuck's mechanical fingers. Against regulation, for sure, but she stopped caring long ago. "We have no secrets here."

"Where did the hypothesis to apply synthetic photons come from?"

Demi squeezed Chuck's hand. And the robotic servos squeezed back. "We had a successful experiment on our ship."

Several hours later, Demi sat on the edge of her bed. She should have been happy—thrilled, infatuated, those sort of things. Chuck stood next to her, and that created the miracle of all miracles.

Except her mind couldn't rest, not when she held the fate of the war in the Horizon. Every passing moment without action put more people at risk. And yet, every possible scenario seemed to create as many problems as it did solutions. The Cluster wanted to keep everything in their established monolith, despite who it squashed. The WM wanted to burn it all down, despite the collateral damage. Both ignored the innocents—and the fact that something had to change, yet neither side seemed to know how to affect it. She couldn't hide out in the well forever. Even here, she realized that the war permeated every moment, every decision, a power stemming from the very existence of conflict. But she couldn't go back to the status quo.

Could anyone?

Demi thought back to the things Matthews had said: "Adaptability through chaos." Maybe she wasn't as good at that as she thought. "I think," Demi said, "I need to stop thinking about this. For now."

"Can you?" Chuck asked. "I may not fully understand the political pressures involved, but I do know your mind." He tapped his body frame, the Lumersian mech equivalent of a human tapping their head. "You are not fond of leaving things unfinished."

He was right. Because Demi's thoughts continued circling, an endless return to the same exact point: the fact that every possible outcome failed to change the underlying equation of the galaxy.

"I have an analogous situation for you," Chuck said. "If you are willing to consider."

Demi laughed at the fact that Chuck existed as a spark yesterday and now he was asking permission to talk. "I'm just happy that we get to have moments. Go ahead."

"Very well. You recall how 620199 said that something was different?" Demi nodded, shortly before she flopped backward onto the bed. "It is a true statement." From the corner of her eye, she caught Chuck tap several buttons on the top of his body unit. A strange whirring came, one that Demi didn't recognize, and despite having just lain down, she propped herself on her elbows for a look.

Then she sat straight up.

The middle protective glass of Chuck's body now slid upward, a subtle color shift as the true photonic body touched oxygen. The light from his body intensified—not brighter, but as if color had volume and everything just got way louder. "Synth is generated from matter. It restored my body. But also . . ." Demi got to her feet, taking slow and measured steps toward Chuck as he spoke. "Organic and synthetic. Two opposites merged together into a new possibility."

Demi put a tentative hand out, which Chuck took. He guided it toward the glowing plane of energy, Demi's palm getting closer and closer until it pierced the photons, floating through, yet experiencing the strangest sense of . . .

Something within that square of *light* resisted her hand.

"Do you understand?" Chuck asked. "I'm mostly myself. But one percent of me is now made of matter. I did not think to check this at all until 620199 said that.

"I needed to understand that new things were within reach before I could embrace the unexpected or the previously impossible."

They didn't say anything else. They didn't have to. Demi just stayed in the moment, taking in the miracle that, for the first time since he'd boarded the ship years ago, she could *feel* him.

CHAPTER 52

✳

DEMI

First, Vice Admiral Krishna appeared on Demi's screen. And she looked surprised.

That may *not* have been a response to seeing Demi's face for the first time in weeks. Instead, the vice admiral may have been taken aback by the pink hue of the captain's quarters' outer window. For a while, Demi felt the same way being back here. But now they had a way out of the now-stable well, courtesy of the Lumersians, and that anxiety faded to the back of her mind.

Mostly, it was just *bright* now, so Demi dimmed the glass dome, a necessity for getting any sleep, given the intensity of the gravity well. In this case, though, she wanted Krishna to see it for herself.

"Captain Kim," Krishna said. "I was half wondering if this was a glitch in the system. The Horizon isn't showing up on any long-range scanners."

"We're not in Cluster space." Demi glanced over her shoulder. "We're quite a ways away."

"How are we communicating?" Krishna asked. "You're well beyond range."

"You might want to ask Oversight about their comms tech."

Demi forced a completely neutral face when she said it and told herself to just *watch*.

The name threw off Krishna, who took far too long to respond. "Oversight doesn't exist. It's a boogeyman myth to scare cadets. You're high enough in rank to know this."

"This tech we're using, it was recovered from a ship piloted by Lieutenant Colin Sadler. He's listed in the GCF records as a research and development engineer." She sent an image of Sadler's profile to Krishna's station. "But he also belonged to that organization that doesn't exist."

Krishna lips pursed as her eyes darted at something—probably someone—off camera. "Okay. That's another issue for another time. You're at the gravity well. That means you got the engine to work?"

"We did." A holographic map appeared in front of Demi, jump points marking their trail. "And we can get it to work again. We can map out all the jump points in the galaxy."

A new face faded into view, one that Demi was not too familiar with, but she knew who he represented. He had human features, but like Neera, his skin carried an ashen gray tint—likely the son of an interspecies couple. And the healing scar across his right eye—well, WM higher-ups probably also got into the field. They didn't have the luxury of bureaucracy to keep them behind desks.

Judging by Krishna's reaction, she knew who he was too.

Demi closed the holo map and straightened up in her seat. "Ah. Now we can really talk. Do we need formalities? Vice Admiral Krishna of the GCF. Prime Minister Britai Kentworthy of the Withdrawal Movement. We're just waiting for one more person . . ."

Kentworthy didn't react. And Krishna, who offered plenty of animated expressions earlier, now sat stone-faced.

Another person arrived, and unlike the last time they were in a meeting together, Demi knew exactly what she was getting.

"Commander Matthews. Good to see you again."

"You're coming through loud and clear," he said, rubbing his chin. "Impressive audience too."

"Now that we've got everyone here, Commander Matthews, you mind sharing where you are and how you're getting home?"

Matthews gestured behind him. "I'm on a WM ship called the Silver Lining. Traveling at a rate that is orders of magnitude faster than our known FTL travel. It should have taken me months and months to get home from the border of Cluster Space. I've been enjoying the quiet on this ship for a little over two weeks now. We entered comm range two days ago. Kentworthy, your propulsion is impressive."

Demi looked over each person on her display. "So, let's look at what we have here. I have schematics for the photonic engine and synth generator from the Horizon. I have the teleportation system developed by Oversight using photonic energy and their long-range comms. Commander Matthews has the WM's fancy new propulsion system. All revolutionary pieces of technology. And I am sitting"— she pointed behind her—"in a gravity well. Created by photonic energy. *Stable* photonic energy, managed by a species called the Lumersians."

"These are all," Matthews said, "good reasons for everyone to listen."

"Now, what's important here is that the Lumersians have control of the well. They can grant access to it. If they want to."

They were on the cusp of something—something far bigger than any of them could have imagined, yet part of her still wondered if this had been worth it. Someone like Macek, who chose to join her to pursue science. Someone like Hikaru, who chose to come out of loyalty.

Someone like Lynn, who died for her beliefs. Someone like Diaz, who died *senselessly*.

So many people died—not just of the Horizon crew, but from the invading WM raiders as well. Scaling back even more, civilians too.

They were all caught up in this confluence of circumstance and violence. And now that Demi stood on the precipice of changing everything, she still struggled with the unnecessary loss of life.

Maybe she always would. But if this worked, it would mean at least her lost crew died for something bigger than all of them.

Demi hit a button on her console.

"I've just transmitted schematics for all that tech to both sides," she said. If Grant were here, he'd remind her to slow down and be present for a moment of this magnitude. No matter how things existed several seconds ago, everything suddenly changed in the most unexpected ways.

"What are you doing?" Krishna said, her eyes now wide. Kentworthy didn't respond, but an audible gasp transmitted over the galactic distance.

"When we came home to war, I tried to keep it away from us. I really tried," she said with a laugh. Matthews snorted at that too. "But that was impossible. It was all-encompassing. It was everywhere. What I have found, though, is that it goes both ways. Everything we discovered aboard the Horizon—from the gravity well, from Oversight, from the Withdrawal Movement—it was our choice to send it back. Your whole war is about resources, right? Resources that drive travel, commerce, the logistics of daily life. I've given you everything to stop that.

"All of these new technologies are within reach for both sides. Which means the previously impossible is now possible."

The two leaders responded with stunned silence.

"You all can keep bickering about the past if you want," Demi said. "Grievances about the way things were, and who did what to who. That's not going to bring back the lives lost. And staying in the past is not going to build a future. But outside of the known are things that just got a whole lot more interesting. Which is appropriate, because space is a rather large place." Space—what a funny concept. For so long, they considered "space" as this sort of amorphous shape they all lived in, and yet now the Lumersians had paths to other universes. "And it's just gotten bigger. All you need to do is get photonic energy from the Lumersians."

"I hear they're pretty friendly," Matthews said with a crooked smirk.

"How . . ." Kentworthy said, pausing for a steadying breath, "how do we do that? What do they want? What currency do they use? You're giving us the data on this tech, we don't have the resources of the Cluster."

Demi shook her head before settling into her chair, a quick scan to check the vibe of everyone involved. They were nervous. Matthews looked like he was trying not to laugh. And for Demi, a calm draped over the chaos that fought in her for so long.

What a strange feeling.

"You're misunderstanding the Lumersians. They don't need minerals or ships or *money*. Ego is not involved here." What was it like to live in a society without those fundamentals? Did that eliminate conflict or just suppress it? "They want knowledge. Trade your science, your *knowledge* with them, and they will help you." The conversation seemed too long for Indy, and the greyhound ended her guest appearance by huffing before returning to her padded bed. "They think mathematically. Try an equation to open communications.

"Like one plus one equals two."

CHAPTER 53

TANAV

Several days ago, Demi cleaned out Lynn's quarters. She'd told Tanav that she expected to find evidence of WM communication—along with Commander Connors's guitar, which never made it back to him. Both predictions proved accurate, and with the war approaching talks for a possibly permanent armistice, a lot of that intel seemed more like historical record than anything else. But she'd also found a small palm-size holo device, the type used for recording keepsake messages.

"I think it's for you," Demi said as she handed it over.

He took it without question or hesitation. But then it sat for days. Every time he considered playing it, every time he even looked at it, an excuse arrived.

Now everything else was complete. Bags packed, duties finished. His storage chip of Lynn's favorites songs was all filled up. Outside, Demi and Neera waited to walk him to the docking bay, where Neera would fly him over to the Lexin ship. They chatted away, and their voices were a good reminder to hurry up, stash the holo device, and watch it later, maybe after settling in.

But no, this was Lynn. This was the Horizon. Their *life* was built here.

It should end here too.

Tanav pushed the device's top button. It hummed to life, then a holographic projection flickered before a miniature Lynn Kohli appeared. She squirmed a little bit, a step from side to side, her long black hair swaying in front of her face as she failed to start several times. Finally, she sighed, shook her hands, and reached over.

An acoustic guitar came into view.

"Hi. God, how do I say this? It's weird. Okay, well, maybe something will happen and you'll never need to watch this. Then none of this matters, yeah? So, let's go with that." She continued to hold the guitar by its neck, the slight vibrations from movement causing a tone from the low E string. "Hi. I said that already. Okay, look, it's . . ." She looked around, then scoffed in frustration. "The actual time doesn't matter. We're jumping again soon. And when we get there, the WM is going to be there. And after that, I may never see you again. So, this is my contingency. I suppose it's to sort out my feelings too." Her face fell as she hesitated. "It's no one's fault. I've chosen the WM. And if we fail with the engine, then maybe you get to the well and you get home. And I'm in jail in some remote system," she said with a laugh. "Or you get home some other way. Or maybe you even joined me. I don't know. I just know that . . ."

Her smile broke, and despite the obvious nerves, her whole tone took on a deep seriousness. "You want to go home. I get that. And I may not get a chance to tell you this, so I'm recording it. Okay? So listen:

"Fuck your family.

"Fuck them. You don't owe them anything. You tell me you know that, you tell me that you don't care what they think, but then you tell me these stories of what you and Thaddea went through— Hello, every single decision you made is because of them. Either to spite them or ignore them or whatever it is, it's because of them. And you don't need them defining who you are. You're better than that. If you only remember one thing about me and us and our time together, I want it to be this message: Make your choices for you."

Now she slung the guitar over her shoulder, and Tanav could see that she formed an A chord with her fingers—fumbly and loose, but they managed.

"There's one of my favorite songs I never played for you. One of those Jenny Lewis songs that punches close to home. But . . ." Her voice trailed off as she strummed to an aimless rhythm. "Given everything. You know?"

"Yeah," Tanav said, "I know."

"This song is about you and them. And they keep taking from you. And you should fight to be happy. *I'm* fighting for you to be happy." Her hand changed, the thumb-strumming switching to individual string plucking. "Even when we're on opposite sides of a war."

This caused her to hold herself, eyes glazing over. "I'm sorry. It's hard to sing and play at the same time. If this is the last you hear from me, I wanted to try. Instead of just playing the track. But still, I don't know how you did it. There's a reason why I didn't want you to hear me sing. No one does, right?" she asked with a laugh. "Okay. For real, this time. If you're going back to them, to Thaddea, then you need to hear this.

"It's called 'A Better Son/Daughter.'"

Lynn cleared her throat and huffed out a breath. Then she switched to an E chord and began to strum slowly. And though her rhythm was a little off—singing while playing wasn't easy to get used to, after all—her pitch was clear, her tone carried a deep soulfulness, and her lilt turned with emotion.

Just like Jenny Lewis.

Tears dampened Tanav's eyes, and he found himself lost in the melody, the richness of her voice, the surprising strength of key for someone who hid her talents from everyone. Before he knew it, she'd finished, and Tanav completely missed the lyrics that Lynn had so wanted him to hear.

"That's it," she finally said after hitting the final chord. "God, I hope that wasn't too embarrassing. Can you imagine, the last thing I leave you with and it's me singing off-key?"

"You weren't off-key," he said softly.

"Okay. Okay, okay. I'm gonna fucking cry if I stay here, so let's see each other again? All right? Even if I'm in jail. You can bring Thaddea if it comes to that. It's okay. It means, like the song says, that you're happy." Lynn pulled the guitar off her shoulder and held it up. "I hope you're happy. I hope *we're* happy, but if that can't happen, I hope you're happy."

The image faded out.

A minute must have passed. Possibly two or three. Finally, Tanav told himself that he owed it to Lynn to listen again, and he nearly started it over when a knock came.

"Tanav," Neera said. "The shuttle's warm-up process has completed."

Tanav paused, stuck between moments. He *almost* ignored Neera and hit the button. But he didn't.

"Right," he called out. "Right. I'll get going."

A replay would have to wait until he had a quiet, private moment. He took one last look at the room he called home for several years, then stepped out to join Demi and Tanav.

"It was Lynn?" Demi asked as they walked down the hall.

"Yeah," he said. "It was what I needed to hear."

"Her intuition was always very accurate," Neera said. "May I tell you something about her?"

This was an odd question, and it took Tanav a moment to remember that they had empathically bonded weeks ago. "Of course," he said.

"Her commitment to the WM caused her a great deal of anxiety. Before I understood it, I detected it. Her feelings about the crew weighed on her." They paused to wait for the elevator. "I know for certain that within those disparate emotions, her feelings for you were the strongest. I believe that after the war, she would have found her way back to you. If the war did not exist, she would have accepted your invitation to go."

Neera's words sank in as the elevator doors opened and they stepped in. Acceleration shifted as it took them up, causing a flutter in Tanav's stomach. The trip was silent, yet Tanav found a strange peace in this. No discussions about crew issues, no need to ask Demi if she was all right, and no further wondering about Lynn—just a comfortable silence. It remained that way as they got to the docking bay and stood before the awaiting transport shuttle, where Chuck oversaw a monitoring station.

"Do you have any last-minute needs before departing?" Chuck asked as he unlatched a power cable.

"Only one," Tanav said. He reached into his pocket and pulled out the storage chip filled with music and turned to Neera. "You okay if we listen to some music on the shuttle ride? These were Lynn's favorites."

ARCHIVE OF OFFICIAL COMMUNICATIONS

Demora Kim
Captain, GCF Starship Horizon

This message is official notice of my resignation from the Galactic Cluster Fleet, effective upon our return to Cluster space. We will dock at Base Theta Seven, at which point I will turn command over to Commander Jonathan Matthews, per intended prior to our detour.

CHAPTER 54

DEMI

"Demi?" Neera called out.

His booming voice came from out front. And before Demi could reply, Indy got up from her bed. The greyhound reached out for a big stretch, her long nose illuminated by a sunbeam through the small house's front windows, and she straightened up, complete with a shake and tail whip. Indy looked at Demi, who offered a quick "Go ahead."

As Demi peered into the yard, she could tell that the last few months living on Earth did two things: First, it made Indy miss Neera way more. Second, it made Neera seem to forget everything on how to handle an excited dog.

"We should rescue Neera. Our dog will not leave him alone," Chuck said, lowering a large paper map of Muir Woods hiking trails. He folded it in half, and then again, but after that, Demi heard as much servo whirring as paper crinkling. She looked at the doorway, then back over at Chuck, who continued to struggle with the map until he just gave up.

"That's a centuries-old problem," she said, and she walked to the porch to find Neera awkwardly petting Indy as the dog circled him, proudly showing off the yellow plush elephant in her mouth.

She looked at the GCF transport shuttle parked on the front of her rural property, the edge of Muir Woods just a five-minute walk beyond the fence line. Such a craft always seemed tiny compared to the scope of capital ships like the Horizon, or even the light freighters that would come and go within the docking bay. But here, it dwarfed the Earthbound vehicles that hauled people around. Especially the pedal-powered bike that Demi had taken to.

"The time has arrived for me to leave. But I must be certain, are you sure you are declining?" Neera asked. "Negotiations between the Cluster and the WM continue to stall. Captain Matthews continues to be consulted on each step forward."

"I did my part. I got them to talk." She turned to Chuck, still marveling at the way natural sunlight hit his photonic essence and changed the color to a deep red. "I trust Matthews to lead them to the finish line. I'm retired. My big mission now is learning how to cook properly."

"She is lucky that I do not need to eat."

"That's right. Table for two, service for one," she said. Indy, seemingly satisfied with Neera's attempts at ear scratches, came back over to Demi and leaned against her thigh. "Correction: one and a half."

Neera dipped his angled chin, his eye narrowing from the bright midday sun. He held up a finger, then walked silently over to the shuttle's open loading bay door, where he disappeared for a few seconds before coming back holding . . .

. . . a GCF comm link?

"Captain Matthews wishes to stay in contact when we are within comm range, given your experience and knowledge. He was worried you might 'take it the wrong way,' given the incident aboard the Horizon," Neera said, using his fingers for air quotes. "I told him you would see the humor in it."

"I'm going to use this just to check in on your progress as his first officer. I expect ace marks all around." Demi had seen Neera through many different circumstances, a whole spectrum of emotions. And though Dywens had a muted gray skin tone, she swore she saw a deepening to them, a flush of blood to the cheeks and face.

"Captain Matthews seems to be satisfied with my performance, though the current political state makes our priorities volatile at times. Peace is tenuous. However, the science ahead of us provides," Neera said, and though Demi expected his gaze to drop, he actually tilted his head upward, "many interesting possibilities."

"I did always tell you to look for possibilities."

"I have told you that I did not want to return to war. But my short time with Captain Matthews has shown me that I am not. I have been given the opening to be part of the peace process." Neera's face flushed again, and Demi opted not to point out how eloquent he was suddenly being.

Instead, she took a moment to be his commanding officer for one more time.

"A word of advice on your new role?" Neera's complexion returned to normal before a quick nod. "As first officer, you can be the voice of reason. Tell him how you feel—even if you disagree. Because when you say that, you can get people to think differently." With that, she took the comm. "So yes, I'll check in. However, I do expect you to bring Tanav on your next visit. Which means they better hurry up and settle this whole thing."

They walked in a line, Demi reaching up to put her hand on Neera's shoulder, the distinct flexible-yet-protective texture of the GCF uniform activating so many sensory memories as they got to the loading door.

T-shirt, jeans, and sandals were much better. And easier to remove dog hair from.

"Where is the Horizon off to next?" she asked as Indy nudged Neera's hand with her nose for a few more pets.

"Charting Sector Kappa Fourteen for convergence points." The Dywen removed a small projector from his belt and held it up, a holographic star chart coming into view. "This is the second convergence mapping initiative since you resigned."

"Your dream," Chuck said, and Demi felt now-familiar robotic fingers weaving between hers. "It is still possible."

Neera's head angled in a way that it rarely did—at least under her command. But she got the sense that he was finally in a space to grow past that. Demi took the half-folded map of Muir Woods from Chuck, unfolded it completely, and held it up. She moved step-by-step, first folding it in half, then half again, then additional folds intuitively driven from the feel of the indentations on the paper. She held up the map in its final form, a picture of redwood trees printed across its front panel, then handed it back to Chuck. She turned to Neera, and usually when they had conversations about options, an impulse tickled her instincts, causing her to pace back and forth.

Yet now, she stood facing her friend, and as the wind blew through her hair, she kept her feet planted. She didn't need to move them, and she looked at Neera's large compound eyes, so capable of brilliantly taking in and distilling information that humans missed.

"I don't need to map the stars anymore," she said. "I have everything I need right here."

ACKNOWLEDGMENTS

I never believed I'd write an original space opera. Readers have asked plenty of times, and despite space opera being woven into my life since a very young age (hello, *Star Wars* and *Robotech*), the idea of all that worldbuilding just seemed incredibly overwhelming.

So this book literally would not exist without my editor, Nivia Evans, asking my agent, Eric Smith, if I'd give it a try. Of course, I'd thought about it—I even had a very loose idea I'd jotted down called *After Voyager*, which was really just a bunch of questions for what someone like Captain Janeway and the Voyager crew would face after coming home. It hinged on two big What-Ifs: What if they had to go back to the place they were stranded, and what if they arrived in the middle of Deep Space Nine's Dominion War?

Once Nivia gave me the green light to actually explore this, the whole project became as exciting—and difficult—as you'd think. So the biggest thanks goes to her, not just for the genesis of this book, but also for patiently combing through iterations of its story synopsis and manuscript. Readers should know one of the big turning points was when she pointed out that the characters were awfully chill for all of these bonkers things happening to them, and I realized I'd written the Horizon's crew to act as calm and dutiful as nineties *Star Trek* crews. Which they're not—they are way messier than episodic TV characters!

Peng Shepherd was invaluable in early plot development. Sierra

Godfrey, Diana Urban, and Wendy Heard provided early insights into worldbuilding and character development—Wendy, in particular, was there for my freak-out about creating Neera's alien species, which is why the Dywens are named after her.

Kat Howard read several iterations of the first half of this book, from the early proposal stage to the final iteration for smoothing out before copyedits. So she saw the complete evolution of this crew, and thankfully she said early on that she "would die for Neera," so I knew that character was sticking.

When I realized that I needed a visual layout for the Horizon to really grab hold of things, I asked Beth Revis, who referred me to artist Marina Charalambides. Marina's wonderful concept art and deck layouts made my job so much easier by simply grounding the actions in tangible geography.

As always, the characters and their voices snapped into place once I figured out actors who could portray them. Demi is a nod to Asians in *Star Trek*, an amalgamation of Demora Sulu and Harry Kim; physically, I imagined a weary and aged version of Jacqueline Kim's Demora Sulu with the vocal bite of Tig Notaro's Jett Reno and tonal intonation of Emily Woo Zeller. The rest of the cast was a little more straightforward: Tanav was Jacob Anderson (particularly with his semi-American accent from *Interview with the Vampire*); Lynn was Ravneet Gill from *Junior Bake Off* (which my daughter was watching while writing this and my brain went WHO IS THAT); Sadler was my friend Colin Donnell (I was only half joking when I told him I'd cast him as a villain someday); Matthews was Jon Bernthal (in Frank Castle mode); and Singh was Rahul Kohli (notice where I put that last name). A lot of names are also easter eggs from *Robotech*, which is still one of my favorite things of all time.

And a shout-out to Jenny Lewis. Like Lynn, I'm a firm believer that she's a poet for generations.

My wife, Mandy, is as big of a sci-fi nerd as me, and we've indoctrinated our daughter into it as well. So sharing all of the pieces that go into a project like this makes it a family affair and extra special, even when the process is difficult.

Finally, the biggest thanks goes to all of the space opera creators who influenced my life—from movies to TV, comics to novels, *Star Wars* to *Robotech*, *Star Trek* to *Mass Effect*. Your brilliance has taken up permanent residence in my brain and shaped who I am today. I can only hope my work here impacts someone just as much.

ABOUT THE AUTHOR

Photograph © Amanda Chen

Mike Chen is the *New York Times* bestselling author of *The Photonic Effect, Star Wars: Brotherhood, Here and Now and Then, A Quantum Love Story,* and other novels, as well as *Star Trek: Deep Space Nine* comics. He has covered geek culture for sites such as *Nerdist* and *The Mary Sue,* and in a different life, he's covered the NHL. A member of SFWA, Mike lives in the Bay Area with his wife, daughter, and many rescue animals.